THE
HASTENING
STORM

C. F. BARRINGTON

HEAD
ZEUS

An Aries Book

Cover design © Dan Mogford
Map design © Mark Clay

MIX
Paper from
responsible sources
FSC® C171272

Printed and bound in Great Britain by
CPI Group (UK) Ltd, Croydon CR0 4YY

Head of Zeus Ltd
First Floor East
5–8 Hardwick Street
London EC1R 4RG

WWW.HEADOFZEUS.COM

THE PANTHEON ORBAT (Order of Battle)

THE CAELESTIA (THE SEVEN)

Lord High Jupiter

Zeus

Odin

Kyzaghan

Xian

Tengri

Ördög

THE CURIATE

Europe Chapter

Russia Chapter

China Chapter

Far East Chapter

US Chapter

THE PALATINATES

The Legion ~ Caesar Imperator ~ HQ: Rome

The Sultanate ~ Mehmed The Conqueror ~ HQ: Istanbul

The Warring States ~ Zheng, Lord of Qin ~ HQ: Beijing

The Kheshig ~ Genghis, Great Khan ~ HQ: Khan Khenti

The Titans ~ Alexander of Macedon ~ HQ: Edinburgh

The Horde ~ Sveinn the Red ~ HQ: Edinburgh

The Huns ~ Attila, Scourge of God ~ HQ: Pannonian Plain

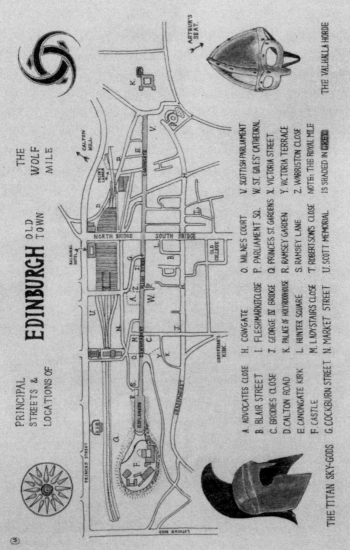

PRINCIPAL
STREETS &
LOCATIONS OF

EDINBURGH OLD TOWN

THE WOLF MILE

↑ ARTHUR'S SEAT.

A. ADVOCATES CLOSE
B. BLAIR STREET
C. BRODIES CLOSE
D. CALTON ROAD
E. CANONGATE KIRK
F. CASTLE
G. COCKBURN STREET

H. COWGATE
I. FLESHMARKET CLOSE
J. GEORGE IV BRIDGE
K. PALACE OF HOLYROODHOUSE
L. HUNTER SQUARE
M. LADYSTAIRS CLOSE
N. MARKET STREET

O. MILNES COURT
P. PARLIAMENT SQ.
Q. PRINCES ST. GARDENS
R. RAMSEY GARDEN
S. RAMSEY LANE
T. ROBERTSONS CLOSE
U. SCOTT MEMORIAL

V. SCOTTISH PARLIAMENT
W. ST. GILES' CATHEDRAL
X. VICTORIA STREET
Y. VICTORIA TERRACE
Z. WARRISTON CLOSE
NOTE: THE ROYAL MILE
IS SHADED IN GREY.

THE TITAN SKY-GODS

THE VALHALLA HORDE

Mark Clay (markclay.co.uk)

*To my brother and sister – who make my world
a better place.*

THE HORDE OF VALHALLA IN THE TWENTIETH YEAR

Strength: 204 shield warriors

Odin ~ Caelestis of the Horde of Valhalla

Sveinn the Red ~ High King of the Horde

Kustaa (successor to Radspakr) ~ Thane of the
Palatinate, Adjutant, Paymaster, Custodian of the
Day Books

Bjarke ~ Jarl (Colonel) of Hammer Regiment –
Heavy Infantry
14 x litters. Total: 114

Asmund ~ Jarl (Colonel) of Storm Regiment –
Light Troops
Arrow Company – 3 x litters = 22
Spear Company – 2 x litters = 14
Total: 36

Skarde (successor to Halvar) ~ Housecarl (Captain)
of Wolf Company House Troop
4 x elite Kill Squads = 38

Freyja ~ Housecarl (Captain) of Raven Company House
Troop
2 x elite Squadron of Scouts = 16

Thegn Calder (Lana) ~ Litter One, Raven Company
Jorunn ~ Litter One, Raven Company
Geir ~ Litter One, Raven Company
Thegn Ulf – Litter Five, Hammer Regiment
Ake – Litter Two, Wolf Company
Stigr – Litter Two, Wolf Company
Unn – Litter Two, Wolf Company

THE TITAN SKY-GODS IN THE TWENTIETH YEAR

Strength: 137 troops

Zeus ~ Caelestis of the Titan Palatinate

Hera ~ Wife of Zeus

Alexander, Lion of Macedon ~ High King of the Titans

Simmius ~ Adjutant of the Palatinate, Paymaster,
Custodian of the Day Books

Nicanor ~ Colonel, Brigade of Hoplite Heavy Infantry
Phalanx: 10 rows of 8. Total: 82

Cleitus (successor to Timanthes) ~ Colonel, Brigade
of Light Infantry
Total: 55. Broken down as follows:

Menes (successor to Olena) ~ Captain of Companion
Bodyguard
Total: 21

Agape ~ Captain of Sacred Band
Total: 14

Parmenion ~ Captain of Peltasts, Archers & Scouts
Total: 20

What Has Come Before

1. Presumed dead, Punnr bursts from the chapel in Edinburgh Castle on the final night of the Pantheon's Nineteenth Raiding Season and rescues Calder from the treacherous Ulf. He then captures the Final Asset for his Valhalla Palatinate.

2. While Calder recovers from her wounds in the secret Pantheon hospital, looked after by a nurse called Monique, Punnr is guest at a grand country house for the Blood Gathering of Scotland. He meets Odin, the Caelestis of the Horde of Valhalla, who presents him with a silver arm-ring for finding all four Assets.

3. Tyler (Punnr) asks his neighbour, thirteen-year-old Oliver, to help him search for his lost sister, Morgan (who was once Olena in the Titan Palatinate). Oliver is a skilled online hacker and sets about his search with gusto.

4. The Rules for the Blood Season are presented. Each warrior wears Bloodmarks to display how many foe he or she has killed. Those with none – Vestales – will be the most valuable kills during the six forthcoming Blood Nights. Punnr is one of these Vestales. Overall, twenty-five warriors must die during the six nights.

5. Punnr and Brante and their Wolf litters take part in the

first three Blood Nights. Punnr's lack of Bloodmarks on his armour, as well as the silver arm-ring from Odin, mark him out and he has to fight for his life on the rooftops of Edinburgh.

6. Tyler meets Brante at a party in the city and discovers his real name is Forbes and he comes from a wealthy background.

7. Tyler follows Lana (Calder) to her house beside the Leith. They share two days together, growing close. Lana makes him promise he will always be there for her in the Pantheon.

8. When Tyler returns to his own house, he is whisked to a distant Hebridean island to prepare for the Grand Battle, the culmination of the Nineteenth Year.

9. Meanwhile, Radspakr knows Tyler is the brother of the missing Olena, who – if she is ever found – knows too much about Odin and Radspakr's dirty deals. Radspakr despatches a killer to Tyler's flat, but the man arrives just after Tyler has flown to the island. As the killer is leaving, Oliver accosts him and gives away that he has been helping Tyler to search for his sister.

10. Radspakr panics and tells everything to Odin. The Caelestis knows he must stamp on these loose ends and arranges the release of a man from Erebus, the Pantheon Prison. This is Skarde, who becomes Odin's trusted killer and joins the Wolf units to seek out Tyler (Punnr).

11. Odin demands the murders of Oliver's parents and the kidnapping of Oliver, who is taken into the dark subterranean world of the Pantheon.

12. On the final Blood Night, Skarde accosts Calder and she realises he is the man who raped her many years before – an attack that also resulted in the conception of her

daughter. Her world falls apart.

13. Radspakr meets with Odin and pays for his failure to silence Tyler with his life.

14. The rival Palatinates are transported to the island and meet in a momentous Grand Battle on white Hebridean sands while the eyes of the world's mega-wealthy look on.

15. At the critical moment in the Battle, Punnr realises his life is in great danger if he remains in Valhalla, so he makes a mad attempt to get to the Titan lines. Brante follows him and they surrender to Agape.

16. Now the Titans must decide the fate of the two friends – and Calder must face her monsters in the Horde alone – as the Twentieth Season awaits.

Prologue

Season – Blood

I t was the cough and hiss of a dustbin lorry that woke her.
She groaned and rolled her neck. Her limbs were as
unyielding as iron and winter had stolen into her lungs.
She was curled against a chimney on the rooftops above
Edinburgh's Royal Mile and during the night she had
slipped to her side, so she eased herself gingerly back up
and ran stiff fingers through her hair.

A weak light suffused the skyline and clouds hung so low
she could almost touch them. Rain had seeped beneath her
armour and its clammy caress made her shiver. Somewhere
the dustbin lorry continued its rounds, but otherwise the
world was blanketed in a pre-dawn silence.

Her mind clawed back to the struggle in the cellar just
a few hours earlier, when Timanthes, Colonel of Light
Infantry in the Titan Palatinate – one of seven rival forces

in the great Game known as the Pantheon – had led thirty Companion Hoplites into the underground depths. They had believed they could surprise their foe and kill Sveinn the Red, but they had been betrayed and the Vikings of the Valhalla Palatinate had been waiting for them. Many Titans died in that cellar, including Timanthes himself, and the rest had scattered back into the night.

Olena, Captain of Light Infantry and Timanthes' second in command, had fought a valiant retreat. The Horde hunted her and howled for her blood, but she had raced for the safety of the rooftops and lost them. Perhaps, in those moments, time was still on her side. She could have used the precious final hours of night to get herself far away, to run from the questions that would be forming in Alexander's strongholds as Titan survivors returned, the identities of their dead confirmed, her own absence noted and the first suspicions roused. But the cold and shock of the whole ordeal had weighed her down. Her limbs succumbed and her mind disintegrated into sleep.

Cursing now, she forced herself to stand, but her legs wanted none of it and she collapsed back in a heap. Perhaps it was already too late. Perhaps she should just sit here, gazing out across the stillness of a new day's birth and let her destiny come to her.

In fact, it arrived quicker than she expected.

A figure appeared on the roof above the Courts. It was track-suited and wearing a cap, and at first her weary brain wondered if he or she was some sort of council worker. A gutter inspector perhaps. Or court employee with good reason to be on the rooftops at this hour. But the figure was too quick. Too sure-footed on difficult terrain. It padded silently between the obstacles, dipping into hollows, checking behind chimneys. A tiptoe along ledges; a leap over wires. Coming ever closer. Lightning quick and lithe, drawing towards her, until she could hear the soft splash of the runner's footfalls in the puddles and the figure finally looked up and spotted her.

Agape. Olena smiled emptily. She should have known. The other woman's blue hair was tucked beneath her cap, but who else would it be?

'Ephesus is filled with the cries of treachery,' said the Captain of Alexander's elite Sacred Band, her tone stone-grim as she came to a halt and eased a backpack from her shoulders. 'Alexander is shell-shocked. Nicanor is leading the interrogations. And Cleitus is howling for blood. It won't take them long to find the answers they need.'

Olena gazed at her erstwhile comrade. 'Why are you here?' she croaked.

'To find you, of course. The Vigilis' feed showed you escaping the cellar, but when you didn't return to Ephesus I feared the Horde had chased you down.' She took a step forward and frowned in consternation. 'But instead you're here, slumped above the Courts. Are you wounded? Is that why you haven't returned?'

Olena shook her head. 'I'm exhausted and broken and near hypothermic, but I'll live long enough for whatever fate the Pantheon decrees.'

Agape processed this for long seconds. 'What are you trying to say, Captain?'

Olena took a long breath. 'That I betrayed our plan to the Horde.'

Agape's eyes drilled into her for an eternity, then she

walked to a slanting roof and leaned against the tiles.
'*Why?*'

'To be with Halvar.'

'You would sacrifice Timanthes and so many of your
Titan comrades for the love of a man from Valhalla?'

Olena nodded. 'I would. Halvar and I have been lovers
since the Sixteenth Year. You've suspected it and you've
kept our secret, and for that I will always be in your debt.
But you have no idea of the hell of it. A love that stretches
across the divide of the Palatinates. A love that would be
extinguished in a heartbeat if it came to light. I couldn't live
with the subterfuge any longer. We needed to be together
and this was the only way.'

'By betraying your Palatinate?'

'By weakening the Companions and giving Valhalla
enough superiority in numbers to have a real opportunity
to kill Alexander at the Grand Battle and so unite the
Palatinates.'

'Unite the Palatinates,' Agape mimicked. 'Halvar and
Olena together under one banner.' She pondered this
information, then flicked her eyes back up to the other
woman. 'And did you think I would be in that cellar with
my Sacred Band?' Olena didn't reply and her silence brought
some kind of finality to Agape's need for answers. 'I loved
you, Morgan.'

The past tense and the use of her true name.

'And I love you too, Kinsley.' Morgan replied sadly.
'But… but it was always Halvar.'

Agape broke her stare and peered away to the smudge of
distant hills in Fife. 'I should kill you.'

Morgan looked at her friend. Just a tracksuit. No sword

4

on her hip, no sign of other blades beneath the garments, and the rucksack seemed too soft to conceal iron. Olena's own weapon still lay in its scabbard beside her. Even if the blood had dried, she was confident a good wrench would draw the blade into the damp air. Olena had been a Titan Captain, a warrior of distinction, skilled in swordstroke and thrust and parry, feared in the battle line.

But Agape was better.

And she knew implicitly that if Agape contrived to kill her, it would be so.

But the other woman made no such move. Instead, she pushed herself off the tiles and returned to her rucksack. 'You have a window. Your absence will have been noted, but they can't draw conclusions until the *libitinarii* have sorted through the carnage in the cellar and officially provided the Blood Count along with the identities of the slain.' She unzipped the bag and threw trainers and another tracksuit on to the wet roof. 'Get into these. Give me your blades and armour. I will deal with them.'

Stiffly, Morgan rose and undressed, handing over each item. Then she pulled on the tracksuit and her cold fingers fumbled with the laces of the shoes. At last she straightened. 'Thank you,' she said quietly.

But Agape would not look at her and busied herself pushing the weapons and armour into her bag. Wrenching the zip closed, she shouldered the load and scanned the rooftops. 'A few hours, maybe until lunch. Then they will come for you. Be gone from the city by then.'

'I love you, little brother.'

Morgan scrawled the final line beneath the note on the kitchen table, tears dripping from the end of her nose and smudging the ink.

She had made her way back to the Craigmillar estate as the city came alive around her, keeping her head low and convinced she would hear an angry shout at any moment. As she climbed the dirty, graffiti-infected stairwell to the sixth floor, she had wondered if Tyler would be home from his usual night-time excursions, or whether he would still be roaming the estate, playing at coke-dealing or passed out in some girl's apartment. Part of her wanted to find him curled in his bed and needed to cling to him, cry into his neck and tell him everything. But the sensible part of her had been satisfied when she found the flat empty.

Christ knows why she had cooked him a lasagne. Some irrational maternal instinct needed to feel assured he would be fed at least for a few days. She had wondered if Halvar would come, yet realised with crushing enlightenment that she no longer wanted to see him. It was all too late. There was nothing they could say or do.

She had no real plan, but decided she would go to her aunt's in the Borders. She and Tyler had not visited since their mother's death, but the rural setting always brought peace and the house was pervaded with the scent of their uncle's pipe-smoke for many years after he had passed away. She knew it was a stupid plan. The Pantheon would have records of all her living relatives and it would take them no time to come calling. But maybe if she just stayed a couple of days, built her strength, then took the car down into England, they might lose the scent.

She packed a few items in a holdall, then went to the

bottom drawer of her dresser and ferreted under the clothes to retrieve a tiny ring box, which she opened gingerly. Inside was the Triple Horn of Odin talisman that Halvar had given her to symbolise their planned union. Wrought in ivory, with a Star of Macedon on the reverse, it was attached to a black neck-cord. Now she took it from the box, returned to the kitchen and rummaged in a cupboard for some tissue paper to wrap around it. She placed the package next to her note and the cooling lasagne, then scanned the room. A heavy fug of tomato and cheese hung in the air, but she had diligently washed all the utensils and wiped the surfaces clean. She checked her watch. Ten to eleven. She must go.

She was about to return to the bedroom for her bag, when there was a thud on the front door. Her hearted lurched. *My god.* She had thought she still had time. Barely daring to breathe, she crept into the hall. Perhaps it was Halvar. But she knew he would never risk coming at this time and, besides, he always used a special *rat-a-tat* knock in case Tyler was at home.

She hugged the wall and the silence extended. Then there was a second thud. She swore under her breath and tried to think. She was on the sixth floor and there was no other exit. Her options were stark: sit it out or fight it out. But sitting it out was never really an option. Sooner or later others would arrive and break down the door.

She stalked to the sink and retrieved a knife she had used earlier to dice courgettes and mushrooms. Then she slunk back into the hallway. *I am Olena, Captain of Companion Bodyguard, and many men have fallen to my blade.*

She unlocked the door and pulled it ajar. Her fingers

C.F. BARRINGTON

loosened and the knife dropped to the floor. She let go of the latch and staggered backwards against the wall.

'No,' she choked, one hand pressed to her mouth and the other held out to ward off the newcomer. 'Not you. Not *now*.'

8

PART ONE

NEW HORIZONS

I

Pantheon Year – Nineteen

Season – Interregnum

Alexander of Macedon – High King of the Titans, Commander of Companions, Protector of Pella, Persepolis, Ephesus and Thebes, Lord of the *Sky-Gods* – stubbed out his cigarette, knelt forward and snorted the blade-sharp line of coke his pageboy had prepared. He grunted and blinked as the floral-scented powder hit the back of his nostril and the diesel undertones slunk down his throat.

God, he needed that.

Only hours earlier he had been on a wind-blasted, gull-infested, blood beach and he was still greased in the sweat, salt and muck of the whole damn exploit. After the klaxon had cut through the frenzy of the Nineteenth Season's Grand Battle like a scythe through wheat, the Titan and Valhalla Palatinates had prised themselves apart and waded to opposite sides of the great bay. Vehicles bumped down to the shoreline and disgorged Vigiles, medics, orderlies and *libitinarii* – removers of the slain. Field hospitals were erected, arms and banners collected, water distributed and cookhouses thrown up, their scents soon blossoming across the dunes and drawing all those warriors who could still walk.

Later, as night descended and the sea drew back once more to reveal swathes of sand, Pantheon planes landed one by one, their wheels ploughing furrows across a battleground washed bare. The Titan regiments gave up their armour in return for jumpers, coats, and boots, then hauled themselves onto the waiting planes and collapsed as the engines roared and took them from those blood isles for good.

'Enter,' Alexander barked in response to a timid knock on the door of his private chamber in the Ephesus stronghold, four floors above Gray's Close off Edinburgh's Royal Mile.

His royal page bustled in, carrying a flight case, which he placed on a gilt table and opened to reveal a thing of beauty – the King's battle helmet. Burnished bronze gleamed in the downlights. Intricate vines wove across the cheek guards. A lion's snout snarled above the eye sockets. And a rich horsehair plume swept over the helm in an unbroken wave of scarlet.

'And what about the rest?' Alexander snapped. It was lost on him that a sovereign's helmet should look less perfect in the aftermath of a mighty battle. There were no chinks in the bronze, no tousles in the plume. For Alexander had spent the duration of the struggle behind his Bodyguard, beside his banners, peering at the carnage from a safe distance.

The boy's eyes bulged with fear. 'My armour,' Alexander

barked. 'My cloak, my greaves, my sword. Do you expect me to do this in only a helmet and undergarments?'

The boy scampered from the room as Alexander grabbed a goblet of wine laced with opium and drank deeply. He dragged an arm across his lips and began to pace. Memories of the Battle flooded back and his gut knotted with exhilaration. He knew it was the coke beginning to work its magic, but he didn't care. He heard again the clamour of his Phalanx as it hit the Hammer's shieldwall, their sarissas splintering limewood shields and breaking the line. He saw once more the speed of his Companions as they launched their ambush against Sveinn's Wolves. The formal Blood Tidings would be announced in a few days, but he needed no certified body count to know Wolf Regiment had been broken in that struggle across the sands.

The boy returned, this time too agitated to remember to knock. He carried the King's cuirass, greaves, cloak and sword, already unpacked from their flight cases, and Alexander forced himself to settle while the boy began lacing his breastplate. A commotion from Ephesus' Armoury bled through the walls as those troopers not already released back to their homes busied themselves cleaning and storing weapons. There was laughter, for the exhaustion of the journey back to the capital had been replaced by a nervous release of emotions as each individual realised they had made it through the annual struggle and still lived. And no doubt there was alcohol. Not strictly permitted in the Armouries of any of the four Titan strongholds, but no one was going to begrudge them their wine tonight.

The boy finished fixing the breastplate and picked up the sword, but Alexander slapped his hands away and belted the weapon himself. Then he waited impatiently while the lad attached the red woollen cloak to clasps on his armoured shoulders. Finally the King snapped his fingers for his helmet and pulled it over his head until his eyes were hidden in the recesses above the great cheek guards. He stalked to a mirror and admired himself. *You'll do.* Even the ancient Lord of Asia himself would approve.

Right, let's get this bloody thing over with.

'For the record, provide your names as given to you by the Valhalla Horde.'

The speaker was Simmius, Lord Adjutant and Keeper of the Books for the Titan Palatinate. Dressed in a grey floor-length tunic, cinched at the waist by silver rope and decorated with a lone Star of Macedon, he also wore a delicate gold mask that did little more than hide his eyes.

He addressed two figures standing in the centre of one of the windowless Bladecraft Rooms. They were tall, fit and straight-backed, though they could do nothing to hide the sheer freight of exhaustion leaking from their bodies. They were dressed only in short tunics and their wrists were bound.

'I am Thegn Brante,' answered the taller of the two. 'Litter Two, Wolf Regiment of the Horde of Valhalla.'

'He didn't ask you for your bloody CV,' growled one of the assembled officers from behind his helmet. Even among the shadows cast by the candles, it was obvious he was a big man with the neck and shoulders of a rugby player. 'Just your name.'

Simmius frowned, but acquiesced with the sentiment.

'Nicanor is correct. Whatever positions you held in the Viking Palatinate ceased to exist at the moment of your surrender. They are irrelevant.' He looked at the other figure. 'And you?'

The man remained silent for a moment, then said simply, 'Punnr.'

Hours earlier Punnr and Brante had been dragged from the battleground, forced to remove their armour, then bound, blindfolded and bundled into a vehicle where they waited as voices argued outside. Eventually they had been yanked out and marched across sand towards the roar of a taxiing plane and ordered into the cargo hold. Frozen, exhausted and unfed, the pair had endured the flight, then been driven another hour and thrown into an upstairs room where they had been untied and informed they could remove their blindfolds. The door was slammed on them and they had sat in the dark, unfurnished space until their jailers returned, this time with bowls of cold water and razors. They were told to shave their beards and then, once their wrists had been rebound, one of the guards chopped at Punnr's long hair.

Alexander was seated in the shadows behind the candles. He played with an object in his hand, running his fingers over its fine engraving while keeping it hidden beneath the folds of his cloak. 'Two questions,' he said at last. 'First, why did you surrender?'

'We were coming to kill you,' replied the tall one called Brante.

'Bullshit!' exclaimed the officer standing between Simmius and the King. 'My Companion Bodyguard had the Lion of Macedon screened at all times.'

Punnr glanced at the man. He had run to fat long ago. His neck was soft and the lips beneath his helmet were sulky, petulant. Cleitus. Commander of the Lights, Colonel of Companions, and successor to Timanthes. Word had it in Valhalla there was no love lost between him and his King.

'We saw an opportunity,' Punnr spoke. 'A clear run around the perimeter of the beach, which would take us behind your lines. We believed we could take Alexander.'

'Bollocks,' Cleitus added succinctly.

'Yet you changed course.' This from the slim officer wearing the silver fish-scale armour of a peltast. His bearing was poised and he spoke slowly with Etonian accents. Blonde hair spilled from beneath his helm. Punnr guessed he must be Parmenion.

Brante shrugged. 'Like your mate said, he had his Bodyguard in the way.'

'So you ran instead straight into the arms of Agape's Band and surrendered.'

'We'd miscalculated. We knew the game was up.'

Parmenion accepted this, but Alexander glowered from beyond the candles. 'So my second question. You – the one called Punnr – why did you wear this?'

Punnr stared long and hard at the object, drawing out the seconds and debating his words. 'It's a Viking arm-ring.'

'The King knows *what* it is,' said Parmenion evenly. 'He asked why you wear it?'

'It was a gift.'

'From whom?'

Punnr stuck out his chin and directed his answer to Alexander. 'From Odin.'

There was a moment of silence, then Nicanor cursed

and Cleitus snorted and all heads turned to Alexander. The King shifted uncomfortably and threw a look to a small camera on one of the walls, wondering if Zeus was viewing. Likely not. The Titan Caelestis had better things to do. He pulled his attention back to the captives. 'And *why* would Odin make such a gift to a junior-ranking Thegn in his Palatinate?'

'I pleased him.'

Cleitus guffawed. 'You've a sweet enough mouth, Viking, but I hear Odin prefers them more Schola age.'

Nicanor laughed, but Parmenion shook his head and addressed Punnr. 'You had better explain yourself more fully.'

Punnr cast his eyes around the room. This was the moment. The moment he had been playing in his head all through the tumultuous journey from the island. His one opportunity. He had hoped someone would notice the arm-ring among his discarded armour. Prayed it would raise enough curiosity. Because without curiosity, no Titan king would hold this audience with captive foe. Punnr and Brante would have been sent packing from the Pantheon and his entire reason for surrendering would dissolve into nothing.

So now he had Alexander's attention, it was time to play the only card he held.

'I pleased Odin because in the Nineteenth Raiding Season I was the White Warrior who successfully claimed all four Assets for Valhalla.'

Alexander sprang from his seat and strode through the candlelight, stopping just a couple of paces from the prisoners. Punnr could feel the King's eyes burning into him from behind the helmet. On either side, Cleitus, Nicanor and Parmenion were all speaking at once. Only Agape held her tongue.

'*You* are Sveinn's White Warrior?' Alexander demanded. 'The one who feigned his death at Old College and cheated my Palatinate of its rightful Assets?'

'I did nothing against the Rules.'

'You pretended to die, then on the next Raid Night you sneaked back into Old College when none of us was present and collected the Asset! That's cheating in my book.'

'Kill him,' said Nicanor.

'This chap here,' said Cleitus, gloating and pointing to one of the guards behind him, 'is Myron. Champion of my Companion Bodyguards. He's so surgical with his blade he can scratch your belly and you'll think nothing of it. You'll laugh at him and tell him he should do better and only then will you realise your first coil of intestine is waving hello. It's incredible how slippery intestines can be. Doesn't matter how much you paw and claw at them, they'll always flop through your fingers.'

The guard was huge. Arms as thick as most men's thighs and a tree-trunk neck.

Alexander turned to Cleitus. 'Who else from the Companions?'

Cleitus thought for a moment. 'Nestor, my lord.'

'I trust he is good?'

'He kills in his sleep.'

'So be it.' Alexander addressed the Vikings. 'The Rules state that no Palatinate may absorb into its ranks any prisoner taken from another Palatinate. Nevertheless, in exceptional circumstances, a sovereign may offer such a captive the opportunity to prove worthy of *replacing* an existing member of the Palatinate. This is decided through the medium of combat. So, Punnr – Odin's favoured White Warrior – and you... what's your name... Brante... I have elected to give you a choice of fates: You may either depart forthwith into the care of the Vigiles, never to play a part in the Pantheon again. Or you may earn your right to remain by proving victorious in combat against my champions. You know of your adversaries – Myron and Nestor. If you decide to fight, then we will meet again in three nights when my troops gather for the Blood Tidings. Be under no illusions, there are only two possible outcomes: victory or death. You have until tomorrow morning to make your choice.'

II

One fire. One measly fire. That's all it took to warm the remnants of Raven Company.

Calder slumped on the sand with her back against a stand of marram grass. It was a clear night and the sea was molten silver in the moonlight. A wind still gusted aimlessly, but with none of the force it had mustered during the Grand Battle when it had seemed intent on sweeping those tiny blade-toting figurines from the vast expanse of beach.

'You okay?' asked Jorunn.

'I'm fine. How's the wound?'

Bandages were swathed around Jorunn's left hand. 'There's barely a scrap of flesh left between my thumb and forefinger, but it'll heal. Must have been a shield rim. If it had been a proper blade, I'd not have much below the wrist to scratch my arse with. It's strange how after a fight, you can never remember how you hurt yourself.'

Calder looked down at her own arms and nodded. She was covered in bruises and scratches, yet she could recall none of them being inflicted.

Jorunn was eating honeyed flatbread and there was more warming on a griddle. She passed one to Calder. 'Eat.'

Calder grimaced her thanks and bit into it, but in truth her stomach was granite and she could barely swallow. There were five of them around the flames. Only five. Sixteen they had numbered on the first day of the year, two litters. But five had been taken from them in the Cull of the Blood Season and of the nine who had stood upon the beach that afternoon, two were being tended in the field hospitals and two more were corpses in the care of the *libitinarii*. She peered through the flames to Freyja and the Housecarl raised her eyes and peered back at her. Then she dropped them again and Calder chewed her bread in silence.

They were perched on the rim of the Atlantic, at the very edge of the world, and night crept infinitesimally over the Valhalla Horde.

'Are you determined never to speak to me again?' Punnr demanded, but there was silence from the pile of blankets in the corner.

It must have been two hours since they were escorted back from the audience with Alexander. They had been given water, bread, soup and even slices of cold beef, which they devoured in silence. There was now a jug and bowl in the corner for their ablutions, as well as a latrine bucket. The room itself was no prison cell. It was plastered and heated and there were empty shelves on one wall. Under different circumstances, it was probably a storage room. Evidently the Titans were unaccustomed to holding prisoners.

'Brante!'

'Don't call me that.' The blankets stirred as his friend pushed himself further against the wall.

'Seriously?'

'You heard Simmius. Our Valhalla names ceased to exist the moment we surrendered.'

'So what am I supposed to call you?'

There was no answer and Punnr lapsed into silence again. His chin was sore and blossoming into rash from the rough shave it had endured. He was shocked by the chopping of his hair, for he had been quietly proud of his tresses, but Titans did not sport beards or long hair and they viewed such refinements as Viking degeneracy, so the jailers had taken grim satisfaction in the ritual humiliation of shaving and shedding.

He tried again. 'We need to talk before they come for us.'

There was another long pause and then Brante poked his head above the blankets and manoeuvred himself against the wall. 'So, talk.'

'For god's sake, what do you want me to say? That I'm sorry?'

'A fat lot of good that is now.'

Punnr bit back a curse and controlled himself. He could just make out the curve of his friend's bald head by the light from beneath the door. Since the shaving, the only hair Brante now owned north of his groin belonged to his eyebrows. 'You were never supposed to be here. You weren't part of the plan.'

'There was a plan? It sure didn't look that way to me. There I was standing in line with my Wolf litter preparing a final defence against the Titan lines coming up from the surf and then I see you way off on the edge of the beach, clambering into the channel and heading for the foe, and I say to myself, *That crazy bastard needs some help.* The next thing I know, we're tearing across the sand towards Agape's

Band – that psychopath Skarde on our heels – and then you're flinging your blade away and dropping to your knees in front of her. And that was the plan? A pretty bloody shite one, if you ask me.'

'Oh for god's sake, Brante, I'm sorry. I told you not to follow me.'

'My name is Forbes.' This last was said in a low, emphatic whisper and there was an angry silence. Then Forbes began again in more measured tones. 'You don't get it, do you, Tyler. Being a Wolf meant everything to me. But now there's no going back to Valhalla. We'll never see those Halls again. Never stand in a Viking shieldwall.'

'I don't know what I'm supposed to say.'

Forbes sighed. 'You're not. I'm just angry with the world, but I know you tried to stop me and it was my decision to come with you. Mine alone. Truth is, Tyler, I came because you're my friend. And I'd do it again.'

Tyler nodded slowly. 'Thank you.'

'Aye.' Forbes grinned sourly. 'Besides, as soon as that bastard Skarde started chasing us with murder in his eyes, there was only one direction I was bloody running!'

'I think he made up our minds for us.' Tyler smiled sadly through the dark. 'By the way, it's Maitland.'

'What?'

'Tyler Maitland's my name. And tomorrow morning I'm accepting Alexander's Challenge.'

'I know,' said Forbes quietly. 'Looks like we'll have one last blood fight together.'

'You don't have to do this.'

'Oh I do, my friend. I do. But first you'll oblige me with one request.'

'Name it.'

'Tell me why we surrendered.'

And so he did. Tentatively at first, but then the words came. He spoke of his older sister, Morgan, who had joined the Pantheon and then disappeared. He explained how his own journey into the Pantheon had been driven by a need to find her and how he had assumed she would be waiting for him among the ranks of the Horde. In fact, piece by piece, he uncovered a much more complex story.

His sister had been a Titan. Olena, Captain of Companions. Somehow she had crossed paths with Halvar outside the Pantheon and they had fallen in love. Radspakr had discovered their affair and revealed it to Odin. Together, they forced the pair to give up secrets about Titan movements and trap the cream of the foe in a cellar during the Eighteenth Blood Season. Morgan had led her troops into that trap, then disappeared, and no one knew her fate. And this drove Odin and Radspakr mad because if it ever got out that they had been using her to leak information and cull Titan numbers, all hell would break loose.

'Then you turned up in their Palatinate,' said Forbes.

'Exactly. I stupidly showed Radspakr a picture of her and said I was her brother. From then on he had a death wish for me. My presence must have terrified him.'

Forbes nodded. 'So he ensured you became the White Warrior. Believed some Titan would finish you off to save him the trouble.'

'And when that didn't work, who d'you think sent Ulf and Erland to gut me?'

'The bastard.'

'During the Raiding Season, I suspect Radspakr dared not tell Odin about me. I don't know why. Maybe he feared Odin's reaction would be fatal for everyone. But then, before the Battle, things got really hot. Odin must have found out. Skarde accosted me, said I was dead meat, said Odin would destroy me. They had Halvar killed – fed to the fishes – and…'

'What?'

'Fed to the fishes. Skarde told me. One less mouth to blab.'

'Christ. That's why he wasn't there to lead the Wolves.'

'Leiv too. Knifed by Skarde. That was when I knew, even if I survived the Battle, the bloodletting in Valhalla would not cease and I'd be the next corpse.'

Forbes sat silently and digested everything. 'So you decided to switch sides.'

'I was always in the wrong Palatinate.'

'But how the hell did you know the Titans would accept your surrender in the heat of battle?'

'Once before Agape had stayed her blade above me and I dared to hope she might do it again.'

'Well, damn lucky for us she did.'

'Halvar told me she and my sister were close. I think, perhaps, the Captain of the Sacred Band knows more about Morgan's fate than she lets on.'

His words drifted away.

'The problem is,' said Forbes eventually, 'you're never going to find out, if we don't survive long enough to ask her.'

'Yeah, things are looking pretty screwed right now.'

Forbes eased himself from the blankets and held out

a hand. 'When we face those Titan bastards at the Blood Tidings, let us be Brante and Punnr one final time.'

Tyler gripped his hand.

The ferry took them from the island, its throaty progress marked by a trail of white through the cerulean waters, like a bridal train curving back to the embrace of the harbour.

Calder stood at the stern rail watching the island recede. She could just make out tiny white houses spotted across the eastern slopes, but the Horde's encampment and the Battle beach were hidden from view. The wind was bitter and she clasped her arms around her.

She had spent barely thirty-six hours on the island and during that time she had been buffeted through a maelstrom of emotions – shock, hurt, fear, ferocity, disbelief – and never found a moment to feel the beauty of the place. Because it *was* beautiful, right then, alone on the stern deck with the dawn sky afire and the dark waters sleeping and the ever-present throb of the engine beneath her. She soaked it all in, then silently vowed never, ever to set eyes on it again and swivelled away towards the warmth of the ferry's interior.

The main lounge was heavy with the scent of sausages and her stomach uncoiled like a serpent waking from winter. The remnants of the Horde sprawled in reclining seats, some asleep, some peering out of the salt-smeared windows, others staring empty-eyed at morning television. She joined the canteen queue behind a group of heavy-set Hammers who looked ready to charge the serving counter with the same gusto with which they had attacked Alexander's Phalanx. She was so drawn to the sight of the feast awaiting that it took several heartbeats to realise the man at the head of the queue had turned around with his filled plate and was examining her. It was Skarde. His parchment-pale skin looked untouched by the ravages of battle and his ice-white hair had been freshly combed. He held her with a glacial gaze, yet there was also something subdued about him, an air of moderation, like a hyperactive schoolchild after a caning by the tutor.

She tore her eyes away and when she looked again he had carried his tray to a coffee machine. She arrived at the counter and pointed mutely at the items she wanted, then steeled herself and walked out among the tables. He was seated halfway up the hall, his back to her. She gripped her tray and walked past, her pace not faltering until she came to the very last table where she pushed herself up to the window.

She tried to focus on her plate, but she felt his eyes crawling over her, pawing at her spine, creeping up her shoulders, tangling in her hair. She prodded at her food, but it meant nothing now. Every pore of her body was fastened on him. She could sense him rising and coming down the aisle, his steps closing on her, his fingers reaching, his breath in her ear.

'He's gone.' Calder jerked at the voice beside her and Freyja pushed a plate of pastries and a coffee across the table.

Calder twisted round. It was true. His table was abandoned, his plate empty. She closed her eyes, gathered herself and turned back to the Housecarl who was biting into an apricot Danish.

'The medics tell me Sassa and Geir are okay,' said Freyja.

'Sassa took a spear strike in her left thigh, but she'll walk again and will be back with us by the summer. Geir was concussed by a pommel in the face. His nose looks like your scrambled egg, but he was always an ugly git, so no one will notice.'

She tried to make light of it, but both were thinking of Gunhild and Siff, who would not be coming back, and Calder wondered if they lay somewhere still on the island or had already been secreted back to Edinburgh or perhaps even now were packed in stiff rows beneath them, deep in the bowels of the ferry.

'Just seven of us then,' said Calder.

'Until the recruitment drive during next Season's Armatura, when we'll replace and replenish. It's the way of the Pantheon.'

'But this *has* been a bad year.'

Freyja inclined her head. 'There's no denying that.'

Calder looked out the window and cradled her cup. The promise of dawn had passed and the sky was greying, the sea like iron. 'Do you think Punnr and Brante surrendered?'

'It looked that way. And if they did, then they abandoned their shield-comrades and renounced their Oaths to Valhalla and it's just as well that they are beyond our blades.'

Calder smiled sadly. 'Abandoned. Renounced.' She rolled the words around on her tongue. 'Only a few short weeks ago he promised me that what we had started together we would finish together.' She stared into her coffee. 'And then he kissed me.'

'You need to forget about him, girl. Forget about them both. They're gone. They're out the Pantheon. Alexander will hand them over to the Vigiles – may have already done so – and the gods know what awaits them after that. If they're lucky, they'll be transported separately to places far from Edinburgh and dumped, with the parting words that if they ever talk about their time in Valhalla or any other detail of what they witnessed, the Vigiles will return and ensure they disappear forever.'

Calder listened stone-faced as the finality of Freyja's words sunk in. Somewhere deep within the recesses of her mind she was aware that Punnr's rush towards the foe was a desperate last attempt to keep alive the trail to his lost sister, but this knowledge did nothing to appease her anger that he had deserted her just when she needed him most. 'He was never worth it anyway,' she said bitterly.

Freyja peered through the streaked window. 'It's Halvar that disturbs me more.'

'Where is he, Freyja?' Calder studied her Housecarl's face and realisation flooded through her. 'You believe he's dead.'

'You don't spend eight Seasons fighting alongside someone and not get to know them. Halvar kept his secrets tight, but I could see he'd got himself neck-deep in some sort of shit. There are few things in this world that frighten men like Halvar, but there were times when I could see the despair in his eyes. He must have seriously upset some powerful people. And I think two nights ago they decided to settle accounts.'

The first peninsulas of the mainland were slithering into view.

'Halvar the Rock,' said Calder quietly. 'Gone as well.'

III

'Name?'

The captives glanced at each other.

'Urquhart?' Forbes proffered.

Simmius tapped this information into his tablet. 'First name?'

'Forbes.'

'And you?'

'Maitland.'

The Titans' Adjutant had not looked up since he had entered their confines, wove between the strewn blankets and balanced his tablet on one of the empty shelves. But now he did.

'Maitland? Spelt m-a-i-t?' His eyes bored into Tyler from across the room.

'Yes. First name Tyler.'

Simmius remained unmoving for a further second, then grunted and recorded the information. 'And your decision?'

'We fight,' Forbes said.

Simmius dragged his eyes up to Tyler's and studied them, recalling memories.

Tyler nodded once. 'We fight.'

★

His caller hung up and the man in the bow tie reached for his laptop and began tapping in passwords to take him through the security levels. He found the footage awaiting him in his ultra-protected private area and spent fifteen minutes watching and sipping a fine Ouzo Barbayannis.

The door to the adjoining dressing room opened and a tall brunette entered attired in a black evening gown. 'How do I look?'

He twisted in his seat and inspected his wife. They had celebrated her sixtieth birthday only three weeks earlier with a stupendous gathering along the Finikoudes beachfront in Larnaca and perhaps these days she was a little heavier in hip and belly, yet despite access to more riches than he could imagine and more opportunities to philander than he could count, in truth he had never desired another woman.

'Sensational as always.' He rose and kissed her. She was taller than him in her heels, but he had always found this attractive.

'Who was that on the phone?'

He stepped back and pulled a quizzical face. '*That*... was Odin.'

His wife inclined her head. 'And what did *he* want?'

'I don't think he really knew. He was full of his usual Yankee bombast. How great the Battle was; neither line giving an inch. How Atilius must be congratulated on his choice of location. Then he said something about being ashamed of *that goddamn pair of yellow-bellies* and assumed I will be doing the right thing and flinging their undeserving arses from the Pantheon.'

31

'What did he mean by that?'

The man seated himself again and pointed to his laptop. 'I wasn't sure, but it prompted me to check some footage Simmius sent me last night. Seems we have two Valhalla prisoners at Ephesus and one of them was Odin's White Warrior in the last Raiding Season.'

His wife chuckled. 'He really won't like that.'

'I suppose not.' He picked his lower lip. Silver-haired, impeccably groomed, with the dark eyes of his Greek-Cypriot ancestry, his features had softened with age but he was still a handsome man. 'But making a direct call to me seems unwarranted.'

'Maybe he had some credibility invested in the captive.'

Zeus looked unconvinced. 'We had our own White Warrior during the Raids. I don't recall her name, much less her fate. And if *she* had been captured during the Battle, I wouldn't have batted an eyelid.'

His wife walked around to her bedside cabinet and extracted a diamond bracelet of such proportions it could have put a Viking arm-ring to shame. 'Our guests are already making their way up from the gatehouse.'

Zeus sighed. 'Of course. Let's go. Odin's just being Odin.'

They made their way to the door, but then his wife paused with her hand on the latch. 'Perhaps when we're done, you should follow it up with Simmius. I've known you long enough to trust your instincts.'

At least the food had improved.

'Fattening us up for the chop,' Forbes suggested archly through a mouthful of sweetmeat.

Word of their decision to stand and fight had been whispered around the Palatinate and it was grudgingly agreed there was honour in this. These Valhalla prisoners might have surrendered in extraordinary circumstances, but perhaps they were not quite the cowards the Sky-Gods had assumed. Their jailers treated them less curtly and the choices of meats, breads, honeys and fruits could not be faulted.

Tyler could not eat. Instead he paced the room. His hands were greased with sweat and his stomach writhed like a nest of vipers. Outside they could hear dozens of feet climbing to the higher floors as the Titans gathered to hear the formal results of the Nineteenth Season and to watch these Wolves die.

'I'm sorry, Forbes. It wasn't meant to end like this.'

Forbes had finished the sweetmeat and was leaning against one wall, stretching his calf muscles. They were still dressed in tunics and sandals, but they had been provided with wrist guards and iron greaves to protect their shins. 'This fight isn't lost yet.'

Tyler bit back his response and then the door swung open and two of their jailers entered. They had discarded their usual masks. Now their prisoners were short minutes from death, they no longer cared about hiding their identities. What they carried, however, was more encouraging. Swords. And not the short stabbing blades of the Titans, but Viking longswords, the ones Tyler and Forbes had hurled onto the sands before Agape's feet. There were shields too – the insignia blackened out with paint, but true limewood Viking shields nonetheless.

A grim, raw-boned officer appeared in the doorway.

'You are not Titans, so you will not carry our blades,' he said simply as the captives strapped the sword belts around them and took the proffered shields. It felt good to grasp the leather bindings again and appreciate the weight of the limewood on their arms. 'I am Menes, Captain of Companion Bodyguard, and you will follow me.'

Forbes leaned close to Tyler. 'I thought this was going to be a dirty knife fight, but look – Wolf shields and weapons. We are the Horde once more.'

They climbed the stairs to the higher floors and came out into a place like no other. A huge, wondrous garden high atop the Edinburgh skyline. Stone pathways wound around borders filled with olive and fig trees, lilies, palms and ferns. From the walls hung great ropes of clematis, ivy and jasmine, above which was a ceiling of glass with a full moon bathing the rooftops.

The earlier clamour had died and now only one voice was speaking, but the garden was filled with Sky-Gods. They stood proudly in their armour, lining the pathways and leaning down from the walkways. They bore no weapons or helmets and heads turned to stare in silence as the prisoners emerged. Tyler's breath caught in his throat. So here were the faces of the foe. The humans behind the bronze. Men, women. Some older, some barely beyond school age. They didn't gloat or leer, nor nod or smile. They simply watched the prisoners and listened to the voice from beyond the olive groves.

Menes prodded Forbes along a path and Titans stepped aside to let them pass. Through the foliage Tyler could see a brightly lit empty space and Alexander sat in state on the opposite side, bare-headed and face contorted in a rictus grin.

There was Cleitus next to him, red and shiny. Implacable bull-necked Nicanor and aristocratic Parmenion. Menes herded the prisoners beneath the boughs of a fig tree and Tyler peered around the Titan circle.

Although there were many female warriors present and he had never looked on her face behind the helmet, he had no doubt he would recognise Agape. And indeed, there she was. Blue hair yanked back into a plaited ponytail. Pale lips. Obsidian brows. Lime eyes. Captain of the Sacred Band and his true captor.

Simmius was saying something about the Valhalla Horde and Tyler zoned back. 'And so, here follows the Blood Tidings for the Horde of Valhalla:

Of the Titan Palatinate killed during the Raiding
Season, the Blood Nights and the Grand Battle of the
Nineteenth Season of the Pantheon:
Lion of Macedon = none
Colonel = none
Captain = none
Platoon Lead or Dekarchos = none
Companions or Band (elite) x 21 = 42 Credits
Phalanx or Peltast x 37 = 37 Credits
Vestales = none
Total Blood Credits awarded to the Horde of Valhalla
Palatinate: 79'

The Sky-Gods greeted this news with a murmur. The numbers represented fifty-eight of their comrades lost during the year and it was a sobering figure. Too many good troops who would no longer share wine with them.

Too many holes in the Titan lines. And almost eighty Blood Credits for the foe meant the Horde could replenish their litters and come at them again in the Twentieth Season.

Simmius allowed the talk to settle, then continued. 'And here follows the Blood Tidings for the Titan Palatinate:

Of the Valhalla Palatinate killed during the Raiding Season, the Blood Nights and the Grand Battle of the Nineteenth Season of the Pantheon:
High King = none
Jarl = none
Housecarl x 1 = 8 Credits
Hersir or Thegn x 3 = 12 Credits
Wolf or Raven (elite) x 17 = 34 Credits
Drengr x 33 = 33 Credits
Vestales x 4 = 16 Credits
Total Blood Credits awarded to the Titan Palatinate: 103'

Cheers thundered around the garden, for every Titan understood the meaning of these results. For the first time in four Seasons, they were in the ascendancy and in the weeks after the Interregnum Alexander could use these Blood Credits to recruit the troopers needed to surpass Valhalla's headcount. No longer would the Horde's Hammer line exceed the Titan Phalanx. No longer would the Wolves outnumber the Companions. This was the turning point.

Alexander raised his goblet to the crowd and the noise was such that it must surely wake the entire Royal Mile. Then from beneath the whoops, a new harmony emerged: a low earthy hum, as though from the roots of the plants themselves. It grew as more voices joined until every Titan was singing. Tyler remembered the sound when their ranks had first appeared through the grasses before the Battle, but he knew not if this was the same battle hymn. Whatever the words, whatever the sentiments, the resonance sent shivers through his bones. While the songs of Valhalla had kindled images of wild ice-bound fjords, these voices were surely the choir of the gods. As the music crescendoed in a sweep of euphoria, Forbes turned to him and the pools of his eyes said everything: *This is it, my friend.*

When the hymn hit its final note, the spotlights dimmed and braziers were lit. The song fractured into a hundred cheers and the King rose from his throne with arms aloft.

'It is time,' he shouted and the Titans thumped their feet and raised their fists. They were a seething mass now, lit only by the braziers and the glow of the moon, and the eye could not tell which limbs were human and which were flora. 'Bring forward the captives.'

'Ready to feast in your afterlife lad?' hissed Menes in Tyler's ear, then pushed him and Forbes into the empty space. The mosaic floor was moonlit pale and flickered with reflected flame. Across it a giant Star of Macedon made from black marble tesserae had been lovingly designed and enclosed by a circle. It was this circle that formed the perimeter of the space and the Titans had arranged themselves around it, careful not to overstep the line.

'Behold,' cried Alexander. 'My champions.'

From the opposite side of the circle came Myron and Nestor – one rhino-huge, the other taut as a bowstring. They carried bronze hoplons, but they were also protected by breastplates and helmets. Sheathed at their hips were shortswords and each gripped an eight-foot dory, the

Hoplite's spear of choice, with its flat leaf-shaped head and counterbalancing iron butt-spike.

'Should have guessed the bastards wouldn't make this a fair fight,' seethed Forbes.

Tyler's heart was pounding at the sight of these bringers of death and his breathing came in short, fast gasps. He caught Agape staring at him granite-faced and wanted to yell at her, but his throat would permit nothing to pass.

Alexander was loving the moment. His arms were still aloft, as though trying to capture the adulation and suck it into him. He stepped from his throne and made a show of clamping a hand on the shoulder of each of his champions, then he turned to gloat across the circle at the prisoners and his eyes were black and vulpine in the crepuscular light. Once he retook his seat, another figure eased from the perimeter. It was Simmius and he waited as the crowd's noise lulled.

'My fellow Titans, the captives you see before you were once soldiers in Wolf Regiment of the Valhalla Horde. Allegedly King Sveinn's most skilled and most fanatical troops.' Pantomime hoots and hisses. 'So, we must ask ourselves, what state of morale, what level of discord, what remnants of harmony, can exist amongst our enemy – holed up in their Tunnels like rats – if their brightest and best warriors run to our lines in the midst of battle and throw themselves at our feet? What clearer sign could we have that our great King Alexander, Lion of Macedon, has led us to overwhelming victory in the Nineteenth Season?'

Simmius waited for the cries to die, then levelled his eyes at the captives. 'Our generous King was noble enough to offer you the opportunity to redeem yourselves and you have duly accepted his Challenge. The rules of this engagement are simple: here and now, you will fight his champions. If any man should step from the circle, he will be thrown from the Pantheon. Of the four of you, when just two remain breathing, these two shall take their places within the Titan Palatinate. Do you understand these rules?'

Simmius swung to the bronze-sheathed champions and they nodded. Then he turned to the captives.

Forbes drew his mighty sword and held it aloft. 'The Wolves of Valhalla!' he yelled and the onlookers roared back, though the jeers were light in number. This crowd might be partisan, but it valued an underdog.

Simmius stepped out of the ring and Alexander flourished a hand. 'Begin!'

Forbes pulled close to Tyler. 'This is the fight we trained for. Everything comes down to this. Stay tight. Lock shields. Protect each other. And don't let the fuckers get behind us.'

Tyler took a juddering gulp of air and dragged his blade from its scabbard. 'Brante and Punnr – one final time?'

Brante grinned savagely. 'Aye. Brante and Punnr.'

And the Titans came at them.

IV

Sveinn was lying and everyone knew it.

Trestle tables had been arranged in rows lining the Throne Room and the Horde was seated shoulder to shoulder. It was supposed to be a feast, but most just picked at the food or sunk themselves solemnly in ale and mead. Many bore the detritus of warfare: broken noses, black eyes, blue bruises, split ears, missing fingers, slings and bandages. And these were the ones who required no stay in Pantheon hospitals.

Calder sat with her Ravens around one table. She had allowed a leg of roast chicken and couscous to be piled into her bowl, but it had remained untouched. She sipped at the mead, which Jorunn had insisted on pouring for her, but the sweet liquor could not warm her. Nor could the fire in the hearth behind. It seemed the heat had gone from Valhalla.

The Wolves hunched along the next table. They ate and drank in silence, but could not stop themselves casting furtive glances at Sveinn's table on the raised dais, for the seating arrangement had a portentous dread about it. Freyja was up there. Asmund too, and Bjarke. Everyone knew these were the remaining officers of the King's Council of War, so there was something wrong about the presence of Skarde. He sat on Sveinn's left, spearing a pork fillet, his face a scowl, his eyes flitting around the onlookers.

The Horde had listened to the formal Blood Tidings given – remarkably – by the King himself instead of Radspakr, but they had needed no telling that the Nineteenth Season must be chalked down as a loss. The final results were not in themselves catastrophic. The Titans' additional twenty-four Blood Credits would allow them to recruit strongly in the next Armatura and close the gap in headcount between the two Palatinates. This was to be regretted, but was nothing exceptional. Rather it was the manner of the loss that tugged at them. The brighter minds quickly drew three deductions: one, it was not the Battle that had been Valhalla's undoing, but the Blood Nights. Sveinn's strategy to hold back his better units had been exposed by the Titans' decision to send out their elite forces. Two, nothing illustrated this more thoroughly than the loss of four Vestales from Asmund's Storm Regiment on one Blood Night alone, essentially handing sixteen Credits to the foe.

And third, the phrase that had reverberated around the walls, the one Sveinn hurried over, rattled and eyes downcast, summed up the Horde's dejection: *Housecarl x 1*.

So now, as the King informed them of the higher Pantheon authorities' need for Halvar's services and his sincere hope that the Housecarl might one day return to Valhalla, they knew he lied. The Blood Tidings said so. You don't add *Housecarl x 1* to the roster if he's only temporarily detained. You don't give the Titans eight Blood Credits and then expect these returned. Halvar was gone. Of that, there was no doubt.

And Sveinn was a pawn in someone else's game. That too

was clear. Sveinn the Red had become Sveinn the Puppet. So there was something inevitable in the way he turned to the Wolf next to him and spoke.

'In the meantime, I have decided that Skarde will be the new – interim – Housecarl of Wolf Regiment. He will join my Council of War in the Twentieth Season and lead a Wolf Regiment rejuvenated by the Blood Credits we have won in this. And he will be afforded all the privileges of a Housecarl's rank.'

Skarde's hard glare fixed on the Wolves, testing them, seeing if any dared respond. Most kept their heads down, but Ake returned his gaze. Words were unnecessary. Her message was clear. *There will come a day of reckoning.*

'Kill them!' yelled Alexander, eyes black pits.

Punnr and Brante had locked shields, but their adversaries were stealing either side, teasing with their dories and forcing the Vikings to bend their wall. Nestor lunged first and drove his spear at Brante's exposed right flank. Brante angled his shield across just in time, but the impact took him back a step and exposed Punnr. Myron saw his opportunity and thrust hard at his lighter opponent. Punnr twisted, took the point on his shield and scythed his sword down onto the dory's shaft. But Myron's grip was rock and the impact jarred up Punnr's arm.

The Titans stepped back. Their spears gave them reach, permitting them to prod and tease at their adversaries' defences, while staying beyond the reach of their blades. They slipped either side of the Vikings and forced them back to back.

'Whatever you do, don't bloody lose contact,' hissed Brante.

As one, the Titans attacked. Nestor went low. Brante was forced to protect his shins, so his backside jolted into Punnr as Myron's spear came driving from high. Only the gods know how Punnr wrenched his face from the path of the blow. The razor edge hissed past his ear and the ash shaft grazed his cheek. He flung his shield up and knocked the spear away. But Myron was not finished. The solid muscle of him smashed his hoplon into his adversary's limewood shield, sending Punnr flying back into Brante and making them both skitter towards Nestor. The latter should have skewered them both, but he was caught by surprise and Brante found himself beyond Nestor's iron point. He swung his sword at his foe's head. It sheared off the Titan's helmet and cut into his shoulder, making him spit a curse and skip backwards.

'First blood to Valhalla!' Brante roared and locked himself against Punnr once more.

Myron bellowed and thrust his dory into Punnr's shield, splitting through it so the spearpoint halted just inches from Punnr's eyes. The giant hauled the weapon back, yanking Punnr with it, then swinging Punnr's shield from left to right like a dog savaging a bone. Punnr lost all contact with Brante as he desperately tried to keep his left arm locked in the shield's leather bonds, for if he lost this, he was done for. The Titan wrenched a final time and the spear came free. Punnr turned his shield in one fluid motion and rammed it edge first into Myron's bull neck, then followed with a sword strike at his leading thigh. The giant got his hoplon down in time, but he was gasping from the blow to his throat and he stepped back, coughing and shaking his head.

He spat at Punnr, then glanced to Nestor and nodded. It was time to stop playing with these Wolves. They flew at them, dories lunging again and again, and then they were in close, hoplons crashing into Viking shields, eyes bulging behind their helmets, snarling and cursing, driving the Valhalla pair backwards. Myron propelled his full weight and Punnr could no more hold him than stop a bolting horse. He fell and Myron came with him, slamming the wind from him and writhing on top like a crazed lover. The giant raised his helmet and brought it down. Punnr's nose should have disintegrated, but he managed to turn his head and instead the blow cracked against the side of his skull. Again Myron pounded him, intent on spraying his brains across the mosaic floor. Punnr yelled and saw stars.

The Titan raised his head a third time and Punnr knew his skull would splinter this time. They were too close for blades, but Punnr reversed his wrist and drove his sword pommel into Myron's throat just as the man was coming down again. It slammed against his windpipe, wrecking it, and Myron's head collapsed onto Punnr's shoulder, a gurgling, choking sound coming from within the helmet.

Above them, Brante grappled with Nestor, but now the Titan was too close to use his dory effectively and Brante's sword hewed at his opponent's hoplon, denting the bronze. Nestor danced backwards to bring himself into spear strike range again. Brante was still off balance and Nestor thrust at his exposed sword arm. The point caught Brante's iron wrist-guard and sheared off, slicing along his arm and smacking into the floor. With a howl, Brante brought his foot down on the point, wedging it momentarily to the tiles, then scythed his blade onto the ash shaft with all his strength. The wood fractured and split. Like lightning, Nestor reversed the broken shaft in his hand and threw the iron-ended butt at Brante's face, but the Wolf was ready and knocked it away contemptuously with his shield. Blood ran from his arm, dripping onto the floor in a russet slick.

Punnr shoved the choking Myron off him and scrambled to his feet, but his opponent was not Alexander's champion for nothing. Despite his bulk, he reared up fast as a cat and set his tree-trunk legs wide apart, shield ready, spear in hand, ignoring the breath still rasping through his smashed windpipe. For a moment the four fighters took stock, sucked oxygen into their lungs and eyed one another. Brante's sword arm was shaking from the wound and Punnr's skull thundered. The pair inched together again.

Myron looked to Nestor and took in the broken dory lying uselessly in two pieces. The smaller Titan pulled his shortsword free and a wordless message passed between them. Time to change tactics. Time for the kiss of blades. Myron swung back his arm and threw his spear straight at Punnr. It buried itself in the Valhalla shield, the point once more driving through the limewood so that it hung immovable like an eight foot-flagpole. Punnr wrenched the useless shield from his arm and flung it to one side, facing his opponent with only his sword for protection.

Nestor's attention had been on Myron's spear throw. With his eyes averted from his adversary, he stepped onto the slippery blood patch and Brante did something no one expected. He charged.

This was no blade craft. This was no practised attack.

This was simple brute force. Nestor was hard as nails, but he was no Myron when it came to bulk and Brante hit him – shield and shoulder – with all the speed and power he could muster. The Titan's feet scrabbled desperately, but they held no purchase on the blood and he went backwards. Brante's velocity was unstoppable. Onwards. Three feet. Four. Five. And suddenly the crowd was parting and Nestor was falling, sliding, thumping into their legs. Beyond the line. Outside the circle.

Brante reared up, heaving for breath and blood trickling from his arm, his eyes bulging down at his vanquished opponent. For Nestor was gone. Out the Pantheon. The Titan crowd erupted. Brante pointed his blade at the man, spat, then turned and walked slowly back towards the others, the noise of the Sky-Gods all around.

Myron had not moved. He was as shocked as everyone else in the garden and now he watched Brante's halting approach. Behind, in the crowd, Nestor clawed himself upright, his mouth slack and his body shaking with anger, unable to grasp the implications of what had just happened. Before anyone could stop him, he stepped back across the line, tore his hoplon from his left arm and threw it like a discus at his receding foe. It was a technique he had attempted many times in the Bladecraft Rooms of Persepolis until he had perfected his aim. The bronze shield spun across the circle and slammed into the back of Brante's neck. If the edge had been thinner, it would have decapitated him. Instead, it flung him face-first onto the blood-slick floor.

There was a moment of silence and then – as Nestor staggered towards his fallen adversary, sword gripped and intent on murder – pandemonium broke loose. No matter that Nestor was a Titan. This was a breaking of the Rules and a breaking of the honour of their Palatinate. Alexander stared wide-eyed from his throne, incapable of taking in the turn of events and unable to quieten the crowd. Nestor was just yards from Brante's prone and senseless body.

And then another figure stepped across the line and bent to pick up the Viking's longsword. Alexander's jaw dropped, cries caught in throats and Nestor halted his approach. For standing above the Wolf, Valhalla longsword pointed at the Titan champion, was Agape.

A stranger sat at Sveinn's table. With all the business of the Blood Tidings, the warriors had presumed he must be a delegate from Atilius and paid him no heed. But Calder watched him now and the kernel of a thought began to seed itself in her gut.

He was young. Or, at least, youngish. In his thirties, with a round, florid face and chestnut hair combed as a mother would style it – lovingly parted, then run in undulating waves across the scalp. His stomach and neckline were testimony to a life well lived and as he cradled a goblet of wine, he beamed magnanimously around the Hall. He was clothed in a bright red robe, buttoned diagonally across his torso, but what Calder peered at now – what no one else seemed to have noticed – was the large silver Odin amulet hanging from a chain around his neck.

An amulet that symbolised Valhalla and one that, therefore, no delegate from Atilius would carry. An amulet just like that which Radspakr wore.

Calder felt a frisson of unease snake through her ribcage.

His beam passed across her table and perhaps she met his eyes. They were chestnut, like his hair, languid and confident. She found herself staring around the Hall. Where *was* Radspakr? Why could she not see him?

As if in answer to her questions, Sveinn turned to the man and held out a hand. The King began speaking, saying something about Radspakr's nineteen Seasons of service, but blood was now roaring in Calder's ears and she could barely make sense of his words. What was that? Retire? Radspakr – as was his right – had decided nineteen Seasons was enough and had chosen to retire!

Radspakr the hawk. Radspakr who wanted her dead, who had sent a killer to her flat, who had directed Ulf and Erland to murder her at the castle. Radspakr was gone?

There was noise around her now, bewildered voices up and down the benches, but she only had eyes for the stranger on the dais. This rotund, jolly man. Kustaa, Sveinn was calling him.

Kustaa. New Thane of the Palatinate. Paymaster. Custodian of the Day Books. Counsellor of War. Lord Adjutant of the Horde of Valhalla.

Kustaa. Who was not Radspakr.

Nestor's rage blinded him.

If he understood the ramifications of being thrown from the circle, he showed no sign. If he recognised the Captain of the Sacred Band awaiting him, he gave no heed. He came at her, all teeth and snarl and spit behind his helmet, his sword arm drawn back for the thrust, and he only stopped when she danced in close, brought her cheek against his bronze faceguard in mournful communion and slipped two foot of iron through his gut. He froze then and the snarl turned to incomprehension. He gripped her, let her take his weight while he studied her features. The flawless ivory of her skin was so wondrous and he felt a longing for life. Then his knees buckled and he crumpled to the floor.

There was an exhalation of breath from the assembled Titans and then a wall of noise. Cleitus was beside himself, purple with rage, gesticulating wildly. One of his Companion Bodyguard killed by another Titan. It was inconceivable, unforgivable. Menes lurked on the perimeter, stone-still, a hand on his sword pommel. Parmenion's sharp gaze darted around the crowd to gauge the temperature. Nicanor argued heatedly with the woman next to him. And Alexander – Alexander was rooted to his chair, fingernails digging into the armrests, utterly bewildered by the turn of events.

Brante was coming round. He raised himself to his knees and winced with pain. He blinked at Nestor's corpse beside him, then reached shakily for his own dropped shield. Punnr's free hand came under him and hauled him to his feet. Myron – thank the gods – was too flummoxed to attack. He hovered several yards away and gawked at Agape. What was he supposed to do? There had only ever been one planned outcome: two victorious Titans and two dead Vikings. Yet now there were five in the ring and, in truth, he was no longer certain who was friend and who was foe.

'Kill them, you imbecile!' screamed Cleitus and Myron heard that clearly enough. He drew his blade and bellowed a challenge.

Wordlessly, Agape stepped to Brante and shoved his

longsword back into his hand, then turned and strode from the circle. The crowd loved this. Nestor had paid the price for breaking the Rules and now Titan honour was restored. They cheered Agape's departing form and they cheered the Wolves. Nicanor was beating his palms and Parmenion grinning. And Alexander was a ghost, a husk, powerless to alter events.

Myron swung his blade in great arcs and the Wolves parted. Punnr shifted right and Myron hit him with his shield, at the same time scything his sword at Brante. The Wolf blocked it with his own shield and then thrust at Myron's exposed flank. The blade found the space beneath the Titan's sword arm where his armour did not reach. It bit through tunic and flesh and sheared off ribs, cracking the bottom of his shoulder blade as it exited. Myron grunted, but refused to recognise the pain.

The Vikings were either side of him now. He held his shield towards Punnr and his blade towards Brante, but he could not hope to defend a concerted attack from both. His brain ticked. At stake were two places in the Palatinate. Two victors. So he only needed to kill one. He chose Brante.

With a speed that belied his size, he exploded towards his target, parrying a blow with his hoplon and hacking his sword into the top of the Valhalla shield. Then fast as a snake, he bent and struck for Brante's legs. His blade hewed into iron vambrace and Brante howled and staggered. Myron reared up and drew his weapon back for the killer thrust, but in the same instant he saw the other Viking in the periphery of his vision and knew his death was upon him. The needle-sharp point of the longsword broke through the soft flesh behind his jaw, split his tongue, breached the roof of his mouth and tore into his cerebellum. Punnr wrenched the blade free and blood and bone and grey brains spattered his tunic.

Myron crumpled and Punnr – caught in the blood-craze of the moment – leapt on top of him and slammed his sword down again, this time into the man's ample belly, so hard that the steel ruptured gut, splintered spine and thudded against the floor itself. He tried to yank it free and would have struck once more, but Brante grabbed a handful of his scraggy hair and hauled him away. Punnr was heaving with rage, his face streaked with spittle. The air was steaming and filled with the tang of blood and death and shit as the Titan's bowels emptied.

Brante swung Punnr round and forced him to focus. And slowly the craze passed. There was noise everywhere. Shouting and cheering. He clung to Brante, needing his strength because his own legs were water, and somewhere over the other Wolf's shoulder he spied Agape. She was utterly still amongst the commotion, her gaze unblinking. She held him with her eyes for a heartbeat and nodded once. He pulled away, shaking his head and starting to laugh deliriously with Brante. There was pain etched across his friend's features and they were both strewn with gore. But none of it mattered.

For they were alive. And what's more, they were Titans now.

V

Lana carried a chair out into spring sunshine and set it on the path beyond her doorstep, where she sat with her breakfast of crumpets and watched the Leith flowing under Falshaw Bridge. There was a late-April warmth in the air. Serried ranks of daffodils lined the banks. Blackbirds vied in the shrubs. But none of this – not even the crumpets – could thaw winter's hold on her heart.

She had departed Valhalla as soon as the Blood Tidings formalities were concluded, marched grimly back to Stockbridge and sunk half a bottle of Pinot Grigio with forty milligrams of temazepam in the hope of blanking out events. Instead, she had lain in her bed, heavy as stone, eyes wide, waiting for night to give way.

Her mind had been overrun by Skarde's face. It hung above her and the darkness only magnified the luminance of his ice-white hair and the crystal-blue cruelty in his eyes. Perhaps, if life had run a different course, she might have been able to move forward from that tangible act of rape. She could have blanked out the details and fenced off the memory of her attacker as a bastard in her past, a brute who had speared through the timeline of her existence and then gone.

But the reality was that he had never left. However much she loathed him, however much she fantasised about burying her knife to the hilt in his heart, she was linked to him by an unbroken thread which, even at the Blood Tidings, tugged at her as it reached across the benches and over the heads of the other warriors and sought out his clenched fist. Because she had carried his baby. She had loved his offspring. She would have given her life to save his child. And the blue of his eyes would always be Amelia's.

As she sat in the April sunshine, she still felt the cold of him pressing down. She rose and took the chair and half-eaten crumpets inside but, in truth, the interior was worse. She forced herself to make coffee and cradled the warmth of the cup as she perched on the sofa. A person's home should be their refuge, their sanctuary, their place of safety, but she no longer felt any security in this house. On that very sofa she had fought for her life and fled from Radspakr's attack dog. And she had also been sitting there when she dropped her defences to another man, let him kiss her, perhaps even wanted him. Now that man had abandoned her.

She reached for her phone and stabbed at the screen until she brought up the number for WW – White Warrior. She stared at it in silence, then tapped the Block button. *It's over, Tyler Maitland. You chose your course and now I choose mine.*

The day stretched into afternoon and she pottered as best she could to keep her mind from the blacker margins. She played music, stripped her bedding and bundled it into the washer-dryer, baked cheese scones and ate some hot from the oven. Gradually it dawned on her that the Blood Tidings had marked the end of the Pantheon's Nineteenth Year and – as the yawning emptiness of the Interregnum beckoned – she possessed in abundance the two things she needed least in her life at that moment: time and emotions.

She knew the scones were an attempt to fill the house with the scent of homeliness, but the act was forlorn. She could have lit a fire in the hearth and run a bubble bath and still the place would feel malign. Only one thought sustained her. It was the image of the man with the chestnut eyes and the double chin and the schoolboy hair. Kustaa was his name. His smile had seemed genuine. His features had looked soft and guileless. Perhaps he really was a new beginning. Maybe, just maybe, she now lived in a world without Radspakr.

As daylight retreated and she faced the prospect of another night in the swaddling arms of alcohol and pills, Lana came to a decision. She pulled on her coat, stepped into the twilight and wended her way up the hill towards the Old Town. Back to Valhalla.

After the fight, Tyler and Forbes were allowed to recuperate in ways they could barely have imagined.

Alexander refused to look at them, so it was left to Simmius to raise his voice above the commotion and confirm them victors. Their weapons and armour were collected and they were led back down the steps, but not to their locked room. Instead they dropped yet another floor and were shown into a large ornately tiled washing area. They stripped off their tunics and stood under the showers, letting the hot flow rinse away the blood.

Forbes clenched his teeth and grunted with pain. A livid welt ran across the back of his neck, but at least his sliced arm appeared only a flesh wound. He cast a sardonic eye over Tyler.

'Nice to see you can take on two Titan champions and come out of it without a scratch.'

When they were done they discovered their soiled garments had been removed. A lean older man sat Forbes by a table and expertly cleaned and bandaged his arm, then sent them both pattering naked to the far end of the shower room where a plunge pool awaited. Tyler dipped an exploratory hand into the water.

'Like ice,' he said and was about to move on when Forbes gave him a firm shove between the shoulder blades. 'Bastard!' he yelled as he emerged puffing and spluttering like a walrus and pulled himself up the ladder.

Forbes was already at the entrance to the next area and he whistled in admiration. Before them was a swimming pool, captivatingly calm and lit from below to highlight a serpent-headed Medusa crafted into the tiling. A scent of aloe rose from its depths and along one edge was seating and a table replete with food and drink.

'Who'd have thought it?' muttered Forbes stretching his bruised neck cautiously.

'We must be three or four storeys above the Mile.'

'Aye. Quite a feat of engineering. To think in Valhalla we considered the showers a luxury.'

Forbes needed to keep his bandaging dry, so Tyler jumped in alone and floated on his back, studying the burnished bronze ceiling. After the heat of the showers and the traumatic cold of the plunge pool, there was a perfection to the temperature and for a moment he had the strangest sensation of being back in his mother's womb.

Forbes was attacking the food when Tyler emerged and together they mauled flatbreads, olives, hams, cheeses, tomatoes and wines. They were animated as the feast invigorated them, but gradually the new reality subdued them and Forbes took himself off to the opposite side and sat with his legs in the water, tenderly massaging the back of his neck with his good arm. They were Titans. Somehow in just a few short days, the Fates had conspired to throw them into the arms of their foe. Valhalla was gone. Friends and allies all lost to them.

At long last the guards returned and indicated the pair should follow them back to the shower rooms, where they found street clothing – boots, trousers, T-shirts and coats. All fitted perfectly and they presumed Simmius must have acquired their records from Atilius' central teams.

Ephesus was silent now. Weapons and armour had been locked away and the troops dispersed back to their homes. Only Simmius remained, seated in his office behind a grand mahogany desk. He welcomed them indifferently to the Titan Palatinate of the Lion of Macedon and informed them that their Titan identities and positions would be confirmed on their return at the start of the Twentieth Season. Meantime, the Interregnum was theirs to spend as they wished. However – and for this statement his eyes rose from the tablet in front of him – they should be under no illusions that they would go unobserved and if he learned of any communications with their previous Palatinate, the punishment would be extreme and final and meted out by Vigiles.

After so many shared experiences since those early nights as Thralls in the vaults beneath Market Street, Tyler and Forbes completed the Nineteenth Season with a quiet handshake and were swept away from the Royal Mile in separate vehicles.

Tyler had expected his driver to take him down to Princes Street and back through New Town to his house in Comely Bank, but instead they continued up the Mile and then along Johnston Terrace, which wound around the southern aspect of the castle. No matter, he thought. It's early morning and the streets will be quiet, so the man's obviously decided to go via Lothian Road and Queensferry.

They drew up at lights and Tyler spied a Tesco Express on one corner. He thought of his flat and tried to remember back to the night he had departed in such a hurry. It was the same evening he had been with Lana by the Leith and they had kissed and then he had drunk too much and been a prick. He had stalked back to Learmonth in a fury, only to find a taxi waiting for him. As he'd hurriedly grabbed a bag, he had no idea he was about to be flown to a tiny island off the west coast of Scotland and then inexorably to a beach, a Battle, a surrender and a new Palatinate. He pictured the creaking stairs and the schnauzer and Oliver across the landing. He thought of his room with its sagging sofa and family photos and he tried to recall what state he had left it in. Two things were certain: it would be cold and whatever remained in the fridge would be inedible.

'Can we make a stop?' Tyler pointed to the Tesco. 'I need a few essentials.' The driver seemed taken aback, but shrugged wordlessly and pulled the car over. 'Oh crap, I've no money. Can I borrow some?'

The man delved into the glove compartment and passed him a fifty. 'On the house.'

Ten minutes later, Tyler returned and the driver eyed his essentials wryly. A loaf of white bread, a bottle of ten-year-old Scapa and two packs of Marlboro. They pulled away, but not north up Lothian Road; instead they went south and then along Canning Street, over Shandwick Place and into an area of upmarket shops and embassies.

'Where are we?' demanded Tyler as they turned into one street of especially impressive Georgian buildings and the car slowed to a halt.

The driver retrieved an envelope from his pocket and passed it over his shoulder. On it was typed *"Callum Brodie Level 6"*.

'Up there.' The man pointed to a modern structure crammed between two stately period properties.

Tyler disembarked and climbed the steps. A glass door slid open and he found himself in a compact minimalist lobby. Ahead was a lift with level 6 labelled *Penthouse*. He selected this and a few moments later emerged onto a marble-floored landing with just one door. He pressed the buzzer, waited, pressed it again and then used the knocker. Silence. He looked at the envelope and broke it open. Inside was a single notelet with four numbers: 8352. He tapped these into a keypad beside the door and was greeted with a click.

The first thing that hit him as he pushed inside was the daylight, so bright it made him blink. He was in a huge room, but all he could take in were the floor-to-ceiling windows running the whole length of the opposite wall, through which morning sunshine was competing with the rain.

'Hello?' he called, but there was no answer. He went to

the glass and found himself looking out across Georgian rooftops towards Fountainbridge in the south. He could see the traffic on Lothian Road and the dome of Usher Hall, and there to the east was a superlative view of the castle. He pursed his lips in appreciation and peered around the rest of the room. It was floored in polished oak. The walls were a golden cream, which complemented three white sofas. There was a gilt and glass dining table, a prodigious white rug and a grand piano in one corner. Whoever Callum Brodie was, he wasn't lacking in a bob or two. At the other end was an open-plan kitchen painted storm grey and a phone was lying on the worksurface. He picked it up and the screen powered up, demanding a passcode. Carefully, he replaced it and dumped his bag of essentials beside it.

A pair of doors led off from the primary living space. He selected the first door and found himself in a leviathan of a bedroom with a super-king bed covered in cushions. There was an en suite too, but he didn't get to view it because his breath had caught in his throat. Piled haphazardly beside the bed were all his earthly possessions. He strode over and rummaged through the boxes. Everything was there except the items he had taken to the island. His clothes, his shoes, his running gear, his dumbbells, his punchbag, his books, magazines, DVDs, his framed photos, even a few mugs and a half-empty bottle of Glenmorangie. He found himself cursing and then laughing. *Bloody hell. Is this serious?*

He returned to the main room and opened the other door, expecting to find a guest bedroom. Instead there was a curling stairway that brought him to a door accessing a blustery, rain-spattered roof terrace, bounded on four sides by waist-high glass and containing another table, set of chairs, sunlounger and state-of-the-art barbecue. The views in every direction were astounding and he stood in the sunlit mizzle and admired a rainbow suspended over Dean Village. *So this is what it means to be a Titan.* He had come a long way since his crack-dealing days on the estate and he found himself wondering what his mother would say if she could see him now. But he pummelled the thought back down into his gut. His mother had worked her fingers to the bone to provide for them on that estate and she had been rightly proud of their little flat. Whatever its limitations, it had been home for Tyler and Morgan and there were times when he would give all the riches in the universe to be back there as a family.

He descended and discovered a fridge filled with provisions. The quantity of fruit and vegetables made his lips curl upwards. The Pantheon wanted its troops to have their five-a-day before it slipped a blade through their ribs. He buttered two slices of the Tesco white loaf, poured a finger of Scapa and collapsed on a sofa. It made sense really, he thought as he chewed and took in the city views. Radspakr and the Horde held records of his old address in Learmonth, so the Titans would want to locate him somewhere new. Still, it had only been twelve hours since the duel and he was amazed at the speed someone had moved his belongings. Then it dawned on him that perhaps they had already cleared his old flat in the days prior. Whatever the outcome of the Ephesus fight, once he had surrendered on that beach, the Pantheon knew he was never returning to Learmonth.

A thought struck him and he popped the last of the bread into his mouth and went back to the phone on the worksurface. He had left his old phone in a box on the island before the Battle. Now he input its passcode into this new phone. The digits were accepted and the home screen opened.

'Jesus,' he breathed.

He tapped through screens and found his contacts all present and correct, as well as a new number for this phone. Again, it made sense. Radspakr had his old number on Valhalla's records, so the Titans would want to start afresh to ensure he could not be tracked by his old Palatinate.

He wandered disconcertedly back to the bedroom and frowned at the boxes of belongings and that was when he spied an item on the bedside table that he had missed. It was a wallet, one he had never seen before. He opened it and discovered his driving licence in a transparent pocket. There was his photo just as it had always been, beardless and several years younger, but underneath was the name Callum Brodie. Slack-jawed, he flipped through the other folds of the wallet. His credit card, his library card, both in the name of Callum Brodie. And a debit card now provided by an entirely different bank. He dropped the wallet and rummaged in the boxes until he found his passport. Photo correct. Date of birth correct. Date of issue correct.

Name: Callum Bloody Brodie.

VI

Calder slipped into Valhalla via the North-West Gate on Milne's Court. There was just the one Hammer gatekeeper, who nodded to her from his control booth. She deposited her coat and bag in reception, crossed an empty Western Hall, passed the silent Practice Rooms and entered Sveinn's Throne Room. Here there was a smattering of warriors idling the evening hours over ale and she waved a greeting to three of Storm's light arrow troops spread across corner benches, but continued into East Tunnel without breaking step.

She came to the door of the Adjutant's quarters, steeled herself and knocked. There was movement from within and she was assaulted by the sudden conviction it would be Radspakr's vulpine features that greeted her. But no – Kustaa opened the door.

'Are you looking for me?'

Calder nodded. 'I was hoping I could speak with you about a personal matter.'

Kustaa seemed surprised, but stepped back to admit her. She had only ever glimpsed the Adjutant's office from the Tunnel and for some reason she expected it to be more impressive, more state-of-the-art. Yes, there were data screens like those at a city trader's workstation, a satellite photo of Edinburgh across one wall and monitors showing live camera feeds around Valhalla and outside the Gates. But look past these and the details became more humdrum. A plastic container with pens, scissors and paperclips. A ruler. A stapler. Several gunmetal filing cabinets. And a flip chart – for Christ's sake – stashed away behind a cupboard. When in god's name had Radspakr ever needed a flip chart?

Kustaa indicated a chair and returned to his desk. 'I haven't mastered everyone's name yet.'

'Calder.'

He consulted his laptop, frowning as he tapped the keys. 'Still getting my head around these systems.'

'Where were you before?' she queried cautiously.

'Back office. Pantheon HR. It might be all glamour and glory in the shieldwall, but someone's got to keep the show running. Ah, here we go. Litter One, Raven Company House Troop?'

'If it's technically a company when there's only five of us left.'

'Hmm, I understand this Season was tough on the Ravens.'

'So what brings you to the Horde?'

'Applications, interviews and references, my dear. Just the same as any other job. I must say it's quite something to be following in the footsteps of someone as exalted as Radspakr, don't you agree?'

'Indeed.'

'His legacy stretches across all nineteen years of the Pantheon. Some might say he was an institution!'

'And some might say the speed of his retirement was all the more remarkable.'

Kustaa smiled vacantly at this and changed the subject. 'So what is this personal matter I can help you with?'

'I want to move from my house in Stockbridge and I understand I need to go through you.'

He checked his screen again. 'Number 4 Reid Terrace? That's not a Pantheon property.'

'No. I was renting it before I was recruited.'

'I see. Well… yes… we have a few properties currently vacant. Do you have a preference for location?'

Calder shook her head.

'And may I ask why you wish to make this move?'

'One of the Wolves who surrendered to the foe at the Grand Battle – Punnr of Litter Four – was a fellow Thrall of mine during the last Armatura. He had a… *thing*… for me and one night after training he followed me home.'

'I see.'

'I told him to get lost and that was the end of the matter. But now he's gone from the Pantheon I worry that my personal circumstances have been compromised.'

Kustaa examined her and there was a sharper light in his eyes. 'I can understand your feelings. Well, give me until Wednesday and I'll get a new place confirmed for you. I can have a team sort the removal process as well.'

She smiled gratefully and watched him tap details into the laptop. 'Can I just confirm that you're now the only person who has access to Palatinate living arrangements?'

'Within the Horde, yes. A change of address will be added to the Pantheon's central database, but it is the Adjutant alone who holds these records within the Palatinate. Is there a problem?'

'No. I simply value my privacy.'

'A commendable attribute.'

She left him and returned to the Throne Room, but baulked at the company of the other warriors. Instead she made her way back to the empty Western Hall and pulled a bench close to the hearth. She gathered some furs and folded herself into them so she could gaze at the flames. There was something calming about a near-empty Valhalla. Despite all the trauma and violence and bloodshed, the timelessness of the Tunnels reassured her and she knew instinctively she would not be sleeping in her house that night.

Later she padded through to the Throne Room and ate a thick lamb stew washed down with two goblets of wine, then took a tea back to the Western Hall and nestled into her place by the hearth.

The flames receded and her eyelids grew heavy.

The day drifted for Tyler. He picked from the fridge and drank too much Scapa. The discovery of his new identity had blown away his earlier exuberance. He had checked some old paperwork he retained and seen that the numbers on his accounts, his passport and his driving licence had also all changed. He logged into the account with the new bank using his old password details and was amazed to find he could not only access it, but it was surprisingly well stocked with additional funds. The name across the top was inevitably Callum Brodie and the guile, skill and, yes, raw power to make these changes so quickly unnerved him.

The only parts of his life, it seemed, which the Pantheon could not touch were the secrets in his head.

Mid-afternoon he made another discovery. While he was scouring through his things, he found a set of keys. He took the lift down to the lobby and located a rear exit. Sure enough, outside was a small residents' parking area squashed between the buildings and parked in the bay marked 6 was his old Vauxhall Vivaro van. He opened up the back and surveyed the familiar duvet and pillows, the ragtag books scattered around, the toolbox and sundry CDs in broken boxes – and in some small way these sights restored him. They were pieces of the real him, untainted by the hand of the Pantheon.

As evening descended and he watched lights come on across the city, he made himself spaghetti bolognaise and opened a can of Grolsch from the stash left in the fridge. The castle was bathed in emerald spotlights. It was a view that wealthy tourists would have paid a mint to experience, but the sheer expanse of the vista made him feel more alone than ever. He toyed with his new phone and pulled up the number for Elsie.

'*Elsie?*' Lana had queried that night in her house. '*Why?*'

'*Say it slowly.*'

'*El... sie. Oh, very clever.*'

He pondered the phone. *Where are you tonight, Lana Cameron? I miss you.* Coming to a decision, he tapped the number and held the phone to his ear, but got only a dead line. He tried again. Still nothing. He sighed and plonked it on the glass table.

He drained the lager and studied the flickering lights across the city, then collected his coat, hat, cigarettes, keys and whisky bottle and dropped six floors to the lobby. He made his way out into the dark parking area, opened up his van and crawled into the back. Slamming the doors shut, he curled under the duvet and lit a Marlboro.

And there he spent the night, illuminated only by the glow of his cigarettes. It felt good to be enveloped by the familiar oily smells and the rough touch of the duvet. It was like old times.

Like the old Tyler Maitland.

She must have slept deeply, for when she finally came round there was morning traffic rumbling on the streets above. Someone had quietly restoked the fire and it was crackling and popping heartily. She rubbed her face and stretched herself from the furs. Breakfast scents beckoned from the kitchens and she followed her nose back through. The morning shift of Hammer gatekeepers were grabbing bacon rolls and a few others were hunched over tables, probably newly woken themselves.

She ate a roll and indulged in two cappuccinos, then decided she would shower before heading back to Stockbridge to begin her packing. She wandered along the North-West Tunnel to the female washing area where the absence of wet footprints told her she was the first of the morning. As always, soft white towels were arranged in baskets beside the mirrors. She took one, stripped and padded into the showers.

The water revived her. She faced the wall and let it

pummel her scalp. The soap in the dispenser smelled divine. She had once enquired what brand it was, but no one seemed to know and a fixation on soap seemed improper in a Viking Horde. She rubbed the bubbles over her torso, then turned to allow the water to massage her shoulders – and opened her eyes.

Skarde was inches from her. So close, his boots were getting wet. His gaze was carnal, his lips drawn back in a leer.

For a second she was paralysed, mind and body blank. Then lightning streaked through her. 'Get the fuck out!' She exploded into a burst of punches, swinging her arms wildly and whacking him in the chest and neck. 'Get out!'

A fist connected with his jaw and he felt that. His right hand clamped around her throat with such force she was lifted from the ground. He thumped her against the wall, then swung her down hard on the tiles, forcing her head into the corner. He was under the shower himself now, the water drenching his hair and jeans. She clawed at his wrist and twisted uselessly under him. She tried to scream but his fingers were dug so far into her neck that it came out as no more than a gurgle. His face was enraged above her, so ferocious she thought he was going to kill her right there and then.

'Where?' he snarled, his eyes burning into hers. 'Where is Tyler Maitland?'

She was choking. Her wet fingers scrabbled at his arm, her legs squirmed and fireworks fizzed across her vision. She could barely grasp his question.

'I'm told little lover boy had the hots for you. So tell me where I can find the bastard.'

He bashed her head against the tiles and she was certain this was her death. Water was pouring up her nose, drowning her even as she gagged. She tried to gasp a reply, but her throat just convulsed.

'What did you say?' He released his grip a fraction and bent his ear to her.

'I don't know.'

'Don't lie, you bitch, you do!' He had a knee on her pelvis to hold her down and with his free hand he slapped her across the cheek. She tasted blood on her tongue.

'I don't,' she pleaded. 'I don't, I don't, I don't.'

He must have spied something in her expression because he eased his fingers. He scrutinised her for several long seconds as though weighing up the truth of her reply, then his eyes slunk down her body. Keeping his grip on her throat, he shifted his knee to take in all her nakedness and when his face returned it had a new expression.

'It took me a long time to remember where I'd seen you. I'd forgotten all about that party. Where was it? Somewhere near Holyrood I think. Christ knows how I ended up there with a bloody load of students. As soon as I arrived, I remember thinking it was going to be too easy. And I was right, wasn't I? Let's face it, girl, it was hardly a memorable encounter. You were a such compliant little rag doll. The whole thing bored me.'

He raised his white eyebrows. 'But look at you now. Who'd have thought my little rag doll would end up in the Horde? Seems you've got some violence in you after all.' He tightened his fingers around her throat again and his expression hardened. 'So let me make myself absolutely clear, because I don't want there to be any misunderstanding. If you *ever* hear from Tyler Maitland or learn anything about his whereabouts, you will tell me immediately. Am I making myself plain?' He dipped his tongue to her ear. 'Because if you don't, I promise you we'll do this again. And next time, I'll allow you to fight. I'll let you punch and kick and bite and scream, because it's the struggle I love.'

He thumped her head against the tiles once more, then released his grip and stood. She sucked in a ragged lungful of oxygen and gulped at the blood and water in her mouth. Only then did he seem to notice the shower drenching him. He peered down at his sodden jeans, cursed profusely and squelched from the room.

For the second time in her life she lay exposed and uncaring after his departure. She gazed at the blue spotlights in the ceiling, placed an exploratory hand to her throat and then forced herself upright. Her legs were jelly and she had to lean against the tiles. She floundered for the shower controls and wrenched them off and the new silence was broken only by her panting breath.

She padded carefully to the lockers and sat for an age with a towel wrapped around her. Finally she dressed, retrieved a comb from her bag and brushed her hair methodically until it was tangle-free. Then she applied eyeliner, mascara and lipstick, and inspected the hard colours against her sheet-white skin.

When she stepped into the Tunnel, there were wet bootprints leading away to the men's washing area where another shower hummed. She paused at the doorway, but other male voices could be heard and someone laughed, so she walked on, eyes fixed steadfastly ahead. From his control room, the new Hammer gatekeeper saw her coming and buzzed the Gate open. He thought she looked pretty damn amazing in that make-up and bid her good day. He got nothing in response.

VII

Renuka Malhotra was performing the dextrous task of replying to a WhatsApp message from her mother in faraway Himachal Pradesh while simultaneously keeping the rain off her screen and navigating around the spring flower borders beside the Scott Monument, when she spotted the woman sitting on a bench, head thrown back and gazing into the heavens. The upturned face was dead to the world. The arms were splayed across the back of the bench. The open mouth was catching raindrops. And the eyes bulged, white like ping-pong balls.

In other circumstances Renuka would have branded the woman a druggy and moved on. But not this time. She glanced along the pathways. The weather was keeping footfall in the Gardens to a minimum and she was distant enough from the Monument to remain undetected by its cameras. So she made her decision.

'Calder?' The woman's head eased forward and assessed her without a flicker of emotion. Her lips were rouged and her lashes blackened and perhaps there were tear trails down her cheeks, but they could have been the rain. 'Are you okay?'

'I'm going to kill him.'

Renuka sighed. 'I know you are.'

If Lana had been planning to elaborate, this response stalled her. She removed her arm from the back of the bench to allow the other woman to sit.

'But when you do,' continued Renuka, 'it needs to be official. It needs to be part of the Game. Within the Rules.'

'Don't preach to me about rules. *He* doesn't conform to rules. He takes what he wants, when he wants and no one ever does a damn thing about it.'

Renuka waited for the bitterness to subside, then said patiently, 'If you take matters into your own hands, they'll crucify you.'

'Do I care? He's *already* crucifying me, Freyja. Every waking moment he's in my head, destroying me from the inside out.'

Renuka looked at her young Raven and saw the ugly grey-blue welts on her throat. 'Those weren't there on the ferry.'

Lana's hand fluttered to the incriminating marks, then she pulled up her collar and turned away. 'They're new. A gift from him an hour ago in Valhalla.'

'I'll tell you this: when the Fates allow – and only when the Fates allow – you will kill him within the Rules. And when you do, I promise you, Calder *Cold Waters*, I'll be there to help.'

They sat in silence listening to the rain patter until Lana said, 'He wanted to know where Punnr is.'

'Punnr? Why would Skarde care where Punnr is?'

'Who knows what the bastard thinks.'

Renuka eyed her. 'More to the point, why would he think *you* know Punnr's whereabouts? You need to level with me.'

Lana held her silence for a moment, then crumbled. 'During the last few months Punnr and I saw more of each other than the Pantheon permits, and Skarde seems to be aware of this. But Christ knows why he thinks I can locate Punnr now. You told me yourself Punnr's either dead or dumped somewhere far away.'

'You're sure that's really what Skarde wanted of you?'

Lana smiled emptily. '*Where's Tyler Maitland?* Those were his words while he was busy throttling me in the shower.'

'I'm sorry, Calder. I promise he'll pay one day.'

'Yeah, he will.'

'You realise you just revealed Punnr's real name to me?'

'It hardly matters now.'

'Perhaps not. Tell me, why were you in Valhalla?'

'I paid a visit to Kustaa, the new Adjutant, to request a change of housing. I no longer feel secure in my current place.'

'Was Skarde there?'

'No.'

Renuka brooded and eventually Lana forced herself out of her introspection. 'What about you? How come you're here?'

'I was heading up to North Tunnel.'

'The Season's over.'

'It might be for some of us. For others there's a thing called admin to catch up on. So has Kustaa sorted you a new place?'

'He said it will take until Wednesday to identify somewhere. Then he'll arrange for my things to be moved.' The rain was getting heavier and Lana stood slowly. 'Thanks for checking on me. I feel better now.'

Renuka frowned in surprise, but nodded. 'Okay. Go carefully.'

The younger woman began walking towards the Academy at the western end of the Gardens while Renuka stayed seated with half-formulated questions buzzing around her head. *Who had provided Skarde with Punnr's real name? What could he possibly want with the ex-Wolf now? And who told him Calder was in Valhalla?*

Skarde might be the iron fist, but the whole thing reeked of higher artifice.

'Hey, Raven. Wait.' She rose and stalked after the receding figure. 'Get your move done on Wednesday, then meet me. Thursday 9 p.m., on Nicholson Street outside the Festival Theatre.'

'Why?'

'Let's just say a Housecarl's priority is to look out for her troops.'

'So is this an order, Housecarl, or a request?'

'Both.'

Lana considered. 'Then I'd better comply.'

'Ensure you're not seen.'

'Of course.'

'And bring a bag. Just a few overnight belongings.'

'Are we going somewhere?'

Renuka turned on her heel towards the Monument. 'I haven't decided yet.'

Hera's phone chimed twice using the notification she had set for her husband's texts on the specialist messaging service used by all the Caelestes. She had flown out of Edinburgh the previous afternoon and was now in the midst of chairing a board meeting on the thirty-sixth floor above West 58th. A late-morning Manhattan sun poured through the windows from a sky of faultless cobalt.

"Seems we have two new faces. Take a look," read Zeus' message. She blanked the screen and returned to the board discussion.

At twelve-thirty they broke for lunch and Hera commandeered the office next door and had her PA bring a crayfish salad while she watched the ten-minute video of the blade fight in the Gardens of Ephesus.

"I didn't expect that," she messaged at the end.

"Not too happy that Alexander lost us those champions," Zeus pinged back. *"They won't be easy to replace."*

"Odin will be furious his Wolves are Titans now."

"Think I might message him. Rub his nose in it a bit."

"Not a good idea."

There was a lengthy pause, then Zeus came back. *"Why?"*

"Just think we should play this cool for now."

There was another long delay. She knew her husband. He would be prickly that she had contended his proposal, but she also knew he would surrender the point.

Sure enough. *"Okay,"* was the abrupt response.

Hera put the phone down and sat looking out at the forest of high-rises around Central Park's lush rectangle. She kept replaying in her mind the image of Agape stepping into the circle and retrieving the fallen sword. The assembled Titans had cheered her for upholding the Rules, righting a wrong, but Hera knew the Sacred Band's Captain too well. Agape had not entered the fray to champion justice. She had other reasons for shaping the outcome of the fight.

And Hera intended to uncover these.

The glass frontage of Edinburgh's Festival Theatre was swathed in a banner proclaiming Scottish Ballet's 'triumphant' production of *Cinderella*. It was just after nine and the interval crowds in the ground-floor restaurant had thinned as they took their seats for the second half.

'It's good,' said Renuka, approaching from across the street.

'Ballet's never really been my thing,' Lana replied.

Renuka inspected her and took in the overnight bag slung over her shoulder, then waved down a taxi. 'Cluny Drive.'

They headed south on Nicholson Street, a pale moon peeking above Salisbury Crags as the last of the daylight faded. 'I always believe there's something balletic in a good blade fight,' murmured Renuka, soft enough for the driver not to hear. 'The poise, the angles, the moments of conjoining. A good blade fight is a dance. You could set it to music.'

'In my experience a blade fight is shock, pain, terror, savagery and just blind bloody luck. I see no art in it.'

The taxi took them south away from the Old Town on its hill, through the Newington shops, past Prestonfield golf course and then east along the Blackford back roads. Fifteen minutes later it dropped them on Cluny Drive and into a very different world. The properties lining both sides were colossal Edwardian semis, each with deep bay windows, double garages, manicured hedgerows and an amalgam of Mercedes, BMWs, Porsches and Range Rovers on the drives. Once the taxi had departed, the evening's silence descended and Lana could believe they were far beyond the city, perhaps in a tiny Borders market town. The hunk of dark behind them was Blackford Hill with its observatory. Years before, Lana had taken the bus out of the centre with a group of university friends and hiked the hill, descending via the banks of the Hermitage of Braid and then wandering back through these affluent blocks. They had joked about which of them would be first to own such a house.

Wordlessly, Renuka set off and Lana slung her bag and followed. They turned into Hermitage Gardens and then took a left into another street. Lana caught occasional glimpses through the hedgerows into expansive front rooms. This was the type of area where curtains were rarely drawn, the denizens buffered by their hefty front gardens and confident in their tangible and spiritual separation from the grimier parts of the capital.

Renuka swooped into a narrow, lightless alley and Lana stumbled behind her. They reached a gate in a six-foot wall and Renuka produced a key.

'I prefer to use the back entrance.'

The gate gave access to a path through a natural arch of foliage and beyond this was a lawn leading to the rear of one of the semis. On a ground floor reconfigured almost entirely in glass, Lana could see a lamplit kitchen and dining area. Renuka led her onto the lawn, then curved right, and Lana spied another building set back amongst the shrubs. This was a modern addition, single-storey, flat-roofed and also walled in glass. Renuka yanked the sliding door ajar, slipped between the blinds and switched on a lamp to reveal an immaculately furnished bedsit, replete with a velvet sofa, reading chairs and rugs over white tiling.

'En-suite shower and bath through there.' She pointed. 'And a kitchenette, but you'll eat mostly in the house.' Lana placed her bag on one of the chairs and looked around wordlessly. 'Keep these blinds drawn after dark,' Renuka continued. 'No need for the neighbours to know you're here.'

'Is it usual for a Housecarl to invite troops to stay?'

'Of course not.'

'Then why, Freyja?'

Renuka faced up to her. 'Because at the end of this Season I have a headcount among my Raven House Company of five and I intend to lose no more. As I listened to you on that bench, I saw a woman heading irrevocably towards one of two denouements: an absence without leave from the Pantheon or a blade through the ribs of the new Housecarl of Wolf Company. Either way your fate would be Erebus or a body bag. So – being the good officer I am – I've decided it's up to me to ensure you avoid those destinies. Now… get yourself settled in, then come over to the house for some food.'

Renuka headed back to the blinds then halted and pondered the other woman. 'We're in the Interregnum now, so perhaps we better know each other more personally. I'm Renuka.'

'And I'm Lana.'

'Those will be our names outside the Season.'

When Lana made her way across the lawn, freshly showered and changed, she found Renuka working on a seafood paella.

'Help yourself,' said the Housecarl, waving a spatula towards glasses and a bottle of white on the island behind her.

The space was an eclectic mix of colours and fabrics. The dining table was reclaimed and surrounded by chairs ranging from antique Georgian to plastic Seventies. There were lamps of all hues, a Persian rug across unstained oak flooring, pot plants and candelabra, and a single wall painted dark green to offset the ivory shades of the kitchen units.

'Is this all yours?' asked Lana, settling onto a stool by the island and pouring wine.

'The furnishings and the flair. The house itself is the Pantheon's, though they pay me enough to own a place like this if I wished.' She retrieved crusty bread from the oven, placed bowls on the island and began scooping the paella into them. 'In a way I'm grateful it's not mine. I can tell myself it comes with the job and I can keep the real me hidden away, ready to come out – spotless and untarnished – if I ever get through this game of ours. That's when I'll go and find my own home. The place I'll end my days in. Does that sound weird?'

'Not at all.'

'Here – eat.' She slid a bowl over and perched on a stool opposite as they chinked glasses.

'And when will you *get through this game of ours*?'

'Ten years is the minimum you have to serve. Survive that and you receive an honorary send-off at the *Agonium Martiale*. But you can extend annually after that if you wish. I've done eight.'

'So you'll leave in two Seasons?'

'I doubt it.' Renuka pulled a face. 'The killing gets addictive. Anyway – what about your new accommodation? Has Kustaa set you up with something decent?'

'It's a real upgrade. A top-floor apartment just off the Meadows. But it's not like this.'

'Ha. They don't give these out to one-Seasoners! You've got to be Housecarl rank to get a semi in these parts.'

'Then I hate to think what palaces they must provide for the Kings.'

'Oh yes, those two enjoy a lifestyle to be envied.'

Lana eyed her. 'That suggests you know where Sveinn lives.'

'Not officially of course – but I *may* have an inkling. That's one of the problems with having two Palatinates in a city like this. There's only so many quality areas you can house your senior officers in the comfort to be expected.'

'So Morningside's swarming with the buggers.'

'I did see Halvar out and about sometimes.' Renuka laughed but then went serious as both of them realised Halvar would not be walking those pavements again. 'There's actually a couple of properties round here with single guys in them and it makes you start to wonder. No family, huge house, never seen them head off in business suits in the mornings.'

'You mean you might have Titan officers for neighbours!'

Renuka shrugged. 'Edinburgh's a small place.'

They emptied their bowls and Renuka poured more wine.

'Why *are* there two Palatinates in Edinburgh?' Lana asked.

'That's one of those Pantheon mysteries no one's ever quite got to the bottom of. What's fact is that the Horde was always here and the Titans began in Athens. Then after the Sixth Season they upped sticks and moved the whole damn circus here. The story goes that it was at the behest of Hera – the wife of Zeus. They're both of Greek-Cypriot origin, but seems she hated the winters in Athens. Those – and his family. Her parents lived in London, while his army of extended relatives were all in Greece, so she pushed hard for a move here. And what Hera wants, Hera gets.'

'But why Edinburgh?'

'Legend has it all seven Caelestes knew each other in the old days. I mean before the Pantheon even started. They were a group and they came up with all this because they were bored and because they were making money by the truckload. It's said Odin and Zeus were close back then. So when Titan overtures in London and Oxford failed, Odin suggested Edinburgh. They thought the very proximity of the two rival Palatinates would add tangible excitement. And – to give credit where it's due – they were right. Having the Titans so close that we can kiss blades every night lends this rivalry an extra edge of excitement.'

Renuka paused. 'But overseeing opposing Palatinates wore their friendship away and then came the Eighteenth Season and something went really wrong between Odin and Zeus. Everywhere we went, we seemed to find Titans for the killing. It was as if someone was telling us where to look. I don't know what was going on behind the scenes, but it was dirty and enemies were made for life.

'It culminated in the weeks before the Grand Battle. There's a tunnel – supposedly secret – which runs from below the Western Practice Rooms and comes out in the basements on Advocate's Close. It's grim and damp and you have to crouch the whole length of it, but one night Sveinn sent two of my Raven litters, all four Wolf litters and three of Hammer creeping along it. What we found at the other end were Timanthes and his Companions. Only the gods know what they were doing coming down those steps, but we took them out that night. It was murderous work. Cramped, bloody.' Her eyes had glazed and she was back in the cellar. 'I killed Timanthes. One of the Bloodmarks on my chest represents his life.'

'How did you know they were going to be there?'

'Like I said, it was dirty that Season. Somebody was telling somebody things they shouldn't know. And those things resulted in a lot of dead Titans. Zeus has never forgiven Odin. And I suspect the legacy of those dark days is still with us. Both Palatinates wage war like it's real now. Not a Game, no Rules. And all the things that have happened this Season – Halvar gone, Radspakr retired, the coming of Skarde – I think they link back to the deeds in that cellar.'

She fell silent and they drank their wine.

'Have you brought me here to protect me from Skarde?'

'I've brought you here to protect you from yourself. To give you some time to sort your head. It's my job to ensure you're fit and ready for the Twentieth Season.'

Lana considered this and nodded slowly. 'Okay.'

Renuka consulted her watch. 'It's getting late. Take the rest of the bottle back to the garden room?'

'Are you going to bed?'

Renuka laughed. 'Ha, no. Strangely enough the Pantheon

has turned me into a night owl. I'll load this lot into the dishwasher and then head to the basement.'

'What's down there?'

'That, Raven, is for another time.'

VIII

Nine weeks. Nine sprawling weeks.

The city was popping with energy. Visitors packed the Old Town. Crowds wandered the Gardens. Café tables lined the pavements *al fresco* style. Greenery burst everywhere, softening the edges and dappling the sunlight.

And Tyler was bored to death.

To begin with he tried to entertain himself. He walked every damn street in central Edinburgh and took in museums, galleries and shows. He toured pubs and whisky bars, listening to a potpourri of foreign accents. He even queued to buy a ticket around the castle. Which was ironic since he had already used a secret tunnel with Halvar last winter to visit for free.

But you could take all the culture, the history, the high cuisine and the summer warmth – and stuff the lot. Because in the absence of the Pantheon, he decided, Edinburgh was just another same-old-same-old city.

He felt adrift without the rhythm of the Conflict Hours and homeless without the welcoming arms of the Palatinates. He would walk past Valhalla's Gates and wonder if they were still manned by a skeleton Hammer crew and whether the fires still burned in the Halls. Sometimes he found vantage points along the Royal Mile and squinted up at the rooflines, trying to fathom which contained Titan strongholds. He had been bundled in and out of Ephesus blindfolded and not yet been introduced to Pella, Persepolis and Thebes, so it seemed surreal that they were up there somewhere, lost to the casual eye of the crowds.

He realised too that he missed the thrill of danger. There had been many occasions during that Nineteenth Season when he squirmed with terror, when the tang of blood in his nostrils had made him want to whimper like a child, but now that these moments were denied him, life's invulnerability was so mundane. Each day stretched inescapably into night and each night passed unruffled.

In his opinion, the Interregnum had arrived at the worst possible moment and left him floating unmoored somewhere between the two Palatinates. No longer was he a Wolf; that much was certain. Valhalla was barred to him and he was most likely viewed by the Horde as a traitor and coward. Yet neither could he make himself believe he was a Titan. To date, under their auspices, he had been treated as nothing more than a prisoner forced to fight for his life. No Titan name had come his way, no place in their ranks identified. As he wandered listlessly around the balmy city, the Pantheon seemed little more than a distant dream and as unreachable for him as it was for the tourists who thronged the streets.

Most of all, he felt entirely and precipitously alone. Every Pantheon comrade was out of reach. Brante had gone north. Calder never picked up his calls. Halvar was fish food and Leiv ashes. Unn, Ake and Stigr were unknowable beyond the Horde. Even Oliver was a step removed now that Tyler had been forced to abandon his Learmonth flat. For the past ten months he had failed to notice that every living, breathing person who meant anything to him was connected to the Pantheon. In the real world, it seemed, he was utterly friendless.

And this discovery sobered him. Or rather – conversely – it turned him to drink. The whisky began in the mornings and continued either side of his afternoon naps. Then it was beers and chasers in the local bars, before inevitable nightcaps leaning against the giant windows of his new abode. On a couple of occasions he even awoke in the small hours to find himself brittle and frozen, reclining in the sunlounger on his roof terrace.

One afternoon, fortified by a couple of stiff malts, he thought, *Damn her*. If she wasn't going to call him back, he would bloody well have it out with her in person. So he took himself from the West End and down through New Town to Stockbridge and navigated his way to her door. His heart leapt when he heard movement in answer to his knock, but it was a man who appeared.

'Is Lana there?' He feared the nightmare that the man would say *yes* and she would come to the door and smile her greetings with her arm around this stranger.

'Sorry, chum, think you got the wrong address.'

'But I was here with her just a few weeks ago.'

The man shrugged. 'We started renting this place a month ago. You'd best try Retties, the agents. They might have forwarding details.'

Tyler retraced his steps heavily and perhaps it was this final blow – this inescapable truth that he really had lost what thin ties had once bound them – which set him studying his maps and tracing fingers along A-roads wriggling between places with strange names. He barely knew what he was seeking and the whole idea was vague as hell, but it was *something*. Something real in his outlandish existence.

He packed clothing and made sandwiches, then spent a night so restless that he rose at four with the first blush of dawn and coaxed his rattling, coughing van out from a sleeping West End and onto the Queensferry Road. Twenty minutes later, second cigarette of the day between his lips, he crossed the Forth just as the sun broke from the waves and awed him with a scene so bewitching that he banged the steering wheel and yelled, *Yes!* and convinced himself he was doing the right thing whatever awaited.

By seven he was past Pitlochry and Blair Atholl and halted for fuel, stovies and head-blowing coffee. By Kingussie he was singing along to the radio and saluting the Cairngorm massif to the east, and by Inverness his bum was killing him. He crossed the Cromarty Firth and finally pulled up outside Tain when he spotted the Glenmorangie distillery ahead. He purchased three bottles of the best stuff and stood in the distillery grounds looking out across the Dornoch Firth. The beaches opposite shone in the sunlight and a Highland breeze buffeted him. How had he spent all his formative years in Scotland and not seen this?

He returned to his van and checked his satnav. Sixteen miles it said, but now on slower roads. He should be there by early afternoon and then – well, Christ knows what then.

From Tain he travelled east onto a finger of land clawing at the North Sea. Until that point his journey had taken him past jostling, tightly packed mountains. Peak after peak shouldering each other out of the way as he passed. His map showed him exotic names: Monadhliath, A'Chailleach, Sgurr a'Choire Ghlais. But now the countryside relaxed into undulating pasture, spotted with clumps of woodland and the occasional lochan. It could have been farmland from much softer southern climes were it not for the windswept presence of the Moray and Dornoch Firths on either side.

Fifty minutes later he halted again at the edge of Portmahomack village curving around a quiet fishing harbour. He was starving, so he took his sandwiches and perched on a stone wall overlooking the firth. The village was no more than twenty dwellings and as he surveyed the whitewashed buildings and the water beyond, he suddenly felt stupid. *What the hell am I doing here?*

There was breeze coming off the firth and it was cold. Summer this far north meant something very different from the temperate streets of Edinburgh. He finished his sandwiches, pulled a coat from the back of the van and trudged down to the village shop.

'I'm looking for someone called Urquhart,' he said to the large lady behind the counter and thinking how daft he sounded.

'Well that'll be first right out of the village, laddie,' she replied without batting an eyelid.

First right out of the village proved to be another three miles along the shore and he was convinced he had missed it when he spotted a pair of pillars and turned up a drive that wound inland to a gravel parking area in front of a house of grand proportions sheltering among a copse of mature oaks. A Range Rover and Audi were already pulled up and Tyler crunched his van next to them.

He grabbed his cigarette packet and stepped out. Sheep

were bleating somewhere and there were crows in the trees. The house was painted white and ignited by the afternoon sun. Its main entrance was reached by steps and at either end stood circular turreted towers. Tyler whistled softly, placed a cigarette to his lips, then thought better of it.

'Can I help you?' A woman appeared at a side gate wearing gardening gloves and surrounded by a coterie of barking spaniels. She was an attractive blonde, probably in her fifties, dressed in a Barbour puffa jacket, brimmed hat and Muck boots and her accent was cut-glass.

Tyler strode over. 'I'm a friend of Forbes.'

She inspected him sternly. 'Is he expecting you?'

'No. It's just a social visit from Edinburgh.'

She arched her eyebrows. 'That's quite a social visit.' She opened the gate. 'Well you'd better come through. Don't mind the dogs – they're all bark and no bite.' She led him around the side of the house to a sloping lawn and raised flower beds. Beyond were sheep fields and then a breathtaking view south to the other side of the peninsula and the Moray Firth. She pulled a phone from her jacket and jabbed at the screen. 'I've sent him a text. He'll be a few minutes. He's down at the stables. Now what did you say your name was?'

'Tyler.'

'Tyler. Hmmm… don't think he's mentioned you.' She deliberated as if this was some kind of problem, then waved her hand dismissively. 'Never mind. Have a seat on the patio and I'll make tea.'

She ushered him to a table, then abandoned him for the kettle. He pulled his coat around him and watched the slanting afternoon light across the fields while the dogs sniffed him suspiciously.

'What the bloody hell?' came a voice from the gate.

'Hello, Forbes. Surprise, surprise.'

His friend walked towards him unsmiling. He was wearing marigold chinos, green wellingtons and a Barbour gilet that had strands of hay stuck to it. His shirtsleeves were rolled up and as he extended a hand in greeting, the scar of his blade wound from Nestor was apparent against the dark hairs on his forearm.

'That's cleared up well,' Tyler commented, not meeting the other man's eyes.

'Had to tell Mum I'd torn it on barbed wire during a morning jog.'

'Edinburgh's full of barbed wire.'

'Yeah well, she didn't cross-examine me.' He took a seat and leaned his elbows on his knees. 'I'll say again – what the bloody hell?'

'Remember the night of your Fettes reunion? You said you came from faraway Portmahomack, caught between the Moray and Dornoch Firths.'

'You've a good memory.'

'Then you told Simmius your surname is Urquhart. I figured maybe there aren't too many Urquharts living up this way and anyone who sends their son to Fettes is probably known in their community.'

Forbes' mother reappeared with a trayful of cups and saucers, an elegant teapot and a milk jug, all in white porcelain, as well as two slices of lemon drizzle cake. 'This is Tyler,' she stated placing the contents individually before them. Her navy cashmere jumper was covered in a fine layer of spaniel hair.

'I know.'

'Seems he's made a *social* trip from Edinburgh.'

'Yes, I've realised that.'

'We don't usually get people dropping in from the capital,' she said and pushed a cup towards Tyler. 'Well, help yourself. I'll leave you to get reacquainted.'

'I'm not sure your mum likes me,' said Tyler once she had retreated.

'She's like that with everyone and she's never good with unexpected visitors.' Forbes poured tea for both, topped up with milk and used silver pincers to drop a single sugar cube into his drink. 'I'm pretty surprised to see you myself.'

Tyler pondered whether to take the hint and tramp back to his van. Instead he twitched his nose and said, 'You're lucky you have somewhere to come. I've got nothing. No parents, no sister, no home to speak of. Edinburgh's a city of three-quarters of a million souls and in these last few weeks I've realised I know none of them well enough to say hi to.'

'So you thought you'd break the Pantheon Rules and come here.'

Tyler was hard-faced. 'I'll not trouble your hospitality further.'

He began to rise, but Forbes placed a restraining hand on his arm. 'Don't be stupid. Now you've made the journey you must stay. There's three spare bedrooms and Mum might not admit it but she loves to show off her hospitality. Try the cake. It alone is worth the trip.'

Tyler settled back and bit into the cake. He had to agree it was bloody good. Forbes had grown his beard again and with his luxuriant eyebrows and bald head he resembled the genie in the lamp. 'Is that to prove a point to the Titans?' Tyler said, pointing to his friend's chin.

'My father hates beards,' Forbes answered as if that was explanation enough. 'I'll shave it off before the Armatura. Anyway, look at you. All short back and sides.'

Tyler acquiesced the point. He had needed a trip to the barber's to tidy up the Titans' hack job and he was pleased with the result. He sipped his tea and looked out at the sheep. 'Do you own all these fields?'

'In a word, yes. The Urquharts are one of the older clans of Easter Ross, but we've not had the means to steward the land for decades so we rent the fields to tenant farmers. It's a convenient relationship. They get access to rare high-quality pasture and we receive the income necessary to keep this old place standing. In truth my ancestors have never been particularly dedicated farmers. Soldiering has always been the focus.'

Tyler could not resist a smirk. 'Then your father must be delighted you've joined a Viking horde.'

Forbes' eyes were filmy, floating across the sunlit fields. 'Sometimes I'd love to tell him just to see his face.' He refocused and realised how cold it had become. 'You brought some stuff with you?'

'In the van.'

'Go get it and I'll show you to a room.'

While he collected his bag, Tyler took the opportunity to smoke a hurried cigarette, then followed Forbes into a hallway full of antiques and snuffling spaniels. They climbed two floors to a bedroom in the eaves with creaking boards, metal bedstead, enamel bath, groaning toilet and views north-west to the hills of Sutherland. There were paintings on the two vertical end walls. Landscapes and cavalrymen. Green and scarlet.

'Dinner's at seven,' said Forbes from the doorway.

Tyler lay semi-conscious on the bed as the crows argued loudly. The tap thumped alarmingly as he filled the sink and splashed his face. Then he smoothed his hair, tucked in his shirt and descended to the dining room.

The dogs seemed to have forgotten him – or at least they had not been informed he was staying for dinner. As he entered, half a dozen of them surrounded him and almost brought the roof down with their indignant barking.

'Edgar! Albert! Oscar!' Forbes marched up the hallway and came in behind Tyler. 'Sorry about them.' He surveyed the table beyond. 'Jeez, why's the woman laid it like that?'

The room was dominated by an oval dining table that could seat ten. Forbes' mother had set two places, one at each end, and left the rest of the table bare. She stepped in from the adjoining kitchen. 'Ah Tyler. I guessed that must be your arrival. A little *after* seven, but thankfully it's only soup for starters. I take it sweet potato and asparagus agrees with you.'

She disappeared and Forbes moved one of the place settings around the table until they could sit more companionably. He retrieved a bottle of wine, poured two glasses and his mother returned with two steaming bowls of soup. 'I've added Stilton for flavour, so I assume you don't have one of those silly dietary intolerances.'

'No, I'm fine thank you.'

She placed the bowls in front of them on mats bearing military crests and departed.

'Is your mother not joining us?'

'No, she'll eat in the kitchen. She often does.'

They sipped quietly at the soup. Tyler felt gauche and inept and could think of nothing to say. He watched Forbes dip his silver spoon away from him, then bring it to his lips and suck gently at one edge. He seemed a different man from the laughing, cheerful favourite of the Valhalla Halls.

'What about your father?' he ventured.

'He'll be travelling back from Aberdeen tomorrow for the weekend. Five years ago he had a mini stroke. No long-term damage, but it was enough to have him eased firmly out of the Regiment and now he's in oil. So he spends his weeks in Aberdeen and comes back up here as rarely as he can.'

It was steak and dauphinoise potatoes for the main course and Tyler's stomach crooned with delight. He had been on the road since four that morning and eaten little but garbage. So he had half demolished his plateful before he spoke again. 'Were you in the same Regiment?'

'Me?' Forbes looked surprised.

'We were in the vaults once in the early weeks of the Armatura. You told us you'd been in the army but Freyja stopped you saying anything more. We weren't supposed to know about each other back then.'

Forbes harrumphed. 'We still aren't. Freyja would have palpitations if she could see us now.' He sawed at his steak. 'Aye, to your question. I was in the same Regiment. The Royal Scots Dragoon Guards. Scotland's cavalry. Formerly the Scots Greys, the oldest Cavalry Regiment of the Line in the British Army. The Urquharts have been officers in the Greys for as long as anyone can remember.'

'So you ride?'

Forbes laughed emptily. 'Yes I ride. If there's one thing my father's done for me, it's instil a love of horses in me. What about you? Ever been on a horse?'

'Oh yes. I whiled away my youth cantering around Craigmillar with the other kids from the estate.'

When they had finished, Forbes let the spaniels lick each plate clean. 'Let's take the drinks to the library.'

'The library!'

Forbes smiled despite himself and Tyler continued ribbing him as he followed him out. 'I mean, the man *obviously* has a library.' He stopped though when they entered the new room. 'Bloody hell.'

At one end was a bay window looking out on the garden, the fields and the distant firth. On the opposite wall was a vast oil painting of a Scots Grey officer in full regalia standing beside his stallion. 'My great-great-grandfather,' said Forbes. 'See that eagle standard leaning against the tree behind him? That's the Imperial Eagle of the French 45th Regiment of Foot, which the Greys captured at Waterloo. Although whether my great-great-grandfather was genuinely present on the field that day is one of those family mysteries never mentioned.'

Tyler looked at the long side walls, both converted to white-painted floor-to-ceiling bookcases and crammed with volumes. He whistled softly.

'Help yourself anytime.' Forbes stoked a small fire and the dogs sprawled out in front of it in a furry pile. 'Up there on the top shelves beside the door is a section on ancient military formations and tactics. There's some good stuff about Alexander and his armies. Take a look if you wish.

It seems pretty relevant for us now. You know, there really was a Sacred Band of heavily armoured Hoplites, but they were Theban, not Macedonian like Alexander. And Philip, his father, destroyed them on the plain of Chaeronea when Alexander was eighteen. It seems the Pantheon picks its classical titbits like chocolates in a box and sprinkles them liberally for effect, but historical accuracy is not one of its priorities.'

'Well,' Tyler mused, swallowing wine and looking around the room. 'You're obviously not in the Pantheon because you need the money.'

'Money's tighter than you think. Look closely and you'll see the peeling paint, the cracks in the ceilings, the woodworm riddling the floorboards. But no – it's not for the money.' Forbes indicated for them to sit in leather chairs by the fire. 'I think I told you long ago about my sighting of that first Titan on a rooftop when I was a schoolboy at Fettes and how it inspired me to read my military history and fall in love with those ancient warrior societies. Valhalla offered me a chance to get as close to those cultures as any person could in this modern age. And I also told you how my father used to speak about the *unity of the Regiment, the unbreakable bonds between men who stand shoulder to shoulder against a common enemy*. After I left the Regiment, I guess I was still looking for that unity.'

'Why did you leave the Regiment?'

Forbes stared at him. 'It didn't suit me.'

Tyler toyed with his glass. 'How did your father take that?'

'He said I demeaned him and the memory of every Urquhart that has gone before.'

They were silent. One of the spaniels was whimpering in its sleep and the sky outside was finally extinguishing, leaving the room in a soft lamplight that made it difficult to work out which limb belonged to which dog in the pile.

'He was right about the unbreakable bonds, though,' said Forbes meditatively. 'But it wasn't the Regiment that showed me. It was Valhalla. When I stood in the shieldwalls on that beach, I was united with my closest friends, shoulder to shoulder against a common enemy and it felt magnificent.'

'And now we *are* that common enemy.'

Forbes raised his glass. 'Aye. But I'm still shoulder to shoulder with my best friend.'

Tyler rose late the next morning and found the dining room empty except for the usual squad of noisy canines.

'That must be you, Tyler,' said Mrs Urquhart putting her head around the kitchen door. 'Nine-fifteen. My, you *must* have been tired. Not to worry, come through.'

She propped him on a stool beside the breakfast bar and cooked sausages and eggs while quizzing him about his life in Edinburgh. For simplicity he pretended he still worked in the university library and she was sufficiently disinterested in this to refrain from probing too far. She was cordial enough and he was grateful for the food, but she had an unerring way of making him feel a complete inconvenience. He stuffed the sausages as fast as he could and asked after Forbes.

'He'll be at the stables. He's always at the stables. Out the front door and down the track – you can't miss it. Don't dally.'

Tyler did dally. He took his time dragging on a cigarette as he ambled down the walled track looking out at sheep-studded fields under a grey sky. A red spaniel followed him, but otherwise he was unobserved. As he approached the stables his nostrils caught the scent of warm hay and there was a wheelbarrow at the entrance full of fresh droppings. He stamped on his cigarette and peered inside. 'Morning.'

Forbes was standing on the exposed concrete floor, using a pitchfork to loosen and spread straw bedding from bales against one wall. There were sweat stains over his shirt and muck on his corduroys. Next to him, secured to rings fixed into the stalls and grazing contentedly from hay nets suspended at head height, were two horses – one large and grey, the other a more compact roan.

Forbes leaned on his pitchfork. 'Morning, fella.'

'Need any help?'

'Aye why not. You happy to get your hands dirty?'

'The last time I saw you in Edinburgh, I was covered in a man's brains.'

'Well say hello to Beatrice and Fergus, the two loves of my life.'

'Which is which?'

Forbes grinned indulgently. There was a light in him that had been absent in the house yesterday. 'Fergus is the big grey. A thirteen-year-old Anglo-Arabian gelding. The speed and endurance of a thoroughbred mixed with the bone structure and refinement of the Arabian. Seventeen hands and a real runner in his day. He used to be my father's before he stopped riding and now he's my boy.' He patted the horse's neck. 'And this beauty is Beatrice. A young cob. Five years old and our stable girl, Marion, has started riding her over the past six months. She's almost fifteen hands now and possesses as gentle a nature as any I've known. Give her a pat – go on.'

Tyler eased around her near side and patted her neck cautiously. Her coat was coarse but warm and he ran a finger through her mane. She seemed entirely inured to his presence and kept tugging at the hay net. He backed off and looked askance at Forbes. 'So what do you want me to do?'

'I've mucked out, washed them, given them their first feed and now I'm just replacing the bedding. So you're in time to help me brush down.' He selected a soft brush from a collection hung on the far wall and came to stand beside Tyler. 'Beginning at the poll – her head behind the ears – work your way down her mane from root to ends, then move on to her body in circular motions in the direction of the lay of her coat.' He demonstrated then handed the brush to Tyler. 'I'll do old Fergus.'

There was something about the simplicity of the task, the sound of the brushes and the gentle munching of the horses on their hay, which made talk unnecessary. Tyler focused on the movement of the brush and the warmth of the body beneath. Occasionally she twitched and at one point she ceased eating and turned her neck to cast one brown eye in his direction.

'Hello, Beatrice,' he found himself saying and Forbes smiled to himself.

When they were complete, Forbes nodded. 'Good job. Now they're ready for some exercise. You coming?'

'You mean... *on* one of them?'

'Of course.'

'Not a chance.'

'Just a walk along the track. If you don't, it'll mean I have to lead Beatrice while I ride Fergus.'

'Me and horses don't mix.'

'There's a first time for everything.' Forbes took a saddle from a bracket on the wall and passed it to Tyler, then led Beatrice outside and tied her loosely to a ring. He took Tyler's saddle and strapped it onto her back, looping a bridle over her nose, then marched back into the stable and re-emerged with a nonchalantly clopping Fergus and repeated the process.

'Is he one of the greys from the Regiment?'

'He's no military horse but – aye – he's near enough in terms of breeding and build. It would have been fellas like him that charged the French bayonets at Waterloo.' He turned with his hands on his hips and grinned. 'Right. Mounting.'

'Seriously, Forbes, this isn't a good idea.'

'Nonsense, look how petite Beatrice is. Not far to fall. I seem to recall this is the man who fell off the roofs over Canongate and landed in a skip!'

'Yeah – and I damn near killed myself.'

'Wear this.' He produced a protective helmet and threw it to him. 'Now over here. Left shoulder next to the near side of Beatrice.' He gave a half-turn to the stirrup. 'Left foot into this. Good.'

Tyler glanced into Beatrice's eye next to him. He imagined she was assessing what oafish lump was about to sit on her.

'Okay.' Forbes was in close to him. 'Take the reins in your left hand and put your right on the waist of the saddle like so. Now swing your right leg up. Make sure you don't brush her quarters. Let's go, soldier.'

Tyler heaved and felt Forbes' hands give him an extra shove until he was seated firmly. 'Shit,' he breathed, but Beatrice barely seemed to have noticed.

Forbes mounted up and then wheeled Fergus gently round so that he could reach down and untie Beatrice. 'Okay, now I'm going to smack her on the rump and we'll gallop full tilt down the track.'

'Don't you fucking dare!'

Forbes barked with laughter. 'Just yanking your chain, Titan. I'll lead Beatrice and we'll walk slowly. All you have to concentrate on is not falling off.'

The horse's muscles moved beneath him and he sat rigid as iron, not daring to shift his legs or twitch his hands. They clopped sedately onto the track and began to ease between the fields. The land rolled away to platinum grey seas on both sides and far ahead a lighthouse sat white against dark sky. Gulls called above and sheep twitched up from their grazing and dashed away as the riders passed. When Tyler refocused, Forbes no longer held Beatrice's bridle.

'Hey,' he exclaimed in consternation.

'What's the problem? Beatrice has walked this track hundreds of times and she's no intention of doing anything different now.'

Tyler tried to relax into the rhythm of the beast beneath him. As the minutes ticked by it became more natural and as she bent into a rise he sensed his body move with her. 'Good girl,' he said involuntarily and he felt a rumbling vibration from her lungs in response.

'Well look at you.' Forbes beamed. They were surmounting a high spot and the views stretched endlessly.

'Look at me indeed. Tyler Maitland from Craigmillar estate riding a damn horse.'

'You're the laird of the land, king of all you survey.'

A breeze rippled Beatrice's mane and he dared take one hand from the reins and run his fingers through the long hair. She twitched her ears and gave a little sideways nod with her head and he found himself smiling. Edinburgh seemed a long way off.

And it was good. It was beautiful.

IX

Elliott 'Eli' Greaves drove around the eastern flanks of Roan Fell with the top pulled down on his Mini Convertible and Coldplay rocking the stereo. The soft rural emptiness of Liddesdale opened ahead and he grinned from ear to ear. Not a bad daily commute. The place could be barren as hell in winter and the road slick with ice, but burgeon the trees with emerald foliage, sprinkle the fields with sheep and slam a summer sky above and it became tourist-brochure beautiful.

He took the corners fast, knowing that oncoming traffic was a rarity in these forgotten folds of land on the Scottish Border between Gretna and his rented house in Jedburgh. To the south slumbered the vast expanses of Kielder Forest and you had to travel several miles to the north before you hit a half-decent A-road. He slowed and turned into a lane where a cattle grid and old iron gate blocked his way. To the unobservant it was nothing more than a private farmer's track. The more initiated, however, would notice the track was well cindered and would spot the camera concealed in nearby trees. After a short delay while his Mini's licence plate was logged, the gate swung open and he proceeded up the lane.

Over the rise and beyond the view of inquisitive eyes from the road, a second gate provided the only access through an eight-foot steel fence-line. This had laser recognition, a guardhouse and a sign reading *Ministry of Defence: Strictly No Unauthorised Admittance*. Eli removed his sunglasses, quietened Coldplay and waved to the faces inside the building. They wore berets and combat fatigues, but they were not solders. Nor was this an MoD establishment, but the pretence was enough to dissuade more intrepid explorers from onward travel. And if online or media enquiries ever became too strenuous, the real MoD had been paid enough to sort out the miscreants.

One of the figures waved back and the gate rolled open. As Eli continued his journey the farmland gave way to new sights. On his left was woodland, but a secondary look revealed rope-walks strung between trunks, timber climbing frames, netting pegged to the ground and flags dotted beneath the limbs. On the other side was manicured grassland ringed by a running track, with a cricket pavilion nestling on the perimeter. He spotted a ten-strong group of teenagers huddled close to the road studying a map and pointing in various directions.

Navigation, thought Eli. It was three in the afternoon and the one hundred and twenty-eight pupils of the Valhalla Schola would be dedicating themselves to outdoor activities as they did every day after lunch. Sport, cross-country, orienteering, obstacle racing, bushcraft and survival skills. He drove slowly past the group – a smile ready on his lips – but none of them acknowledged his presence and he continued on towards the main campus. The first building was a grand specimen. Three floors of wisteria-clad

Victorian red-brick, decorative cast-iron guttering and a clock tower. The place had once been a genuine private school for the sons of wealthy Lowland Scots. It had been commandeered as a hospice during the wars and then used as a sabbatical centre for Methodist clergy, before going on the market fifteen years ago and falling into the hands of more elusive owners.

He pulled into the shade on one side of the building and waited for the hood to close, then grabbed his shoulder bag and strolled onto the main quad. Originally this would have marked formal gardens behind the main hall, but now it was laid to lawn and surrounded by blocks of classrooms. He walked to the far end and dropped down steps to enter the staffroom. As always, he was greeted by an aroma of stale coffee and cigarettes. A few of his colleagues were huddled in armchairs, marking workbooks and conversing quietly.

One waved. 'Afternoon, Eli. You on lates today?'

'Yes. I swapped with Cristina. But not an overnighter – just until eleven. All quiet so far?'

'Pretty much. Some of the third-years got into a scuffle and it became bloody, so the Praefecti removed them.'

Eli sighed heavily and dumped his bag on his desk. The Praefecti were always getting called in too soon. The Schola was home to some seriously mucked-up kids and fights were such a daily occurrence they could almost be timetabled. He and Cristina were paid handsomely to be the Schola's mental health experts, to counsel the kids, help build their inner strength and give them a shoulder to lean on in the harder times, but what was the point if the Praefecti waded into every fist fight and roughed up the perpetrators?

He grabbed a filter coffee and stared moodily out the rear

windows, which overlooked a new rose garden constructed specifically as a place of peace for troubled young minds. 'Where are the Initiates? I've got them at four.'

'Out with Frog on the Blue Trail. Year Two are doing Nav. Years Three and Four are bushcrafting somewhere.'

For simplicity the Valhalla Schola was divided into four "year" groups, but in reality kids of any age from eight to fifteen passed through the hands of the Venarii teams and ended up here. They were grouped by experience rather than age, so a nine-year-old could find him or herself alongside a twelve-year-old in the first Initiate Year, and the duration of Year Four varied considerably as each individual awaited the opportunity of Blood Funds to allow them to progress to the Palatinate Selection Board.

Eli checked his watch. He still had forty minutes before his class and the sunshine looked a damn sight more appealing than the stink of the staffroom. 'I'll go and see how they're doing on the Blue Trail. Check Frog's not ripping their heads off.'

He retrieved his sunglasses and exited to the rose garden. The scent was intoxicating and he paused to note the Latin names of different varieties and to listen to the buzz of bees. In the warmer months he often used this garden for his classes and sometimes brought more needy individuals for mentoring.

A decade earlier he had qualified with a PhD in Counselling Psychology from Strathclyde and moved into local government social work. His reputation had grown and seven years in, he had received an email purporting to be from a private school working with children from particularly difficult backgrounds. It was from Piper

Mallard, the head, who seemed to know a lot about his career to date and intrigued him enough to agree to meet. When this smart, eloquent lady explained to him over coffee the scale of the challenge and the size of the reward package, he became even more interested and embarked on several more rounds of recruitment interplay with her before he realised his prospective employer was the Pantheon.

He had baulked at this. *No way*, he said to Piper in a late-night email. He could not condone the violence-for-money culture of the Pantheon and would never allow himself to be a part of it. But she had persuaded him to meet again and this time she had given him the speech that would change the course of his life. She told him of the Lost Children, the tens of thousands of youngsters who disappeared in the UK every year, slipping through cracks in the care system, disappearing from residential homes, foster families and temporary placements; or falling victim to drugs, theft and sex gangs before they could even become a statistic.

He knew all this of course from his social work, but then she painted a new picture of youngsters rescued from these destinies. Taken by Venarii parties and provided with dedicated schooling, world-class training and potentially a well-paid and properly structured career path. Not only were they educated, they learned to become brethren and part of a team. They were given a moral code and taught the importance of discipline. Above all, they were shown how to value themselves and cherish the bonds with their compatriots, so that even those who never graduated to the Pantheon itself could be returned to the real world with once only dreamed-of prospects.

'But let's not pretend the journeys of these Lost Children

are always smooth,' Piper had said in her soft tones, her big eyes behind her glasses never straying from his. 'These are tough kids we're talking about and they've already been put through life's shitty grinder. They've seen and experienced things most of us never dare think about and so their transformation into dedicated, morally worthy warriors is going be to strewn with pitfalls. And that's why we need you, Eli.'

She had let this statement hang, waiting for him to bite. And, of course, he had.

'Why me? You think these youngsters need some token counselling?'

'It's precisely because these kids require far more than token counselling that we need someone like you. The Pantheon takes the long road when it comes to finding the best people and we've watched you for a lot longer than you realise. We know what you've achieved; we know the difference you've already made to individuals and families. You have experience and you have... a way with you. And these are things we need. So we want you to head up the mental health team at the Schola of the Horde of Valhalla and to use your skills to take these vulnerable youngsters along their rocky emotional paths to a far better place. In short, we want you to help us change their worlds.'

There and then she had won him over. Her words, her voice, her eyes and the huge remuneration figure she had scrawled on a napkin.

Eli made his way out of the rose garden and climbed into surrounding woodland. Tracks weaved through the trees, marked by blue, red or yellow splashes on trunks. He followed the blues and strode past a row of hanging tyres, a water jump and an eight-foot obstacle wall. Eventually he saw Jo "Frog" Fraser standing further up the trail and waved to him. Frog was an ex-Marine and now one of the Schola's Hastiliarii – a weapons, combat and fitness instructor. The two tutors had cordial enough relations, but agreed on little. Frog believed you built *esprit de corps* through common hardship, pain and grit, and he had no time for Eli's psychological mumbo-jumbo.

Just as Eli was approaching, he heard running footsteps behind and turned to see a skinny blonde girl of about thirteen, dressed in the standard black athletics garb of an Initiate, leading the pack. She was soaking wet and streaked with mud and her face was set in a rictus of misery, but she maintained her pounding pace straight past him.

'Go, Meghan,' he called and applauded.

They were never given the surnames of pupils, so he only knew her as Meghan. She was ten months into Year One and had spent the first twelve years of her life in and out of foster care, where she had been physically and sexually abused. She rarely spoke. Even when he took her aside for one-to-one development, he could get little more than monosyllabic answers from her. Yet from the moment she had arrived, she had dedicated herself to success. She was well turned out at the dawn roll calls and attentive during morning lessons, when she would silently make notes. She could outrun, outclimb and out-think most of the other Initiates and at night, in the hidden underground cellars, she launched into her Combat training like someone who had real scores to settle.

She was gone in a flurry of earthy footprints and then there were a dozen more runners, each of them known to

Eli. The youngest was Alfie, aged nine. A tubby little thing of Jamaican origin, with fat arms and chestnut eyes, who displayed a cocky attitude to everything, except when he was crying quietly into Eli's arms.

There was a pause and then two more figures emerged. The first was Gregor, a thickset, angry eleven-year-old. His file had told Eli he had been taken from the streets of Glasgow where he was a runner for one of the drug gangs. He claimed to have experimented with pretty much every substance known to man and was mouthy and opinionated. So much so that in his eight months at the Schola to date, he had managed to get into fights with many of his seniors in Years Two and Three. On one memorable occasion he had even kicked off with a cadre of Year Fours who were being specially trained to comprise the Perpetual intake for the Twentieth Armatura in a couple of months. These were the cream of the Schola, aged sixteen and above, primed in the use of shield and steel, and they had barely known what to make of this fist-flying young thug.

'Well done, Gregor. Keep going.'

'Fuck off, Greavsie,' came the panted response, along with two fingers.

Eli had seen this mentality often enough to know it was wafer-thin. Underneath would be a frightened child desperate for support. Gregor provided Eli with a dilemma. His professional conscience wanted to find the key to unlocking the child, but he also knew the toughness Gregor displayed was exactly why the Pantheon liked him so much.

And then came the final runner. At thirteen, he was old for an Initiate and he was a head taller than Gregor, but he was thin and his face had the complexion of someone much younger. He had none of Gregor's hard edges, indeed he exuded a fragility that seemed out of place in Valhalla's Schola. And Eli's files told him why. Here was a real rarity in the Pantheon. This was a boy who had been loved. This was a boy from a proper home, from a middle-class upbringing, who had gone to normal schools and enjoyed normal friendships. To all intents and purposes, he simply shouldn't be here.

Four months it had been now. In the first weeks he had been like a rabbit in headlights, with eyes wide and mouth firmly closed. But Eli had worked with him. Little by little he had prised words from him and discovered – to Eli's surprise – that what opened him up the most was talking about the Pantheon.

He seemed to know things, this enigma of a lad. Things he probably shouldn't. When Eli could coax him, he would rattle off figures about Palatinates and facts about Caelestes, troop numbers and battle tactics. And occasionally he would ask if he had been brought to the Valhalla Schola because of someone called Tyler. Eli had no idea who this Tyler was, but the lad seemed accepting when told it was indeed Tyler who had arranged his presence in the Schola.

He was also informed he would be able to see his parents after the first eight months and Eli hated this lie, because his parents had been killed in unfortunate accidents. Lying, however, had a calming effect on the boy, so Eli stuck to the fabrication like everyone else. Yet this was the nub of the issue. The Pantheon never took recruits from the arms of family and that alone made this lad unique.

Eli watched him as he stumbled by. 'That's the way, Oliver. Two more laps.'

A hundred yards down the track, Frog waved them through and then the two men stood separately and waited several minutes in stillness until they heard footsteps again and Meghan reappeared, still out in front. She pounded past Eli without a glance, followed shortly after by Alfie and the others. Eli applauded and then turned to look back along the track, but the last pair failed to appear. He returned the way he had come and dropped over a slope towards the eight-foot climbing obstacle at the bottom, from where he heard a commotion and realised the two runners were rolling around.

'Hey,' he shouted. 'Cut it out.'

Gregor had got himself astride Oliver and was raining punches on his face and torso, while his opponent tried to shield himself with his elbows. 'Don't you ever get in my way, weirdo,' Gregor was hollering as he slammed down. 'I'll break your fucking face.'

'Hey!' Eli shouted again and grabbed Gregor by the collar of his black T-shirt. 'Get off him.'

He threw the boy backwards and attempted to prise Oliver's arms open. Gregor raised himself, cursing, and launched into Eli with a series of wild punches. The teacher was so taken by surprise he could only hunker down in defence. He felt knuckles impact his shoulder and then his head and was trying to rise when another voice yelled, 'Enough!'

A rough hand appeared in Eli's field of vision and threw Gregor to the ground for a second time. It was Frog. 'Don't you ever, EVER, hit a member of staff, boy!'

Gregor knew better than to antagonise Frog. He stood and glared at them both, but kept his fists at his sides. Oliver rose as well. He had a bloody lip and an eye that looked as though it would blacken rapidly, but Eli had expected to see bewilderment or even tears. Instead, the lad appeared unfazed and simply wiped his arm across his mouth.

'So what was that about?' demanded Frog.

'Weirdo there was getting in the way on the climbing thing.'

'So you thought you'd punch his lights out.' Frog sighed then pointed at the obstacle. 'Get on and climb it – both of you – then clear off and run your final lap.'

Oliver wordlessly took up position several strides from the Challenge, ran at it and used his willowy height to grab the top and pull himself over. He dropped to the other side and jogged up the hill without a look back. Gregor puffed and cursed, then lumbered up to the obstacle and leapt for the top. His weight brought him back down and he swore and jumped again, but to no avail.

Frog pushed him out the way and bent with both hands linked. 'What you should have done, boy, is get that other lad to hoist you up, then you could both clear the obstacle. But obviously you're too bloody dumb to think of that. Here – put your foot in my hands and try again.'

Gregor stepped angrily into Frog's palms and the Hastiliarius launched him up the wooden wall until his fingers found purchase on the top and he could haul his body over. With a whump, he fell to the ground on the other side, picked himself up and loped away.

Frog turned to Eli. 'You should just let them fight – that's what they're here for.'

'You're saying I shouldn't have interfered?'

'They need to work out their own pecking order. I only got involved because Gregor was hitting you.'

Eli brushed dirt from the front of his shirt. 'These kids have coped with some crap in their time and if we don't help them sort it out they'll be too messed up to be any use to the Horde.'

'You do your nicey-nicey stuff in the rose garden when it says so on the curriculum and leave me to get them ready for battle.'

'Just show a bit of care with Oliver, okay? You know he's different. He's no Lost Child. Someone must have their reasons for wanting him here.'

'Yeah, yeah.' Frog waved over his shoulder as he began making his way up the slope.

'To turn them into half-decent warriors,' Eli called after him, 'you first have to know what makes them tick.'

X

'He's back,' observed Forbes after they had returned Beatrice and Fergus to the stables, picked out debris from their hooves, sponged them down and left them to browse on refilled hay nets. Tyler was exhausted and more than ready for another offensive on Mrs Urquhart's lemon drizzle. Now there was a second Audi parked out front and those two words were Forbes' only comment.

Mrs Urquhart emerged with tea in white porcelain again, this time with sandwiches accompanying the cake and dogs accompanying the sandwiches. Tyler was chomping into prawn mayonnaise between rye when a male voice spoke over his shoulder. 'Taylor, I believe.'

He wiped his hand on his shirt and took the man's own outstretched hand. 'It's Tyler.'

'Major Urquhart,' the man said seating himself opposite. He was dressed in cherry chinos, a V-neck jumper, check shirt and regimental tie. 'Such an unconventional name. I don't believe I've ever met a Tyler before.' Forbes' mother brought him a cup of tea, which he took without acknowledging her. 'So what brings you to these parts, Tyler?'

'I came to see Forbes.'

Urquhart sipped his tea. 'Hm. Yes, well he does seem to be

spending an inordinate amount of time back up here these days. What's the matter, doesn't our capital have enough to entertain young men like you?'

'Young men like us?' Forbes asked testily.

Tyler cut in. 'It gets too full of outsiders in the summer. It's impossible to get anything done.'

'And what is it you do, may I ask, which gives you the opportunity to come here?'

'I work in a library.'

'How delightful. You must see our own modest library. The family has garnered quite a collection over the decades.'

'I've already shown Tyler,' said Forbes. 'He's particularly interested in some of the ancient history we have.'

'Indeed.' Urquhart glanced at the mess Tyler was making with the prawn sandwich. 'There are some valuable volumes, so handle with care if you please.'

Tyler bit back a facetious remark. 'I gather you're in oil.'

'Principally in an executive capacity. I lead on image and perception.'

'Really? For oil?'

Urquhart pierced him with his eyes. 'How did you get up here?'

'In my van.'

'No doubt a van powered by oil. So don't give me any of your flower-power bullshit about saving the planet because you need oil just as much as the rest of us. We all have to drive.'

Tyler reached for lemon cake and bit into it, peering out at the gloomy fields. 'Funny how not that long ago everyone rode horses and only the rich drove cars. Now everyone drives cars and only the rich ride horses.'

There was a sustained silence and then Forbes said, 'I'm teaching Tyler to ride.'

'Not on Fergus.'

'Of course not. But he tried out on Bea today and he's quite a natural.'

'I'm delighted to hear it. Every man should know how to ride.'

Tyler wanted to needle the man. 'I gather you've stopped these days.'

Urquhart ran the tip of his tongue around his lips and dropped hawk eyes on Tyler. He had his son's height and build, but strangely retained a fuller head of neatly cut silver hair. 'My cavalry days are sadly over, though it was not long ago that I still led the Dragoons' ceremonial mounted troop at Edinburgh Castle. There's been an Urquhart in Scotland's cavalry for generations.' He glanced at his son. 'Until now.'

Tyler wanted to tell him that his son was swifter and more deadly with the sword than any of his damn Waterloo ancestors; that when he ran with Wolves he was a terrifying sight to behold; that he had held his ground in the ferocious hell of a Viking shieldwall; that he proudly displayed on his chest the Bloodmarks of those he had killed; that the scar on his arm was from a blade fight to the death; and that he was most likely paid more each month to do this than any oil company could ever reward his old man.

But he resisted. Instead he popped the rest of the cake in his mouth and threw a final morsel to an airborne spaniel.

'So do we have the pleasure of your company over the weekend?' enquired Urquhart swallowing the last of his tea.

'Yes we do,' said Forbes. 'He's staying as long as he wishes and I want to see how far we can get with his equestrian training.'

Urquhart made a noise in his throat at this and rose. 'Well, I'll see you both at dinner.'

'What the hell's his problem?' demanded Tyler as soon as the man had departed.

Forbes watched the dogs for several moments and then said, 'He thinks you're my boyfriend.'

Tyler gazed at him open-mouthed and then burst out laughing. Forbes scowled, but when Tyler slapped him on the knee he started grinning himself.

'Can I ham it up at dinner?'

'No!' But Forbes' shoulders were shaking with mirth now.

'Please let me.'

'Don't you even think about it.'

'*Oh, Forbes dear, be a darling and give me a thicker sausage.*'

Forbes' eyes were watering with glee and Tyler leaned forward and grabbed him. 'What a pair we are,' he said rubbing his hand over his friend's bald head. 'What a bloody pair.'

And if the major was watching, he would have been disgusted.

For the remainder of the weekend Tyler went with Forbes to the stables and dedicated his time to feeding, grooming and exercising Beatrice and by Sunday evening Urquhart had departed for Aberdeen again and the house breathed more easily.

'I wish we hadn't left her,' Tyler said the following day.

They were walking the horses east towards the head of the peninsula.

'You mean Calder?'

'I miss her.'

They reached a gate across the track and Forbes manoeuvred Fergus so he could undo the latch. 'I think perhaps your journey in the Pantheon has come to mean more than just finding your sister.'

Tyler considered this as they clopped downhill to a meadow that sloped away to the sea. 'When Radspakr recruited me, I was preoccupied with a belief I could find Morgan. But maybe my journey did change. I made friends, I got strong. When Sveinn chose me as White Warrior I was scared – yes – but also proud. And the Blood Season bonded us even more.'

'And yet your search still drove you to do the unthinkable at the Battle.'

'In truth, there were push factors as well as pull.'

'Meaning?'

'Meaning that even in the short time we've been in the Horde, I could feel it changing. The loss of Halvar. Of Leiv. The ranks of the Wolves pruned and tattered. Sveinn looking weak and old. Radspakr plotting. Then that psycho Skarde. It all hit me as we defended that line on the beach and suddenly I was thinking of Morgan and walking towards the Titans.' Beatrice shook her head and whinnied softly, eager to increase speed on the soft grass. 'And – if I'm honest – even Calder changed. On the island she was so cold towards me. So distant. She wasn't the woman I thought I knew.'

'I suspect that girl has more demons than all of us.'

Tyler played with Forbes' words in his mind, pulled them apart, then said, 'She must never know I told you this, but she lost a child.'

'Oh no.'

'It was a girl – Amelia. Lymphatic cancer or something. Almost three when she died.'

'My god.'

They drifted to the edge of the field and looked out across silver water.

'So perhaps it's actually loss that binds us,' mused Forbes.

'What do you mean?'

'You lost your sister. Calder lost her daughter. And I lost my father.'

Tyler tried to process this, but before he could respond the other man patted Fergus' neck and wheeled him, then took hold of Beatrice's bridle and turned her gently too. 'Come on, this is far enough for today.'

The horses got the message and began to retrace their steps up the slope.

The man known in the Pantheon as Cleitus, Colonel of Titan Light Infantry, waited outside a locked glass entrance to one of Edinburgh's leading curry houses and glanced up and down the street. It was after midnight and the restaurant had closed over an hour ago, so the street lights revealed only dim outlines of chairs stacked on tables. The night still held a whisper of warmth and he was dressed in shirtsleeves. Groups of pedestrians wandered the pavements refusing to give up on their nocturnal entertainments. A party of men with Scandinavian accents jostled past wearing kilts over their jeans and tartan berets. A couple dressed for the theatre hailed a cab. Cleitus pulled a face. He could see why the Pantheon took a holiday at this time of year.

'Come on, damn you.'

There was a flicker of light from within the building and a turbaned staff member approached carrying a torch. He unlocked the door and held it open for his visitor, then sealed it again and led Cleitus to an elevator at the rear.

'Second floor,' he said and accepted a roll of notes with a curt nod.

When the elevator doors opened Cleitus thought he must have pressed the wrong button because the place was still wreathed in gloom. But as he stepped out, he saw a single table pulled up against panoramic windows, the shadow of a waiter bending over to retrieve plates, and a lone occupant, lit from behind by a lamp. His stomach oozed at the scent of spices and he thought how welcome a jalfrezi would be just now, but he also caught the whiff of cigar smoke and realised the waiter was removing used crockery.

'I've ordered us coffee,' stated Odin as Cleitus approached.

'You invited me here just for coffee?'

'I didn't invite you, I required you. And if you think I'm going to ruin a fine curry by sharing it with a goddamn Titan, you're even more of a fool than you look.' Odin pointed with his cigar to the chair opposite and Cleitus sat heavily. 'Here. Cuban. Finest money can buy.'

He proffered an open box. Cleitus hesitated then took one, snipped the end with the cutters provided and leaned forward to draw on the tabletop candle. Odin watched him. Normally he would avoid such meetings like the plague and send a reliable lieutenant instead, but these days he seemed to be running low on reliable lieutenants. Kustaa was grasping and avaricious but way too green. And Skarde – well, put Skarde in the same room as Cleitus and one of them would come out in a body bag.

'So?' he demanded once the waiter had brought coffee.

'So, we've not traced him. It's the Interregnum. People disappear.'

'In a city this size?'

'You should have thought about it before the Blood Tidings. I could have put a tail on him when he left Ephesus, but the strongholds have been closed since then.'

'Goddammit, before the Blood Tidings we all assumed your champions were going to carve him up.'

Cleitus banged his coffee cup down. 'He would have been if that bitch hadn't intervened.'

'Just as well she did, because I never wanted him carved up. But nor did I expect you to lose his scent so fast.'

Odin scrutinised the black pinprick eyes in the podgy face of the man before him. A strange beast, this Cleitus. Every now and again Odin paid him for a snippet of information, but the bloody man only ever gave him small stuff. He could never be enticed to bring the tastier morsels to the table. Nothing about strategy or resources or unit numbers. Because bloody Cleitus considered such matters sacred to the Game and providing them to the enemy – no matter the size of reward Odin offered – was beyond the pale.

That was why Morgan Maitland had been such an asset for Odin. She *had* been prepared to give him all he desired in terms of Titan plans and movements. And all so the stupid cow could be with the man she loved. Cleitus – for his part – knew her only as Olena and he hated her with a passion for betraying his Companions and sending them to their deaths in the cellar that night during the Eighteenth Blood Season – but he assumed she was a lone traitor and had no inkling that Odin had been running her.

Now Cleitus seemed to hate Tyler too, but only because the bastard had killed his vaunted champions in front of the whole Palatinate and made him a laughing stock. He knew nothing of Tyler's link to Olena and probably assumed Odin wanted vengeance on his Wolves for switching sides.

Odin jabbed across the table with his cigar. 'So my ex-Wolves were free to depart your strongholds the day after the Blood Tidings and now you have no goddamn idea where they are until they wander back again at the start of the Armatura?'

'That's pretty much the nub of it.'

'Can't you bloody well lean on Simmius? He'll have all their details.'

'Simmius doesn't take kindly to being leaned on.'

Odin swore and glared out the window at the lights along George Street. 'Drain your coffee and fuck off.'

'What?' Anger rose like a red tide in Cleitus. 'I've only just arrived.'

'Bearing F-all with you!'

'You invite me to one of the city's finest restaurants and all I get is two minutes and a crap coffee!'

'What you get is bloody well rewarded – but only when you bring me something useful. So get lost.'

Cleitus' hand drifted to his hip where on other occasions he would have found the hilt of his shortsword. Odin noticed the movement and gave a predatory smile. 'You wanna make this a problem, cowboy?'

Cleitus weighed the malice in the eyes before him and forced himself to cool. This was one of the Pantheon gods – a Caelestis – and he had the power to make people scream like babies before they died. He stood stiffly, dropped his cigar into the half-drunk coffee and marched away.

'You hear anything, you reach me through the usual means,' Odin called after him, scowling at the wasted cigar.

So what the hell now? the Caelestis asked himself. Having one missing Maitland was ball-ache enough, having two smacked of incompetence. Simmius' Titan databases were unobtainable. Atilius' central teams had proved impregnable to corruption over the years. And besides, even if he could get access to their records, it would never go unnoticed. The power of a Caelestis might seem without limit, but breaking into Pantheon records of any kind was deemed high treason due to the potential leverage this might have on the vast sums of money wagered each Season by the world's elite. Odin had been playing with fire when he drained Olena of every useful nugget of information about Titan movements and he was playing with fire again.

So what now indeed? Even if he could locate Tyler Maitland, he could hardly have him killed. The circumstances of his surrender on the battlefield had been unprecedented and his victory over the Titan champions momentous. That meant his star was too high simply to be murdered in his bed. But Odin was also beginning to suspect that Tyler's rush into the arms of the Titans did not imply he had any new idea about his sister's whereabouts. Indeed his surrender had been a wild lurch in the dark, a stumble on his journey to finding her.

Goddammit, if truth be told, in all this time the one

person who had come closest to catching the scent of Olena's trail was that kid. The one who had lived across the hall from Tyler. He'd managed to trace her to a networking site where she was employing the username *Torchlight96*. Then he'd hacked into the site's database and discovered the username had last been activated back in December by someone called Olena Macedon. Damn clever.

'Brandy!' Odin yelled across the room and the shadow of a waiter leaning against the wall scuttled away.

The kid, Odin pondered through the window. The damn kid.

XI

During the days that followed, Tyler perused the Urquhart library. He focused on the shelves beside the door where Forbes had said the ancient civilisation volumes were kept. Many were old, leather-bound and exquisite and Tyler thought his mother would have loved to touch them. She had never been a reader, but she would have venerated them simply as objects to be placed on show alongside her antique collection in the flat he grew up in. Touching them, Tyler realised, was about all you could do because their pages were brittle, their covers crumbling and the language inside arcane.

There were other books that were more accessible and he browsed through sections on Egyptian pharaohs, Roman society, the Phoenicians and Sumerians, Phrygians and Scythians, the Hittites and Illyrians, Tocharians and Thracians, the Medes, Chaldeans and Nubians. He learned of long-lost places with enchanting names: Mitanni and Tartessos, Elam and Akkad, Minoa and Babylon. He absorbed himself in kings and warlords: Genghis and Attila, Tamerlane, Rameses, Cyrus the Great, Tiglath-Pileser, Sulla, Hannibal and Scipio.

And then he found Alexander.

Tyler read voraciously of the boy king from Macedonia who conquered half the known world. His birth in Pella, his father Philip II and his mentor Telamon. His first Battle at Chaeronea outside Thebes where – just as Forbes had said – the Macedon army defeated the Thebans and destroyed the Sacred Band. Tyler travelled with Alexander across the Hellespont into Asia proper, to Troy and then the field of Granicus where he planted his Lion Standard against Darius the Third of Persia. He rode with him at the head of his wedge of cavalry into the shallows of the river and tore into the Persian horse. Tyler imagined cavalry fronts numbering in their thousands, the mailed cataphracts of Media and Darius' own heavy knights on huge Parthian chargers. He marched with Alexander to Ephesus and Halicarnassus and then to the Battle of Issus where Darius escaped with little more than his pride.

Tyler found himself immersed not only in the hours before dinner, but also late into the night armed with wine or whisky. One time Forbes padded into the library to discover him out for the count in a leather armchair, a map of Alexander's Afghan campaigns on his lap and a spaniel on his feet.

Tyler was with the young Lion of Macedon as he entered Mesopotamia, then Babylonia and on to the mighty Battle of Gaugamela where, legend has it, Darius met him with war elephants and a million men. But even these could not stop Alexander, and Tyler followed him through the Persian Gate, walked the streets of Persepolis, crossed the Caspian Gates and never left his side as he conquered Media, Parthia, Bactria, Sogdiana and on into India itself.

Names sprung at Tyler that he already knew well.

Parmenion, Alexander's senior general. Black Cleitus, Commander of the Royal Squadron of Companion Cavalry and destined to be murdered by Alexander himself. And Nicanor, Commander of the Royal Guards Brigades. There were new names too: Hephaestion, Alexander's closest friend; Leonnatus, his Bodyguard; Olympias, his mother; and Roxane, his Bactrian bride. And then there was Corona and Bucephalus, his trusty mounts.

He found himself picturing the beings behind all these names while he groomed Beatrice. His mind dwelt on arms and weaponry, squadrons and strategy, fronts and feints, wedges and oblique orders. And sometimes he spoke of these with Forbes and there was fire in the eyes of both men.

It was midweek and Tyler rose while the morning was still young. He dressed and crept downstairs in time to see Mrs Urquhart heading through the wall at the end of the garden to take the dog pack on its early walk. He made himself coffee and toast and wandered down to the stables with a cigarette. The sky was clear, but there was a breeze rustling the trees, which grew heavier as he left their shelter.

Fergus was still lying on his straw bedding and simply turned his head to watch Tyler enter. Beatrice, however, was standing waiting for him. Despite the summer season, both were rugged at night for warmth in this northern latitude and they were secured by means of a log and rope system, which extended enough to permit them to lie down, but also retracted under the weight of the stone "log" so they did not tangle their feet.

He reached into the stall and cupped his hand for Beatrice

to nuzzle. She sniffed him cautiously but lost interest when she could discover no tasty snack. He stroked her forehead and ran his hand gently over her ears while Fergus looked on. The previous evening, Forbes had set out fresh bales of straw and Tyler now retreated to these and sat with his back against the wall and legs pulled up to his chin. There was something about the earthy smell of the straw and the quiet movements of the animals that brought him peace and he allowed the morning to mature in their company.

After half an hour Forbes arrived and peered at him through the door. 'Have you been disturbing my lovelies?'

'We've just been contemplating each other.'

Together they began the morning ritual They fitted headcollars to the horses and secured them more tightly, then threw up the rugs and brushed their flanks to remove any stains acquired while lying down for the night. Tyler filled their water troughs while Forbes gave them their first feed. Then the pair mucked out together and Tyler wheeled the droppings away to where they were piled to dry as manure, while Forbes broke up the bales and spread new straw. It was hard work, but Tyler felt energised by it. Gone were his days of sloth in the capital.

They returned to the house to fortify themselves with more coffee and then it was time for the horses to be exercised. They saddled up and fixed the bridles and Forbes watched as Tyler mounted without aid. As they walked down the walled track, Mrs Urquhart was returning with the dogs. Forbes halted the horses but neither set of animals seemed perturbed by the other. The spaniels flowed around the horses like a stream around stones and the two larger beasts waited with infinite patience. Mrs Urquhart bid good morning and passed by without further words. Forbes touched his knees to Fergus' flanks and the big grey moved on. Tyler imitated the movement and was delighted to feel Beatrice step forward.

They came to a gate giving access to one of the fields and Forbes leaned down and unlatched it. Sheep skittered away. 'We'll take this route and wend our way to the lighthouse.'

Tyler guided Beatrice onto the grass and faced her towards the end of the peninsula.

'Let's ease them up to a trot,' proposed Forbes.

'Okay. I'm in your hands.'

'Can you hear each of Bea's hooves? One, two, three, four. When a horse walks it places each of its hooves on the ground at separate times, so we call it "four time". When they shift up to a trot there are only two beats to a stride because the horse springs from one diagonal pair of legs to the other, hitting the ground just twice.'

'And what's the rider doing while the horse is springing? I fear the answer may be falling off.'

'You'll be fine. The key is all about keeping your body relaxed and going with the movement. Lean your torso forward – like so – then let yourself be raised by Bea's movement and returned to the saddle without any loss of balance. Okay, pace her forward, then nudge with your knees and she'll know what to do. Let's go.'

He touched Fergus' flanks. Tyler swore quietly and did likewise. Beatrice broke into a trot and suddenly there seemed to be an earthquake shaking the peninsula and Tyler was crashing about in his saddle. Whack, whack, whack. His backside thumped against the leather, jarring his whole body and rattling his teeth.

'Relax your legs,' Forbes called. 'Hip, knees, shoulders, elbows – everything needs to be supple.'

The field was disappearing beneath Beatrice's hooves and they approached a gate so Forbes leaned in and pulled her bridle until she came to a stop. He opened the gate and they walked through. 'Let yourself rise with her, become one with her rhythm. Now come on, let's go again.'

Forbes nudged Fergus and Tyler took a breath and flicked his knees against Beatrice once more. They were off.

'Feel her motion,' Forbes yelled.

And then something clicked and Tyler did feel her motion. He found himself rising and falling with her and no longer was his rear smacking against the saddle. The whole thing became fluid and they were trotting and he was grinning from ear to ear. The wind buffeting his face, the ground rolling past and the power beneath him. Forbes whooped and gave the horses their head and they whipped down the slope.

Too soon another field boundary appeared and Forbes came in close to grab Beatrice's bridle. 'Whoa, girl.'

They came to a stop, all four breathing heavily. Tyler patted his mount's neck and whispered congratulations to her.

'I think you enjoyed that,' laughed the other man. 'And that was just a trot. When the time's right, we'll go somewhere flat and let you feel what they can really do.'

They exited the field onto a tarmacked lane and made their way along it for a further mile until the road finished at the entrance to the lighthouse grounds. There they dismounted, secured the horses to the gate and followed a shoulder-wide path as it wound over heather-clad slopes to the beckoning sea beyond. Tarbat Ness Lighthouse reared above them, blinding white in the sunshine, with swallows swooping in and out from its upper reaches. Forbes found a flat rock and they lolled down. The heather clamoured with insect calls, but the sea breeze was enough to keep any midges away. The water was afire with light and broken by legions of white horses.

Tyler pulled out a cigarette pack. 'Mind if I smoke?'

'Be my guest.'

They were silent for a long time, letting nature assault their senses. 'Remember right back in the early weeks,' Tyler mused, 'when we knew each other only as Thrall II and Thrall VI – you pulled me off Princes Street and gave me your short and medium reasons for being in the Pantheon? You spoke about them again in the library the other night, but what you divulged was really just the same thing reworded – all that stuff about unity of the Regiment and shoulder to shoulder.'

'So?'

'So I'm still waiting for the long version you promised all those months ago.'

'I don't remember promising anything. And it's not a long version, just a deeper one.' Forbes watched the waves for such an age that Tyler began to think he would get nothing more out of him, but then he sighed, dropped his eyes to the heather and spoke.

'If you'd asked me about my father and the problems between us, I'd have told you it's none of your damn business. But you didn't. You asked me about the Pantheon. So I'll give you your answer.

'I spent just over two years in the army. Three terms

at Sandhurst for military skills and officer leadership development, graduating as a second lieutenant. Then up to Leuchars with the Dragoon Guards for more specific training on the Jackal 2s and light armour reconnaissance and assault operations. Foolishly I got close with someone there – another young officer – and I thought my feelings were reciprocated. Looking back, I think they probably were, but he got scared and chose to cover his tracks by revealing to the rest of the RSDG Mess many of the things I'd said.

'Ironically, if I'd joined the military in the ordinary ranks, things might have been different. No doubt some knucklehead joker would have taken this information and baited me until I beat the bloody crap out of him. And that might have sorted it once and for all.

'But no, as expected of all Urquharts, I joined as an officer and those braying snobs were far more subtle. There was never an action tangible enough for me to take public offence, no solid wrongs that I could right with my fists. It was always just an aside here, a wink there, a whispered double entendre, a grouping of heads over drinks that never included me.'

'I'm sorry, Forbes.'

'I don't want your damn sympathy. It's *me* I'm furious with because I made it an issue in my mind. The more I worried about it, the more I convinced myself I couldn't fit in. I *let* them make me feel different! And by doing that I also let them win. I resigned my commission, took a place in Edinburgh and spent a year working for a law firm and blaming everyone else for my misfortune.

'But gradually I realised what a fool I'd been. There

are prejudices the world over and whenever you come up against other people's prejudices the only thing you can do is walk right on through without allowing them to divert your course.

'So when another frontline battle group came looking for me – this time with their Venarii parties – I saw a second opportunity. And *that's* why I'm in this Pantheon up to my damn neck. To prove to myself – and perhaps to others – that you can be what you want to be in this life as long as you believe in yourself.'

'Well said,' murmured Tyler and it looked as though Forbes wanted to add more, but words failed him and he leaned back on the rock, chewing his upper lip.

Tyler struggled in the wind to light another cigarette and shifted himself uncomfortably on the rock so that he could look out to the horizon. 'You know, they say Alexander – not the bastard in Edinburgh, the real one, the one thousands of years ago – they say he was gay. His best friend, Hephaestion, was most likely his lover and his marriage to Roxane was a sham.'

'What's your point?'

'That history remembers him as Alexander the Great. We are defined by our deeds and nothing else.'

There was an irascible silence from Forbes, but he seemed to accept the statement. He shifted forward in a sign that they should depart. 'And now I think this subject has been well and truly aired, so let's never speak of it again.'

'One final thing.' Tyler grabbed his arm and Forbes stopped his movements and scowled, daring him to meander over old ground. 'I want you to know you've already found that unity you crave so much.'

'What the hell's that supposed to mean?'

'That I'd stand shoulder to shoulder with you against anything. And – I've not wanted to admit this – but I'm so thankful you came with me on that beach. God knows what I was doing because I could never have actually gone through with the whole bloody surrender on my own. In fact I could never have done any of it without you.'

Forbes looked hard at him, then slowly removed his arm from Tyler's grip. 'Come on. No matter how often I've shown them, those horses never learn how to clean themselves.'

'Visit again in a few weeks.'

It was Friday morning. Tyler had been at the house above Portmahomack for over a week and Major Urquhart was due back that afternoon. So the two friends had come separately to the same decision: it was time for Tyler to return to Edinburgh. He leaned out his van window and shook Forbes' hand.

'Won't your mum mind?'

'She'll be fine. The room's already set up for you and it's easy enough to cater for an extra place at meals. Just avoid the weekends when the old man's around.'

'Wouldn't want him thinking it's getting serious between us.'

Forbes grinned and released his hand and Tyler clattered down the drive and turned left for the village.

Back to the city. Back to the crowds and festivals and muggy streets. Back to his rooftop eyrie overlooking the West End. Back to Callum Brodie.

But now – as he gunned the old engine beyond the

village – he was no longer afraid of the emptiness of life. He thought about the house on the hill with its crow-filled trees and spaniel-infested rooms. He thought about his friend and the things they had said. And he thought about Fergus and Beatrice, waiting patiently in their stable for breakfast.

And he knew he would be back.

XII

It seemed to Oliver that no one at the Schola of the Horde of Valhalla ever saw a sunset.

During daytime there was a single absolute rule: no noise. You walked quietly between lessons. Breaks were opportunities to chat, but not to overexcite. Even the afternoon sessions outdoors must be undertaken with minimal fuss. Through these means, no passer-by in Liddesdale would hear the cries of youngsters and wonder at a school so remote.

But in a world of drones and long-range photography, the Schola authorities could never militate against a spy on the hillsides. How could they stop someone watching from a distance and witnessing things that did not belong in a normal school?

Simple. They went underground.

Every night after dinner, elevators took the students down to floors beneath the quad and their world became skyless and subterranean.

Oliver exited the elevator with nine others and hurried to the male changing rooms. Frog and his team of Hastiliarii allowed only eight minutes from leaving Hall to parading in the Arena fully kitted. Any longer than this invoked shouting and press-ups. He reached his locker and scrambled into his black T-shirt, shorts and sandals. Year Two wore green tops, Year Three red and Year Four graduates were permitted breeches, boots and belted Viking tunics. A couple of red-topped Year Threes, although no older than Oliver, shoved him out their way and he had to let them pass before he could jog down the corridor with the other Initiates and line up in the Arena.

'Move it!' yelled Frog. 'What d'you think this is? Bloody St Trinian's? Playtime's over. You belong to the Hastiliarii now.'

'Get that line straightened!' shouted Spade, his deputy. 'An arm length apart like we showed you. Come on, you morons. Don't make me come over there to sort it out.'

Oliver pulled himself into line and reached out to touch his fingers against Meghan's shoulder. He had never heard her speak, but she often looked at him. Perhaps it was just silent messaging between fellow thirteen-year-olds or perhaps she liked his own quiet fortitude. He never really knew, but he felt some kind of bond with her. *We'll get through this together*, her eyes seemed to say and he would nod in reply.

Knuckles banged hard into his other shoulder as Gregor lined himself up as well. Oliver still had shades of purple around his eye from the fight on Blue Trail, but he knew their vendetta was not personal. The eleven-year-old thug simply roughed up everyone.

'Ten... shun!' hollered Frog and the Arena became rock-still.

'Eyes front, you mongrel,' murmured Thumbs, walking along the Year Two lines.

The three Hastiliarii wore boots, T-shirts and combat fatigues. Each was ex-military, but they were also ex-Pantheon and that made them stars in the eyes of their students. After serving their country, they had dedicated more than a decade in the shieldwalls of the Horde before being allowed to retire from the front line to train the new crop. They were all in their fifties, clean-shaven, skin-headed and flaunting Valknut and Triple Horn tattoos on their toned biceps.

After the inspection, they got the years running in tag teams, made harder because the floor of the Arena was covered in sand. Oliver stumbled across the length of the great underground space until he could slap Meghan's palm and she took off in the opposite direction. He stood with hands on hips, catching his breath, and watched her reach the other end and tag Gregor. Tiered seating rose around the perimeter, which allowed the Hastiliarii to gather their students and observe demonstrations. If blood was lost during these exertions, the sand soaked it up just as it would once have done in the heat and noise of Ancient Rome's gladiatorial Arenas.

Oliver was uncertain of the exact date that night, but he thought it must be early September, which meant he had been at the Schola for five months. He could recall only snippets from the early days in the Pantheon Hospital and nothing of how he had come to be there. He remembered grunting goodnight to his mum, spending an hour online, then getting under the duvet in his room overlooking Learmonth Gardens. When he awoke he was on a hard bed in a locked white room. He was aware of figures coming and going, prodding him and murmuring, but they must have got him drugged up to the eyeballs because he kept drifting in and out of consciousness.

Even in his sedated state, he remembered feeling terrified. His brain was incapable of grasping where he was and his visitors were cold, formal, making no effort to reassure him. He wondered if he had suffered some kind of accident or maybe a seizure in his sleep and he kept thinking his mother would surely come through the door any moment.

Blood and urine samples were taken. Fingers checked under his eyelids. Hands assessed his muscles. Stethoscopes explored him. They forced him out of bed and made him stand on wobbly legs while his limbs were measured and his ears examined. He recalled a particular pair of eyes – hard and cruel – which belonged to someone who seemed to be in charge. He would arrive and issue curt orders to his colleagues and look at Oliver as one might observe a mouse in a trap.

It was several days into his captivity when they must have reduced the sedative because he was at last able to think properly. There was movement in the corridor beyond the opaque windows and his door beeped. A new nurse entered. She appeared flustered and looked behind her before closing the door quietly and slipping over to his bed. He saw fear in her eyes, but then she did something no one else had done since he found himself trapped in that room. She smiled at him.

'Hello, Oliver. How are you feeling?' She was a black woman and she had a kind face. 'My name's Monique. I don't usually work in this part of the hospital, but a friend asked me to come check on you. Are they treating you okay?'

'Which friend? Where's my mum?'

'Your mum's fine. I'm sure they'll allow you to see her soon.'

'Is she here?'

'Not at the moment, but don't worry yourself about that.'

'Which friend?'

'Her name's Calder. She seems to know you.'

Oliver frowned and shook his head irritably. 'I don't know anyone called that. What does she look like?'

'Slim. Curly blonde hair. Big blue eyes.'

'How old?'

'Maybe mid-twenties.'

'Mid-twenties! I don't know any girls that age.' He scowled again and then a thought occurred. 'Do you mean Lana? Tyler's friend?'

Monique considered this. 'Maybe that's her name in the real world. I only know her as Calder in the Pantheon.'

'The Pantheon! What are you talking about? Where am I?'

Monique checked the door and then looked back at him. 'They haven't told you?'

'No one's told me anything.'

'You're in the Pantheon Hospital. I work on the wounded wards.'

'But… but I'm not wounded.'

'No, this is the Assessment Wing where they decide if you're the right quality to join.'

'Join? What do you mean? Join the Pantheon? Did Tyler do this? Last time I saw him, I said I wished I could be part of the Horde.'

Monique had never heard of Tyler, but she guessed Oliver

needed some kind of confirmation. 'Yes, it's all Tyler's idea. He's sent you here to be assessed.'

'What about my mum?'

'She's fine with it. You'll see her in a few days.'

'What about school?'

'School?'

'I'm supposed to be at school.'

'Don't worry about that. The Pantheon has sorted everything. Has the doctor been to see you?'

'There's a man who comes and asks me questions. I don't like him.'

Monique nodded and her eyes were pools of sympathy. 'None of us likes him, but he's important. He's the Assessor. You need to answer his questions well. Whatever you do, don't allow him to put a cross by your name.'

A figure walked past the opaque windows and Monique held her breath. The footsteps receded and she looked back at Oliver, studying his face. 'Do you *really* want to join the Horde?'

'I... I think so. If it means being with Tyler.'

Monique made up her mind. 'Then you're in the right place.'

'But I don't like it here. Can you get me out?'

'I can't do that. But I'll tell Lana you're okay.'

'And my mum.'

Monique nodded curtly. 'And your mum.' She rose from beside him. 'I must be going. I shouldn't be here.' She slipped back to the door and looked out, then turned to him, smiled and waved once. 'Remember – impress the Assessor.'

When the doctor with the cruel eyes next visited, Oliver was feeling stronger. 'Do I fit your criteria?' he asked as the man busied himself looking at notes at the end of the bed.

The Assessor raised his gaze. 'What do you mean by that?'

'The criteria to join the Pantheon.'

The man replaced his notes and walked slowly around the bed, stare like a cobra's. 'Who's been talking to you?'

'No one. But I'm not stupid. I see the Odin insignia on your ring and I can make out silhouettes through the glass. I know the shape of a Vigilis helmet when I see one.'

The Assessor examined him wordlessly for many seconds. 'And what does a boy like you think he knows about the Pantheon?'

Oliver met his gaze. 'Seven Palatinates. Five cities. September will mark the start of the Twentieth Year. The Horde of Valhalla comprises approximately two hundred shields, divided into Wolf, Hammer, Raven and Storm regiments. During the last Raiding Season, Valhalla's White Warrior claimed all four Assets hidden at Calton Hill, West Princes Street Gardens, Old College and the castle. These have given King Sveinn real strategic advantages in advance of the Grand Battle, which is probably taking place even as we speak.'

The man peered into Oliver's soul unblinking, then returned to his notes and scribbled something. 'Shooting your mouth off like that can be extremely dangerous,' he said grimly and departed.

That night Oliver was escorted down flights of stairs and bundled into the back of a windowless van. As the vehicle lurched around corners and the journey grew beyond the first hour, he succumbed to the terror again, feeling it clutch at his throat. He wept. Long, earthquake sobs alone in the back. He cried for his mum, for his bedroom and his old life. He cried for the sheer unknowingness of all that was happening to him. But the van kept moving, the miles rolling away beneath its tyres, and by the time it slowed he had long ago exhausted his tears. He hunched silently until the engine stopped and the suspension swung as the driver got out. There were footsteps on gravel and muted voices and then the doors sprang open and cold night air pawed at him.

A woman stood alone, lit by lamps and the cool glow of the moon. 'Hello, Oliver.' She was tall, with sleek hair and the glint of glasses. 'My name's Piper and I'm the head teacher.'

She held out a hand and he took it cautiously and stepped onto a cinder drive. There was a large building behind her with others beyond and he sensed trees all around. Instinctively he knew he was a long way from Edinburgh.

'Welcome to the Schola of the Horde of Valhalla.'

That was when it hit him. There would be no mother waiting for him. No school to attend the next day. His life had taken a sharp and violent new route and he was powerless to stop it.

'Is Tyler here?' he asked quietly.

'Er… no,' Piper replied uncertainly, but then added, 'I'm sure you'll see him soon enough. Meanwhile I'll escort you to your dormitory so you can get a little sleep before roll call.'

Oliver followed her in silence, his eyes flitting constantly. Gone was his confidence from the day before. Now he felt more alone than ever and a small voice at the back of his brain was whispering to him: *This is the Schola. They have you now. You're going nowhere.*

Thumbs the Hastiliarius was yelling at him and suddenly his mind was back in the Arena. 'Move it, you cretin! I said staves.'

The other Initiates were already running to the equipment area and he stumbled after them. Years Two and Three had peeled away and were exiting the Arena to work in the adjoining Practice Rooms. Booted and belted Year Four were heading to the Armouries to collect shields and blades. These seniors would form up in squads and fine-tune their shieldwall tactics – for in just a couple of weeks, the Horde would spend its Blood Funds for the Twentieth Season and many could find themselves called to join its ranks as common trooper Drengr. A few – the best of Year Four – had been set aside as Perpetuals to go forward to the notorious *Sine Missione* and test themselves against new Thralls who had been recruited directly from the outside world. Those who survived would join the Palatinate as young officers – Thegns.

Oliver reached the equipment area and Meghan shoved a wooden stave at him. The fifteen Initiates cantered back to Thumbs and he split them into groups of five.

'Attack Circles. Let's go.'

Gregor grabbed Oliver by the back of the neck. 'You're in the middle first, weirdo. I wanna break your kneecaps.'

Frog and the other Hastiliarii used this routine regularly at the start of Combat and Oliver's bruised bones knew the Rules well enough. As the middle person, he must defend himself against attacks from the other four. If they could rain enough blows to fell him, they won. But if he could use his stave to knock any part of their bodies, they were out and he could win by staying on his feet long enough to remove all four from the Game. Only head strikes were not permitted because these resulted in too many students hospitalised.

Thumbs whistled through his teeth and they were off. Oliver knew the trick was to keep covering the full three-sixty degrees with his stave. They would hit him each time he presented his back, but they had to retreat fast to avoid his next pass.

Meghan struck first. A hard blow into his left collarbone and he winced. He swung back at her and felt a second hit land on his buttocks. Then Gregor was in behind him and his stave cracked against Oliver's spine. He stumbled under the blow, but would not allow his knees to bend. They'd be on him then in a blizzard of impacts until he crumpled entirely. He spun fast and caught one of them on their wrist.

'Out!' called Thumbs, who was prowling between the groups. And now Oliver had more space. Even if one of his assailants slunk behind him, he could always keep two in his field of vision.

Meghan attacked again, but she was slower this time and he could have swung into her with ease. Gregor was expecting this and went for his own sly offensive, but Oliver sensed him coming and ignored the opportunity to take out Meghan. Gregor's blow struck hard against his upper arm, but the boy was too slow to retreat and Oliver's stave rapped his fingers.

'Out,' came the cry.

'No fucking way,' spat Gregor. 'He missed.' With a growl

he stepped in to belt Oliver again, but a figure strode through the circle and whacked him around the back of the skull.

'You heard them,' said Thumbs. 'You're out, you little turd.'

Gregor glared at Oliver, but stepped back and lowered his weapon. The Hastiliarius moved on and Oliver was left with only two opponents. Now the odds were stacked in his favour and he launched himself towards the other Initiate, knocking her shoulder even as she hit him on the hip. Defeated, she dropped away and he turned on Meghan. They eyed one another. If it had been a fair duel, she would probably have the better of him, but in this game he only needed to make contact while she still had to ground him. She attacked with force and their staves traded blows as though it were a sword fight. She broke through and hit him in the stomach, which bent him double.

Seeing her opportunity, she raised her weapon to bring it down on his back, but quick as lightning he swung his own stave and caught her ankle. There was no power in the blow, but the rules were the rules. He had made contact and she pulled out of her attack.

'Nice one,' said Thumbs from beyond the next group as Oliver stretched himself up and rubbed his painful hip. Meghan threw him a look of respect and he took a long breath, privately savouring his victory.

'You,' called Thumbs pointing at Gregor. 'Get in the middle. Let's see if the others can knock a milligram of sense into your thick bloody skull.'

Oliver shifted to the outer ring, weighed his stave in his hand and looked at Gregor. There were several hours of Combat still ahead of them and only at eleven would they be permitted back up to their dormitories to collapse into sleep before reveille at six-thirty.

Thumbs whistled once more and the Initiates attacked.

XIII

In the weeks after first entering Renuka Malhotra's home, Lana hardened in mind, body and heart.

To begin with Renuka forbade her even to leave the house, let alone return to her new accommodation overlooking the Meadows. She split their days into three parts. The late, lazy mornings spent alone constituted the hours of Awakening. Lana would throw open the bifold doors on her garden room and listen to birdsong, bees and raindrops. She fuelled herself with coffee made from the kitchenette, but gradually attempted to emulate Renuka and drink mostly camomile and fennel teas. It was during these hours, Renuka said, when one's soul should adjust to the rhythms of the natural world, when one should live only in the present. The patio in front of Lana's room was a morning suntrap and, little by little, as she took in the beauty of flowers, the intricacies of leaves, the whir of insects, the rooting of robins and the tick-tick of blue tits on the feeders, she felt her ghosts tiptoe away.

The two women came together for lunches of pick-and-mix salads, falafels, hummus, perhaps some mild dhal and rotis, fruit and sparkling spring water. Then the afternoons were devoted to the Finding. They would adjourn to a sparsely furnished front room and there Renuka taught her the fundamentals of Yogic asana postures, pranayama breathing exercises and pratyahara contemplation.

'When one object is perceived, all others become empty,' she said as she arranged Lana in a cross-legged upright posture. 'Fix your attention on the point between your eyebrows. This is the third eye. Merge your mind and senses on this point and listen to your heart chakra.'

Lana was never sure she was doing it right, but she hovered somewhere on a border between deep concentration and dreamless sleep, and when she came round she felt resurgent. Renuka taught her about the seven chakras of her body and placed her in various simple yoga positions and Lana was never bored or rebellious, perhaps because she knew this was a vital part of her rebuilding before the Pantheon came calling once more.

One afternoon Renuka said, 'Meditate on the feeling of pain,' and this time she watched Lana as she fought wordlessly with her demons.

At the end of each session, they separated and showered, read, listened to music, and reunited for dinner. Then, when they were fired and ready and the hour was late, Renuka led her down to the basement for the final phase of the day: the Reckoning.

She had divided her basement into two areas. In the first was a gymnasium complete with cross trainers, chest and shoulder presses, leg curls, treadmills, turbo-cycles, rowing machines, weights, dumbbells, wall-to-wall mirrors and a headbanging sound system. To dance beats they worked through their routines building sweat, heart rates and muscle.

Then they went through to Renuka's Combat Arena. The floor was cushioned and the walls lined with targets. From the ceiling hung two training pells constructed of stiff canvas and filled with sand. There were also standing pells, which could be hauled into place and locked to the floor. These were man-sized wooden poles around which Renuka had ingeniously placed thick cardboard tubes, then taped pool noodle padding and finally wrapped several layers of canvas. The two women selected wooden swords and Renuka forced Lana to go right back to the basics of her blade craft, to the concepts of power, energy, accuracy and range.

'To be a good swordmaiden, your feet, your trunk and your arms must all coordinate to focus the strike.'

She watched Lana as she practised her thrusts and feints. She made her change the angle of her attacks, come from high, low, left, right, move in and out of range. Sometimes they stood together and studied their movements by slowing down and cutting at the air. Other times Renuka fixed weights to Lana's wrists so that it required twice the effort to attack. When they were finished with the pells and suitably attuned, they faced each other and sparred. Renuka was careful not to bruise her opponent, but in the early days she opened her up too easily and the wooden blade would touch Lana on every part of her body.

After three weeks, Renuka was suitably reassured that Lana had arrived at a better place in her mind and was not about to disappear or murder Skarde in cold blood, so she allowed her more freedom. Lana took herself back to her apartment and enjoyed a sprinkling of shopping sprees into the city centre, but she kept slinking back to the house below Blackford Hill, hooked on the three-fold training regime and increasingly dependent on Renuka's companionship.

Towards the end of June, Renuka departed on a month-long trip to Himal Pradesh to be with her extended family and Lana found herself at a loss. She spent a few days in Kirkcudbright with her own mother who still believed she worked for an estate agent in the city. Lana summoned the strength to maintain the subterfuge and together they shared lunches in the town and browsed the charity shops. But ever since the death of Amelia, Lana could not shake the feeling that she teetered on one side of a vast chasm and her mother was unreachable across the divide. She explained this by telling herself that having loved and lost her own daughter she could no longer be a loving daughter for someone else.

Frustrated and befuddled, she escaped Dumfries as soon as feasible and returned to her apartment in the capital. There she sprawled in front of an atlas and thought about the tens of thousands of pounds sitting underused in her bank account. She had not left Scotland since her year in Thessaloniki, since her skin had been kissed by a Mediterranean sun and a Mediterranean man, and that seemed a lifetime ago. She ran her finger over continents. Where? She thought of Renuka in Himal Pradesh and her stories about orchards and mountains. She reflected on the yogic teaching that had become so critical for her in recent weeks and she made her decision. It would be India – though she would never dream of disturbing Renuka's family time.

Instead she selected a luxury tailor-made journey offered by the type of travel company she had spent her younger years abhorring and embarked on a sixteen-day tour of the subcontinent. The mayhem of Delhi. Dawn pinks over the Taj Mahal. Clattering bicycle tours through bird sanctuaries. Bumping four-by-four drives. The noise of Pushkar camel market. The blue city of Jodhpur, the pink city of Jaipur and every other colour of Rajasthan. The punch of the midday sun. The stench of open latrines. Monkeys on temples. Rainbow saris. Dust under the eyelids. Chai drunk at roadside stalls. *Paan* sellers on bicycles. Perfume bazaars and the scents of *falooda* and *rabri* sweet markets. Agreeable waggling heads. The haunting eyes of beggars. Wandering cows. Peacocks at sunrise.

And then the exhilaration of early morning game drives through Ranthambore, staring into the trees, leaning out to gawp at giant footprints in the dust and finally the heart-stopping moment rounding a corner and finding a full-grown female tiger resting languidly in the shade of an acacia tree. Lana would never forget the majestic condescension in the beast's eyes as she rose and retreated from the irritant of the vehicle. For a few precious seconds she was the manifest wild, strolling between the trees, and then she was gone.

When Lana landed in Edinburgh again and walked through customs, she felt a fraud. For she brought with her the colours and smells and heat of India undeclared in her heart.

It was August now and the Festival was in full swing. Queues snaked from every conceivable venue and diners spilled across pavements. Lana found herself enjoying the buzz. It was hardly the beautiful madness of Delhi, but the crowds provided an anonymity that she valued. She took to sitting outside cafés wearing outsized sunglasses and watching people. If there were off-duty Vikings among them, she would never have known and the blade-sharp suspense of the Blood Nights seemed a world away.

She bothered with none of the shows. The opportunity to observe the fiction of others held no attraction, because participating in the Pantheon felt like fiction enough – all the more so during this summer Interregnum when reality reimposed itself and relegated the helms and cloaks and *brynjar* of the winters to mere fanciful thoughts.

Renuka flew back and the two women resumed their training regime. Lana hoped to spend more time at her own apartment, but Renuka was nervous about unwelcome eyes observing her comings and goings from the house. So she fell into a pattern of sleeping in Renuka's garden bedsit during the weeknights and reserving the weekends to be alone above the Meadows. Once again, as the neighbours settled under their duvets, the two women burned calories in the gym, then attacked the pells and each other in long hard bouts until the sweat poured from them and their lungs juddered.

One hot night in mid-August Renuka retrieved a case from her storeroom and opened the clasps to reveal a pair of magnificent Viking longswords.

'I had them made specially by an artisan in Hamburg and they're correct in every detail.'

Lana grasped one and it felt like an old friend. The balance, the weight, the grip. It was a Raven blade in every sense and it surprised her how much she had missed the steel in her hand. She ran her thumb cautiously along one of the edges, but found it blunt.

'Designed to draw blood, but not to kill,' Renuka said in

answer to the question in her eyes. 'Now then, Thegn, show me your worth.'

They attacked and the weapons were swift after the wooden proxies and the clash of steel reverberated from the walls. Lana remembered the first time she had watched Renuka fight. It had been in the vaults many moons ago during the Armatura and the Thralls had witnessed a demonstration of the art of blade combat between Housecarls Freyja and Halvar. Renuka had danced around the bigger man's attacks and stung him time and time again with the point of her wooden weapon. Now Lana felt like Halvar. No matter how fast she moved, how neatly she turned her sword, Renuka kept waltzing around her, dipping beneath her defences and smacking her lightly with her blade. In a genuine struggle with sharpened iron, Lana's life would be bleeding away through the padded flooring.

'Remember that third eye at the centre of your brow,' Renuka panted. 'Focus on it. Don't try to anticipate my moves. *Feel* your own strokes. Let the sword become an extension of your mind and let your instincts drive your limbs.'

They battled on. A blur of blades. But still the Housecarl danced effortlessly to victory. Lana realised this was the critical test. She must match Renuka at her own game and only then would her mentor be satisfied. So each night the steel swords were brought out and Lana flew at her adversary. Her movements became second nature. The weight of the weapon became part of her body. She lost sense of the aches and gasps. Her feet began to dance. Her wrists flicked seamlessly. Her mind flowed clear and fast.

And one night deep into the small hours, with the stink

of sweat hanging heavy in the air and the ring of steel a constant melody, Lana slipped under Renuka's guard and swung her blade lightly into the Housecarl's throat. In that moment their movement ceased. Their breathing subsided. Renuka lowered her sword and stared at the Raven, her cinnamon eyes hard-rimmed but bright with a new respect.

'A perfect death strike.' She nodded slowly and swept strands of hair from her cheek. 'You've come a long way since I found you on that bench. You've worked hard and learned well. And now, Thegn Calder of Litter One, Raven Company House Troop, you are ready.'

PART TWO

HEPHAESTION

XIV

Tyler had been chowing down on omelette and chips in his West End apartment when his phone pinged with a terse WhatsApp message from an unknown number: *Crichton's Close. 10pm.*

Five seconds later, it deleted itself.

It was the ninth day of September and he had been starting to wonder about the silence from the Titans, but he should have known the Pantheon would contact him only when it was good and ready. What had Radspakr said a year ago? *No one ever finds the Pantheon. We find you.*

Over the last two months, Tyler had returned to the Urquhart farm on three further occasions, each timed to avoid Forbes' father. While the spaniels began to treat him like an old friend, Mrs Urquhart remained as coolly distant as she had been on his first visit. Tyler was perturbed about this, until he realised she was the same with her son and he understood just how useless she must have been for Forbes during his emotional battles with his father.

On each trip, Tyler lived for the moments when he first walked down the track and greeted Beatrice. She would cast a baleful eye on him and maybe swish her tail, and he guessed his feelings were unrequited, but he loved her nonetheless. She was tended by the stable girl, Marion, a seventeen-year-old local lass back from her summer break, who watched Tyler coyly beneath an auburn fringe.

'You've got a fan,' teased Forbes whenever she was out of earshot and Tyler would bat him away, but he had to admit she looked great in her riding boots and jodhpurs.

Whatever the weather, the two friends would saddle up and explore the peninsula and every day Tyler grew more confident. On one occasion during his final visit, Forbes led them onto a thin strip of beach stretching along the Dornoch shoreline. The horses already knew the feel of sand beneath them and the easy flat terrain ahead. Their tails flicked up and they became high with anticipation. Bea eased into a trot at the merest nudge from Tyler's legs and she was ready for more.

'Shall we take this up a notch?' shouted Forbes over his shoulder as Fergus pushed ahead.

'Let's do it.'

'Okay, you need to move your outside leg back behind the girth strap and give her a definite nudge. That will be the signal for her to shift into a canter, something we call "three time" and...'

But Forbes' instructions were lost because Tyler had moved his leg back and Bea was away. Tyler felt her great neck moving backwards and forwards and he adjusted his arms to the flow as they drummed over the sand.

Forbes drew level. 'That's it. Hips and legs totally supple. Keep low to the saddle. You're a natural!'

Gulls rose in a panic. The ground disappeared. The air flew around him. His mount's muscles worked in a perfect rhythm and he felt more alive than perhaps ever before.

Fergus was pulling ahead, his mighty frame powering Forbes across the beach. And Tyler shouted in delight.

What a moment. What a breath-taking, wondrous moment.

When Tyler returned to Edinburgh, he took these feelings with him. He nurtured them and fed on them to give him the positivity to get through the remaining Interregnum weeks. He walked the streets with a new enthusiasm and imagined Titan skyline walkways above. He browsed bookshops and purchased volumes on Alexander's campaigns – his armies, his generals, his tactics – and he took these back to his new apartment, devouring them on the floor beside the great windows. He began to dream of his future in a new Palatinate and to believe that he had done the right thing during the Battle. He would befriend Agape and find the trail to his sister and things would work out.

He thought sometimes about Oliver and his mum in their flat across the hall in Learmonth and wondered how things had worked out after his parents separated. Tyler felt terrible that he had left the lad in such a rush, before flying to the island and never been back. One time he strode to Stockbridge and made his way to the gardens outside his old place, but he was careful to keep hidden by the trees in case Oliver was watching from his window.

The boy still had Tyler's laptop and it was tantalising to wonder if he had managed to discover anything more about Morgan's whereabouts, but Lana had been right when she warned him that he might be placing the lad in danger and he could no longer take Oliver on the journey with him. Too much had changed. Bad as it made him feel, he must forgo contact. He would buy himself a new laptop and perhaps in a few more months, when he better understood his Palatinate and the dust from his surrender was settling, he would find the right circumstances to get in touch again.

And now it was the second week of September and Tyler was climbing up the Mound towards his appointment in Crichton's Close at ten o'clock. The city slumbered after the Festival crowds and there was the first tang of autumn in the night air. A train eased out of Waverley beneath him, one of the long-distance ones to Inverness, and he remembered taking just such a journey with Halvar and Freyja and the rest of the Thralls on their way to the showdown at the *Sine Missione*. He could picture their faces as though it was yesterday and even recall what they had eaten: salmon fillet followed by chocolate sponge. The thought drew a smile, which withered on his lips because of the eight in the carriage that night, half – Erland, Vidar, Hertha and Halvar – were now dead.

He asked himself why his mind was needing to reminisce and decided it was because the clock had turned a full year and the scents and sounds and feel of the night were just like those when he had taken his first faltering steps into the arms of the Pantheon.

He paused to light a cigarette and a girl passed him on her way up to Lady Stair's Close. He decided he would take the same route and then cut down the Mile to Crichton's Close. The steps were steep and when he reached the top he heaved a breath and pushed up the brim of his hat. The woman was a dozen yards in front, but then she veered to the left and stopped in the shadows of the far wall. He glanced at her, wondering if it was his presence that had made her halt, and then noticed other figures around the perimeter of the Close. They were tucked into the shadows and keeping their distance. No one spoke, but their eyes shifted to him – as though they had been waiting for someone to emerge from the steps.

No. Surely not. This can't be what I think it is.

Tyler eased back towards the wall of the Writers' Museum. A man with a cap pulled low over his features crested the steps and headed to the first figure in the shadows. There was a murmured conversation and then he moved to the next. Tyler was transfixed.

Early September. Ten p.m. Lady Stair's Close. The old tenements. The dull glow from the lamp. Am I seriously in the middle of this?

He looked towards the exit onto the Mile and remembered standing in that exact place, leaning on the railings in his long coat, shoulder-length hair then but the very same hat on his head and the same brand of cigarette between his lips. *Christ, just the blink of an eye ago.*

The man completed speaking with each figure and slouched towards Tyler.

'Password?' he hissed, keeping his face down.

Tyler dragged on his cigarette and let the smoke drift under the man's cap. 'Sorry, mate, don't know what you're talking about.'

The man peered sharply at him, then nodded gruffly and walked away towards the Mile, drawing the others behind in a ragtag procession. Tyler followed and stepped into the brighter lights of the Mile just in time to see four limousines pull away. Emotions ignited in his gut. He could feel himself with them in those cars, nervous adrenalin behind their blindfolds, bumping against one another as they were swept towards the Horde and the training vaults and the excitement of everything to come. And suddenly he envied them.

Bells were striking the hour and he tore himself away from his reverie and ran down the Mile. He dashed past the Kirk of St Giles and on to Tron Kirk and South Bridge, then further still towards Canongate Tolbooth. The Mile got narrower here and darker. He was panting and could feel a slick of sweat around his groin. At last the tight entrance to Crichton's Close appeared and he veered inside.

'Where the hell have you been?' demanded Forbes.

Tyler waved an apology and tried to catch his breath.

'It's not me you need to be apologising to.' Forbes indicated a woman waiting at the bottom of steps leading to a smartly lit door.

She gave Tyler a withering look, then ascended and the two men hurried after her. When they were close enough, she indicated a row of buzzers and pressed the one marked A&K Finance, then raised her face to a camera. The door clicked and she took them into a hallway where different offices led off each side. They followed her up three flights of stairs and finally saw a door labelled A&K Finance. It opened as they approached and a man stood aside to let them pass.

'Evening, ma'am.'

'Evening, Terence. I've got the newbies.'

Without breaking step, she took them across a room filled with empty desks, then through another door to a ladder. A hatch opened and Forbes glanced at Tyler, then followed the woman up. They found themselves in a bright vaulted loft space, which extended above dividing walls for as far as the eye could see.

'I am Rhea,' the woman said. 'A peltast in the Brigade of Hoplite Light Infantry, and tonight I've been tasked with introducing you to the four strongholds of the Titan Palatinate. But first you will meet with the Adjutant.' She pointed in one direction. 'Changing rooms, pool, preparation and eating areas, then through to the Bladecraft Rooms, Armouries and the roof exits.' She swivelled and indicated behind them. 'This way for administration, officers' quarters and the strategy rooms.'

Forbes puffed out his cheeks. 'Who would have believed it, eh?'

Simmius was awaiting them at the door to his office when Rhea led them through the administration wing.

'You're late. Hardly a promising start.' He swept them into seats in front of a desk and sat himself opposite, while Rhea closed the door and waited outside. 'I suppose I should say welcome to Persepolis. You are currently four floors above Crichton's and Bull's Closes in the stronghold that lies most distant from central Old Town and furthest from the Valhalla Tunnels. It gives us excellent access to the lower end of the Mile and means that in any footrace we can have troops in numbers around Holyrood, Parliament or Arthur's Seat long before the Horde.

'Persepolis is second only to Ephesus in terms of size and contains the same facilities except the Gardens. Pella and Thebes are more compact and do not house Bladecraft training halls or swimming pools. As you know, Ephesus spreads above Gray's Close on the southside of the High

Street. Thebes is eight hundred yards further up the Mile on the northside over the junction with Cockburn Street. And Pella can be found on Brodie's Close looking out to Lawnmarket at the top of the Mile.

'By telling you these locations I'm giving away no state secrets. We have known the whereabouts of Valhalla's Gates for years and Sveinn's officers are fully aware of the entrances to our strongholds. Ravens may even have made it onto the rooftops to identify our exit points, but they would never consider an attack on terrain so alien. Let me be clear, you will never pass through the street-level entrances in Titan uniform. These are civvy rights of way only and some – like the one below us – are shared with other legitimate businesses. Titans only ever come and go from the roof exits.'

Simmius scrutinised the new recruits. 'What I'm going to tell you next is highly classified, so I will remind you that should you ever cross paths with one of your erstwhile colleagues and let slip these details, I will personally ensure Menes has the pleasure of slitting your ball sacks before slitting your throats. Is that clear?'

Tyler and Forbes nodded silently.

'On Conflict Nights, strategic needs dictate a mix of Titan units may be found in any one of the strongholds. In general, however, Alexander and Nicanor's Heavy Brigade base themselves at Ephesus due to the numbers involved; while Menes and his Companions locate themselves here in Persepolis. Parmenion's peltast scouts will be found in Thebes because of its central location; and the Band usually starts from the high ground of Pella where they can sweep fast in any direction. Unless you hear otherwise, the pair of you will base yourselves in Thebes. If you are required to arrive at a different stronghold, you will be messaged in advance.'

Tyler glanced at Forbes. 'Does that imply we're going to be peltasts?'

'There's been much debate on that question. Alexander was all for dumping you in the Phalanx where the basic recruits start, but there's no denying you've had a year's experience in Valhalla's Wolf units so you could be wasted with the Heavies. You're hardly flavour of the month with Cleitus and Menes after killing their champions. They will not countenance you in the Companions. So peltasts, it is.'

'What about the Band?'

Simmius eyed him. 'You two in the Sacred Band? Don't be ridiculous. Now – when we are finished here, Rhea will escort you to the other strongholds. Afterwards she will return you here and I suggest you begin your training in earnest. You have the early weeks of the Armatura Season to become peltast-class. That means becoming versed in the use of the Titan javelin, as well as our shortswords. I will also arrange for you to have rooftop practice. You will need to be proficient in moving at pace across the higher elements of our capital's Old Town. You must learn the best eyries for concealment and reconnaissance, and you will need to know the precise locations of ropes for descent and rapid ascent. Some of our troops pride themselves on being world-class urban climbers. You can't hope to become that good, but there's no point joining the Sky-Gods if you're going to fall off the first building you traverse.'

Forbes grinned. 'Tyler's already done his fair share of that.'

'Yes. I seem to recall the Conflict footage revealing we have a certain well-placed skip to thank for young Tyler's continued existence.' Simmius paused and said darkly, 'Not many of my colleagues have yet realised you were responsible for the death of a Companion on that rooftop. I would advise you keep it to yourself.'

He let them think about this, then began again more brusquely. 'So – let us move to matters of identity. I've drawn up a shortlist of names and I will allow you to select from these.' He began to prod at his iPad. 'Let me see, where did I save them?'

'I have a request,' said Tyler.

'I don't do requests.'

'If the identity is not already taken, permit me to be Hephaestion.'

Simmius broke off from his searching and peered at Tyler. 'Well now, there's a name. Tell me, what gives you the right to make suggestions?'

'I've been reading about him.'

'And?'

'And – he was a distinguished Macedonian general who, according to the Roman historian Quintus Curtius Rufus, was also the dearest of all Alexander the Great's friends.'

'You fancy yourself a friend of the King's?'

'As a Titan, I aspire to give the best of myself to his service.'

Simmius harrumphed sceptically, but refrained from condemning the proposal out of hand. 'We don't have many troopers who bother to learn the heritage of this Palatinate and I will admit it's refreshing to come across one who has. So you're a historian?'

'I like to know what I'm getting myself into, so I spent my time constructively during the Interregnum.'

'Hephaestion was Alexander's closest boyhood friend and rose to become one of his best generals, the innermost of his inner circles. Giving such an identity to a Viking turncoat may raise the bile of some of my colleagues who also know their history.'

'I will prove myself worthy of the name.'

Simmius turned this over in his mind. 'Perhaps you will,' he said quietly, then began to input the details. 'So we are agreed. You will be Hephaestion, friend of Alexander.'

'He was also commander of the Companion Cavalry.'

'We don't have cavalry.'

'I'm aware of that.'

There was a moment's pause and then Simmius looked to Forbes. 'And I suppose you have a special request too?' he asked facetiously. 'Apollo, the son of Zeus perhaps? Or Achilles, the greatest of all Greek warriors?'

'I figure it's best to keep my head down, so you make the choice.'

Simmius consulted his list and deliberated for a few moments. 'Are you a stoic, my friend?'

'I can endure most things without fuss when I'm required.'

'Then you will be Diogenes. A philosopher and founder of the Cynic movement and school of Stoicism.'

Forbes shrugged. 'A philosopher. It could have been worse.'

'So we have it. Hephaestion and Diogenes of the peltast scout units led by Parmenion, Brigade of Light Infantry commanded by Cleitus.'

As Simmius tapped in the final details, Forbes winked at Tyler and whispered, 'Heph and Dio.'

Heph and Dio.

It was agreed.

XV

It was three in the morning when Rhea escorted the new Titan pair back to Persepolis. They had spent an hour in each of the other strongholds asking every question they could think of about locations, routines, protocols, armament and personalities. Then she had taken them up onto a few of the easier rooftops to get a feel for the city at that level and gauge their head for heights.

'Hephaestion,' Simmius called, still in his office at that hour. 'A word.'

'Sir?'

'You have a breakfast appointment.'

'I do?'

'Seven-thirty at the Balmoral.'

'O... kay.'

'I suggest you find a triklinion couch in the dining area and get some sleep. I will ensure you're woken in good time.'

That appeared to be the end of the conversation, so Heph joined Dio and explained he would be remaining in Persepolis.

Dio raised his eyebrows. He had shaved off his beard when he left Portmahomack and once again the eyebrows were the only feature on his head that revealed his natural hair colour. 'Moving in exalted company?'

'God knows. I'd rather be collapsing in my bed.'

'I plan to return on Wednesday to begin sword practice in the Bladecraft Rooms.'

'I'll join you. Goodnight, my friend.'

Heph consumed some bread, cheese and wine in the dining area, then spent an uncomfortable few hours on a triklinion couch, which ancient Greeks had used to recline while eating. He was shaken awake by one of the kitchen team.

'Six-forty-five, sir.'

'Christ, already?'

He bathed and threw an espresso down his throat, then descended through the loft hatch and exited into a grey dawn. The air was chill and he lit a cigarette, thrust his hands into his coat pocket, pulled down his hat and strode up to North Bridge and the Balmoral.

'May I help you, sir?' asked a uniformed manager behind reception in the vast entrance hall painted in soft pastels to set off its dark wood furnishings.

'I have an appointment.'

'With whom?'

'I don't know.'

'I see. May I have sir's name?'

'Er... Tyler.'

He consulted notes hidden behind the counter. 'Ah yes. Step this way, sir.'

Tyler removed his hat and followed the man. In over twenty years living in Edinburgh, he had never set foot inside the Balmoral. Such establishments had no place for his type.

The manager showed him into a hexagonal and colonnaded room with an opaque glass ceiling, allowing the best of the morning light to illuminate its features. On every available wall space were intricate paintings of trees, accompanied by huge mirrors, which lent the room even grander proportions. Beside the columns were big blue pots with mature palm trees reaching for the daylight. White linen-clad tables were dotted across the floor accompanied by peppermint velvet armchairs. All were empty, except one in the far corner under the largest tree, where a slim brunette dressed in a cream business suit awaited them.

The manager led him across. 'Your guest, ma'am.'

The woman rose with a smile and extended a bronzed hand for Tyler to grasp. 'Good morning. Please do join me. What will you have?' she asked, seating herself again.

'Coffee's good.'

'And I'll have another pot of Darjeeling,' she said to the manager, to which he bowed his head and retreated. 'I apologise for the early hour. My husband and I have a flight mid-morning. He prefers his breakfast in bed, but I like to take the air in the Gardens whenever we're in Edinburgh and then enjoy this wonderful room. Have you been here before? It's the Palm Court. I'm told it's rather popular for afternoon tea.'

'Never.' Tyler glanced around. 'It's pretty quiet.'

'That's because it's not open yet. Champagne?'

'Why not?'

The woman reached for a bottle of Dom Perignon in an

ice bucket beside her and poured a flute for Tyler. 'When I'm travelling in the middle of the day, I find bubbly at breakfast helps me sleep on the flight.'

'A couple of beers usually sort me out.'

She raised her glass in salute and he did likewise. They drank and then she swept her hand over the table. 'So, we have fresh fruit, yogurt, olive bread, sweet breads, tahini, thyme honey, pastries, grilled sausages from Trikala, Graviera cheese from Naxos, Froutalia omelette from Andros, farsala halvas and almond sweets. Please do tuck in.'

Tyler helped himself to sausages and olive bread and cut a hunk of cheese, biting hungrily.

'I understand you are to be Hephaestion,' the woman said watching him. Despite the hour, her shoulder-length hair looked professionally blow-dried and her make-up was immaculate. Gold hung from her ears, throat and wrists. 'A good choice.'

'I'm afraid you have me at a disadvantage,' said Tyler between mouthfuls.

'Does the name Hera mean anything to you?'

He shook his head.

'In Ancient Greek mythology, Hera was the wife of Zeus, ruler of the gods.'

Tyler stopped chewing. 'You're the wife of Zeus? And he's upstairs having breakfast in bed?'

'I wanted to meet our latest recruit.'

'There are two of us actually.'

'Your friend was loyal to follow you on that beach and we should all have more friends like that. But we both know he only did it because you were so determined to change sides. Something much stronger than friendship drove you into the arms of our Sacred Band.'

They were interrupted by the manager returning with coffee and Darjeeling.

Hera poured her tea, added a drop of milk and took a new tack. 'I can't begin to tell you how delighted we were to see you make Odin look such a fool. By all accounts, he's raging. Two of his elite Wolves changing sides at the climax of the Battle, when the Curiate and every other Pantheon investor was watching. Over the last few Seasons of treachery and bloodshed, I've been praying for a chance to give him a black eye. So please see this breakfast as a token of our gratitude.'

'With pleasure,' said Tyler, helping himself to sweetbread and honey.

Hera sipped her tea. 'So how did you spend the Interregnum.'

'Riding horses.'

'Really?' she exclaimed with delight. 'Are you good?'

'Only just learning, but I took to it like... well, like a duck to water.'

'My husband and I own a thousand-acre stallion farm in Bluegrass, Kentucky, and I try to get there to ride as often as my timetable will allow. For fifteen years now, we've been breeding some of the best young sires in America. But I first learned to ride as a young girl at my uncle's farm near Pelasgia in the foothills of Mount Othrys in central Greece. My first horse was called Persephone, after the goddess of fertility, and she was my best friend in the whole world.'

Tyler did not reply and Hera quietened and recomposed herself. She studied his face as he tested the almond sweets and she thought about what she had learned of him from Simmius and Agape. Zeus believed she was eating alone, but she had needed to see this new man for herself. Needed to look on his features and hear his voice. *So this is you, Tyler Maitland. You've come at last.*

'Whenever we get new blood into the Palatinate, it can be refreshing to obtain their early perceptions before they become tainted by the authority of those in charge.'

'So do you make a habit of inviting every new recruit to breakfast?'

'Let's just say the circumstances of your arrival make you a special case.'

Tyler accepted this and drank his coffee.

'Well?'

'Well what?'

'I'd like to hear your observations on what you've gleaned so far about our Palatinate.'

Tyler finished his coffee slowly, then sat back and looked at her. 'Okay, if you really want my views... You say you want to give Odin a black eye, you say you're delighted to make a fool of him, yet for the last nineteen Seasons the Titan and Valhalla Palatinates have been stuck in stalemate. Every year you slug it out in the Raiding Season and the Blood Nights and the Battle, and a few troops die and then they're replaced with Blood Funds and the whole circus starts over again. That's pretty much the situation in a nutshell, am I right?'

'No one can claim we were not the outright victors last Season and we have the Blood Funds to prove it.'

'And you'll spend those funds as you always do on

enlarging the Phalanx, adding a few peltasts, strengthening the Companions. Just the same old, same old.'

'We earned over a hundred Credits last Season. It's our first opportunity in four years to become the larger Palatinate.'

'But so what? Will those additional troops make any real difference? You'll simply go on fighting it out as you do every year. Nothing will change.'

'So what would you have us do?'

'You've lost sight of the bigger picture. You've forgotten what really counts.' Tyler paused to gather his words. 'Alexander the Great himself never lost sight of what mattered. That's what gave him so many victories. Every time he came up against the massed armies of Darius, he remembered the one thing that could always make the difference.'

'And what was that?'

'Kill the King.'

Hera laughed. 'Kill the King?'

'That's what Alexander had at the forefront of his mind in every Battle. Get to Darius. And Persia's million troops counted for nothing. Kill one man and victory was his. That's all it took.'

Hera's smile was fixed across her features. 'No one's killed a King with a sword in their hand in the history of the Pantheon.'

'That's because no one's attempting anything completely unexpected.'

'And you think the Titans can?'

'Perhaps.'

Hera grew serious. 'Go on.'

'Do you know what made Alexander's armies so effective?'

'Tell me.'

'Speed. Alexander could move his forces across the battlefields so fast they could strike at exactly the right place at exactly the right moment.'

'And how did they do this?'

Tyler allowed himself the hint of a smile. 'By using the squadrons of his Companion Cavalry.'

Hera laughed again. 'Horses?'

Tyler leaned forward. 'Every year at the Grand Battle both Palatinates shuffle around on foot, emulating each other's formations. The Hammer shieldwall against the Heavy's Phalanx. The Wolves matching the Companions strike for strike. No one ever gets past the Bodyguards of either King. Can you imagine the impact of the unexpected arrival of horses on such a battlefield?'

'Do you have any idea how expensive horses are in the Pantheon? We could use all our Blood Funds on them and still only buy ten at most.'

'Think what havoc ten riders could cause to an enemy taken by surprise.'

Hera inclined her head and looked at the dregs of her tea. 'Well, I did say new recruits could bring refreshing perspectives.'

'And you asked for my honest opinion. This Titan Palatinate should be seeking to emulate the greatness of its Alexandrian heritage. The Lion of Macedon roared across Eurasia with an army of mounted knights, but you are content to slug it out shield to shield with the Horde.'

'So you would have Zeus expend our Blood Funds on mounted knights? I know what his response will be.'

'I'm simply saying that if you think about things very, very differently, you have the opportunity not just to give Odin a black eye, not even just to maul him – but to utterly destroy him. To leave him in the mud, defeated, destitute and without a Palatinate.'

Hera looked at him for several silent moments. 'It's been interesting to meet you, Hephaestion,' she said at last.

'Thank you for breakfast.'

'Can you find your own way out?'

'Of course.' Tyler rose and tucked in his chair, then paused. 'I'm sorry if I spoke out of turn. I'm not used to champagne at eight in the morning.'

'You gave me your honest opinions and for those I'm grateful. Good day, Heph.'

'Have a good flight.'

It was two in the morning when the Boeing 727 Executive jet taxied to a halt and Lana still had no idea where she was.

Five hours earlier she had followed Freyja's instructions and made her way to the southern side of St Andrew Square with an overnight bag, where she came upon twenty other members of the Horde loitering on the pavement. They all wore civvies and Lana found herself adjusting to the sight of Bjarke in a Hearts football top, Asmund in brogues and Sveinn sporting green corduroys and a golfing jumper. Skarde was there too, leaning alone against the railings, smart jeans, blue polo-neck jumper under a brown leather jacket. He stared at her as she joined the group, but she kept her eyes averted.

Freyja approached and smiled. 'Good. That's my Ravens accounted for.' Lana spied Jorunn behind her and three others, including Geir who had recovered from the pommel in his face and Sassa, also wounded on the beach. It was good to see them fit and strong after the Interregnum. 'Five of us, as there are five from each of the other units. Twenty in total, plus Sveinn.'

'Where are we going?'

'We've been summoned.'

A coach pulled up and they slung their bags in the lower storage. It whisked them to the airport, where the Boeing took off just as last light deserted Scotland. Lana had never travelled in such luxury. The plane's interior comprised leather sofas stretched along the walls, gilt tables fixed into thick carpet, flower bouquets, fruit bowls and a bar area that filled most of the rear third of the passenger area. She squeezed herself onto a sofa with Storm archers and was served a variety of hot and cold assortments during the three-hour flight.

Now, as she disembarked to another executive coach, her face was caressed by warm night air. *Where the hell are we?* She sat next to Jorunn and gazed out the window as the coach pulled away, but it was only when they eased onto a motorway that she glimpsed a passing sign: *Roma 30km*.

Rome. *My god.*

Everything about the name caught at her, teased her.

After twenty minutes the first tendrils of the city grabbed them and they weaved through intersections, which were deserted at that hour. They passed shops and apartments and crossed a river and then Jorunn prodded her and pointed. Rising to their left was a giant oval structure. Three storeys of beautifully lit arches running in symmetrical perfection one above the other before crumbling away to nothing. The Colosseum. Something tingled in Lana's spine.

The coach took them ten minutes further and pulled up in front of wrought-iron gates, beyond which stretched a softly lit terraced garden. Top-hatted doormen saluted and ushered them through. There were fountains and tables and statues of ancient Roman dignitaries and staff waited with trays of sharp Campari sodas. Some of the Horde settled onto seating and began to laugh and converse, but Freyja marched back from reception and handed key cards to her Ravens.

'I suggest you get some sleep. Tomorrow is yours to spend as you wish. Feel free to explore the city, but also take time to rest because you're going to need it. Be in reception tomorrow evening at eleven. I'll see you then.'

Lana took herself up to her room on the ninth floor. It was a modern space, tinged with art-deco Valentino influences and huge windows that opened onto a private balcony. She dumped her bag, stripped and showered, then wrapped herself in a robe, made a large gin and tonic from the fridge and wandered onto the balcony. The night was still warm and broken only by the Valhalla stragglers in the garden. Beyond the hulks of surrounding buildings, Lana could just make out illuminated lines of columns and she wondered if these were the remains of Ancient Rome. The centre of the old city. The beating heart of empire.

It was four o'clock when she finally tucked into bed, but she set her alarm for eight and discovered a tray of pastries, fruits and coffee waiting outside her door. She ate on the balcony, revelling in an Italian sun and a heart-breaking blue sky. Freyja had omitted to say pack for heat, so she had to make do with a T-shirt, jeans and trainers and was thankful she had thrown in a pair of sunglasses. She dropped to the garden, where four Hammers were breakfasting on eggs. One was Ingvar and she realised all of them were Berserkers. She had a memory of them snarling and cursing on the blood beach, working themselves into a rage, but now they waved to her jovially and wished her a good day. *I've fought tooth and claw alongside these people*, she thought. *I've feasted with them, trained with them, hell – lived with them, but I don't know them at all.*

It was still cool in the shade as she strode through the streets, but when she progressed onto Via Dei Fori Imperiali, the wide thoroughfare cutting through the city's heritage area, sunlight embraced her. On her left crouched the Colosseum and stretching away to her right were the remains of Rome's age-old Forums. She had beaten the tourist mobs, so she walked quietly along the broad pavement and embarked on her own journey of discovery.

Over the course of the morning, she wandered among the skeletons of great buildings. She peeped into roofless basilicas; stood under arches commemorating victories she would never know; gazed at lonely columns that had once enjoyed the company of others; and imagined the beauty of temples where now only foundations remained. She climbed Capitoline Hill and pondered treasures behind inch-thick glass in the museums, then ate ice cream in the sun on Michelangelo's hilltop square. As the day matured and visitors arrived in waves of selfie-snapping, she took herself to the quieter Markets of Trajan and explored the different levels of cellars and storehouses, imagining the clamour that must once have echoed around these walls.

'I like it here,' said a deep voice when she reached the top and Bjarke came next to her. He was in shirtsleeves and wraparound shades and he stood looking out at the bustle of the Forums across the Via. He smelt of leather and denim and gum. His beard was still braided and his tattoo writhed across his throat, but somehow his huge presence felt at rest under the Roman sun.

'You've been here before?'

'Aye. A few times. I like to sit up here, just being quiet and taking it in.'

'I never had you down as the quiet type.'

'We're all full of surprises.' A flash of teeth within the beard, still not looking at her. 'Take you for example. You're a hell of a surprise.'

'In what way?'

'You're alive and prospering. And I wasn't expecting that.' Now he turned to her, but his eyes were invisible behind his glasses. 'Your boyfriend was a stupid bugger on that beach. Gone and left you all alone. But you're a survivor and that's something I can respect.'

'Are you threatening me?'

He seemed to find this funny, but then he stilled and considered her. 'Just the opposite, little lady.' He swivelled away and returned to his seat. 'Get some rest. Long night ahead.'

She ate lunch outside a corner café near the Trevi Fountain, but hated the elbowing crowds, so she lost herself in a warren of old streets. Some hours later she came upon a hidden piazza and gazed at a domed building at one end. She knew of this place, had read about it somewhere. It had been a Roman temple, then a Catholic church, built by Emperor Hadrian as a place to worship all the gods.

She smiled softly. Somehow, on that afternoon in the sunshine, with a Horde of Vikings waiting for her at the hotel and a night of expectation looming ahead, it felt right to be standing on that spot, watching pigeons strutting around the dome of the original Pantheon.

XVI

On most nights at eleven-fifteen, the Via Dei Fori Imperiali would still be sprinkled with tourists wandering back from restaurants and enjoying the floodlit ruins. But tonight, as the twenty-strong Horde of Valhalla strode onto this wide boulevard, nothing stirred. Calder stole a look towards the Colosseum and saw a line of figures blocking the road. Not helmeted Vigiles, but modern soldiers with guns. Whoever bestowed privacy on the Pantheon that night obviously possessed power enough to call out the Italian army and close the centre of one of the world's great cities.

The group crossed the Via and approached the northern entrance to the vast Forum area. Sveinn had gone ahead earlier and the Horde progressed in a disjointed mishmash with Bjarke leading the way. They were still dressed in civvies and resembled nothing more than a large coach party exploring late. But coach parties were not usually waved through the ticket barriers by armed soldiers, nor allowed to thread their way across the ruins in shadows. They crossed lawns, skirted walls, weaved between columns and eventually approached the bulk of a hill and a larger building. Bjarke and Asmund led them into this and they began to climb up a long curving internal slope.

'The emperor Domitian's Imperial Ramp,' said Freyja next to Calder. 'It joins the temples, markets and Courts of the Forums below to the houses and palaces of the rich on the hill above.'

'How do you know these things?'

'This is not our first summoning to Rome and it won't be our last.'

They reached the top of the mighty ramp and came upon tree-lined gardens lit with lamps and rows of burning torches. Ruins rolled away as far as the eye could see, but these had a different feel from the colonnaded grandeur of the Forums below. They were more intimate and suburban, nestling into their gardens, and the view over the city was breath-taking. Calder could see why the rich of Ancient Rome would have chosen this spot to build their houses.

'This is the Hill of Palatine,' said Freyja.

'Palatine?' repeated Sassa. 'As in Palatinate?'

'Our Palatinates are named after this very place. It is one of the seven hills on which Rome was built. Seven hills. Seven Palatinates. Tonight, my Ravens, you are welcomed to the Summoning of the Seven.'

'It marks the beginning of the new Season,' Geir chipped in. 'There is a Summoning every year, but not always in Rome.'

'Seven?' mulled Calder. 'You mean we're not the only ones here?'

'Oh no.' Freyja smiled. 'It's time to meet the Pantheon's other players.'

Figures materialised. This time it was Vigiles in their full armoured regalia. They spoke with Bjarke, then signalled for the Horde to follow and took the group along winding footpaths until they came to ancient steps leading into the earth. They filed down, dropping away from the starlight, but finding instead the harsher glare of temporary fluorescent strips, which illuminated rooms off each side of a passage.

'Hammer first right,' shouted Asmund after conferring with the Vigilis. 'Storm first left. Wolves and Ravens further down. We have fifteen minutes to ready ourselves.'

They discovered chests labelled with their names and filled with their war apparel. No one cared about separating the genders and Calder found herself stripping next to Geir.

'Are we fighting?' she breathed at him.

'No blood tonight, lass. Don't you worry.'

A few paces away, Ake, Unn, Stigr and the other two Wolves groped with leggings and tunics, hoisted *brynjar* mail over their heads, tied hair back, belted longswords, fixed wrist guards and pulled down helmets. And there was Skarde in one corner, silently transforming himself into a god of war. Freyja reached into a chest and retrieved the Raven banner wrapped around its pole.

'Tonight you carry this,' she said handing it to Calder. 'Unfurl it when we step into the night.'

The other Ravens were watching her.

'Why me?'

'Because you're a Thegn. The only one left in my company and that makes you my number two. It's time you became the young officer you were recruited to be.'

Calder took the banner and glanced at the others. But they were grinning and Geir winked at her.

Raised voices came from the passage, and the Wolves

and Ravens took up their shields and joined Hammer and Storm. They progressed down the passage, iron clinking and eyes peering through their slots. Somewhere ahead the scent of animals rose.

The passage expelled them into a larger room, ringed with braziers and with a stone ramp leading up to doors. Sveinn was awaiting them in the centre, dressed regally, his silver-streaked beard shining in the flames and his armour polished bright.

'What does the fool look like?' hissed Geir.

For Sveinn was standing in a Roman war chariot, with a driver holding the reins beside him and two black stallions waiting patiently. The horses bore scarlet plumes and the sides of the chariot were adorned with giant eagles painted in gold. Hanging from a pole fixed to the rear was the banner of Valhalla, the Triple Horn of Odin.

'They've done it on purpose to make him ill at ease,' said Freyja and, indeed, Sveinn clasped the chariot's edge awkwardly and his jaw beneath his helm was frozen rigid.

'Who has?' asked Calder.

'The Legion, of course,' said Geir. 'We're in Rome. This is their party.'

As the Horde settled around their King, Calder became aware of the hum of voices above.

'Sounds like our audience awaits,' said Jorunn grimly.

'The Curiate?' Calder asked.

'There'll be a right repellent mix up there,' Geir answered through gritted teeth. 'Aye, some will be the Curiate. And god knows who else – bent politicians, banker wankers, military cronies, tech billionaires, CEOs, la-de-da lords and ladies, old-school grandees, mob bosses and black market shysters – and not a single moral fibre between them.'

'They pay our salaries,' commented Sassa.

'They pay to watch us die and don't you forget it.'

A single thudding crash silenced the room and the Horde held its breath for a heartbeat. Then the sound came again, and a third time. The voices above grew in excitement and the crashes fell into the rhythm of dozens of drums.

'Showtime.'

The drums beat a tattoo and there was a roar from the crowd.

'First one's coming out,' said Jorunn.

'Aye.' Geir nodded. 'That'll be the Titans.'

Feet beat the ground over their heads and the crowd went wild.

Freyja looked to Calder. 'Fix your shield high on your arm and leave your blade sheathed. You'll need both hands to keep the flag aloft. Let them know the Ravens are on this damn hill.'

Another roar.

Jorunn looked to Geir. 'The Warring States?'

'That would be my guess. They'll be accustomed to the chariots at least.'

'Us next,' said Freyja.

The stallions pawed the ground and Sveinn clutched his chariot rim. Bjarke turned to the assembled warriors with fire in his eyes. 'This is it, Valhalla. There may be no blood spilt tonight, but you still put the fear of god into them. Make them shit at the prospect of ever facing us in a shieldwall. Are you ready?'

The Horde yelled its response and when Bjarke drew his

blade, fifteen others followed suit – all except the banner bearer for each company.

Vigiles on the ramp waved signals, the drums beat with a passion and the great doors swung open. The charioteer rippled his reins and the stallions broke into a trot. Sveinn jolted, almost fell, then forced himself upright as a cry tore from his warriors and they ran up the slope.

As she emerged into the Roman night, Calder could take in nothing. The ramp was steeper than it looked and she was struggling to unfurl the banner. There was noise all around and flashes of fire from burning torches. The drums pounded their incessant rhythm and her Ravens strained next to her. They were in some kind of huge elongated pit, ringed by stone walls with braziers around the rim. There was grass underfoot, but also the stumped remains of columns extending away along the length of the enclosure. The drums came from above and there were more banners up there and more flames. And there were people too. Hundreds of them, yelling and applauding.

But she had no time to look properly. Sveinn's chariot was already flying down the centre of the turf and Bjarke was leading a full-throated charge. The Horde cried hell to the skies and threw themselves forward and all Calder could do was let the Raven banner fly free and add her own voice to the challenge. A hundred paces away, over the heads of Valhalla's front lines, she could see another group of twenty figures, and as the braziers lit their bronzed armour and shields, she recognised the Titan foe. Their hoplons rammed together, bristling with lethal dory spear points, and they braced themselves for the oncoming Vikings.

For a moment Calder thought anarchy had taken hold. Sveinn's chariot had disappeared to the far end and the two sides seemed about to carve into each other, but Bjarke ploughed to a halt inches from the line of sharpened iron and brandished his longsword high above his shoulders, hurling curses at the enemy. The Horde crowded round him and screamed their abuses and beneath the Titans' bronze helmets the insults flew back. Then a new sound released the valve and Calder glanced over her shoulder. A third group of warriors launched themselves at Valhalla's flank, stopping just short of a blade strike. In the flickering light of the torches, she could see the knee-length robes of these new soldiers, their armour of leather strapping and their egg-shaped leather helmets above their eyepieces. Several were armed with bronze swords, but others carried crossbows and many bore long iron-headed spears with slashing axe blades fitted.

She might not have recognised them in the dancing light had Jorunn not named them earlier in the Tunnel. Now Calder took them in with mouth apart. Back in Scotland, most people could list the seven Palatinates. They were all famed and the overseas ones were considered even more exotic and untouchable than Edinburgh's pair. Kids collected Palatinate stickers. The web was filled with artists' impressions of every unit, every weapon, every scrap of armour. And here before her was China's very own Palatinate. The Warring States led by Zheng, Lord of the Qin and ruled by their Caelestis, Xian.

The crowd was going crazy, almost drowning out the drums, but the show had barely begun. A new cacophony arose at the opposite end and more newcomers made their entry. The twenty figures came in two lines, with none of the bluster and war cries of the first Palatinates, but their silence was just as imposing. They wore knee-length robes of scarlet with blue tunics beneath, green silk trousers tucked into boots and pointed iron helmets with a vertical metallic gold plume rising from the lip over their eyepieces. Many were women, but the men among them sported curling moustaches.

'So the Sultanate has brought its Janissaries to the party this year,' said Geir next to her. 'Don't be fooled by their lack of armour; they are the second best foot soldiers I've ever witnessed.'

Calder knew well enough of their reputation. She clung to her flag and peered at their lines. The Sultanate, based in Istanbul, led by the imperious Mehmed the Conqueror and ruled by their Caelestis, the ancient Turkish god Kyzaghan. In ancient times, the Janissaries were believed to be captured Christian children, raised into Islam as slave soldiers and trained to become the most fanatical units in the entire Ottoman empire.

A new commotion tore from the other end of the enclosure and Calder gasped and almost dropped her banner, because thundering towards them was a wave of horses. Each animal was compact and sturdy and the twenty figures on their backs rode with a lightness of touch, at ease in the saddle, at one with their beast. They wore leather armour and spiked iron helmets with leather neck guards and earflaps. They carried small circular shields and some held composite bows, while others brandished curved sabres.

The Palatinates stepped back and hunkered down before this wave, but the riders reined their beasts and howled in a single coordinated challenge with their weapons held high above their heads. The other Palatinates screamed back and Calder found herself yelling and shaking her Raven banner, but more in exhilaration than anger. For this was the Kheshig and she had always loved them. Something about them was so wildly romantic. The soldiers of the endless plains. The great Mongol army of Genghis who had once ruled the known world and who worshipped Tengri, the god of the unfathomable skies.

But she had no time to take them in properly because beyond them the night was coming again. A new blackness, a thundercloud rolling towards them. This time the horses were even smaller, shaggy and unkempt, with long straggling manes and as black as midnight. They hurled themselves at the lines of warriors and the Kheshig troops had to yank their mounts to one side, for these new arrivals showed no sign of slowing.

The crowd roared and Geir grabbed at her. 'Get back, you fool. You'll be flattened.'

These riders were whooping and black horsehair streamed from their helmets. The Palatinates splintered as the horsemen flung themselves into the gaps, kicking out at their unmounted adversaries and spitting and cursing. The animals passed so close to Calder the knee of one rider thudded into her shoulder and she was smothered by a noxious stink of sweat, blood, excrement and unwashed bodies. Even as her stomach heaved, the horsemen broke through the crowd and wheeled at the far end of the enclosure, still whooping, and their horses snorting in the darkness and drumming their hooves.

'Bastards,' spat Geir. 'I guess you don't need any introductions to that lot.'

And Calder didn't. There was no mistaking those wild horse soldiers. Loved and hated in equal measure and revered by anyone drawn to the darker side of humanity. For these were the Pantheon villains. The anarchic Palatinate from Hungary's Pannonian Plains. Attila's Huns, led by the Scourge of God himself and overseen by the most feared of the Caelestes, Ördög.

There was a long pause in proceedings. The rival lines settled and the crowd's noise lulled. Then drums crashed again and the night was broken by the blare of trumpets.

Geir cursed. 'Trust the buggers to add a fanfare. Here they come. Everyone curtsey to our bloody superiors. The almighty, unconquerable, top dog of the Pantheon. The Legion.'

No horses this time. No chaotic, screaming charge. But Calder sensed the Horde around her drawing themselves up to stand firm against this adversary. Their glittering armour, red leggings and rounded helmets with elongated ear and neck pieces needed no introduction. Nor did their curved rectangular shields or their short pilum spears. The whole world knew what a Roman legionary looked like and the world also knew of the empire they had forged, the foe they had defeated. They came not with flags, but with eagles, and they marched in a V-formation, ten troops on either wing, with the lead place taken by an officer in shimmering gold.

'Is that Caesar?'

'Hard to tell. I suspect he's with the other Kings at

the far end. So it's probably Augustus, the boy king and heir apparent. He's got more bloody gold on him than Tutankhamun. Prissy shit. Put him in the Valhalla Tunnels for a few nights and we'd roughen the crap out of him.'

The Legion marched between the rival Palatinates and came to a halt in the centre of the Stadio. As the trumpets built to a climax and hit a final note, the drums ceased at last and spotlights flicked on to illuminate eight figures standing along the rim of the far wall. Every voice hushed and the stillness was deafening after the turmoil. In the distance a police siren wailed and somewhere a lone bird called from the shrubs, frightened by the night's hubbub.

A figure at one end of the line detached itself. He was robed in a simple red tunic and silver face mask and he was unmistakably Atilius, Praetor of the Pantheon.

'My friends,' he said, addressing the crowd around the rim and not the troops below. 'Was it Mark Antony or Shakespeare who coined the phrase *Friends, Romans, countrymen – lend me your ears*? It seems appropriate tonight. Here we stand once more on the eve of a new Pantheon Year. The Twentieth. Has it really been twenty years since the Seven who stand beside me created this great Game for us? I think we owe them a huge debt of gratitude.'

The crowd broke into applause, but there were none of the hoots and cheers of before and Calder understood why. These were no rock stars or sports idols. These seven figures were the founders and rulers of the Pantheon and quite possibly the most terrifyingly powerful people on earth. Governments quaked before them. Militaries and law enforcement were corrupted by them. Stock markets blossomed or crashed on their whims. And in the Pantheon

– perhaps even in the real world – you lived or died by their word.

Atilius was speaking again – recounting events in the Nineteenth Season and building anticipation for the year to come – but Calder's eyes were roving over the Seven. They were dressed identically in full-length gold robes and giant wrap-around helmets with the images of their respective gods engraved upon each. She had seen Odin and Zeus like this at the *Agonium Martiale* at the start of the Raiding Season on Arthur's Seat, but the Seven together created a spectacle of a different kind. There was something ominous about their stillness and the lack of any visible humanity. Even their hands were hidden in the folds of their robes. Only their statures provided any real clue about the people beneath. She could see Odin's belly, and Zeus, slight and short. At the end of the line Ördög was a giant of a man and next to him Kyzaghan was grossly overweight. But it was the central figure that held Calder's eyes. The one with the bearded visage of Jupiter engraved on the helmet. The one who must be Caelestis of the Legion. This figure was different.

Somewhere within Atilius' speech, the spectacle of the night lost its lustre. The arrival of each Palatinate had been a stage-managed extravaganza, like fireworks at the start of a Super Bowl, and the crowd had loved it. But now the audience stirred restlessly as Atilius droned.

Below them in the Stadio, action had given way to tension. Warriors' blood had been high as they raced from the Tunnels. Wired for battle, ready to attack at the smallest provocation. Now they fidgeted and eyed each other in the dark. Janissaries glowered shoulder to shoulder with Titans, and Huns seethed silently on horses alongside Mongols. Even when Atilius flourished an arm down at the assembled fighters and the crowd raised a cheer, the blades that were brandished in response waved discontentedly. Resentment rippled through the lines. You could not take trained killers and make them stand like schoolkids. It was dangerous. A single spark somewhere – perhaps a foot on a neighbouring toe or a whispered insult – and flames would roar through the whole assembly. *Damn the Twentieth Year. Let's do it now. Eye to eye. Blade to blade. We can sort out the victors in one blood-soaked hour.*

'Get a flippin' move on,' hissed Geir. 'What's the idiot waffling about? There's a Hun over there and I swear if he looks at me one more time…'

'Cool it, Raven,' said Freyja.

Finally Atilius came to an end. He wished the warriors of the Palatinates good grace and told them if death came for them, they must face him bravely. He wished the gathered crowd good fortune and hoped their choices this season would bring them wealth and gratification. He swivelled to check if the Caelestes wished to add anything, but none acknowledged him. Then the lights illuminating them flicked off and the troops were forced apart again as seven chariots bearing the seven Kings of each Palatinate processed along the centre of the Stadio and disappeared down the ramps.

And that was it. The crowd began to drift away in search of better pleasures amongst the Palatine Gardens and warriors herded themselves back to their respective Tunnels, with occasional backward glares and mumbled insults. Whomever had planned the night should be sacked – or maybe skinned alive if that's what the Pantheon did when its entertainments failed to hit mesmeric heights.

Calder trudged behind her Ravens, but her mind was still on the Caelestis in the centre of that line of Seven. The figure who had been different. It didn't trouble Calder at all, but it intrigued her. Jupiter, King of the Roman gods, ruler of the firmament, Lord of the Legion and most powerful Caelestis in the Pantheon, was a woman.

'You are beautiful tonight.'

It was Freyja who put into words what others already thought.

When they had returned to the rooms below the Stadio, they found new boxes labelled with their names and containing clothing of a far finer quality than their armour and tunics. Now Calder was sheathed in floor-length silver, her shoulders and neck bare to the moonlight, her hair pinned up, a silver amulet around her throat and a silver mask over her eyes. Freyja wore ocean blue and the night swam with her.

The gardens of the long-lost denizens of Palatine Hill had been transformed into playpens by the Pantheon. Soft, luminous lighting glowed amongst the shrubs. Flaming torches lined the paths. Seating sprouted in the quietest spots. Champagne rivers flowed, joined by tributaries of vodka, gin, whisky and tequila, studded with islands of coke and pills. There were mime artists, dance troupes, conjurors and escorts paid by the hour. Food stalls plied the air with intoxicating scents and musicians performed behind hidden corners. Decadence piled upon the ruins of decadence.

Freyja and Calder explored and wherever they went, eyes followed them. They accepted flutes of champagne and wandered through the gardens of the House of Livia where a hog roasted alongside champagne bars. They witnessed debauchery between the crumbling walls of the Temple of Magna Mater and lingered in the quieter grounds of the House of Augustus where jugglers performed. And eventually they were drawn by ethereal music floating from the wide lawns of the Palace of Flavius, where they discovered a chamber orchestra and couples dancing elegantly across the grass. The onlookers comprised the most powerful ranks of the Pantheon, attired in immaculate evening dress or the black robes of the Curiate, and senior officers from the Palatinates mingled in their masked finery.

A waiter bowed and offered the Ravens new flutes of champagne.

'You're attracting attention,' said Freyja.

'I think we both are.'

'I don't mean generally.'

Calder followed Freyja's gaze over the heads of the dancers and caught her breath. A figure stood unmoving amongst the guests and returned her look with an unblinking silence. He was the most magnificent sight she had ever witnessed. His radiance dazzled her. His golden hair lit up the night. Lights flickered across his golden robes. His face behind a golden mask was sculpted, flawless. Acolytes fawned around him. Palatinate officers dipped their heads. Fat men in tuxedos, with rings like ingots, vied for his attention. But in that moment, he had eyes only for Calder.

'Be careful,' warned Freyja.

Calder held his gaze, then finally tore her eyes away. 'Who *is* that?'

'That, is Augustus. Caesar's heir apparent. The next King of the Legion. Many say he holds the key to the Pantheon in the next decade. He leads the Praetorian Guard and while Caesar may command the Palatinate, once Augustus is in the melee of the battlefield, he takes orders from no one. They say he has the ear of the Lord High Jupiter. Some even believe he is her son.'

'He's magnificent.'

Freyja nodded. 'Aye, he is. He's also dangerous and a spoiled shit. He wants for nothing. His every desire is granted. The most truly pampered son of a god. And when he doesn't get his way, he's a vicious bastard. So if he comes over here, you're either going to have to dance with him or let him down *very* gently.'

'Don't be ridiculous.'

Calder focused on the orchestra. She knew she was beautiful that night and felt incredible in her silver dress. The champagne warmed her, made her tingle for the first time since Skarde had come back into her life, and she found herself toying with the idea of dancing with the son of a god. Perhaps it would not be so bad. Perhaps it would be thrilling.

And even as she flirted with this idea, she sensed the man approach. 'May I have the pleasure?'

She turned, a half-smile on her lips. But it was not Augustus. The figure with his hand extended towards her wore a bronze mask adorned with a scarlet plume. He was dressed in a velvet tunic, belted with a sash, and knee-high boots over leggings. Every inhabitant of the Palace of

Flavius watched her and waited for her answer. And behind them all, she could feel the glare of Augustus as he dared her to accept.

She passed her glass to Freyja, smiled cautiously at her suitor and took his hand. They processed onto the lawn and he drew her to him. His arm slipped around her waist and she gritted her teeth at being so close to a man again. The strings soared and they began to move, hip to hip, ear to ear.

'Which Palatinate are you?' she asked and she felt him laugh lightly.

'Has this Roman night really blinded you?'

She drew back and examined the eyes behind the mask. And realisation flooded through her. 'Punnr!'

He laughed again. 'I don't go by that name now.'

'My god, I thought you were gone forever. Thrown from the Pantheon. What are you doing here?'

'I'm an invitee like you.'

'But how?'

'Keep dancing.'

'What?'

'Everyone's watching. Keep dancing.'

She had stopped without realising and the onlookers could see her staring into his eyes. With an effort, she began to move her body again and she felt him press himself into her. She wrestled with her questions. 'How can you be here? I thought I'd never see you again.'

'They accepted me. I'm a Sky-God now. Alexander wanted me here to show off his new acquisition.'

They were caressed by the music as they glided across the lawn, but her head pounded.

'And my name's Heph. Hephaestion if we're being formal.'

'What about Brante?'

'He's okay. He's Diogenes now. He sends his love.'

She was incapable of coherent thought. She was dancing on the Hill of Palatine and she was in the arms of Tyler. His mouth was turned towards her ear.

'I've missed you so much,' he whispered.

'Don't say that.'

'It's true, Lana. My heart skipped when I saw you in the Stadio.'

'Don't speak like that. Just don't.'

'They've moved me to the West End in Edinburgh, but not far. We can still see each other.'

She could not reply. Shock and anger ran through her. And emotions that were deeper still. He was alive and he was here, holding her. But he was a Titan. And, far worse, despite all his promises, he had abandoned her. She remembered the last time they had been intimate. They had cuddled on her sofa and her words had been: *We started this together and we'll finish it together. Promise me that.*

I promise, he had said and kissed her.

Then – as her life fell apart with the return of Skarde and she perhaps needed him more than ever – he had deserted the Valhalla lines in the final minutes of the Battle and rushed into the clutches of the foe. Promises, promises.

'I can't do this,' she said as his arms took her around the lawn of Flavius.

'Don't say that again. That's what you told me in your apartment. You said we had to wait until the dangers of the

Nineteenth were over and then we could be together in the Interregnum. And I believed you.'

She stopped dancing and disengaged from his arms. 'I mean it.'

'Everyone's watching, for god's sake. The whole damn lot of the bastards. Just dance.'

She stepped gingerly back into his embrace and moved woodenly to the music.

'They're all jealous as well,' whispered Heph. 'You're so damn beautiful tonight and I'm the luckiest man on Palatine Hill.'

She craned her head back and looked into his eyes behind the mask. 'Don't you understand? We can't be what we were. We can't ever go back to that.'

'Of course we can. No one will know.'

She held his eyes. 'Tyler – *we're foe now*. What we were has no meaning now.'

He screwed up his nose. He wanted to argue, wanted to dash her logic. 'The Pantheon doesn't have eyes everywhere.'

'That's not the point – and you know it.'

'Dammit, Calder. I'm not giving up on us.'

'Yes you are,' she said quietly, looking into his eyes. 'We both are. So now you need to shut that mouth of yours and dance with me one final time.'

She placed her cheek back on his shoulder and there were pinprick tears in her eyes. The orchestra played and the onlookers oozed desire and the stars twinkled over Rome.

And they danced.

When it was over she would walk away forever because he was a Titan now. And because he had destroyed her faith.

But in that moment, amongst the palaces of Palatine, she surrendered to her emotions and danced with the enemy.

They caught him as he strode through the shadows of the Palatine ruins, his eyes on the ground and his mind on Calder.

They were big men. Grips like iron. Thick necks and chins scraped smooth by razors. Roman chins. Roman plumes above their masks. Roman cloaks across their vast shoulders. He struggled and swore, but they kicked his feet from under him and forced him onto his knees on the grass. Arms pinned his shoulders. Fingers held his neck in a vice.

And then came Augustus.

Wordless and golden. He nodded to the men and they tore Heph's mask away and forced his face up. Augustus studied the kneeling man, his face expressionless, unlined, smooth and perfect behind his own golden helm.

'Who are you?' he demanded softly.

Heph twisted his shoulders and cursed and the men kicked him. 'Piss off,' he spat and they hit him and gripped him even tighter.

Augustus approached and peered at him with his head tilted. 'Who are you, Titan?'

'My name is Hephaestion. And I answer only to Alexander.'

A cold smile licked across Augustus' beautiful lips. 'That old clown. His brains are addled and his reputation in tatters. He is nothing.'

He brought his face close to Heph's and searched his eyes, staring into his soul. For a moment, uncertainty flickered through his gaze and then he blinked and the golden features were smooth once again. 'And you too are nothing,' he said dismissively and swung away.

As the men laid into Heph, bludgeoning him with their fists, smashing his head, tugging his hair, kicking his ribs, all he could see was the golden figure receding back to his adoring throng.

XVII

'**B**uongiorno, sir.'

Tyler swore through broken lips and squinted at the bedside clock. Just after seven. Someone was knocking on his hotel door and calling him. He groaned loudly in an effort to make the idiot disappear.

'Sorry, sir, but message is you meet lady in reception at – er – *sette e mezza.*'

Tyler hauled himself upright, every bone in his body protesting. He limped to the door and peeked around it. 'What the hell?'

The hotel manager's eyes widened in shock at the state of him '*Sette e mezza*, sir.'

'Seven-thirty? Are you serious?'

'Seven-thirty – yes, sir. Very serious.'

Tyler shook his throbbing head and started to close the door. 'Okay, okay. Message received.'

'Oh and, sir.' The manager flourished a booklet at him. 'Your passport.'

'My what?'

He took the document, closed the door and leafed through it. Sure enough, Callum Brodie's passport. Only problem was Tyler hadn't brought this with him from Edinburgh.

He shuffled over to a mirror and stared at his beaten face. His lips were cut and inflamed. One eye was black and swollen. There were scratches and bruises around his throat and a thousand other aches unseen beneath the tunic that he still wore from the previous night. The Romans had been professional. Nothing was broken or openly bleeding. No lasting damage. Just a routine beating because – well, because that golden prick simply felt like giving him one.

He showered carefully, threw his things in his rucksack and stalked down to reception, where the lady in question was Agape.

She greeted him with: 'You look shit.' But refrained from asking questions.

There was a car waiting and it pulled away as soon as they were seated in the back. Agape smelt of mint and orange. She was wearing jeans, boots and a fitted jacket, and her eyes were sparkling emeralds, her make-up perfect.

'How come you can look so bright after two hours' sleep?' Tyler mumbled.

'Practice. You have your passport?'

'Yes. Although why everyone thinks it's okay to keep breaking into my apartment and taking my stuff is beyond me.'

'That's a copy. Simmius has a stash for everyone. Rumour has it he gets them from the best forgers in Bombay.'

'Naturally. So where in god's name are we going at this hour?'

'Another little flight.'

'Just us?'

'Yes.'

He stared morosely out at Rome, the low sun snapping on and off as they passed buildings. He thought about Lana. How wonderful it had felt to hold her and then the way she had disengaged on the final note of the orchestra and left him without a backward glance. He clenched his knuckles at the memory of Augustus and wished he'd had just once chance to lay a punch on that perfect complexion. Just enough to make him remember. The man's henchman would have beaten him black and blue, but it would have been worth it.

They arrived at Fiumicino Airport within thirty minutes and headed through the first-class lounges to security.

'No private flights this time?'

'Well, this isn't strictly Pantheon business. We're under the radar, so to speak. Here's your ticket.'

He glanced at it and puffed out painful cheeks. '*That's* our destination? Jeez, I hardly even know where that is.'

It took an hour before they were finally airborne, by which time they were already into their second glasses of champagne. His throat hurt when he swallowed, but the bubbles loosened him and he tried to relax. He glanced at his companion when he thought she wasn't looking and decided that Lana had an innocent beauty and Freyja a powerful one, but this woman's allure was terrifying.

'If we're not strictly on Pantheon business, what do I call you?'

She turned her emerald eyes on him. 'You call me Agape.'

'Glad we got that one sorted.'

Italy rolled away beneath them and they were served a breakfast of fruits and tarts by stewards who stared at

Tyler's bruises. He ate with caution and gazed moodily out the window at sunlit sea and then waves of endless scrubland. Agape was quiet and he thought she was asleep, but when he fidgeted, she opened her eyes.

'Can I ask you about last night?' he asked.

'Meaning?'

'Meaning, my first year was a rollercoaster, what with trying to stay alive and all. So I never had a chance to think about what lies beyond. Seven Palatinates. The Game. Can you tell me about it? How does it work? Who fights who? Who wins? Who loses?'

Agape glanced around. The seats in first class were far apart and no one was paying them any attention. She extracted a gold-nib fountain pen and began to create a triangular arrangement on a paper napkin. When she had finished, she handed it to Tyler. 'That's it. The Pantheon.'

Legion

Huns   v   Sultanate

Kheshig   v   Warring States   Horde   v   Titans

'No one's ever shown me this structure.'

'We keep it pretty tight. Don't need the media all over it, although the fan sites worked it out long ago.'

'Tell me about it.'

Agape checked around again and then leaned in, her scent stealing into his lungs. 'When it all began, the seven founders each started with the same funds and the same troop numbers. During the first five years it was pretty much anyone's game, but victories on the field and shrewd gambles off gradually sorted a pecking order. Some

Palatinates became much more powerful than others and a flat playing field was no longer realistic. So the Caelestes got together and agreed this structure.'

'And it hasn't changed for the best part of fifteen years?'

'Pretty much.'

'Let me get this straight. For three-quarters of the history of the Pantheon, the Titans and the Horde have just been slugging it out in one half of the bottom tier?'

'I suppose that's one way of looking at it.'

'Has there been *any* movement?'

'The Huns and the Kheshig traded places a couple of times in the early years. If a Palatinate reaches a troop number that is disproportionately higher than its opponent, it can challenge the Palatinate in the level above. They then fight it out and the winner takes or retains the place in that higher level. But over the last decade the Huns have consolidated their position in tier two. They came to a tacit agreement with the Sultanate that they're both happy to ensure no more challenges from below.'

'So what's the Legion do right up there, sitting pretty on those heady heights?'

'They wait and watch and each year's victor between the Huns and the Sultanate gets to challenge the Legion in a mighty battle.'

Tyler thought of that golden bastard Augustus again. 'Let me guess. The Legion always wins.'

Agape dipped her head.

'And the only *other* way to shake things up is to kill the King of your direct opponent and combine two Palatinates?'

'With a sword in the hand. That would indeed shake things up, but it's never been done.'

Tyler scowled at the diagram, furrows of concentration. 'Isn't... isn't it boring? I mean for the Curiate and the investors. If nothing ever changes?'

Agape thought about her words. 'Let me put it like this: the Pantheon's like a mega-corporation. It's not important if its staff are bored. It's not even important if its customers are unexcited, as long as the sales keep rolling in. Profit is the only motive. Profit for its shareholders.'

'Meaning the Curiate.'

'The Curiate – yes, they're the Pantheon's investors. But there's also the much larger outer ring of invited players whose money keeps everything oiled. But who are the really big winners? The Caelestes of course. They're the founders, the owners of each Palatinate, the real money-makers. In their day they were perhaps the most successful capitalists on earth. They made fortunes beyond imagination and spent them by creating a vast capitalist game. And they *designed* it to be stable. To be – as you put it – boring. Why? Because stability means the money keeps flowing to the top. For them, that's what it's all about. Profit, heaped on profit. You can never take the greed out of a capitalist. The fact that the profits are earned from our spilt blood just adds to the frisson.'

Tyler ran a tongue delicately across his sore lips. 'So it suits them that the Palatinates can't change places?'

'Everyone's making money, so why rock the boat?'

'Except they left in one Rule that still has the power to throw it all up in the air.'

Agape nodded. 'Kill the King. And that, Tyler, is why we're on this flight.'

He stared at her, trying to pull her thoughts from the garden of her eyes. 'What's that supposed to mean?'

'It means Hera enjoyed her breakfast with you.'

XVIII

They landed in Istanbul before midday and spent a two-hour wait lunching in the first-class lounge. Their Turkish Airlines flight took off just before one-forty local time and Agape soon pulled a mask over her eyes and extended her seat into a full-length bed.

'You don't get that in cattle class,' said Tyler, scrolling through the film list.

Agape peeked one eye out. 'I suggest you do the same. It's a ten-hour flight and local time is six hours ahead, so we'll be landing at the start of a new day and I will expect you to be functioning.'

She pressed a button and a screen rose between their seats, leaving Tyler partially cocooned against the window. He bolted 2000 milligrams of painkillers, washed down with whisky, and slumped, thinking of Lana. Through the frenetic activity of their departure from Rome, he had carried with him a heavy emptiness in his gut. He had hoped against hope that she might be present on Palatine Hill and when he had held her in his arms, she had felt so delicate and priceless and his heart had drummed. But there had been a finality about her words. *We're foe now.* Try as he might to dispute this, he knew she was right. And he hated himself for this acceptance.

He drifted into an uncomfortable, troubled sleep in which he was once again struggling against the fists of his attackers while calling to a receding Lana, and only came round when the cabin lights turned on and the crew served breakfast. Agape was awake, reading a magazine and looking pristine.

They landed at seven local time and dawn fire was just slithering over a vast black mountain range.

'Bloody hell,' swore Tyler as he hobbled across the tarmac to passport control and his breath spiralled in plumes. 'It's freezing. I only packed for Italy.'

When they reached the arrivals hall a thin man with a broad crooked-toothed smile splitting his lined features stepped towards them holding a card saying *Miss Agap*. He shook their hands earnestly. 'Hello, my friends. My name is Nergui. It means *no name* in Mongolian. I am your host and guide for this trip. Welcome to Ulaanbaatar and Chinggis Khaan Airport, named after the great leader.'

The place looked tired and run-down. The only retail outlets were *Tom n Tom's Coffee* and *Memories of Mongolian Handicrafts*. Nergui noticed their appraising looks and hurried to assure them that a new airport was under construction. His vehicle, however, was a brand-new LandCruiser with nuclear incense and the heating cranked up to sauna levels.

'Pantheon money?' Tyler asked quietly and Agape nodded.

As they pulled out the airport, Nergui pointed over his

right shoulder. 'Ulaanbaatar that way, but I take you straight to Gorkhi-Terelj.'

'How long is the journey?' asked Agape.

'Seventy kilometres. Maybe one hour. You like Mongolian music?'

'We do, but not now.'

They travelled on arrow-straight tarmac through a grey landscape sprinkled with breeze-block buildings and discarded detritus and Tyler thought it looked like nothing he had imagined. The sky was fathomlessly clear, but the sun's light seemed only a watery version of its brilliance in Rome. Nergui was happy to play the role of guide and chattered away with facts and figures about his country. They were, apparently, four thousand feet above sea level and summer temperatures could rise to forty degrees in the Gobi desert to the south, while winters could drop to minus forty. They were driving north-east and the mountains ahead were the Khan Khentii, with the main peak rising to two and half thousand metres. Nergui said Mongolians considered these hills the spiritual heart of the world.

There were prayer beads wound around his rear-view mirror and an amulet engraved with a winged horse swinging low enough to catch the smoke from a smouldering incense stick on the dashboard. Tyler had seen the symbol on the shields of the Kheshig riders in the Stadio Palatino and he asked Nergui about it.

'It is a wind horse, my friend, in honour of Tengri the great god of the Blue Mighty Eternal Heaven.'

They forked left off the main highway and the landscape changed. Grass replaced the gravel and the plateau began to roll and crumble into ridges and hillocks. Clumps of birch forest were scattered across the slopes and when Nergui steered them over a rise they saw a river winding down from the mountains.

'The Kherlen. One of the three holy rivers. We are in the heart of the land of the Great Khan.'

The road led them to a herd of hotels and rows of Mongolian traditional ger tents. 'These for the tourists in high season.' He turned in his seat and grinned his crooked teeth at them. 'No tourists now. And also no road. We get bumpy.'

The tarmac stopped and he launched onto a track with gusto. They lurched their way through the grasslands, crossing a wooden bridge over the Kherlen, and entered a forest. They arrived at an army control barrier and a high fence leading off into the trees either side. A soldier stepped to the window and conversed harshly with Nergui. Tyler picked up the word Kheshig and they seemed to come to some kind of agreement. The barrier was raised and they progressed for a further twenty minutes of bumping and rolling.

Finally they topped a hill and below them, contained by a bend in the river, was an encampment of fifty ger tents, with smoke rising from a few.

'The Kheshig's summer grazing grounds,' said Nergui. 'Almost empty now. Genghis took two *arbans* to Rome for the Summoning. Most of the other troops have moved west to their *ordu* – their military camps – ready for the Twentieth Season. But don't worry—' he grinned in the mirror '—Belgutei the Jurtchis – Quartermaster of the Kheshig Palatinate – is here with two arbans. And the guard back there told me Borte may still be somewhere in the area with a *jagun*.'

'What's a jagun?' asked Tyler.

'A jagun is ten arbans.' There was silence and Nergui peered at them in his mirror. 'These are the units of the Kheshig. An arban is ten mounted men. They are together until they die. A jagun is a hundred horsemen.'

'Let me get this straight,' said Tyler leaning between the front seats. 'You're saying most of the troops have gone west but there's still a jagun around here and that's a hundred horsemen?'

'Correct.'

'So how big is the Palatinate?'

'Three and a half jaguns.'

'Three hundred and fifty mounted troops.' Tyler glanced at Agape.

She smiled thinly. 'A force to be reckoned with.'

They pulled into a parking area on the edge of camp and a man strode from the nearest ger to greet them. He was short, but solidly built, with greying hair and beard, and wearing a belted black felt coat and riding boots.

'Agape.' He smiled and took her in an embrace. 'It has been too long.'

'It is good to see you, Belgutei. Thank you for staying back in the summer camps to meet us.'

'If it had been anyone else, I would have delegated the responsibility, but how could I resist seeing you?'

She introduced Tyler as Hephaestion and Belgutei took in his beaten face without comment.

'Who knows of our visit?' she asked the Jurtchis.

'Just Tengri's people and me.'

'Not Genghis?'

'I don't think our King would welcome Titans in his Kheshig. Besides, he's still in Rome and will then be heading to the military camps to prepare for the Twentieth Season. So it's just a few hands here at the moment. Borte's somewhere up in the hills around the eastern grazing grounds, but isn't scheduled to bring the jagun here.'

'So we can keep our heads down.'

He laughed. 'Yes, Captain. Hera wanted your visit to be kept our little secret. Come – you too, Heph. We have food waiting.'

Nergui waved them goodbye and they followed Belgutei towards one of the gers with black smoke billowing from its flat canvas roof. He glanced at their light attire. 'I'll find you some deel coats. Summer has long gone and you'll be needing them.'

They bent to pass through the felt doorway and Heph found the roof inside was so low he had to remain partially dipped. The air was smoky and acrid, but warm. Felt lined the walls, stretched across wooden beams that bent up to a hole in the centre of the roof, through which the pipe from a large wood burner reached for the sky. The floor was wooden and layered with rugs. Cushions ringed low tables, on which were arranged an assortment of covered bowls.

Belgutei signalled for them to sit and ostentatiously removed the lids from each bowl. 'Steamed dumplings, fried dumplings, mutton stew, roasted khorkhog – a speciality – rice, cheese and milk sweets. But first, tea.'

He reached for a steel teapot and poured a mug, grinning as he handed it to Heph.

Agape was smiling too. 'You're too hard on the poor lad, Belgutei.'

Heph took a sip and his eyes bulged. He swallowed hard and his stomach rolled over.

'He kept it down.' Agape laughed.

'What the hell was that?' Heph spluttered.

'Milk tea,' said Belgutei, delighted. 'We like it with salt and butter.' He reached for a second pot and poured three mugs. 'Here is some western tea. We just wanted to see your face.'

'You've had milk tea before?' Heph demanded of Agape.

'Once. At a Summoning in Istanbul. Belgutei played the same trick on me.'

Thankfully the rest of the meal was delicious and afterwards the Jurtchis showed them to another ger, which was divided down the centre by a wooden lattice covered in felt. 'This will be your quarters. Women always on the right and the door always facing south. Get yourself changed and we can begin. I will await you outside.'

They found clothes laid on their respective beds. Silk undershirts, felt tunics, leggings, riding boots, and black sable overcoats. The garments were heavy, but comfortable and when Heph had pulled them on, he sat quietly listening to the rustle of Agape beyond the lattice.

'Why is the Kheshig happy to have us here?' he mused. 'The Pantheon is a game of death, so I assumed there would be no love lost between the Palatinates.'

'There isn't on the battlefield. But at other times, the relations between the Palatinates are rarely as clear-cut. Over the years, the more seasoned among us have got to know our rivals. We meet at Summonings and other key events. We see their actions on feeds. And, naturally, we learn to respect some of them, just as we loathe others. Belgutei and I have known each other for a long time and occasionally we share advice if it's not to the disadvantage of our Palatinate.'

Agape came around the lattice. 'But this little visit was arranged by Hera. A request direct to Tengri. Like I said on the plane, the seven founders all knew each other well in the early years. They might never have been friends, but they were certainly partners in the burgeoning Pantheon enterprise and they would communicate frequently and even meet to forge the Rules. And that goes for their wives and partners too. As the Seasons have unfolded, greed and blood have inevitably changed the dynamics. The founders retreated into their Palatinates. Some – like Odin and Zeus – have found reasons to detest each other. But others – such as Hera and Tengri – have remained close enough to communicate and offer up select favours.

'Genghis, the King of the Kheshig, is another matter. He might answer to Tengri, but he guards his military secrets jealously and our presence here is possible only because he is still in Rome. Make no mistake, Belgutei is taking a genuine risk by hosting us, so we keep our heads down and do exactly as he says. Understood?'

When they emerged, Belgutei appraised them with a satisfied smile and then led them towards wooden blocks at the edges of the camp.

'I understand you are a horse lover,' he said, placing a hand on Heph's shoulder.

'Well...'

'The West remains obsessed with thoroughbreds and

Arabians, but you will fall in love with the creatures we keep here.'

They stepped into the dark interior of one of the blocks and the smell immediately took Heph back to the stables at Forbes' house, only now the stink was much stronger.

'Behold, the horses of Mongolia,' said Belgutei proudly. 'The steeds that conquered half the world.'

As their eyes adjusted, they made out a group of twelve short, stocky horses, untethered and free to roam the straw-filled building. They were a mix of blacks and duns, with large heads and very long manes and tails, and – to Heph – looked ill-bred and insignificant compared to the regal grandeur of Fergus. There was a man standing to one side, wrapped in an ankle-length deel tunic.

'This is Yul, one of our Horsemasters,' said Belgutei and the man smiled and nodded. 'I'm afraid these are all the stock that remains at this camp. Twenty travelled to Rome. Two hundred are now stabled in the winter valleys. And a hundred are with Borte to the east. Come, see.'

Belgutei had the manner of a French vineyard owner introducing his latest vintage. He eased Heph towards the animals and watched with satisfaction as he stroked one of them and ran his fingers through the shaggy mane. Agape leaned against the doorway, her face tight and serious.

'These specimens are pampered,' explained Belgutei. 'They are the prized possessions of the Kheshig Palatinate and provided with everything they need. But they are the lucky few. Most Mongolian horses are never stabled, even in the harshest winter months. They need no food substitutes because they graze on grass all year round, digging it up from beneath snow if they have to. They drink only once a day and will quench their thirst in winter by eating snow. They need no hoof care because they roam constantly. They are, at once, little more than wild horses, yet utterly obedient to their master.'

He came close to Heph and watched him stroking each mount in turn. 'The Mongolian soldier carried everything he needed with him and that meant no complex logistics, no lengthy supply chains. Each warrior would have four or five mounts and he could keep riding all day. His saddlebag was made from a cow's stomach, so it was waterproof and inflatable. It had pouches to hold dried meat, water, cooking pots, clothing, a knife for sharpening arrows, needle and thread and his weapons. No obstacle was too great. Arrive at the banks of a river? Simple. Strip. Pack your belongings into the cow stomach. Then swim your horses across. Dress. Remount. Move on. Whole armies could be over in a few hours. Like this, Genghis' jaguns could travel faster than the wind, circle an enemy and appear where they were least expected.'

Belgutei's gaze switched to Agape. 'Today our Kheshig's troops have only one mount and their saddlebags are not stomachs, but we still train and equip them for self-sufficiency. We still move like the wind and we don't require supply trains. That's what makes this Palatinate successful as a force based around the horse. If, however, you really are considering a Titan cavalry, you will not be so unencumbered. You need to think about this.'

Agape nodded in reply and glanced at Yul the Horsemaster.

'Don't worry about him,' said Belgutei. 'The only words he knows in English are Manchester United.'

'Manchester United,' said Yul happily and wagged his head.

'What do you think?' asked Belgutei, returning to Heph.

'They look strong.'

'For the ancient Mongol warrior, they provided everything. Not only did they transport us, their leather clothed and armoured us. Their tails and manes provided the hair for our bowstrings and the braid for our ropes. We used them for hunting and sport, and in winter we lay beside them for warmth. Sometimes, when things got tough, they even fed us. Now you will ride?'

'Oh, I'm...'

'Of course you must ride! You will be aching to try them.'

He shouted something to Yul, clapped an arm around Heph's shoulder again and walked them back into the midday light. Once they were several paces from the building, he gave a high-pitched whistle twice followed by a single low one. There was a pause and then two horses wandered out and came to stand beside them.

'They may have wild hearts, but every one of them knows the whistle of their master.'

Yul threw saddles and bridles over both horses and lengthened the stirrups on one for Heph's longer legs.

Belgutei grabbed a stirrup and held it up. 'We Mongols developed these from the Chinese in the sixth and seventh centuries. They are the single most essential piece of equipment for controlling the horse and they allow our warriors to ride without reins and use their bows. But do you understand what this means for you?' He peered at Agape and Heph, but they had no answer. 'It means the cavalry of Alexander rode into battle a thousand years before the invention of the stirrup and if you Titans want mounted soldiers, you may be required to ride without the use of them.'

'No stirrups,' Heph exclaimed, remembering how their aid had allowed him to rise and fall with the rhythm of Bea. 'That would be impossible.'

Belgutei shrugged. 'Maybe you will be permitted. Maybe you won't. Politics will decide. We might like the armour of the Legion, but we are never going to get it.'

Yul was grinning and offering the reins to Heph, so he steeled himself. The mounts looked so small compared to Fergus, even a couple of hands smaller than Bea. Perhaps it wouldn't be so bad. But his body still ached from his beating and he grimaced as he fumbled placing his foot in the stirrup, held the saddle and reins, and swung himself up. The horse stood idly and Yul mounted up next to him.

'Just onto the grassland and back,' said Belgutei and spoke to Yul.

Heph shot a look to Agape, then flicked the reins. The horse reacted like lightning. No gentle clip-clop walk. Instead it broke straight into a trot. Yul shouted something in an encouraging tone, but Heph could find none of the rhythm he had practised with Forbes. His backside jolted hard against the saddle, his arms stiffened and his legs lost contact with the stirrups. They careered from the camp and the horse, sensing it was in charge, picked up speed. Heph was thrown all over the place. His teeth rattled in his skull and shockwaves surged up his spine. There was a moment of clarity when he knew he was going to fall, but then Yul veered alongside and grabbed Heph's reins. The two animals came to a halt and Yul turned them on the spot and began to lead them back to the pair of figures in the centre of camp.

'Okay,' he said, still grinning.

Agape was cold with fury as Heph dismounted. 'Hera said you could ride.'

'I told her I was learning.'

Agape shook her head and swore, so Belgutei played the diplomat, guiding them both away from the horses. 'Maybe some tea,' he said. 'No butter or salt.'

They sat on blankets on a small hillock not far from the camp and ate mare's milk cheese with their tea.

'In summer,' said Belgutei, 'these grasslands are a carpet of flowers and you can't hear yourself think for the song of skylarks.'

Neither of his guests commented and he let them eat in silence as they stewed. Eventually Agape spoke, stabbing at a piece of cheese. 'How long does it take to get good?'

'A lifetime. But you don't have to be good, you have to be shocking.'

'What's that supposed to mean?'

'The strength of cavalry is in speed and shock. Great skill is unnecessary, you just have to be able to break through and then you can kill at leisure.'

'Can we do that in six months?'

Belgutei sighed and used his teeth to slide cheese from his knife blade. 'Time isn't the essence. If you have the funds, you can buy horses and you can buy capable riders and you can train them to break through an enemy line.'

'If it's that simple, why does the Kheshig pride itself on skills built up over years?'

'Our situation is very different from yours. We are the

Palatinate of Genghis and we are, therefore, entirely cavalry. We face a Warring States foe who knows everything about us and who has developed tactics specifically to counter light horsemen. We are also required to fight like our ancestors and that means mastering the use of the composite bow while in the saddle. To ride without reins and fire a bow takes years. To ride without reins and fire a bow accurately takes twice as long.'

He glanced at Heph who was drinking his tea in sulky silence. 'You, however, need only a fraction of these skills. To grasp the reins of a horse in one hand and a lance or sword in the other, then gallop at a foe who is not expecting cavalry, is not complicated. You can do it in six months.'

They mulled this over and their silence was lost among the vast silence of the grasslands.

'So tell us the "buts", Belgutei,' said Agape after a while. 'There are always "buts".'

The Jurtchis took his time refilling each of their mugs from the big teapot, then slurped noisily as he studied the horizon. 'As you wish. Firstly, there is cost. You will need ten Blood Funds for every horse. If you can't train up any of your current warriors and you want to buy riders, you'll need another four funds for each because mounted troops are classed as elite. So Zeus will need to study his budgets and know what size of unit he's realistically going to be able to get.'

'How on earth have you afforded three hundred and fifty?' Heph spoke up at last.

'Prices were different in the early years when we managed to win the bedrock of the Kheshig Blood Funds. Everything's inflated like crazy since then.'

'What else?' pressed Agape.

'There will be all kinds of auxiliary costs: stabling, forage, saddlery, transportation. These won't need to be taken from your newly won Blood Funds, but they still have to be assimilated into the ongoing budgets of the Palatinate.

'The real Challenges, however, are strategic, not financial, so you have to ask yourself if cavalry really serve a purpose in the Titan Palatinate. I have three points: one – to my mind, you are located in one of the world's most beautiful cities, but Edinburgh's Old Town is no horse country. Your Raiding Seasons and Blood Nights will continue to be contested on foot. Two – you have no power over the choice of battlefield. You may well imagine your horsemen sweeping across plains like these, but what if Atilius selects a dense forest for your next engagement? Three – no one has tested just how strong that Viking shieldwall would be against horses. What if they hold? What if they form into squares like the British at Waterloo and your horses sweep around them instead of breaking through? You will have squandered huge amounts of Blood Funds on an instrument that proves to be blunt at the critical moment.'

Belgutei let them think about these things and there was a long silence. Not far off a marmot popped out a burrow and raced across the grass, but they were too absorbed to notice. Belgutei could see from their faces that the dream of Companion Cavalry was already dying and perhaps they had barely believed it in the first place.

'But,' he said enthusiastically, 'there is one more "but".'

Agape looked up. 'Go on.'

'But – I am a Mongol horse warrior to my bones and I can assure you that before the age of the gun, cavalry was the single most powerful weapon any army could wield. The speed and violence of mounted troops cannot be underestimated. Buy prudently and use them effectively, and they could be the wisest choice you've made in twenty years.'

His guests looked unconvinced, so he patted them on the back and rose. 'Come. Yul is dying to show you everything we do for our horses.'

For the remainder of the afternoon, Heph helped Yul to brush and clean all twelve horses and – through a series of signs and grins – learned about Mongol equipment and exercise regimes. Agape hovered at the fringes, taking her fact-finding mission seriously but still livid with Heph for not being the rider she had thought him.

As the sun lowered and the shadows of hills marched across the camp grounds and cold sprang from every corner, Belgutei strode back from his ger and signalled Yul to bring out one of the horses. Beckoning Heph close, he drew a short hunting knife from his sleeve and jabbed it into a vein in the horse's neck. Heph recoiled as blood spurted out in a thin fountain, but the Jurtchis was already holding a leather cup to catch the precious liquid. He sheathed the knife, pulled out a poultice of dried grass and mud from a sack in his pocket and pushed this against the wound until the bleeding ceased. The horse seemed entirely unconcerned by the whole episode.

'Remember I told you how Mongol horses provided sustenance for their riders? This is how they did it. When rations were low and the going was tough, they would cut the vein like so and drink the blood neat or mixed with milk. In this way, they could be sustained for days.' He held out the cup. 'Try. It is good.'

Heph attempted to deflect the invitation, but Agape stepped forward, grasped the cup and swallowed. She passed it to Heph, wiping a trail of blood from the corner of her lips, and he took a breath, dipped his face to the rim and sipped the hot, thick substance. Once again his stomach rolled and his eyes watered, but he held the stuff down and handed the cup back to Belgutei.

The Jurtchis grinned. 'By such acts of ingenuity, the Great Khan led his hordes across the world and no one could stop them.'

Swaddled in felt and fur, Heph and Agape sat around a blazing fire and stared in wonder at the brightness of the heavens above a Mongolian plain. They had been joined by some of the other warriors remaining in the Kheshig's summer grazing camp, several of whom – to Agape's delight – were women. She examined their knives by firelight and one of them brought a bow and they laughed when she could not draw it. For a heartbeat, Agape's pride was stung into anger, but it dissolved among the female mirth.

Earthen pots were loaded with lamb, carrots, onions, potatoes and hot stones, then sealed and cast on the fire. This was the famed khorkhog dish and the contents came out steaming and barbecued. They ate with their fingers and merrily burnt their mouths. Belgutei poured beakers of airag, which was fermented mare's milk, and three times dipped a finger and flicked droplets onto the ground. 'One for Father Heaven,' he said. 'One for Mother Earth and one for our ancestors.' Heph and Agape copied the actions and gulped the sour drink. It was better than they had expected, but they were still pleased when the vodka came out instead. When they had eaten their fill of the lamb, flour dough pancakes were cooked on griddles, covered with sugar and butter and passed around.

As the vodka oiled friendship, pipes and drums and horse jaw harps were produced and the Titans were honoured with a performance of Mongolian three-tone nasal singing floating above a chesty drone. Heph thought it was the eeriest sound he had ever heard the human voice produce and lay entranced. As the evening grew late and the cold pressed down on them, the warriors filtered away to their gers and Belgutei bid them goodnight.

'Don't extinguish the fire,' he said. 'A Mongolian fire always goes out naturally.'

Agape and Heph remained curled in their furs, a bottle of vodka between them. The stars blinked and from somewhere a horse whinnied.

'I'm still surprised by all this advice he's so happy to give us,' Heph mulled. 'Isn't he fraternising a bit too eagerly with the enemy?'

'You saw the structure I drew on the napkin. We sit firmly on the opposite side of the pyramid from the Kheshig. In nineteen years, we've never had to face them and even if one of our Palatinates was promoted to the next tier, our paths would still not cross. The chances of us ever becoming direct foe are negligible. Besides, if we are indeed mad enough to invest in a mounted unit, it's hardly going to be at a scale to threaten Genghis' jaguns.'

Heph considered the logic of this, then rolled to peer at her.

'Do you know why I surrendered to you at the Battle?'

'Tell me.'

'Because Halvar thought you knew my sister well. Said you and she were close and you might have more information about her disappearance.'

Agape shifted to look at him. 'I guessed we wouldn't get through this trip without that subject coming up.'

'You can hardly blame me. You've obviously known since an early stage that I'm her brother. Let's see – you've *not* killed me at least twice now. Once on Calton Hill when we were searching for the Asset and once on the Battle beach. Isn't that negative Blood Funds or something? Shouldn't you have a Bloodmark removed for *not* killing a foe?'

'There's still time to rectify that.'

'I'm serious. Tell me about my sister. Is she alive?'

The Captain nodded slowly, staring into the flames. 'I think so.'

'Do you know where she is?'

'No, nothing concrete.'

'And there's no way to contact her?'

'Not by any of us.'

'Shit.' Heph gulped his vodka and heaved a sigh. 'Odin was going mad searching for her. He used her in the Eighteenth Season; he set her up. And now I'm so worried that if he finds her first, he'll kill her without compunction.'

'Heph, you need to understand that Odin might seem terrifying to you, but he's actually a small-time player compared to the real powers in the Pantheon.'

'Meaning pricks like that Augustus?' he demanded sourly.

Agape stared at Heph's bruised face. 'Did you run into him in Rome?'

'We had a little misunderstanding.'

Agape shook her head in quiet disbelief. 'Try to imagine for one moment, you muttonhead, the sort of people who terrify Odin. The sort he'll do anything to ensure don't find out how he used your sister to cheat the odds. So far, his cheating and your search for Morgan have gone under their radar and it has to stay that way or...'

Agape broke off and looked at the ground, uncertain she should be saying such things and aware the vodka was lubricating her tongue.

'Or what?'

'Or it all comes tumbling down.'

'What does?'

'The whole thing. The Pantheon.'

There was silence except for the crackle of splintering wood.

'What the hell are you talking about?' demanded Heph eventually, his words slurring. 'Just because my sister betrayed the Titans and Odin cheated some odds?'

'Of course not. Odin *thinks* it's just about his cheating, but actually that's nothing compared to the real issues.'

She clammed up again and Heph exploded. 'Well don't stop there! What are the *real* issues?'

'Keep your voice down. These gers have ears.'

'Just tell me.'

She peered at him, her green eyes black and gold in the flames. 'I honestly don't know. I wish I did.'

'Then who does?'

'Hera. It's she who pressed on me how dire the situation is.'

'Christ,' Heph swore to himself. 'I'd never even heard of her until a couple of weeks ago. How is she involved?'

'Like I said, I don't know the details. I just know the magnitude. Hera is a powerful voice in this Palatinate and she moves with the real powers when she needs to. If she says things are as serious as this, she knows what she's talking about.'

Heph rubbed his face and took a deep breath. 'What the hell is going on? All these secrets, all these revelations. Did Halvar know more than he let on to me?'

'He was simply a loved-up fool, quite out of his depth.'

Heph lapsed into a forlorn silence and then said more quietly, 'Bloody hell, Agape, this is all getting so crazy, I don't really know where to turn or what to do.'

'Well, perhaps you don't do anything.'

'What?'

'I mean it. If Morgan's alive, which I believe she is, then I think she's somewhere safe. She wouldn't have made it for this long if she wasn't. But if you keep blundering about looking for her, you'll draw attention and that might put her in danger.'

'So I just sit around doing nothing?'

'For a time. You can focus on being a Titan and – besides – you may have a new cavalry unit to develop.'

Heph looked at her. 'You think so? I thought you'd given up on the idea.'

'I'm coming round to it.'

They were quiet as Heph tried to analyse her advice.

Perhaps she was right. Perhaps his actions *were* endangering his sister. 'Do you think Halvar's dead?' he asked slowly.

'It depends who took him. If it was Odin, then he may yet live deep in the bowels of Erebus. But if it was the greater powers – if they've got wind of your search – he's long gone from us.'

Heph peered at her. 'What does your gut say?'

'I think Odin took him.'

'Why?'

'If it was the powers – we'd all be dead by now.'

XIX

'Come with me,' said Eli Greaves, tapping Oliver discreetly on the shoulder. 'You have a visitor.'

It was four in the afternoon and although the day was damp, Oliver had been sitting on a concrete step in the rose garden with a selection of Initiates. As part of the daily mental health hour, Eli had asked them to take pen and paper outside and each list down their individual strengths. Meghan was writing studiously, Gregor was crushing ants and Oliver had been staring at the yellowing trees, thinking how ironic it was that before he was sent here he had been utilising his strengths very effectively for Valhalla, finding them all four Assets in the Raiding Season. And how had the Pantheon repaid him? By removing him from all access to technology, forcing him to run around obstacle courses and swipe at people with staves, then having the gall to ask him what he considered his strengths.

As he rose and followed Greaves, he felt the eyes of the others on him because in this place no one ever had a visitor.

'Is it my mum?' he asked once they were out of earshot.

Eli glanced back, compassion scrawled across his face. 'No it isn't. Not this time.'

Piper Mallard, the head, was waiting for them in the

staffroom. She nodded to Eli and beckoned Oliver to follow her. The pair crossed the quad and entered the wisteria-clad main house with its creaking carpeted floors and wood polish essence. She escorted him upstairs, paused to inspect him up and down, then knocked on a door and stuck her head round.

'I have Oliver Muir for you, sir.'

'Good, good, show him in.'

A plump man was sitting behind a table, beaming at him. He was dressed in a check shirt and blue chinos. His face was blotchy and his hair combed into waves.

'Come, lad, sit. Good of you to break off from your studies.' Despite the smile, his eyes held no humour.

Oliver approached and perched on a seat. The man pushed a glass of orange juice towards him and poured himself a cup of black coffee, then looked back at the door. 'Thank you, Piper, that will be all.'

Once they were alone he steadied his eyes on Oliver. 'Do you know who I am?'

Oliver shook his head.

'I am Thane of the Horde of Valhalla.'

Oliver frowned. 'You're Radspakr?'

The man chuckled. 'I was warned you would know more about our Palatinate than is good for the health. No, Radspakr retired. My name is Kustaa. I'm here at the behest of the Caelestis of Valhalla himself, Lord Odin.'

If this was supposed to impress the lad, it failed. Oliver maintained a steady gaze on the glass of orange juice and waited for Kustaa to continue.

'How are they treating you?'

Oliver shrugged. 'What am I supposed to say?'

Kustaa eyed him and picked his words. 'You know, Oliver, our Palatinate doesn't only need recruits who can swing a sword. There are other roles for more intelligent people away from the front lines. I oversee all the support teams for Valhalla. Under my authority sit Finance, Estate Management, Procurement and Tech and some of my best people have come from the Schola system.'

He paused and tested his coffee, pulling a face at the bitterness. 'Lord Odin tells me you had quite a hand in Valhalla's successes during the last Raiding Season. Without your technical support, Tyler Maitland – Punnr the White Warrior – would not have discovered the four Assets which gave us such advantages at the Grand Battle. Odin is very grateful to you both. One of the ways he wants to show his appreciation is by helping Tyler to locate his sister, Morgan Maitland. Lord Odin knows you were very involved in this search. He already knows you tracked her to a chat room and…'

'How does he know that?'

'From the hard drives in your home, which we copied when…' Kustaa drifted into silence.

'When what?' Oliver demanded, his face pinched tight.

'It doesn't matter. We're digressing. My point is that he believes your skills could be extremely useful in finding her. So he has proposed that you spend some time in Edinburgh in my Operations Support Unit with the express purpose of continuing your search for Miss Maitland.'

Oliver chewed over this and then asked, 'What does Tyler think?'

Kustaa laughed and his next words were uttered without thought. 'Tyler doesn't even know you're here, lad.'

Oliver's brows creased in a frown. 'Doesn't know I'm here? Then who decided I be brought here.'

'Odin of course.' Kustaa stopped as he saw Oliver's troubled expression and began to wonder if he was wading into waters much deeper than he had expected. He continued more slowly. 'Odin and Radspakr were so impressed with your attempts to search for Morgan Maitland that they decided your skills must not be wasted and you should be inducted directly into the Pantheon.'

'So it was nothing to do with Tyler.' Oliver had dropped his gaze and his words were more to himself. He was lost somewhere, scratching at memories from the night of his abduction and also thinking about the final time he had seen Tyler. They had been sitting on the stairs just before Tyler left for the Grand Battle and he had warned Oliver to be careful. *There are people in the Valhalla Horde who would react very badly if they knew you were looking for my sister.*

Kustaa was becoming uncomfortable with the train of conversation. 'Look, lad, this isn't really up for discussion. The decision's made. I was just trying to make you feel positive. This is an opportunity for you to get more involved in your new Pantheon life. Usually Schola kids don't get anywhere near the Palatinate until their third year when some are selected to be pages and dressers and weapons cleaners for the troops. So think yourself lucky. On Monday you will start in my OSU in Edinburgh and you will continue your search for Morgan Maitland. I take it that's clear?'

Oliver nodded mutely.

'Good. Welcome aboard, Oliver. I trust your skills will prove decisive in Lord Odin's search.'

★

Heph spent a restless night in the ger, snuggled under sheep's wool blankets to limit the deadening cold. They were woken by a smiling young man with a tray of tea, who refused to leave until they understood his name was Oktai. Heph drank his tea, then hauled on his clothing in the sub-zero temperatures and stepped outside to give Agape some privacy.

The sky was a pale faultless blue, the sun still far behind the hills and the gers drenched in dew. The cold was a physical assault on his lungs and the sting of it made his eyes water. But it was the silence that tugged at him most, as though the whole world had stopped. When he moved his feet to circulate his blood and moaned at the pains in his spine, he feared he was disturbing a continent.

He strolled between the gers, imagining busy summer grazing grounds with the full Palatinate gathered. As he rounded the ger they had lunched inside, he came upon Belgutei standing beside the canvas outer layer, dressed in a deel tunic and felt hat, and Heph's eyes lit up because the Kheshig Quartermaster was smoking. Belgutei inclined his head and grunted, then reached into his tunic and retrieved a small tin containing five thin roll-ups, which he proffered.

Heph took one, then leaned in when Belgutei flicked a lighter. The tobacco was black and bitter, but god it felt good.

'We're not permitted these,' Heph said. 'Ancient Vikings and Greeks didn't smoke, so neither can we.'

Belgutei raised an eyebrow. 'Foolish rule.' He pointed

a stubby finger at Heph's bruised face. 'You are a troublemaker?'

'Some people think so.'

'We have marmot ointment, which will help.'

'I'm good, thanks.'

The Jurtchis spied Agape emerging, stamped on his stub and ushered them both into his tent. Over flatbreads and tea, he explained that today the remaining troops would demonstrate the art of good cavalry and when they stepped back outside they found ten Kheshig soldiers saddling up horses outside the stables. Belgutei led the pair from the camp and onto the grasslands. He had removed his ankle-length deel and now wore a leather tunic belted over breeches and boots. The grass was soaking from dew, but the ground was hard. Belgutei said it was aerated by millions of field mice burrows and he pointed out tiny birds flitting over the stems and gave them names that meant nothing to his guests.

They made their way between gentle slopes and arrived at a line of wooden poles driven into the soil, each with a target fixed atop. The camp was a mile back, smoke wafting gently from some of the gers and the glint of sun on 4X4 windscreens in the car park beyond was the only hint that this was not still the land of the true Genghis.

'So,' said Belgutei. 'Have you seen them?'

Heph and Agape peered along the crests of the slopes, but nothing moved.

'This is the *surprise* of cavalry,' the Jurtchis continued. 'It's not all about noise and power. Good horsemen – *light* horsemen – can be silent. They can disappear. We've known this for centuries. Tens of thousands of the Great

Khan's troops could bypass whole armies, swing around them, spring the noose, and the enemy never even knew. It requires a precise understanding of the landscape and total command of communications.

'Perhaps this will be the most important skill of your Companion Cavalry because I suspect Zeus will not have the funds to recruit many mounted troops. You will be small in number and so you need to go unnoticed. Not for you the cacophony of a full charge. You will be furtive. You will slink towards your prey – and then come on them like thunder when they least expect it. Just as my arban is doing right now.'

He raised his eyes to look over their shoulders and the two Titans spun round. Flying towards them in sustained silence were five of the horsemen. They had already covered half the ground from the summits of the slopes and their ponies were at full gallop. If this had been a real Battle, if they held blades of death above their heads, they would have been on the tiny group in seconds and slashing down.

Even as Agape and Heph took this in, they were aware of a new rumble reaching through the soil and they swung again to see the other five troops charging at them from the opposite direction. Instinctively, they stepped in towards Belgutei and hunkered down, and only at the last moment did the two sets of horsemen curl around them in an avalanche of hooves. Then they were gone. Joining together seamlessly into the ten-strong arban unit once again and tearing down the valley, still without a syllable uttered.

'What is the number of your foe?' asked Belgutei.

'You mean the Horde?' Heph checked.

'Two hundred,' confirmed Agape.

'And their shieldwall?'

'Hammer Regiment is a hundred strong.'

Belgutei mulled this. 'A hundred single-file, fifty double-file.' He looked at the line of targets and paced to one of them. Down the valley the horsemen were wheeling. Belgutei raised an arm, then returned and paced the same distance the other way to another pole, and raised his arm again. 'That's the approximate length of a double-file shieldwall at fifty shields each. The front rank will have their shields interlaced and their bodies angled. The troops behind will have weapons ready over the shoulders of the first rank and shields pushed into their backs for additional resistance. They will be expecting an offensive straight at them. Now watch.'

He waved and the distant horsemen immediately broke into a canter, forming into a tight wedge. They increased pace and swept over the grasslands like a hawk on a mouse.

'Imagine your Viking enemy,' said Belgutei. 'They will be tightening their wall. Yelling at each other to hold fast. Stamping their feet into the ground. Wedging their shields. Preparing for the blow.'

The arban closed on them and the earth rumbled beneath their feet once more. Fifty yards from impact, they suddenly sawed the reins, broke into two and streamed around the two outer poles, which Belgutei had signalled to represent each end of a shieldwall. They were round in seconds and turning back in on the small group.

'Imagine the chaos,' shouted Belgutei over the drumming of hooves as the two groups passed each other just yards from them and wheeled away once again. 'The shieldwall will disintegrate as Vikings turn, but it will be too late. You will be at their backs already, your blades splintering their spines.'

Heph and Agape looked at each other, eyes wide in understanding.

'Now I suggest we stand aside,' warned Belgutei and they followed him away from the poles. The arban was coming again, now in a tight diamond shape, a single lead horsemen acting as the point. 'I told you cavalry was all about speed and shock. Here comes the shock. Think again of your Viking shieldwall. This time my soldiers have no intention of rounding the ends. This time it is all about the breakthrough.'

The gap between the two most central poles was only five or six yards, but the unit was packed tight now, the horses' flanks almost touching, their hooves working as one. At the critical moment, the Mongols finally let loose their tongues and screamed a challenge. They tore between the poles, so close to the bystanders that the air rushed over them and the smell of horse and leather and sweat stampeded down their throats. They were gone in a heartbeat, disappearing up the valley and the peace of the land returned, birds chirping as though nothing had occurred.

'A two-file shieldwall against that?' Belgutei asked archly. 'I think not.' He checked the faces of the Titans and was pleased with the expressions he saw. 'Yesterday I told you about the weaknesses of cavalry and today I have shown you their strengths. You must return to Edinburgh and give your reports to Zeus. He will decide.'

'Our gratitude for the demonstration, oh Jurtchis,' replied Agape.

He chuckled. 'There is one more. I throw it in as a – what

do you say in English – a freebie? It serves no practical purpose for you, but it is a spectacle nonetheless.'

The troop was approaching, trotting easily over the grass. All except one who was still a distant figure on the horizon. 'That is Tuya.'

One of the riders came forward and handed Belgutei a bow. He grasped it and beckoned the Titans to close around. 'The Mongol recurved bow. An instrument of beauty and ultimate power. It takes a year to make a good bow. Layers of wood set in perfect harmony to create the flex. A cork handle for grip and lightness. But – look at the ends – this is where the magic takes place. The "ears" of the bow are made from staghorn and bend in the opposite direction. The string loops over these. When the archer draws, the horn extends. When the archer releases, the horn bounces back to its original form, thus providing huge power in excess of what the wood alone can achieve. An arrow will leave this bow at three hundred kilometres per hour and at fifty metres it will go through two centimetres of wood. Nine hundred years ago, these were the armour-piercing cruise missiles of their day.'

He ushered them away from the targets again. The other riders had eased to the side and now only Tuya waited on her horizon. Belgutei waved his arm and she steadied her mount, then began to canter towards them.

'You are about to witness the pinnacle of hard training. Weeks of falling so hard there's blood in your urine. Months of whirling sticks and balls and bags to get the horse ready for the noise of a bowstring over its head. Years of learning to release an arrow only at the split second when all four hooves are off the ground. The perfect moment. The heartbeat of peace within the tumult.'

Tuya thundered towards them and Heph realised she was not holding the reins. Indeed only her thighs gripped her horse. She sat ramrod straight, yet he could also understand from his own early lessons how supple her body must be, how she must be instinctively flexing with the precise movements of her mount. She carried a bow and brought it up with her left arm. An arrow was already notched and two others were clasped between the fingers of her left hand. With her right arm she drew back the string and then she paused, waiting for the moment, that heartbeat of peace.

Before the onlookers could register, she released and there was a loud thud as the arrow buried itself in one of the targets. In a second she had picked another arrow from her left hand, fitted and released. This buried itself into another target. And then she was past and they were about to cheer, but the show was not over. Even as her horse galloped for the distant horizon, Tuya whipped the final arrow onto her string, turned in her seat and fired it behind her. Heph's jaw dropped as a third thud told them the arrow had flown true. With infinite grace, Tuya faced forwards again and slowed her horse with a nudge of her knees. Without looking at them, she trotted back towards the camp and the other riders followed.

Belgutei stood with hands on hips, a grin cracking his face in two. 'Well,' he said. 'I believe that means it's time for lunch.'

They started back, lost in thought about what they had witnessed. The camp was a mile distant and as they walked amongst sunlit grasses, a distant murmur came to them. Belgutei halted and frowned at the slopes behind. Heph followed his gaze and then called a warning. Mongol horsemen were streaming towards them. Not just ten. Not even fifty. A multitude. Stocky steeds and lamellar armour, the wind horse on their shields, and bare-headed.

'Borte and the Nightguard jagan,' said Belgutei with a glimmer of concern in his eyes. 'They must be undertaking a wide loop today.'

Agape glowered. 'Our visit is supposed to be low-profile. A hundred horsemen were not on the agenda.'

It was too late to do anything. The riders had seen them and were cantering directly for them. As they neared, the front ranks began shouting hotly and gesticulating.

'What's their problem?' growled Agape.

Belgutei shouted back, but this was greeted only with more angry responses.

'Close your eyes.'

'What?'

'Do as I say.'

'We are not about to...'

'They are not wearing their masking helmets and will not allow outsiders to see their identities. You are Pantheon. You should understand.'

Agape fumed, but understood.

The riders were almost on them and the Titans forced their eyes closed and bent their heads just in time to feel the jagun arrive. The ground trembled and the noise and movement of horses was everywhere. The troops still hollered and Belgutei was arguing back. Horses whinnied and snorted and thrummed the earth. Riders creaked in their leather and called to each other. Heph could sense them coming in close and inspecting. There was dust in his mouth and the stink of an army in his lungs. He kept his eyes screwed tight and wondered if the razor-sharp curve of a scimitar would embed itself under his ribs.

The anger cooled and at last Heph felt the horses beginning to flow away. There were whoops and the weight of threat lifted. The hooves receded, the ground settled and the voices grew distant.

There was a long pause and then Belgutei said evenly, 'You may open your eyes.'

The jagun was pouring over the opposite slopes, bypassing the camp and returning to their own bases in the east. But seated on a horse just twenty yards away, with a scarf wrapped high to hide facial features, one rider remained watching the trio.

'My friends, may I introduce Borte, Colonel of Horse for the Nightguards.'

The rider said nothing. Hard eyes between the folds of the black silk scarf. The Titans returned the gaze and the steppe was still.

Then Borte yanked the reins and the sturdy Mongolian steed spun and galloped up the slope in a whirl of dust as the last of the Kheshig Nightguards disappeared over the skyline.

PART THREE

FULL CIRCLE

XX

Quartermile. An expanse of luxury, state-of-the-art offices abutting the green swathes of the Meadows and built above a warren of cafés, bars and high-end shops. These premises had rapidly become the most sought after in Edinburgh. The penthouse suites in particular, with their commanding views and plethora of terraces, attracted the most astronomical prices. The sort of location a lord of industry might choose.

Oliver was escorted through reception by a monosyllabic man who had driven him the ninety-minute journey from Liddesdale. A pass was scrutinised by security guards who telephoned ahead, then indicated a lift to the upper floors. The doors opened on more security personnel and Oliver was required to raise his arms while scanners snaked around his body.

When he was waved through, he found himself in an understated waiting area with a single unlabelled door. After a short delay the door buzzed open and a woman with an unnaturally blonde bob and heavy make-up stepped out. She was old enough to be Oliver's grandmother and wearing a smart skirted business suit with very high heels, accompanied by a thundercloud of perfume. She beckoned him inside with a curt nod.

They entered a spacious open-plan office with floor-to-ceiling glass along each side, leading out to rain-spattered terraces. The place was divided into four distinct clusters of desks and there was a kitchen, eating area and several enclosed meeting rooms. In total he could see about fifteen heads bent over terminals and each one popped up to inspect him, then dipped back to their work.

'Right,' said the woman in clipped tones. 'I understand you're from the Schola and you've been assigned to us. I am also informed you have Level 3 clearance and I can therefore tell you that this is the Operations Support Unit for the Valhalla Palatinate. I assume you already know that?'

Oliver nodded.

The woman weighed him up dubiously. 'How old are you?'

'Thirteen. Wait, no...' Three weeks earlier, in the never-ending routine of the Schola, he had marked the passing of his birthday with a few silent tears in his dorm bunk, dreaming of his mother and the cake she would have baked for him. 'Fourteen.'

She pulled a face and sighed to ensure he knew his presence in the unit enjoyed none of her support. 'It seems Kustaa, the new Quartermaster, wants you to work on a pet project of his. Has he briefed you?'

Oliver nodded again.

'Okay – well – he must have faith in your skills. I'm the COO of the unit, chief operating officer. You call me ma'am and you report your progress to me and only me. Understood?'

Not even a nod this time, but she let it go. 'We're divided into Treasury over there; Estates, which oversees the running and maintenance of all Palatinate property including Valhalla and our Schola; Procurement, which deals with supplies, equipment and catering; and finally Tech in that far corner, where you'll be sitting. My office is the door over there, where I do not expect to be disturbed.'

She fixed Oliver with a mascara stare. 'Let me be clear about your ground rules. You will not leave the premises under any circumstances. You may use the kitchen facilities and take air on the terraces, but you do not go back through security until your driver is ready to return you to the Schola at the end of each day. The lift over there goes only to the floor above, which is the private office of the boss when he's in Edinburgh and no one has access except me. Is that clear?'

The lad gave a shrug, his eyes blank, his face expressionless.

'Staff are permitted to bring nothing into these premises, least of all phones. We run on ultra-secure servers, our internet firewalls are of the highest order and activity is closely monitored. All social media is blocked, as is email and any other form of communication, and you have been granted only basic access to our systems. I have been fully briefed on your task and I will review your activity on a regular basis. Jed is my Tech manager and your point of contact. He has, however, not been told the purpose of your presence with us and you will not discuss it with him or any of the others. He can help you with broader queries and show you the system, but if you have any questions more specific to the task, you will ask only me. Kustaa seems to think you display aptitude to be useful to the unit in the future, so you are also to be introduced to some of the primary activities of the Tech team, all within the scope of your level-three clearance. Jed is authorised to induct you more fully. Is there anything I've said that is unclear?'

Oliver shook his head, but refused to meet her eyes.

'Right.' She marched him over to a corner desk, separated by a few square feet of carpet from Jed and three other Tech employees. Her blood-red nails clipped over the terminal keys. 'That's you logged in. If you click here, you'll see you have one folder on your personal drive. It comprises all the documentation our previous Thane – Radspakr – gathered in regard to the person you are searching for. I've looked through already and there is nothing confidential, but you will still ensure the contents remain for your eyes only. And now, you'd better begin making yourself useful. Kustaa expects results.'

Jed was the polar opposite of his boss. A dark-haired, overweight twenty-something, with thick glasses and fingers in a packet of crisps, but smiling eyes, who said in a heavy Glaswegian accent, 'Did she give you the "*call me ma'am*" speech? Don't worry about her. Aurora's her Pantheon identity, but she gives everyone the ma'amship speech when they start. She's just an accountant who crawled her way up the greasy pole and she's damned if she'll let anyone up behind. So is Oliver your real name?'

'Of course.'

Jed raised an eyebrow. 'Okay, well in here we all have aliases, but if you're just Oliver, then that's fine with me. Her ma'amship tells me you're seconded from the Schola for a few weeks on a private project, but I'm also supposed to induct you into the world of Pantheon tech. You'll find our systems are as locked down as they get, but there's some fun to be had with them once you know the basics. Make a drink, get yourself settled in and we can have a chat later. Meantime, shout if you need anything.'

Oliver sat at his new desk and looked out surreptitiously at the city beyond. What none of them knew – least of all that strutting cow – was the hurricane of emotions beneath his quiet exterior.

During his weeks at the Schola, his survival instincts had kicked in and the endless repetitive structure forced him into some sort of tolerance of his predicament. He believed his mum would visit soon and he was convinced Tyler was behind his new circumstances. The Valhalla White Warrior must have taken Oliver's wishes literally and found a way to induct him into the Pantheon. It was startling and frightening, but he could not deny a certain thrill. So, when Kustaa's indiscretions had revealed that Tyler knew nothing of Oliver's predicament, thrill was replaced by foreboding.

And now this – *this*. Suddenly he was back in Edinburgh and his mother was so close, just across the rooftops. She worked in a jewellery shop off George Street and he could walk there in fifteen minutes. He wanted to run onto the terrace and scream for her. Yell his soul out until the police arrived and rescued him. Desperation bubbled in him and he had to screw his hands so tight that the nails dug grooves into his palms.

'Hey – you okay?' Jed was peering at him. 'You want to come get a brew?'

Oliver shook his head. 'No,' he said, taking a deep breath. 'I'm all right.'

He crammed his emotions back down his throat. So the

bastards wanted him to find Morgan Maitland. For now at least, it seemed he had no choice. He opened the single folder on his personal drive and saw it mostly contained random documents, which must have been copied from Tyler's old laptop. Utility bills, old emails, screenshots, scanned payslips from Tyler's job at the library. The usual electronic detritus from an average life. He flicked through a few of the files, then closed the screen and dredged up recollections. He could barely even remember where his own searches had taken him all those months ago. *Torchlight96*, that was it. He believed he had found her in an obscure chat room and *Torchlight96* was her username, but what on earth had been the website? He was damned if he could recall.

He closed his eyes and cleared his mind, then pulled up the unit's specialised browser and began to search.

Zeus' arrival in Ephesus was intentionally understated. His chauffeured Bentley dropped him where the mouth of the Mile flows out to meet the bulk of Holyrood Palace and he walked up the sloping street, dallying by some of the shop windows and enjoying the late morning sunshine. He and Hera had just returned from a short break on their yacht moored off St Kitts and he was pleased Edinburgh had not greeted him with arrow-shafts of rain.

He turned off the Mile about halfway up at a backpackers' hostel, slipped around the rear to a discreet door and climbed an internal staircase to the fourth floor. As he had expected, Ephesus was empty. The choice of a lunchtime meeting meant only a few souls trained in the Bladecraft Rooms, so he progressed unnoticed.

A guard was stationed at the doors to the gardens, dressed in black T-shirt and combat boots.

'You are?' asked Zeus.

'Ezio, my lord. Heavy Infantry.'

'We are to be undisturbed.'

'Yes, lord.'

Zeus pushed through the doors, then paused to enjoy the scents of petal and greenery. It had cost a pretty penny to create this place, but he was proud of the achievement. To him, it resurrected the lost gardens of ancient Macedonia and he loved knowing they thrived here in secret above Scotland's capital, an abundance of foliage and gently dripping silence.

Alexander and Simmius were at the main table and they both rose and bowed their heads.

'Morning,' said Zeus with a brief wave. 'Or is it afternoon? My body clock is all over the place as usual.'

'Just after midday, sir,' said Alexander and stepped aside to offer Zeus the principal seat.

'No, you stay put, I'm fine here.' Zeus eased himself into a chair opposite while Simmius retrieved a demitasse cup and a copper-handled briki from a nearby hotplate.

'I took the liberty of ordering, my lord,' he said, pouring viscous black coffee into the cup.

'Ah, perfect. Kafette?'

'Of course and organic.'

Zeus sipped appreciatively and reached for a plate of koulourakia biscuits.

'So,' he said through a mouthful of buttery crumbs. 'Let's get straight to business. We've all seen the Blood Fund counts for last Season, but perhaps – Simmius – you can impart the numbers again for the purposes of clarity.'

The Titan Adjutant pushed specs onto his nose and consulted his iPad. 'After a particularly confrontational Nineteenth Season, we ended the year with one hundred and three Credits, my lord. This can be set against Valhalla's total of seventy-nine.'

'A fine victory,' said Alexander squinting small eyes at Zeus. 'And one we must build upon this year with a successful recruitment drive.'

'Indeed.' The Caelestis studied the king's strained features, the storm-cloud blotches beneath his eyes and the parchment-frail skin stretched across his skull. *My god, the man looks half in his grave.* He had heard rumours of Alexander's coke and opium habits, but had underestimated the physical toll these were taking on a soldier he had once admired.

Alexander consulted a sheet of paper. 'We currently trail Valhalla by thirty-five troops, so my proposal is that we spend the bulk of our funds on basic one-Credit hoplites from our Schola to ensure we outnumber our rivals at the start of the Twentieth. I suggest an intake of ninety-one standard ranks: forty to the Heavies; twenty-five to Companions; nineteen to the peltasts and seven for the Band. We will spend our remaining twelve Credits on three Dekarchos officers from outside the Pantheon, who will be trained and distributed among the units as required. We could afford only one Dekarchos last year – Lenore, our White Warrior in the Raiding Season – so an intake of three will ensure a strong bloodstream into the officer cadre.'

Zeus pursed his lips and remained silent.

'What do the numbers say?' Alexander growled to Simmius.

'Such a recruitment programme would add ninety-four

troops to our ranks and bring our total to two hundred and eight. Almost certainly matching Valhalla's count, if not making us the larger Palatinate for the first time in several years.'

Alexander's eyes were hard on Zeus. 'Seems a pretty fine plan to me.'

'Indeed,' repeated the Titan god.

And perhaps it was a fine plan. On the surface it certainly seemed more so than the one Hera had pushed on him interminably while they soaked up the sun off St Kitts. She had been exhilarated by her new idea and unrelenting in her persuasion, and he could never resist his wife at her most potent. He had promised he would give the absurd concept a shot, at least a test run.

On arriving at Ephesus, he had intended to explain the new thinking to Alexander, but now he scrutinised the king's ravaged features and snatching, suspicious eyes, and he came to the fateful conclusion that he could not bring this man into his confidence. He let the silence hang as he considered his next words.

'A thorough plan, but now permit me to extend an alternative one. We have spent the last twenty years hacking away at the Horde with the same tactics, rarely taking them by surprise, our numbers waxing and waning but never amounting to a total that might shock our foe. Well, enough is enough. This year, I have decided to take a different approach.'

'A different approach, lord?' Alexander repeated, suspicion-laced.

'I will give Cleitus another ten Companions because he lost too many at the Battle, and I will allow Nicanor thirteen more Heavies for his Phalanx as a gesture. But the remaining seventy Credits I'm keeping. We will see out the Twentieth Year with this reduced troop count and then add the seventy Credits to next year's newly won funds in one giant recruitment campaign next summer.'

No one spoke. The garden dripped around them and an ambulance siren wailed somewhere over the rooftops.

'You're *keeping* seventy Credits?' Alexander confirmed at last.

'Let's call it investing. With the right tactics, the new troops I *am* granting should give us enough to hold the Horde this Season and we will be in a better position to invest properly for the next.'

Alexander felt the heat rising in him. 'Valhalla already has a hundred and forty warriors. If they recruit sensibly, they will likely field over two hundred for the start of the Raiding Season. Your plan gives them a sixty-head advantage before a single blade has been drawn.'

Zeus bit back a retort and attempted persuasion. 'Imagine the shock when we field double the number of recruits at the start of the following year. We will bide our time and plan for unimagined victories in the Twenty-First.'

But Alexander was shaking his head, blinking fast as he tried to get his mind around this sudden new challenge to his carefully prepared plans. 'No. It's nonsense. I refuse to countenance it.'

The King had overstepped a mark.

'My decision is not up for debate. You will accept it and act upon it, or I will find a new King who will. I suspect Cleitus yearns for your crown.'

Alexander's hands were squeezing compulsively on

the table and Zeus could see the muscles twitching in his cheeks. Was this fool of an addict really the man he wanted commanding his Palatinate?

'So, we are agreed,' the Caelestis concluded, standing. 'You will ensure the troops are the best prepared they have ever been to face down the Viking threat and we will hold seventy Credits until next year. In the meantime, you will speak of this to no one.'

Alexander stared blackly at his master and gritted his teeth. 'Understood,' he confirmed with a twist of his lip.

Zeus nodded and turned to depart. 'Simmius, walk with me to the Gate.'

The two men left Alexander simmering in the gardens and made their way back through the deserted haunts of Ephesus.

'I sense you are unhappy with my proposal,' commented Zeus as the other man walked silently by his shoulder.

'Surprised, my lord, that's all.'

'You think I should spend the funds?'

'I think if we do not, Valhalla may make untold gains this Season.'

Zeus stopped and leaned in to his Adjutant conspiratorially. 'Of course I'm spending the funds. But I don't want that fool knowing.'

'Lord?'

'I am planning a new unit. Very small, but expensive and with an impact potentially tenfold its number. They will be trained, equipped and kept in the utmost secrecy. Not one Hoplite, not one Titan officer, not one member of the Curiate – no one – will know of their existence. Understood?'

'My lord, it's not good form to keep secrets from the Curiate. They make their wagers based on known facts.'

'It's been done before,' Zeus replied acidly. 'We're covered under *ruse de guerre*. Necessary Battle tactics. The Legion have played enough tricks in their time.'

'Am I permitted to know this particular *ruse de guerre*?'

Zeus considered his Adjutant for several long seconds, then dipped his head. 'Horses, Simmius. Ten Credits a pop, not including the rider. I understand Diogenes is an accomplished rider.'

'The ex-Wolf?'

'He will be Horsemaster. And his friend, Hephaestion, can join him.'

Simmius' eyes locked on to Zeus at the mention of Hephaestion. 'Is that wise, my lord?'

'If memory serves me correctly, one of them was the victorious White Warrior of the Nineteenth Season and both of them demonstrated courage in the extreme to make their dash across the battle lines on that beach. They then marked the start of their time with us by sending Alexander's champions to their deaths.' Zeus smiled thinly. 'I rather admire their spirit. Besides, it may be good to keep them away from the other troops for the time being. They can focus on training the new squadron and the rest of the ranks can forget about them. We will recruit the other members from within our current Brigades. I assume you can identify those with horse riding experience?'

'I can.'

Zeus made to continue to the Gate, then drew back and said in more conciliatory tones, 'I'm not yet fully convinced myself. This new unit has ten weeks until Christmas and the *Agonium Martiale* to prove its worth. I assume you have plenty of replacements ready at the Schola if we decide to change tactics before the formal commencement of the Combat Seasons?'

'The whole of Year Four is primed and desperate to be accepted.'

'Good man, then we have our Plan B. And Simmius?'

'Lord?'

'Not a word.'

XXI

Calder shivered. The seasons were shifting. Winter's touch was once again fingering the air and the vaults were thick with chill. Could it really be a year since the Pantheon had shouldered its way into her life? How could a time so crammed with memories pass faster than a sword strike?

Around her, eight figures with no names gasped and sweated. They pummelled sandbags. They staggered with stone weights. They climbed ropes, dropped into press-ups and shadow-boxed in corners away from the candlelight. On the left shoulder of each an even number had been stamped in Roman numerals; numbers that were now their identities. For they were Thralls and must earn their names.

In the vault next door another eight with odd numbers on their shoulders trained equally hard. And between them Freyja paced – just as she had done for the past six Seasons – observing, noting, castigating. *Speed. Strength. Violence. The Three Pillars of readiness.*

'It has to be you,' she had said three weeks earlier when she had first walked Calder back into the training vaults of her own Armatura.

'But I'm not ready. How can I do this after only a year?'

'Halvar is gone. Leiv is dead. Asmund *will* not. Bjarke *should* not. And Skarde *must* not. You are a Thegn, my only officer in Raven Company and I want it to be you. Sveinn agrees.'

Valhalla's Council of War had decided to spend their seventy-nine Blood Funds on forty-seven Drengr from Year Four at the Schola and eight new Thegns. Accordingly, Kustaa's Venarii parties tracked twenty-three potential Electi recruits on the streets of the city and handed over twenty-three Triple Horn amulets. Five were returned to the yew tree in Greyfriars and two were no-shows. So that left sixteen Thralls who turned up wide-eyed and shaking for their first induction. Before them was a journey like no other. They would learn, they would train, they would fight and some would die, and in December Valhalla would bring eight before Charon the Ferryman at the Oath-Taking.

Calder circled the figures as they strove, contemplating their faces and wondering at the stories behind each. At first, she had felt gauche in her role as their instructor, but to her amazement, the Thralls hung on her every word. And when she and the Housecarl took wooden swords and sparred, their audience watched as though witnessing a battle between gods.

She ran an appraising eye over her class and felt their sweat warming the vault. They were a good bunch this year. Five lads and three women. Tough, athletic and determined. They wanted this. They wanted to be there at the Oath-Taking. It came off them in waves. Two in particular stood out. Thrall XIV had a confidence that reminded her of Brante and Thrall X had silent steel shades of the Punnr she first knew.

She had said as much to Freyja at the end of the fourth session.

'Hardly the best role models,' the Housecarl had said harshly.

'But X and XIV are strong and fast. They would make good Wolves.'

'So you would have us hand them to Skarde?'

Calder had not thought of that.

The recruits were tiring now. The repetitions were grinding them down. As if reading her mind, Freyja entered from the adjacent vault with her eight pupils in tow and Calder called a halt. Amid the panting silence and the fug of body odour, the Housecarl and her deputy wordlessly rearranged candles to illuminate a hexagon marked on the flagstone floor. Calder bent and placed bowls of burning oil in each of the six corners, while Freyja positioned herself in the centre and observed her audience.

'In pairs,' she said, without embellishment. 'One on one. The first one to leave the hexagon loses.' Memories flooded back to Calder. Of Brante and Vidar battling like rhinos. Of Hertha grabbing Calder's foot mid-strike and dragging her from the hexagon. Of Erland twisting Punnr's balls until he bleated and yanking him across the perimeter.

'No rules,' said Freyja.

'No *rules*,' breathed Calder.

When it was over, Calder gathered them around her and tried to recall Halvar's words. '*Get your stance right... Keep your chin down... Keep moving, but not bloody dancing like a monkey... If you can't avoid a punch, step into it... Finally attitude. Your opponent may be a giant piece of horseshit, but make the bastard wonder if you can win.*'

As she spoke, the Thralls eyed her pensively. They were shaken. They were bruised, scraped, bloodied. And, more than that, their instructors had wanted to see the beast in them. To survive in that hexagon, they had needed to find their anger.

Week three. Mid-October. And the Pantheon had just got nasty.

Tyler sat bleary-eyed in the back of a Saab as his driver took him over the Forth in the pre-dawn glow of a cloudless teal sky. It was too early for the mass of Edinburgh's commuters and only a few headlights shot past on their way to the city. The car slipped north, then curved west around the dozing suburbs of Glenrothes and into gently rolling farmland. Despite the lateness of the season, hay bales still waited in fields. Farmstead lights winked at them from hillocks. They crossed the Fife border into Perth and Kinross, circumvented the rugged Ochil Hills and descended the deep slash of Gleneagles. Finally, as the clock on the dashboard flicked past seven and the eastern horizon blushed rose, they turned into a thin potholed drive that ran up to a farmhouse with several stone barns.

There was Agape waiting beside a gate, dressed in long Barbour boots, wax jacket and brimmed hat. Tyler stepped out and raised a hand to her, but she did not respond. As the car backed up and the driver killed the engine, the farm door opened and Forbes emerged carrying two mugs of tea.

'Hey, mate. Want one of these? I can get another.'

Tyler shook his head. 'You're here early.'

'I've been here all night. Seems this is where I'm going to be laying my head for the foreseeable future. Damn comfortable actually. The owners were encouraged to sell a month ago and now it's Pantheon. I think they've had the builders in.'

They walked over to Agape and she accepted one of the teas, blowing on it silently and taking her time to drink before speaking without preamble. 'So, you have your wish, Hephaestion. Zeus has given his consent. This place is now the headquarters of the fledgling Companion Cavalry of the Titan Palatinate – all seven of you. But know this: Zeus did not come to his decision lightly. One hundred and three Blood Funds would have filled our ranks and made us a force equal to our Valhalla foe.

'But now we won't be calling up such a host from the Schola. Our ranks will not swell with fresh hoplons. Nor will we recruit Electi from outside. There will be no new Dekarchos officers. Instead, seven horses await you in those barns. Seventy precious Blood Funds. If one goes lame or is hurt or proves unsatisfactory, it will not be replaced. You have seven and only seven. Tell him, Diogenes.'

'They're beautiful, Heph. They arrived last night. Arabian. All stallions. Fourteen to fifteen hands, which is not large by modern standards, but closely matches the warhorses of Alexander's cavalry. Great bone structure, strong legs, good disposition. Four chestnuts, three greys. They've been well trained and know how to carry a rider.'

Dio's breath, warmed by the tea, steamed in the morning air and his eyes danced.

Agape spoke again, just as the first rays of sun slanted across the Ochils. 'Let me be clear. Zeus has not yet made his final decision. You have until the *Agonium Martiale* on the second night of the new year. If you are not what he expects by then, the Companion Cavalry will be disbanded and seventy graduates from the Titan Schola rapidly assimilated into our lines.'

She drained her tea and slung the dregs into the bushes. 'So it's down to you whether these beasts belong to the shortest-lived unit in Pantheon history. Diogenes, you are Horsemaster, entrusted with the welfare and training of our cavalry. But Hephaestion, this madcap scheme is down to your meddling, so you will lead. If you succeed and the unit exists beyond the *Agonium Martiale*, then you will be Captain of Companion Cavalry.'

Heph glanced at Dio, but he simply nodded his head. A distant engine turned them as a minibus made its way up the potholed drive.

'They are arriving. Before they do, you will hear me out. No one knows of this experiment beyond Zeus, Hera, Simmius and those of you about to gather in this yard. And it will stay that way. You are all excused from your units. The officers have been told you are required for vital Palatinate business. They are curious and suspicious, but accepting. This cavalry does not exist. No one in the higher Pantheon knows of it, nor indeed must they ever. What good are seven horse warriors deprived of their element of surprise? Breathe of this to no one.'

The minibus was pulling up, curious faces peering at them. 'Diogenes, you will care for the beasts night and day. Hephaestion, you will be brought here each morning. Use your time wisely. You are the Valhalla traitors and there are many who would gladly see you fail.'

She handed her mug to Dio. 'Now, I will leave you to your introductions. Good luck, Titans.'

She strode past the van without a glance at the group alighting and dipped into the car that had brought Heph. It returned down the drive, followed by the minibus, leaving a huddle of five new arrivals waiting in the middle of the yard.

'I guess it's over to you, boss,' said Dio.

'You don't resent it?'

'You're the man, Heph. Always said you were. I'm happy to follow where you lead.'

'Even if my leadership on a horse is going to be bloody suspect?'

Dio laughed. 'We've time to improve that. Now we'd better meet our cavalry.'

Heph strode towards them and began to raise his arm to shake hands, but when he saw their hostile expressions he stopped short. 'Welcome. I expect you've been briefed about why you're here?'

'Only that we're being seconded from our units for a few weeks,' answered one of the two women. She was thickset with short dark hair and probably in her forties. Her accent was Borders and her tone cold.

'Let me introduce myself.'

'We know who you are,' said a burly silver-haired man in a cashmere jumper. 'We saw you fight. You're the Valhalla turncoats.'

Dio stepped up to Heph's shoulder. 'You have a problem, grandfather?'

The man bristled and squared his shoulders. 'My instructions were to come here, so here I am. But I'm taking no orders from Valhalla scum. And you ever call me that again, boy, and it'll be the last thing that comes out your mouth.'

'Leave them be, Zephyr,' said a slim figure standing a little apart from the group. He had a neatly combed blonde hair and the hint of a Teutonic accent. He looked fit and wore combat trousers and a cotton shirt with the sleeves rolled up.

'So – we will try again,' Heph said, choosing to direct his gaze at the man who had just spoken. 'My name is Hephaestion and I am in command of this unit, as directed by Agape and Zeus himself. This is Diogenes, Horsemaster.'

This last word caught their attention.

'In the stables behind us we have seven Arabian thoroughbreds freshly arrived and gagging to be ridden.'

The group glanced at each other.

'We're here to ride?' the dark-haired woman said dubiously.

'We are indeed. And you are?'

'Maia. Bodyguard to Alexander, Companion Light Infantry.'

Heph turned to the silver-haired man. The man debated for several seconds, then said, 'Zephyr. Nine years Phalanx frontline, Brigade of Heavy Infantry under Nicanor.'

By his shoulder was a kid, not yet out of his teens, lanky brown hair and a cautious smile, who reached for Heph's hand. 'I'm Pallas and I'm also in the Phalanx, but only second Season and still in the back lines.'

Heph smiled and shook, then shifted to the woman who had not spoken and something sparked in his memory. Her hair was tied back in a bun, but wisps hung across her pale cheeks and the strands were vivid red. She stared at him frostily. 'We've met.'

Heph inclined his head. 'I think we may have.'

'Lenore. White Warrior of the Titan Palatinate.'

Good god. It really was her. Heph had never seen her unmasked. 'We spoke at the Blood Gathering after the Raids back in March. You called me an arsehole.'

'I called you a cheating arsehole.' Her voice was just as he remembered it. Exquisite soft Scots. 'Now it seems you're a cheating arsehole who changes sides.'

Zephyr chuckled and Heph fought an angry retort.

'Now, now,' intervened Dio. 'I think it's time we all started to get along.'

Heph forced himself away and looked at the final figure. 'And what about you?'

The blonde man met his gaze. 'Spyro. Sacred Band.'

'You're one of Agape's Band?'

'This will be my seventh Season.'

Heph glanced at Dio, who raised his eyebrows.

'I'm glad she could spare you. Now, shall we meet our mounts?'

He started to move towards the gate, but Zephyr stalled him. 'First tell us why we're here.' His stocky legs were planted on the gravelled yard and he was going nowhere until he had his answer.

'Okay,' Heph replied. 'You are indeed owed an explanation. You're here because you are all experienced riders in your spare time. Zeus has invested in seven Arabian stallions of the highest quality and he expects us to train as horse soldiers. We have until the *Agonium Martiale* to prove to him that we're good enough and if we do, he intends to use us in the Grand Battle as his new elite shock troops. We are to be the first Companion Cavalry.'

'Seven of us?' Maia said incredulously.

'Yes – seven,' answered Heph, visibly irritated.

His words hung in the morning air and there was a long silence as he fought to control his anger.

At last, Spyro shrugged, stepped towards the gate and waved for Heph to go first. 'Then lead on, Hephaestion. Let's see these mounts.'

XXII

During the first two weeks of Oliver's internment in the Operations Support Unit, he made minimal progress in his quest for Morgan Maitland.

He had rediscovered the chat room unearthed by his investigation earlier in the year, but the unit's browser firewalls and his own limited user rights meant he was unable to access these forums because they were classed as communication portals and thus strictly blocked. Indeed, even the most basic internet searches brought back ragged results because all media outlets were censored. There was a Morgan Maitland who worked in HM Revenue and Customs in London and one who owned a hair salon in Wisconsin, but he knew implicitly none of these was Tyler's sister and he found himself simply going around in circles.

If even a single molecule of his heart was dedicated to the task, he might have complained, but the reality was he couldn't care less. He glowered in his corner and cast sideways glances at the city beyond the terrace. His home was out there, no more than a mile away. What right did these people have to hold him in this rooftop prison?

For the first few days Aurora eyed him suspiciously, but when she realised he was achieving next to nothing, the heat went out of her. She saw him as just a kid in the wrong place. Out of his depth and time-wasting. If he couldn't find what Odin was seeking, it wasn't her problem. Jed showed him some of the broader tasks performed by the Tech team; the camera feeds at Valhalla's Gates; the locking and laser controls for security; the ultra-secure messaging services; and the image and video libraries from previous Seasons.

Oliver wanted to see feeds from the cameras of the Vigiles, but Jed explained these were managed only by Atilius' Pantheon-wide teams.

'Everything not specifically linked to a Palatinate – like the Vigiles, Pantheon recruitment, the hospitals, transport, event security, and all technical support for the Caelestes and Curiate – that's all run by Atilius.'

'And where are his teams based?'

'Some say London. Some say Rome. My money's on a huge Pentagon-like complex in the middle of nowhere.'

It was Oliver's twelfth day when Aurora came clopping across the room. 'Kustaa dropped this by yesterday. Something left in his office by his predecessor. Says it might be useful.'

It was Tyler's laptop. Old, cheap and bashed about, but unmistakably the one Tyler had placed in Oliver's keeping before the Grand Battle.

'I've disabled most of the functions,' she said. 'All communications are blocked and I have full administrator rights, so don't get any ideas. The hard drive's already been explored, but you might as well look yourself if Kustaa thinks it's worthwhile.'

Once she was safely back in her glass cage, he eased open the laptop and his fingers hovered over the keys. Either she severely underrated him or she was congenitally stupid, because she had just handed him a computer that wasn't part of the ultra-secure servers with a browser unrestricted by specialised firewalls. Moreover, if he covered his tracks well, she would have no way of reviewing his activity.

Keeping his eyes on the room, he scanned for Wi-Fi signals. Three came up from the offices on floors below and one was not password-protected. He selected it, but a message flashed up saying *Access Denied. Contact Your Administrator*. It took him three minutes to remove her ma'amship's rights, make himself the new administrator and get online. He forced himself to pause and take stock. She was on the phone in her little booth. Jed was deep in coding and no one else was paying him any attention.

There was only one thing on his mind. Get a message to his mum. Let her know he was okay and tell her he was trapped in this Quartermile office. But he quickly realised communicating with her was more complicated than it seemed. She had never been one for Facebook. WhatsApp was useless because he had no access to a phone and he had long forgotten if she ever possessed an email address. He wondered if she was contactable at the jewellery shop, but could not remember what it was called or the street it was on. Swearing silently, he resorted to Google and input her name in the hope it might cough up something useful.

And that was when the appalling pieces of his old life began to tumble around him. Press articles. Police briefings. Discussion threads. Death records. The body of Mrs Patricia Muir, aged forty-two, had been found in the bedroom of her property on Learmonth Place on the morning of April twenty-eighth. The coroner's report concluded she had been suffocated in her sleep up to four nights prior. There were no signs of forced entry, but shoe prints, DNA from a pillow and CCTV footage of a Mitsubishi registered to Mr Trevor Muir, aged forty-six, suggested her estranged husband had been present in the house on the night in question. Police, therefore, had been keen to ask him about the death of his wife, as well as the disappearance of their only son, Oliver Muir, aged thirteen, on the same night. The discovery of a Sunray motorboat registered to Mr Trevor Muir and floating off the Isle of May, along with sundry clothing belonging to Mr Muir and his son Oliver had led police to believe a further tragedy may have taken place at sea. Both Mr Trevor Muir and Oliver Muir were listed as officially missing, presumed drowned.

Oliver deleted his search, removed the Wi-Fi history and returned admin rights to Aurora, then with shaking legs made it to the toilets, where he locked himself into a cubicle, fell to the floor, heaved and cried until he had nothing left.

Everything after that was a blur. He was returned to the Schola in the back of a van, then it was dark and he was fighting with someone. Next he was in his dormitory with the faces of the other Initiates around him, but he was still shouting and Praefecti arrived and dragged him through the corridors to the sick bay. Maybe he was sedated or maybe his body simply ran out of energy, but he stopped fighting and yelling and wanting to tear the place down. Days disappeared. He lost all track of time. Mr Greaves was there, talking to him in a soft voice whenever he was conscious, though his words meant nothing.

Gradually his senses came back. Perhaps they stopped the drugs. Perhaps his brain just said enough is enough. He was transferred to the dormitory again and he lay alone for a day while the other Initiates were at their classes. His terror subsided. His anger cooled and the next morning they forced him out of bed with the others and told him he must return to the usual Schola schedule.

After morning classes, Mr Greaves took him aside. He asked him if he was okay and Oliver was too numb to think what a stupid question this was. There were black blotches round his eyes and his skin was parchment pale. Grimly, he nodded. Yes, he was fine.

Mr Greaves looked hard at him, then slipped a corner of paper into Oliver's hand. 'This is my mobile. If you ever need someone to speak to – day or night – call me.'

But what Eli Greaves could not see – what none of the scanners outside the door of the Operations Support Unit would pick up when Oliver at last returned – was that he brought with him a new darkness. When he once again sat at his corner desk with the leaden skies of Edinburgh all around and listened to her ma'amship lecturing him, he carried in his gut a dreadful new conviction, an implacable thirst for revenge.

The police were fools. The media, peddlers of fiction. His father had nothing to do with the murder of his mother. He knew this in his heart. The Pantheon had murdered his parents and – come what may – he would make someone pay.

XXIII

The place was as bleak as she remembered it.

The floor was littered with glass, bricks and patches of nettles. The windows were broken. Graffiti sprawled on every surface like lichen. The air managed to be at once stale and much colder than the night beyond. When she had stood there a year ago, moonlight had poured between the columns, but now rain pattered on the roof and leaked through every seam. Somewhere a generator rumbled to ensure corner lighting augmented the stuttering candles before they gave out and left everyone fumbling like moles.

Calder peered through the door, which was still off its hinges. Beyond the dais where Kustaa had begun the evening's proceedings with a short speech that lacked all of Radspakr's rhetorical flair, she could just make out her Thralls standing stiffly in two rows halfway down the disused warehouse. Freyja was with them and Kustaa was calling them up one at a time, and Calder knew they were being given their names. She ached to hear, but the distance was too far and the rain too persistent in its thrumming.

There were twelve Thralls now. Four had failed the grade as their training in the vaults had become more brutal. When she had been given her name in the Nineteenth Season, she had stood there with just five others – Punnr, Brante, Hertha, Erland and Vidar. She remembered their shock as Radspakr had called forth eight Perpetuals and introduced the Thralls to their competition.

The memory made her shift from the doorway and look over her shoulder. Ten figures stood in a silent line disappearing down the darkened corridor, waiting for her signal. All wore black T-shirts and carried training shields and wooden swords held loosely at their sides. There was no fidgeting or betrayal of nerves. Their posture was relaxed, yet disciplined and she thought they looked more formidable than she could ever have imagined. So here was this Season's competition. The best of Year Four from the Schola. Ten Lost Children. Ten Perpetuals who would each fight – and no doubt kill – for their place as one of the nine Thegns called up to the Horde this year.

Calder pondered the numbers. Twelve Thralls. Ten Perpetuals. For eight places. It would be a hard fight in the forested slopes beyond the Great Glen in a few weeks.

She heard her name and spun back to the doorway. The Thralls were all back in place and Kustaa was beckoning impatiently in her direction.

'Follow me,' she whispered, but the Perpetuals were already coming, walking with grim purpose towards her. She stepped through the door and descended the dais, hearing the detritus crunch beneath her boots. She could sense them snaking out behind her, their training weapons held in confident hands, their stares boring into the group of Thralls. Ahead of her, she could see the faces of her twelve charges and read the shock in their eyes.

Calder brought the Perpetuals to a halt in line in the

centre of the warehouse and then gave way as Freyja took charge.

'Perpetuals!' the Housecarl bawled with the same parade-ground voice she had used the last time Calder stood in that place. 'Present arms!'

Ten shields locked and ten sword arms swept up. The newcomers took a unified step forward and held.

'Perpetuals! Advance!'

They marched towards the Thralls.

'Halt and brace!'

They stopped twelve paces from the Thrall lines, their eyes boring over their shield rims.

Calder peered at her pupils. Over the last weeks she had come to know them as well as anyone can in the confines of the vaults. They were a tough bunch. Competitive and driven. But they had not yet handled training weapons and shields, and now they stared at the Perpetuals as if they were ghosts. Calder recalled her own first impressions of these apparitions a year ago. She had just been congratulated by Radspakr and given her name and she was feeling undeniably pleased with herself. Then Ulf and Gulbrand, Signe, Einar, Eluf, Havaldr and the others had stepped into her life and she had understood in a heartbeat what fearful challenges still lay ahead. Now she could see this realisation spreading across the faces of her Thralls and she felt she had betrayed their trust by keeping the secret of these rivals from them.

'Advance attack!' yelled Freyja and the ten newcomers came at the Thralls, sweeping the air with their wooden blades. Just before the moment of impact, they halted and presented their weapons, only a hair's breadth from the

Thralls. There was silence as the lines eyeballed each other, weighing up the opposition, searching for tell-tale signs of weakness.

Calder remembered it was the moment when Punnr had not been able to resist a comment. '*Is that all you got?*' he had whispered to the man in his face. He must have thought his defiance had gone unnoticed by the other Thralls, but Calder had heard him and she had caught the expression in the Perpetual's eyes when he had snarled back: '*Look out for me.*' Little had they known at the time, Ulf was not the forgiving type.

'Perpetuals! Slope arms,' Freyja ordered and the ten took a half step back and swept their swords onto their shoulders.

It seemed the moment of greatest tension had passed. To their credit, the Thralls had held their ground and Calder was ready to lead the Perpetuals away, when something must have been said. A whispered exchange. An insult. A cocky curl of the lip. It was enough to make Thrall XIV lunge at the throat of the youth in front of him and then all hell broke loose. The lines collapsed. Bodies slammed into each other. Fists flew. Rivals grappled. Wooden blades thumped against bones.

Kustaa was shouting and waving his arms ineffectually, the bedlam utterly beyond his control. Freyja hauled a Thrall from the mass and hollered at her. Calder stepped in too and shoved a Perpetual. For a second the man thought to swipe his sword at her, but the fire in her eyes stopped him and he controlled himself. Freyja was in the centre of the carnage by now and she had Thrall XIV by the scruff of the neck, yanking him up from where he was twisting on the floor with one of the Perpetuals. She threw him backwards, took a breath and yelled with all the force in her lungs, 'Get in line!'

Somehow her sheer presence broke through their anger. Fists paused. Bodies slowed. She dragged the Perpetual to his feet and Calder shouldered one of the female Thralls.

'Get in line!' the Housecarl roared again, volcanoes in her eyes, and the figures broke apart, shuffling back into order. She glared around her and waited until the lines were straight and no one moved. 'Perpetuals. Retire.'

The ten stepped smartly backwards.

'Left face.' They spun on their heels towards the dais.

'And dismiss.' The Perpetuals strode to the platform, filed through the door and were gone.

Kustaa shifted uneasily, his mouth open and his eyes bouncing round the room. Freyja turned back to the Thralls. 'You just showed me that you really want this. But you ever – *ever* – break order again and I'll tear you apart before I throw you from the Pantheon.' She let them think about this. 'Tomorrow night we move to sword and shield practice. Now get out of my sight.'

The Thralls trudged disconsolately out to the waiting cars.

'May Odin fortify you,' Kustaa called after them, then glanced at the two shieldmaidens and beat a hasty retreat.

Freyja approached her fellow Raven. 'That's never happened before,' she said, hands on hips.

'Someone obviously incited the situation. To be fair, we set them up for confrontation by marching them into each other's faces.'

Freyja harrumphed. 'We train them hard now.'

'I know.'

'I don't just mean to punish them. We train them hard because we have to now. Enmity has been forged tonight and when we release them in the *Sine Missione*, that forest is going to drown in blood.'

Oliver was not sent back to the Operations Support Unit for a fortnight and in that time he came to understand three things.

First, he was a Lost Child now and, under such circumstances, there were worse places to be than the Schola. The unremitting structure of Schola life allowed no time for him to wallow in grief and he was surrounded by other Initiates who had not seen their parents in years or maybe never known them at all. The mindset of those around him was: *Take the hit, then get up and hit back harder* – and, as if to prove the point, Frog and his Hastiliarii bawled even louder at Oliver.

The second thing he understood was that his absence from the OSU was not on compassionate grounds. An almighty row had broken out between the staff of the Schola and the OSU. Mallard and Greaves were furious that a secret they had successfully kept from Oliver for six months had been blown and they suspected the leak must have occurred during his time at the OSU. But no one seemed to know the specifics of how he had found out and he wanted it kept that way. So he muddied the waters. He dropped hints that he had overheard casual talk at the Schola weeks earlier and his breakdown at the OSU was a case of delayed response to trauma. He doubted Greaves believed him, but it was enough to have everyone scratching their heads.

Third, Oliver convinced himself that no matter how his parents had spent their last moments and who had been present to witness their demise, the authority behind the actions was Odin. The Caelestis seemed to believe that Oliver could find him Morgan Maitland and must have judged the lad should be taken from his old life. For that, he needed the parents silenced. A new urge seeded itself in Oliver. He must meet Odin, look this man in the eyes and scour them for guilt. He must know for certain if Odin was responsible. And if that meant he must get serious about the search for Morgan Maitland, so be it. Find a new lead, impress her ma'amship and perhaps he would be given the chance to get closer to the Caelestis.

When Oliver finally returned to the penthouse offices on Quartermile, Tyler's laptop was gone. Aurora hovered in her cubicle, raining ice stares on him and wondering why Kustaa wanted this troublemaker back in her unit. But Jed had hit the nail on the head when he said she was just an accountant who had grappled her way up the greasy pole. Silently Oliver promised himself, she would never see him climbing that pole behind her until it was too late.

'Does Odin ever come here?' he asked Jed in a low voice one afternoon. 'I mean actually to this office?'

Jed cast a sideways glance at him. 'Sometimes. When he's in town.'

'Perhaps over Christmas?'

'If you owned a fistful of tropical islands, would you spend Christmas in Edinburgh?'

Oliver conceded the point with a twitch of his nose.

'But,' continued Jed, 'he's always here in the new year for the *Agonium Martiale*.'

Of course. The *Agonium Martiale* on the night after Hogmanay. The annual parading of the two rival Palatinates below Arthur's Seat. It was an occasion favoured by the presence of both Caelestes.

That was it then. That was his chance.

The fledgling Companion Cavalry trained every day and while their early hostility failed to dissipate, its sharp edges at least rounded.

It helped that they loved their horses. On the first morning, Dio had led them to the stables and they recognised instantly the quality of these fine Arabian mounts. As each ran appraising eyes over frame and muscle, and wordlessly calculated which beast they would make their own, Dio had steered Heph to one of the greys and indicated with a raised brow that he had already taken the opportunity to choose the most suitable for his friend. At fourteen hands, this one was smaller and finer-boned than Fergus, but muscle rippled across his withers and any fool could see he had been born to run. He twitched his tail arrogantly when Heph ran a hand along his spine. His flanks were dappled, running to obsidian on his legs and mane, and his eyes coal black. His name was Boreas, god of the north wind, and Heph loved him.

There was tension when Spyros, Zephyr and Maia all wanted the same chestnut called Skylla, but the deadlock was broken when Spyros waved offhandedly and declared that a lady should have first choice, leaving Zephyr no option but to accede. They saddled their beasts and fixed bits and bridles with the assurance of riders who had done this many times. Heph copied Dio, who had stood proprietarily beside the largest chestnut – named Xanthos – wearing an expression that would brook no debate.

When they led them out, they realised these horses were not only strong and swift, but well trained. The beasts walked easily beside their new riders and stood firm as Dio, Maia and Zephyr placed feet into stirrups and mounted. The others followed suit and Dio led them on the first of many circuits of the field. As they eased up to a trot, it became apparent to all that Heph was the least experienced. His mount, Boreas, trotted confidently enough and responded to commands, but Heph's posture was rigid with nerves and he creaked arrhythmically against the movements of his beast. Zephyr spat derisively and Lenore shot Heph a look that would wither forests.

As evening slunk across the hedgerows, the minibus and car returned and waited in the yard as the riders brushed and fed their new mounts. They bedded them in individual stalls to avoid conflict between the stallions, laid straw, filled hay nets and settled them for the night. Lenore, Maia and Pallas were already in the bus when Spyros wandered casually into the farmhouse, peered around the kitchen and headed upstairs to open each of the bedroom doors.

'I'm staying,' he announced on his return.

'Why?' Zephyr demanded belligerently.

'My orders are to become an integral part of this new unit and my horse doesn't live in the city.'

Dio inclined his head in agreement.

'Suit yourself,' Zephyr responded brusquely and bent inside the minibus.

Heph watched the two figures at the farmhouse doorway

as his car took him down the bumpy drive and he felt the heat of embarrassment prickle up his neck. He was the leader of this group. He should be setting the example. So why the hell was he heading back to the city in a comfortable Saab? That night he threw together a bagful of belongings and the next morning as he arrived once more in the farmyard, he told his driver he would not be needing him again.

It seemed the others had come to the same conclusion because they alighted from the minibus with their belongings in hand. There were not enough rooms to go around and when Heph threw his bag beside the kitchen hearth and announced he would sleep there, young Pallas grinned and dropped his rucksack there too.

They spent their daylight hours with their mounts. At dawn, after steaming bowls of porridge, they trekked to the barns in the early chill and fell into the rituals of experienced stablehands. They checked the horses over, tied them up, then mucked out, cleaned water buckets, adjusted rugs and gave them their first feed. By eight, they were saddling up and emerging to the grey light of another November morning. Throughout each day, they walked, trotted and cantered around the field. They split into halves and circled. They constructed obstacles to weave around and small jumps to negotiate. They took the horses onto the surrounding lanes and slipped through gates to explore changing terrain. And there were smiles.

These Titans might still view the grander enterprise with cynicism, but there was no hiding their delight at taking Pantheon pay to spend hours in the saddle. Middays saw second feeds for the stallions, while the seven riders retired to the farmhouse for soup and hunks of bread, which Dio warmed in the oven. When the afternoons grew late and the light receded at a gallop, they brushed the horses, picked out their hooves, rugged them up, shook out bedding and gave them a final feed, then the fire was stoked in the farmhouse kitchen and meals prepared. Lenore and Pallas slid easily into helping Dio with curries, casseroles and tagines, while the others sat on benches and contemplated the flames. As the evenings passed, there were long silences and violent arguments, which flared from nowhere and spluttered fitfully. But there was also good food and alcohol and the warmth of a fire and tensions began to thaw as each of them grew more at ease with the company they kept.

In fact, Heph could have been excused for believing it was going well. Zephyr might be forever cantankerous, Spyro distantly aloof and Lenore marble-hard whenever he glanced at her, but they all rode confidently on their new steeds. They cantered in formation, knee to knee, and on fine days took the beasts up to a gallop without the line disintegrating. Even Heph found himself improving and they scowled at him less and seemed content to follow his directions.

The *Agonium Martiale* was still four weeks away and it was good, Heph thought. Zeus could not fail to be impressed.

Then one morning a van pulled up carrying wooden crates. As they wrenched them open in a yard thick with frost and discovered fur pelts, strange new bridles and ten-foot lances, it dawned on them that what had been achieved so far was only the first of the tests this infant cavalry must pass.

XXIV

'Does it seem strange?' asked Freyja, toying with a glass of Chardonnay.

'It feels like only yesterday,' said Calder as she stared at the rushing night beyond the train window. 'I can remember what we said, what we ate, how we felt. I could pretty much walk down the carriage now and point to the seats we were in.'

'If she could, what would your new self tell your old self?'

'Run. Get out while you can.'

'Really?'

Calder shrugged. 'Maybe not. But if I told my old self she'd be the only one of our group of six still standing in Valhalla in twelve months, she would never have believed me. Three dead and two deserted. I'm all that's left.'

She swivelled in her seat and looked down the empty carriage to where the new Thrall cohort was clustered. Ten of them now. Two more had fallen by the wayside during the weapons-training weeks. Ten Thralls to meet ten Perpetuals to compete for eight places as Thegns in Valhalla. There was a certain neatness about the numbers, but Calder shivered at the incontrovertible maths that dictated the coming days must rid the process of twelve young people.

The Thrall pair who reminded her of Punnr and Brante were still present. Thrall XIV had earned the name Rangvald. He possessed the height and ability of Brante, but he wore his temper for all to see. It was him who had kicked off the brawl in the warehouse when they first clapped eyes on the Perpetual contingent and Freyja had roasted his bollocks for that. Thrall X was now Sten. His quiet drive conjured in her visions of the early Punnr, limping and sickly, yet irresistibly magnetic, but Sten was a plainer, less charismatic version.

There was Estrid too, a girl with the most beautiful cream complexion and soulful chocolate eyes. Kustaa had said she was from Taiwan originally, but he would give away no more. She had entered the vaults one night with a flower in her hair, yet was the fastest of them all with a blade.

They had finished their food and were talking quietly and drinking the wine. Calder could see the strain on their faces and wished she could be part of their conversation. She remembered her own nerves as a similar train swept her through the night to her fate.

'We should tell them what they face,' she said, turning back to Freyja.

'We didn't tell you.'

'I wish you had, instead of sending me into that place without a clue.'

Freyja rained hard eyes on her. 'No you don't. Do you really think you'd have wanted to stew over the news that you'd find weapons caches and be expected to kill to win your place?'

'It might have saved Hertha,' Calder replied tartly, but did not push the subject.

Sveinn's Mead Hall at the heart of the castle in the heart of nowhere was just as she remembered when they arrived close to midnight, but as they settled to food and fire and furs, it pined for the ghost of Halvar. It needed his presence, his rich voice conjuring tales of Asgard, Niflheim and Vanaheim. It needed his bulk filling these nervous Thralls with the spirit to be the best of themselves. But they had never known him and so they bit at their food and grinned restlessly as they listened to Freyja instead and watched the flames dance.

It was the first time the Housecarl and her deputy had spent downtime with their charges outside of the vaults and Calder felt closer to them than she had ever done. She told herself it was just the mead, but she knew in her heart it was because this moment of togetherness was so ephemeral. Later, as the fire dwindled and they wrapped themselves in furs and drifted into sleep, she felt Rangvald's leg reach out and touch hers. His eyes were moons in the dark and his mead lips so close.

'Go to sleep,' she whispered. 'You have a trek tomorrow.'

They gathered beneath the beams in Sveinn's Mead Hall on three further occasions, drinking and bonding, and in between they trained and marched and prepared. Atilius arrived and spoke to them, purple-smocked as ever. Kustaa was there too. He floated around the perimeter of proceedings, listening and watching, seemingly as jumpy as the Thralls. Then on the penultimate evening, they heard helicopter rotors on the lawns to the east and Calder felt a new presence oozing down from the higher floors of the keep and permeating the stones themselves. Lord Odin had come to witness the contest.

Finally, it was the inevitable dawn when the vehicles came and she watched her recruits leave, like mothers must have done down the ages when their sons went to war.

Valhalla sent them into the forest in fives and for this, at least, Calder was thankful. She had always known the choices of the year before had been unprecedented. Back then, she and the others had crossed through the boundary fencing in pairs – one Thrall, one Perpetual – and she remembered the consternation in Freyja's eyes. It was a decision that had come from much higher authorities and could only result in a faster blooding of blades.

But now, Calder and Freyja watched the live feeds on monitors in an antechamber off the Hall as a horn sounded over the forest and the first group of five Thralls – dressed in fur hats and russet cloaks fastened with a Triple Horn of Odin clasp – was herded through the fence line in the murky drizzle of a Highland winter's morning, followed by the second at a gate three miles further round the perimeter. For a moment, one figure looked straight into the camera of the Vigilis in the watchtower. It was Estrid. Calder would have recognised her alabaster skin anywhere. The deep pools of her eyes bore into the lens, then she blinked once and turned to follow her companions.

At the same moment, two similar groups of Perpetuals stalked through two similar gates, moving with confidence and purpose. Calder knew such groupings should mean each weapons cache could be discovered without opposition and then it would be easier to build shieldwalls together and fend off attack. Perhaps, this year, the *Sine Missione* could be decided by the first eight to reach the tower and hold it, without the outpouring of blood last year's decisions had provoked.

But the gods had other plans.

Calder had no idea how long she gripped the edge of a table as she stared at the live feeds, barely daring to shift her eyes, while Freyja sat sullenly next to her and ate grapes. Kustaa would be surrounded by his screens in Radspakr's old office and Atilius and Odin prowled the upper reaches of the keep, so it was just the two Ravens who witnessed events unfold in the small antechamber off the hall.

The two groups of Perpetuals moved like lightning, jogging down tracks away from the fence. Calder had always suspected the Perpetuals were fed information and now they seemed to know what they were looking for. Camera traps at path junctions showed them briefly debating, then loping onwards, covering the ground, dropping ever deeper into the forested glen. The Thralls, by contrast, walked cautiously, eyeing the trees and spending an age pointing and arguing at each branching of the track. There was rain in the air and they kept their hats firmly pulled down, so it was difficult for Calder to make out individual features, but she recognised Rangvald's height and thought Estrid still loitered at the rear of the first group.

The Perpetuals discovered their respective weapons caches while the Thralls were still wandering. From the drone footage high above, Calder could see the silent thoroughness with which they armed. Swords, spears, shields. Then – like wolves – they scented the air and made their selections. Group one went south on an approximate course to intersect the first Thralls. Group two chose west to cross the river, then tracked the far bank to find their prey. Calder glanced at Freyja, but the Housecarl would not meet her eyes.

To their watching audience, the progress of the Thralls seemed glacial. Calder remembered covering ground quicker when she had been in that same forest, but perhaps this was because she had been with the Perpetual Einar and maybe he kept her moving. Maybe he knew about the weapons awaiting them and took her at pace towards them.

The second group of Thralls reached a junction above the river and the Ravens watched from a camera feed on a nearby pine as the five of them gesticulated. The lens brought Calder and Freyja close enough to touch them. They could see the expressions, sense the argument.

'What are you doing, you fools?' Freyja demanded.

'Oh god, no,' Calder breathed.

The Thralls were splitting up. Amid much waving of angry arms, two took the path north along the bank and three dropped towards a bridge.

'What the hell are you thinking?' Freyja could not control her exasperation and smacked the table.

The feed switched to a drone high above and as it panned out it caught Perpetuals weaving between the trees, heading for the bridge. They would come across the lone pair first and it was only minutes before they spotted them. The Perpetuals fanned out and closed. The two Thralls had seen them but did not realise their opponents were armed. They stood their ground like the brave individuals they were and Calder buried her face in her hands. She did not need to witness these deaths. When she looked again, Freyja's face was rigid and the Perpetuals were jogging south along the track, spears bloodied.

The feed switched again to a clearing on the other side of the river. The first group of Thralls had finally come across their cache. They were examining the weapons and strapping swords to hips.

'Thank god,' said Calder. It was Rangvald's and Estrid's group. The muggy morning meant they had removed their hats and she could also recognise Sten.

But the camera revealed more movement in the trees to the north and the other five Perpetuals stepped into the clearing. They came in line, but held their weapons loosely and waited for their opponents. The Thralls burst into activity, grabbing shields and spears and shouting instructions to each other. They pulled themselves into a ragged shieldwall and set their legs apart with spear points wavering in the drizzle. The Perpetuals walked towards them in casual disarray and then flung their spears. Two drove hard into the shields of their foe and a third took a Thrall full in the face and dropped him like a stone. Rangvald could be seen raging at his three remaining companions to close the gap. Silently, the Perpetuals drew swords and brought their shields together in a rigid wall. And then they were upon them.

To Calder, watching a feed from far above, the two lines seemed to embrace and curve in a sinuous dance, but she knew the reality would be a kicking, cursing melee, the thump of shields and the cloying fear of a foot slipping on rain-soaked earth. From amid the chaos, she spied a pattern emerging and could almost sense the inevitable before it even happened. Rangvald fought like a god in the centre, stabbing with his spear and keeping his adversaries at bay, but they were bending around the edges and letting him come.

'Stay in line, you fool,' Freyja hissed.

But Rangvald's blood was singing with the conflict. He thrust his spear into a shield and left it hanging, then tore his sword from his hip and waved it wildly above his head. Calder knew he would be goading them, just as he had done in the warehouse and calling on his companions to follow him. But Sten and Estrid could not move on the flanks because their adversaries were snaking around them. Then the fourth Thrall stumbled and the blades of two Perpetuals jabbed into her and that was the moment of collapse. Rangvald was deep between the Perpetuals. Sten and Estrid could not hold. They turned and ran for the cover of the trees and their foe allowed them because they had larger prey to gorge on. They closed the circle and Calder watched as Rangvald beat and cursed and swung his blade, screaming into the implacable faces of his five attackers as they cut him down in the centre of the clearing, hacking at him and then stamping on his body until there was no movement. One of them looked up at the whine of the drone and pumped a fist at the camera. Then they sheathed their swords, collected their spears and ran after Sten and Estrid.

Now events for the watchers descended into a clutter of chaotic moments. The players no longer kept to paths and the tree cameras only picked up occasional flurries of movement. The drones tried to follow the packs from above, but the density of the forest meant their audience could only witness the action properly when the trees gave way.

The day stretched into afternoon. The rain came heavier and still the Raven pair sat in their antechamber and strained to decode transient images. From what they could tell, the three remaining Thralls from the second group had crossed the river, discovered their weapons cache without hitch and climbed one of the switchback paths on the other side, steering towards the tower on the hill. But they must have spied or sensed pursuers because they stopped on a bank halfway up and decided to abandon the path. Threading into the trees, the forest closed over them once more.

Of Estrid and Sten, there was nothing.

An hour passed while the screen switched from one view of sodden foliage to another and then, at last, a camera trap on a trunk caught Perpetuals. The Ravens could not tell which group, but there were only two now, not five, and they had lost their swagger. They looked tired and chilled. Their blades were drawn and one gripped his arm and grimaced at a hidden wound. They glanced briefly at the camera, then hurried out of frame.

The minutes leaked away. Outside the winter sky was darkening beyond the rain and, within the claustrophobic spaces beneath the forest's canopy, night would already be reclaiming its throne. Calder's nerves were shredded and even Freyja was pacing in and out of the doorway, needing to get away from the screen, yet desperate to miss nothing. At last, the drones picked up movement high on the hill. Five cloaked figures, running in a line up a thin track in the direction of the tower. At first the Ravens assumed it must be one of the Perpetual groups, but then they noticed there was a larger gap between the first figure and the rest and it dawned on them that this was a chase.

They were desperate to identify the lead runner, but the rain veiled everything. The incline was steep and the person was obviously tiring. They slipped in the mud and hauled themselves up.

'Come on,' Calder found herself urging. 'Keep moving.'

Freyja was beside her. 'Whoever it is, they don't have much left in the tank.'

Just as it seemed inevitable that the chasing pack would catch their prey, a sixth figure appeared from the trees behind the group and threw itself uphill. A blade flickered and the last in line of the pursuers collapsed. The other three turned, took in this new threat and flung themselves back down the path. More blades swung and the group fused, but the track was thin and the three assailants could not take advantage of their number.

'If that's one of our Thralls,' Freyja said grimly, 'I honour their courage, but they're not going to survive this.'

Beyond the walls of the antechamber a hubbub broke the evening gloaming. Rotors. The *Sine Missione* would end at dusk and Valhalla's helicopters were preparing to collect those still standing.

And then the unexpected. The first figure – the one who had been chased up the path – refused to use the opportunity to disappear. Instead they turned and charged down into the melee, cleaving the gloom with their sword.

'Are you coming?' Freyja demanded as she strode to the door.

'What?'

'It's time to get them.'

Calder tore herself from the screen, but her Housecarl was already gone. She stared again at the struggle before her, then swore and dashed from the room.

The elements raged as she ran onto the lawns and the

rotors flung the rain into her face. She hauled herself into the first cockpit beside Freyja and the castle disappeared below them. Calder had no idea how the pilot could navigate. Rain pounded the glass and it seemed to her that there was nothing but a sea of night beneath. But within minutes they were dropping and she could make out the tower.

The three helicopters landed on an open patch of ground and the Ravens were out, carrying blankets and bent beneath the rotors, then running across the last few hundred yards to the tower. There were four figures awaiting them and Calder felt a stone in her gut as she saw no face she recognised. The Perpetuals were striding towards them, but then they stopped and looked down the hill. Two more cloaked figures were running desperately towards the group, blades lost, boots slipping in the mud. Perpetuals too, but Calder's eyes were drawn to a spot in the trees behind them. Was there movement in the dark or simply the writhing of branches in the onslaught of the rotors?

The pair reached the main group, collapsed and looked back. There was a long pause and then two more souls stepped from the trees. They walked calmly now, their hats lost and their cloaks thrown wide and Calder gasped with relief. For they lived. Estrid and Sten.

The *Sine Missione* had chosen its eight.

The Ravens gave blankets to everyone and herded them into the helicopters. If anyone else still breathed on those hills, they would be found in the morning by the *libitinarii*.

Pressed against a shivering Perpetual and listening to the thrumming of the rotors as they were carried back to the warmth of the castle, Calder's elation drained away. She thought of the weeks in the training vaults. The figures

THE HASTENING STORM

pounding the apparatus. The faces that gazed at her as she
demonstrated each fighting move with Freyja. Sixteen they
had started with. Then twelve at the naming ceremony and
ten on the train north.

And for what? To recover from this place just two.

In the hours to come she would grieve. She would
pace her living quarters and cry for those she had lost and
ask herself again and again if she had trained them well
enough, if she had prepared them properly for the tests
that night.

But for now, all she could do was stare down at the
infinite blackness and pray she would never lay eyes on that
forest again.

XXV

'This is a bloody joke,' spat Zephyr, slinging his skin saddlecloth on the ground.

A watery December sun had risen, but it was enough to melt the frost that had dusted the farmyard when they first emerged. Heph sat on a fence, smoking and watching his unit come to terms with the contents of the crates. At first they had assumed the pelts were underlays to be placed beneath their current saddles to minimise any discomfort for the horse, but it was Lenore who put paid to this theory.

'From the size of them, these look like *lion* skins and I suspect putting one under a saddle is going to ruin the fit against the horse's back. Besides, look at the straps stitched to each pelt. These are designed to go around the girth. Who's going to girth a lion skin and then girth a saddle on top?'

Her question needed no answer.

'Someone's having a laugh at our expense,' said Spyro solemnly, inspecting the iron snaffle bits and basic bridles that were also packed into the crates.

'So you're saying we use these instead of our saddles?' asked Pallas.

'That's the damn idea, lad,' replied Zephyr, stalking away

and leaning against the farmhouse door with his hands in his pockets.

Lenore was crouching over one of the crates, still examining the pelts. 'How would we fix stirrups to these?'

'No stirrups,' said Heph from his perch.

All faces turned to him.

'Completely bareback?' Maia demanded and Heph nodded.

Zephyr laughed. 'Well, you can play your merry games, Viking boy, but count me out.' He shoved the farm door open and disappeared.

Lenore and Maia followed and from the kitchen their raised voices could be heard.

Spyro looked at Heph. 'If you still want a Companion Cavalry, Hephaestion, I think it's time you got off that fence and showed some leadership.'

He was right. Heph stamped out his cigarette and strode into the farmhouse with Pallas and Spyro tracking him. The others were standing around the kitchen table, the atmosphere as taut as a bowstring. Zephyr had his phone in hand and looked on the point of calling for a taxi to whisk him away from these idiots. Lenore had her arms tightly folded and refused to meet anyone's eyes.

Heph deliberately pulled out a chair and seated himself, and Spyro took another, reversed it and sat astride. Pallas stepped to the sink and filled the kettle.

'What are you doing?' hissed Maia.

'I figure we all need tea.'

And no one could argue with that.

'Okay,' said Heph over the kettle rumbling on the stovetop. 'I didn't see this coming any more than the rest of you. But now that it has, it sort of makes sense. If we really are going to be the first seven members of a Companion Cavalry, then we have to do it properly.'

He looked at Zephyr and the older man held his gaze as Heph continued. 'You're right, I was a Viking boy last Season and I stood on the opposing side at the Blood Battle, but I saw you, Zephyr, you and the rest of your Phalanx. I saw how you carved a trail of death across that beach step by step. Nothing could stand against your sarissas, no force could hold you in place. And you know why?'

'Because we're the best,' the Titan Heavy growled. 'No Viking Hammer wall is going to stop us.'

'And why are you the best? Because you've spent years emulating and mastering the techniques of Alexander's ancient Phalanx warriors. Your skills are those that won him the fields at Granicus and Issus; that ground through the limitless Persian hordes at Gaugamela and the Indian lines at Hydaspes. The death you bring with your sarissas is no different from the devastation wrought by the Heavy Brigades of Perdiccas and Craterus. You stand in the front line of an ancient Macedonian Phalanx reborn.'

They watched him now, caught by this unexpected oratory, as Pallas silently placed mugs of tea in front of each.

'So it must be with us. We can't claim to be a Companion Cavalry if we are not true to what they were. Alexander tore across the known world in 300 BC, centuries before the widespread use of stirrups and saddles as we know them today. So we must ride as he did, with nothing but those skins.'

Maia sighed and shook her head and Zephyr murmured obscenities at the back of his throat.

'What's the matter Phalanx-man?' Spyro asked clutching his mug. 'You afraid of falling off?'

'Fuck off, Spyro.'

'The Huns do it,' interrupted Lenore.

'Do what?'

'Ride without stirrups. The Mongol Kheshig jaguns use saddles and stirrups because these items had been invented by the thirteenth century when Genghis Khan came to his prime, but Attila's Huns were nine centuries earlier and they rode without them. So the Hun Palatinate now forgoes them as well.'

'But they've had twenty Seasons to hone their skills,' protested Zephyr. 'We've got weeks.'

'So maybe,' mused Spyro, 'we shouldn't be sitting here drinking tea.'

From beyond the farmhouse walls they heard heavy footfall on the gravel in the yard. Pallas leaned over the sink to look out the window and grinned from ear to ear. They all herded back to the front door and there was Dio seated on Xanthos, stirrup-less, saddleless except for the lion pelt, his left hand gripping a new bridle and his right holding a lance.

'So are we doing this or not?'

And so they did.

They grabbed the other cloths and bridles and followed Dio and Xanthos back to the stables. As they busied themselves strapping the pelts to their mounts, Dio explained quietly to Heph that he was no expert in bareback riding, but he had on occasion walked Fergus from the stables without bothering to saddle up and he had also spent time in his family's library reading about the principles and techniques of such riding to better understand Alexander's horse troops.

When they were ready, he insisted they all wore safety helmets and then led them onto the grass. The frost had melted and it was soft and squelchy underfoot, but perhaps this was for the best.

'Okay, mounting,' he said. 'Not easy, but not as hard as you think. With the rein in your left hand, take hold of a big clump of mane as high up towards the ears as you can. Then grab more mane with your right hand down by the shoulder. The power must come from your left arm. Use it to pull yourself off the ground, then use your right to guide yourself onto your mount's back. Like so.'

Dio eased up in one flowing motion and Xanthos stood nonchalantly as though nothing had happened.

What followed was a mess. The Titans' would-be elite cavalry struggled and swore and slipped and fell as their mounts peered at them balefully. Pallas made it first, his light frame lending him wings. He whooped and grinned at Dio. Lenore got her leg over and manoeuvred upright, but she must have brushed her horse's back because it jolted forward and she slid straight off. She wiped herself down, refused to look at anyone and grabbed a handful of mane once more.

'Sorry, boy,' Heph whispered to Boreas, feeling bad about using his mane like a length of rope, but Boreas just watched his struggles out one eye and waited. By the fourth attempt Heph could hold himself high enough with his left arm to hoist his right leg over the great spine before him and then he slithered inelegantly into position.

Spyro was up too, keeping his horse calm and still, and

Lenore stayed put on her second attempt. But heavier-set Zephyr and Maia were still grounded and staying that way. Zephyr's face was black with fury again and when Dio dismounted, retrieved one of the crates and told him to stand on it, he let loose a tirade.

'Just use it,' Dio said, unimpressed and went to collect another for Maia.

To begin with, as they walked their beasts around the perimeter of the field, it wasn't too bad. It felt alien to be without the control of stirrups, but they could feel the movements of their mounts much better beneath them and natural riding instincts came to the fore.

'Don't sit as far back as you normally would in a saddle,' called Dio from the front of the line. 'Pull yourself up towards the withers and let your legs hang straighter down the sides. Keep your top half loose and grip your horse with your thighs. Hold him there. Feel him there.'

They followed his example, but when he eventually pulled them into an exploratory trot, all advice went out the window. Maia was the first to fall, slamming onto the turf and lying winded. Heph toppled next. He knew he was losing it, but even though he grabbed at Boreas' mane again, it was not enough and the ground rushed up to punch him. He sat in the mud, thankful for his hard hat and ruefully considering what a journey they still had to be capable of smashing through Hammer's shieldwall. Boreas had stopped and was contemplating him, no doubt wondering whether this idiot wished to ride him or not.

And in this way, the days became weeks. Pain became a way of life. They fell constantly. They snarled at each other and stormed away swearing they would never go near a bloody horse again. They limped into the farmhouse at dusk and groaned as they moved. Heph discovered blood in his urine but told no one. Pallas fell badly and dislocated his shoulder. They called an ambulance and he disappeared to hospital in Perth, but was back with a sling and a grin two days later. Every one of them had bruises and cuts across their bodies and sat silently in the evenings with hollow eyes.

There was still so much to achieve. Christmas was approaching and they had not even brought the horses to a canter, nor begun to consider lance and sword work from a saddleless stance. Perhaps it would all be too much. Perhaps Zeus would see this new unit for the foolish experiment it was and spend his Blood Funds more wisely on reinforcements from the Schola.

But they knew they were getting somewhere. They could feel their horses in new ways – the sweat, the muscles, the breathing. They were each becoming at one with their mount. Each growing as riders. And secretly, they were starting to desire the prize.

To fly like their ancient forebears.

To feel the exhilaration of the charge and the yards closing in a breathless rush towards a bristling enemy line.

XXVI

Parmenion's peltasts armoured up in the Prep rooms of Thebes, their eyes shifting constantly to the new face.

Four storeys below, the Royal Mile was as silent as a corpse. Two-thirty in the morning on the second night of the new year, with an icy fog enveloping the Old Town, and the world was asleep.

Hephaestion dressed diligently. The feel and fit of Titan armour was new to him and he had never noticed before that the peltasts wore a different rig from the Hoplites of the Phalanx and Companion brigades. The peltast shields were oval instead of round and their torsos were protected by scale armour rather than heavy bronze cuirasses. He held up the leather jerkin covered in hundreds of small overlapping plates and was surprised to discover its flex. Parmenion wore such a piece when Heph and Dio were first interrogated after the Battle, but his had sparkled silver, whereas this one was bronze and in need of polish. It would provide little defence in the hack and thrust of a shield line, but such close-quarter combat was supposed to be left to the heavily armoured Hoplites. Peltasts were light troops, armed with javelins and tasked with screening the assault units.

He struggled to pull the scales over his head and wedge his arms through the sleeves. Just as he was cursing silently he felt hands take the shoulders and tug it until the scales fell into place. He jumped up and down to allow the weight of the coat to find its own fit, then nodded his thanks to a peltast with streaks of silver surfing the sides of his hair, but the man stepped back to his own preparation without acknowledging him. Heph belted the Titan's traditional shortsword around the scales, tightened his boots and then picked up a helmet that had been waiting for him in his allotted locker. Like all Titan helms, it was rounded and comprised a prominent nose piece that divided the eyeholes, and cheek guards that wrapped round at such height that they hid the face. Once in place, only the eyes of the wearer would be visible.

Peltast helms, however, went without the plumes of the Companions and Band. He wedged on the helmet and noted the perfection of its fit. It seemed every item in the Pantheon arrived tailored for the individual. Weapons had already been collected from the Armouries and now he copied the others as they thrust their left arms through the grips of their oval shields, clutched two javelins with the same left hand and took a third in their right.

Twenty minutes to the hour and the peltasts were ready.

It had only been that lunchtime when the phones of the seven would-be mounted troops buzzed in their farmhouse kitchen. Diogenes the Horsemaster would remain, but Alexander required the others returned to their original units for the *Agonium Martiale*. None of the team had commented, but all knew it was because of them that the Titan Palatinate had such a scant intake of fresh blood in the lines, so the King needed every head he could muster for this grand opening to the Raiding Season.

Heph followed his peltast colleagues up to the Theban rooftop above Cockburn junction, where youngsters from the Schola waited to cast rope ladders over the side. Parmenion was there, his helmet gleaming damp in the fog. There was movement on the street below, the sound of boots marching up the Mile. The Companions would be coming from Persepolis with Alexander and Black Cleitus at their head. The youths threw their ladders and Parmenion swung out into the void. With shields strapped to backs and javelins gripped in one hand, his troops followed and Heph went with them.

'This will play havoc with their cameras,' yelled Freyja over the noise.

As it did each new year, the Horde had come to the valley beneath Arthur's Seat and was roaring its presence. Its ranks had been replenished with Schola Drengrs and new Thegns, and Valhalla once more numbered over two hundred. Bjarke led a Hammer line of a hundred and fourteen. Asmund had four litters of archers and light spear troops. The Wolves were again a force. Thirty-eight, just shy of five litters, with Skarde swaggering at their head. And the Ravens too were something more than the wreckage of five they had ended the Nineteenth with. Two litters now and it seemed right that among their intake were Estrid and Sten. Since the calamity of the *Sine Missione*, Calder had felt drawn to these two survivors and it was good they stood behind the Raven banner.

The fog had risen and hung above their heads, giving them a clearer field of view but denying the overhead drones opportunity for any proper footage. The watching Curiate would have to content themselves with images from Vigiles headcams and the occasional camera fixed to a tripod. Just as last year, the valley was ringed by flaming torches and on a platform behind the warrior lines, Odin surveyed the scene. And just as last year, the Titans had yet to make their entrance.

'I want you at the Council meetings,' Freyja said in Calder's ear.

'Me? In what capacity?'

'Interim Captain of Ravens.'

Calder stared at her Housecarl. 'What about you?'

'I'll be there – don't be alarmed. But I'm to be the King's military adviser this Season and so I want you present to speak for Raven Company.'

She checked around to ensure no unwanted eavesdroppers, but the Berserkers were already goading themselves into rages and the hubbub was too great. 'Sveinn needs a voice of reason beside him and without Halvar, he knows it must be me. Kustaa is Odin's man through and through, and a wet fart to boot. Bjarke is Bjarke. And now we have the pleasure of a mad sadist leading our Wolves. Hardly a pretty bunch. So I will advise our King on strategic matters in council and you will represent the Ravens.'

'As you wish,' said Calder, imagining the small Council Chamber above Sveinn's Throne Room heavy with the presence of Skarde.

There was a roar from Hammer's lines.

'And so we are graced,' said Freyja looking up the

fog-infested slope on the other side of the valley. 'Fashionably late as ever.'

It was an important night in Valhalla's OSU and four members of the Tech team were hunched over their terminals, while across the room Aurora sat restlessly in her office. Outside, the fog hugged the Quartermile buildings. Oliver had asked if he could join the night shift for this special occasion and she had made a meal of considering it before giving her consent on the strict understanding that he was just an observer. She phoned Eli and told him the driver should come for the lad at five the next morning.

'Is this as good as it gets?' asked Oliver as he stared at his computer.

'Pretty much,' replied Jed, not taking his eyes off his own screen. He was conducting a strained conversation with someone called Golan who was standing on the flanks of Arthur's Seat operating Valhalla's single drone, and Oliver could pick up snippets of Golan's irascible comments over Jed's speakers.

'Give me a break. If I go any lower, I'll literally crash into Sveinn's helmet!'

The reason for their tension was the quality of the footage on the screens. Valhalla's drone was equipped with infrared cameras, but these were doing little more than bathing the fog in a harsh green glare. Flames could just be seen sparking below, sometimes accompanied by clumps of ghostly green humanity, but it was a visual muddle and everyone on the Tech team knew it.

'You got Atilius' feed yet?' Jed demanded of one of his colleagues.

'Just coming through.'

Jed's screen split in two and a second video feed appeared alongside the footage from Valhalla's drone. On this one, the flaring green fog had been replaced by bubbles of reds and yellows.

'Jeez, even the Pantheon's thermal imaging isn't making much headway.'

'At least it's not just us then,' commented a bald man dryly.

Jed accepted the point. On such occasions, it was the footage from Atilius' central Pantheon teams that always fed live to the Curiate, but Odin liked to use Valhalla's drone as an additional source of images for this own reference. If the thermal imaging from the central team cameras had been unaffected by the weather conditions, then Jed's Tech team would have no doubt been roundly bollocked by their Caelestis for using only infrared. As it was, the fog was beating all-comers.

'Guess it's the ground cameras then,' said another team member.

'Hmmm.' Jed was dubious. 'Not really good enough. Nice for the detail, but they won't pick up the grander scale.'

Both feeds were showing new blotches approaching the mass in the centre.

'Here come the Titans,' said the bald man.

Jed leaned into his mic. 'Hey, Golan, are you seriously telling me this is the best you can do?'

Expletives burst from the speakers. 'I'm flying blind – you do realise that?'

'Says here you're at ten metres. Try bringing it to five.'

More colourful language, but Golan complied and for the briefest of seconds the fog relented and the screens filled with masses of green-tinged figures ranged across the hillsides. From behind his own computer, Oliver leaned forward and captured a surreptitious screenshot. The next moment the fog reached out and imprisoned the drone once again.

Aurora came prancing across the office and Oliver thought he had been spotted, but her lasers were set for Jed. 'Get that drone down further.'

'Golan, did you hear the boss?'

'I'm not going lower than five. I'll literally be hitting armour and anyway it won't show anything more than the ground cameras are picking up.'

Her ma'amship considered pulling rank, but in the end she simply glared at Jed and told him it would all be on his head, then retreated to her lair. A look passed around the team and then they hunched back over their screens.

Silently, Oliver pulled up his screenshot.

The Companions went first, headed by Menes, with the Lion Standard of Macedon stirring the fog behind him. As they shouldered past Heph's unit and disappeared over the lip of the hill, the noise from the valley redoubled.

Zeus had prioritised spending some of his Blood Funds on resurrecting his broken Companion lines and now they numbered a respectable twenty-one. But everyone knew it should have been many more. Rumours were flying among the ranks. A hundred and three Blood Funds could buy a huge intake of troops. Why did they not see forty Companions? And why not a hundred and fifty Heavies in the Phalanx, instead of the seven rows of twelve that followed the Companions into the valley?

Some said that Zeus had tied his purse strings and no new troops were coming this Season. There were tales of Cleitus and Nicanor yelling blue murder when Alexander informed them. But others said the reinforcements were being held in reserve and would be with them soon. Whatever the truth, the Titans on that hillside peered at their numbers and listened to the tumult of the enemy in the valley and cursed their luck.

Parmenion raised his javelin, cast an appraising eye over his twenty peltasts and signalled the advance. Heph remembered the year before when he caught his first glimpse of the Titan foe as they sped like gods out of the night and now the peltasts around him broke into a sure-footed run and poured over the edge. Heph was caught in the moment, adrenalin coursing through his veins, and he threw himself down the slope. He was one of them now. One of the wondrous bronzed Titans bursting out of the night, and a grin split his features.

Yet, even as his heart pounded, the noise of Valhalla hit him like a wall. He could see them now, the banners he knew so well, the horns and the painted shields. As his peltasts pulled into position flanking the stationary Phalanx, he realised this was the first time he had looked on the Horde since last Season's Battle. His friends were out there. Ake, Stigr and Unn. Freyja. Asmund. And Calder. And now they hurled hatred at him, filling the valley with the threat of violence. Ingvar and his Berserkers were already staggering and cursing towards the Companion frontlines, axes aloft, beards frothing. Behind them, every Viking smacked sword against limewood shield in a rolling thunder of defiance.

The noise raised to fever pitch as they recognised the blue plumes of the Sacred Band dancing out of the fog and, once more, Heph wondered how the event did not collapse into wholesale slaughter. Somewhere an invisible hand kept these warriors on a leash and as Atilius strode into the middle of the valley floor, growls caught in throats and passion cooled.

The Kings came to meet the Pantheon's Praetor. Alexander looked glorious in his scarlet-plumed gold and Sveinn's silver mail sparkled in the flames. Heph remembered being right there behind his King the previous year, dressed in white armour and not yet appreciating the challenges awaiting Valhalla's White Warrior in the weeks to come. Now Sveinn was accompanied only by Radspakr in his Thane's robes. But was it Radspakr? Heph squinted through the dark. The man wore the same robes and mask, but he looked plump and well-lived, with none of Radspakr's spartan frame. Heph frowned. Why would Radspakr be absent on such a night?

Atilius was speaking and blood bowls had been produced. Alexander stepped away from Simmius, dipped his plumed head, spoke his words and splashed blood onto the Horn of Odin symbol on Sveinn's shield. Then Sveinn growled phrases and splashed more blood across the bronze Lion of Macedon on Alexander's hoplon. The Oaths were complete and the first of the two Conflict Seasons could begin.

Atilius was speaking again and handing scrolls to the kings, but Heph's mind was wandering. He was thinking how many Valhalla looked that night. Lines and lines of shields spreading between the burning torches at each perimeter. A Palatinate fully resourced by its new Blood Funds.

And then he was imagining Dio asleep in the farmhouse, the embers of a fire in the hearth, the fields empty and silent, and seven horses bedded comfortably on new hay, waiting for their riders to return.

There was something eating at Oliver.

It was four-thirty and the show on Arthur's Seat was well over. The feeds had been turned off and the rest of the Tech team had already departed.

'You not leaving?' Jed asked as he sorted his bag and logged out.

'Driver's due at five.'

'Looks like it's just you and the boss then.'

'I thought you said Odin shows his face here when it's the *Agonium Martiale*?'

'Odin does what Odin wants. He's been standing on a freezing hill for the last hour, so I guess he's now somewhere nice drinking a malt in front of a good fire.' He shouldered his bag. 'Right, I'm off. Have a good trip back to the Schola.'

Oliver was left alone in his corner. He checked her ma'amship stewing in her office, then pulled up his screenshot. Despite the momentary retreat of the fog, the image was poor quality and the figures blurred into amorphous green masses. Even so, the drone had been at just the height and angle to capture the full lines of both Palatinates.

Cautiously, he began to tap keys. He created alternate versions of the image and aligned them in layers. He added filters, toyed with luminosity, opacity and exposure. He minimised noise and fine-tuned white balance, shadows and highlights. And little by little, warriors coalesced before his eyes.

'What are you up to?'

Christ. He snapped the image closed just as she appeared at this shoulder.

'Just logging out.'

'Where's your driver?'

'You said he should be here at five.'

'Well, you're not hanging around in here on your own. Get packed up and wait outside with security.'

She strode away towards the toilet areas and Oliver brought the image up once more. He squinted at the figures, willing his eyes to discern faces. *Are you out there, Tyler? Which one is you?*

At that moment the door to the OSU buzzed and a bearded man appeared, wearing a long raincoat and a scarf. He glared at Oliver, glanced in Aurora's empty office and then stalked to the lift and took himself to the upper floor.

Oliver sat dumbstruck, blood pounding in his ears. He checked around again, but it was still only him in the office. Forcing himself to focus, he saved his image to a shared drive, powered his terminal down and rose from his desk. He crept towards the toilet area and listened. Nothing. She was probably in there shovelling on more mascara. Heart thumping in his throat, he edged to the lift and pressed the button. There was an interminable wait and he was convinced an alarm must go off and guards would burst from outside and rush him, but all that happened was the lift slid open with a gentle sigh. He stepped inside and before he had time to think, he felt himself rising and then the doors were opening and there was Odin pouring himself a brandy beside a grand mahogany desk.

'What the hell are you doing up here?'

'I come bearing gifts.'

'Who are you?'

'Oliver Muir.'

Odin cocked his head. 'Is that supposed to mean anything to me?'

Oliver stepped into the room and tried to keep his voice from quivering. 'You asked me to look into the disappearance of Morgan Maitland.'

Odin eyed him suspiciously and then pointed a finger over his glass. 'You're the kid.'

The kid with a dead mother and a dead father, Oliver thought and his mind filled with images of them. He stared into the man's features for a glimpse of guilt or remorse or even remembrance.

But Odin just seated himself comfortably behind his desk and scowled at the intruder. 'Well spit it out. Have you found something on that Morgan woman?'

Oliver clenched his fists and forced his brain to focus. 'Can I show you on your computer?'

Odin waved him over. 'It better be worth my time.'

Oliver came around the back of the desk and leaned in to clasp the mouse. He could smell the damp on the man and the heavy musk of his aftershave. His grey hair had frizzy ends and was balding at the back. There were more hairs on his ears and a boil on his neck. But from this angle, he could not see into the man's eyes, could not glimpse the sliver of guilt that would convince him of Odin's hand in the murder of his parents.

Barely able to breathe, Oliver pulled up the computer's filing system and clicked on the shared drive, then selected the image he had saved.

Odin sighed. 'You're showing me a picture of tonight's shit-show. I was there, kid, I don't need a bloody picture as a keepsake.'

'I've enhanced it. It's still hazy, but it's possible to count individual shields and helmets.'

'And?'

'The Titan Palatinate had one hundred and eleven troops at the end of last Season and they won a hundred and three Blood Funds. They should have two hundred or more shields in this shot, but I count only a hundred and thirty-six.'

'So?'

'So where's the rest?'

Odin rubbed a palm into his eyes. 'It's damn late, kid. I'm tired, I'm hungry. I've been freezing my nuts off up some Scottish hill. And you're bending my ear counting goddamn Titans. There's no Rule saying every warrior has to be present at the *Agonium Martiale*. Zeus can field whatever number he wishes.'

'But,' said Oliver, struggling to keep his argument intact. 'But, if you were Zeus and this was the first time in years that you could amass more troops than your enemy, wouldn't you put every last one of them out there on that hill?'

Odin was silent. He placed his brandy on the desk and gave Oliver a long hard look, then squinted at the screen.

As he did, the lift hummed and the doors slid open once more.

'Oh my god, a thousand pardons, my lord!' Aurora burst into the room. 'I'll have him punished for this. It'll never happen again.'

'Get lost,' Odin growled without taking his eyes off the screen.

'My lord?'

'The kid's helping me with something. So clear off.'

Lost for words, her eyes boring into Oliver, she backed herself into the lift, pressed the button and stared at them until the doors closed.

'So,' Odin mused as though there had been no interruption. 'You say there's a hundred and thirty Titans in this shot?'

'A hundred and thirty-six, not including Alexander and Simmius. That makes them at most seventy short.'

'Does anyone else know about this?'

'Just me. The quality of the footage was too poor to see the shield lines properly. This was the only decent image and I've had to enhance it big time.'

Odin eyed him shrewdly. 'You don't miss much, do you, kid?'

'My mum used to say I missed nothing. She thought I was a young Poirot.'

'Bright woman.'

'She's dead now.'

'Yeah, well the worst things happen to the best people.'

Oliver's throat clamped. *What?* His head drummed. *What did this bastard just say? The worst things happen?* He tried to control his breathing. *Why would he phrase it like that?*

Odin glanced sharply up at him, conscious of the lad's sudden silence. Then he sucked his teeth and waved Oliver back around to the other side of the desk. 'So if you're such a damn good Poirot, then you can tell me what secrets you've been revealing about Morgan Maitland. That's what you're *supposed* to be looking at.'

Oliver's energy had deserted him. His limbs hung heavy. A pain blossomed at the back of his skull. 'I can't find anything more about her,' he said slowly, avoiding the man's gaze.

'So you're wasting my time.'

'My only lead takes me back to a chat room I found last year, which Kustaa said you already know about.'

'Bloody useless.'

'It's impossible to dig deeper when access to all external comms is denied in this place.'

'I want results, not excuses. Maybe I just send you back to rot in the Schola.'

Oliver screwed up his eyes. Everything about this man – his arrogance, his nonchalance, his supreme belief in his own power – reeked of guilt. Behind Odin's scowl, lay the implacable coldness of a viper. A man who killed for convenience.

Oliver forced his brain to function. 'The chat room is a dead end. We need to go back to when the whole thing began, when Tyler's sister first disappeared. When was the last date she was seen?'

Odin scrutinised him. 'What goddamn use is that?'

'We have camera feeds. Maybe something was captured on one of them.'

The Caelestis reached for his brandy and drank silently,

his eyes flint over the glass. 'Okay, I'll have someone check.'

'Date and time.'

'You'll get what we have. And you better damn well have more results the next time we meet. Now clear off as well.'

The next time we meet. Oliver walked wordlessly to the elevator. Those were the words he needed to hear because he was not finished with this man yet.

'And tell that stupid boss of yours that if I have any more visitors up here without permission, I'll string the lot of you up.'

XXVII

While Odin had taken the quickest route off Salisbury Crags and dropped down a torchlit track to his chauffeur on the southern curve of Queen's Drive, Zeus decided to wander north along a slim path that weaved above Hunter's Bog towards Holyrood and the Mile. The valley was empty now, purged of the seething lines of warriors who had marched over its lip and back to their strongholds as soon as the ceremony had ended.

Zeus had removed his ceremonial apparel, covered his identity with a simpler mask, and set off along the track with only his security detachment following at a discreet distance. The way was illuminated by lanterns dug into the tussocky ground and the going muddied his shoes, but he pressed on to the far rim of the valley, where the twinkling mass of the city revealed itself.

He glanced at the fog looming above like an ominous inverted ocean and decided the conditions had been a lucky bonus. His Titan units had looked too light and his troops had whispered sullenly about the lack of fresh blood in their companies, but had the elements cloaked his gamble from the eyes of Valhalla? That was the question eating him as he descended to a Range Rover.

'Could you see it?' he demanded as Hera emerged from the back seat to greet him.

'Not much. The drones were useless, but the ground cameras provided a more palpable sense of proceedings.'

Zeus removed his mask, embraced her and then helped her alight once more. 'We looked thin. Nothing like Odin's masses. I worry this plan is foolish.'

The vehicle took them quietly from the hill and Hera poured him a flute of champagne. 'We can't give up.'

'We can and we should. I cannot afford to start the Raids without our ranks filled with seventy Schola hoplites.'

'Stand fast, my love. We've made our choice and we must watch how fate plays out.'

'Not this time. This Palatinate is ours to share – we have always said that – and your wishes are mine to uphold, but this time I must insist. I cannot risk the whole Season with a plan that's, at best, a giant gamble.'

Hera leaned forward and tapped the shoulder of the driver, who nodded and turned the car onto Horse Wynd.

'Where are you taking me?'

'I have a little surprise for you.'

They approached the southern entrance to Holyrood and the ceremonial gates swung open to admit them. They progressed along the drive and pulled up beside a fountain in the grand courtyard fronting the Palace.

'Why do I have a feeling I'm not going to like this?'

Hera slapped his arm. 'Stop being so churlish and get out.'

The Palace was only dimly lit and the fog pressing down exacerbated the silence. Zeus walked round the vehicle to stand beside his wife and peered moodily into the night.

'Well?' he pressed, but she did not answer because a sound came to them from beyond the southern wing of the building. The snort of a beast. Then the rat-a-tat ring of iron-shod shoes on paving.

'Is that what I think it is?'

'A present for you. Lovingly wrapped and sent from our new Perthshire farm holding.'

The peal of hooves built momentum and then a single mounted figure burst around the corner and steered towards them.

Zeus took an involuntary step back, but Hera placed a restraining hand on his elbow. 'Study him. See his glory.'

And she was right. For rider and beast were indeed glorious. A knight from the storybooks of old, dazzling despite the gloom. He came at them clutching a lance, a cloak rippling from his shoulders and a great scarlet plume cresting his helmet. Bronze gleamed – shoulder guards, cuirass, greaves. His charger pounded the paving, muscles pumping and mane boiling around his grip. They reached the vehicle and he pulled back so hard that the horse rose on its hindlegs and boxed the night air, braying in magnificent indignation.

Zeus was enraptured.

Hera grinned and prodded him. 'This is Diogenes, Horsemaster of your new Companion Cavalry. The last time you saw him, he was fighting for his life and for his place in your Palatinate.'

The rider calmed his mount, couched his lance and waited.

Zeus walked cautiously to him and reached out to touch the horse's snout. He stroked the fleck of white above its eyes and the beast nickered in appreciation.

'What is she called?'

'He, my lord. He's ungelded, a stallion. Arabian, fifteen hands and he's called Xanthos.'

Zeus moved around the stallion's shoulder, feeling the mane and inspecting the lion skin that was draped across its back.

'You ride without a saddle?'

'Aye, lord. True to the ways of Alexander's horse soldiers.'

'Is that difficult to master?'

'We have trained hard in the weeks you have given us.'

'Are the other six as impressive?'

'They can ride, lord. We will be ready for you.'

'Imagine,' said Hera. 'Imagine seven of them like that, hurling themselves towards Odin's shields.'

Zeus nodded, still examining the horse. 'You could ride Xanthos against a Hammer wall?'

'Not yet, lord. But give us the three months until the Battle and – aye – he will ride against them. They all will. A shock unit like no other.'

For long moments, Zeus kept his hand on Xanthos' flank, as though feeling for his mighty heartbeat. Finally, he stepped back and took in the knight once more, letting his eyes roam over plume, armour, lance, lion skin and stallion.

'The flower of Greek knighthood,' Hera said. 'Imagine how proud your mother would be back in Ekali.'

Zeus took a deep breath and exhaled, then turned to his wife and a slow smile of surrender spread across his features.

Sveinn the Red, King of Valhalla, was stoking the fire in the

Council Chamber when Calder entered. His back was bent and his face curtained by long silver tresses. He sighed when he straightened and there was pain behind his eyes. Calder thought him a man whose prime had slunk away in the months since she had last beheld him on the Battle beach.

'Come, Raven,' he said with a thin smile, briefly touching his abdomen through the folds of his robe. 'You are welcome at my Council.'

Last year Calder had watched Punnr mount the steps to the Council Chamber, but she had never herself set foot up here. It was less impressive than she expected, with just the smallest of windows in the top corner, now shuttered to prevent uninvited eyes from the night beyond. A desk and armchairs were arranged around the fire, but the rest of the room was dominated by a generous table, brightly spot-lit and ringed by the other Council members, all standing and eyeing her.

Sveinn pointed to the desk. 'There's coffee. Help yourself, then we will begin.'

The gaze of the others shifted back to the table as she quietly poured a coffee and slotted herself between Asmund and Kustaa. The new Thane wore his usual woollen robe and amulet, with his hair combed into waves. He smiled at her, but the expression was wary and his eyes fluttered nervously around the others.

Freyja stood beside Sveinn, her hair twisted tight into a rope down her back. She shot a cursory glance at her interim Housecarl, then returned her attention to an exquisite map of central Edinburgh that decorated the tabletop. Its colours shone under the lights. Green for the parks, purple and gold for the key buildings, and the roads and closes named in black oil. The Gates of Valhalla were shaded red and on the rooftops over the Mile were four distinct areas painted in blue and bearing the names Persepolis, Pella, Thebes, Ephesus. Calder had never known the precise locations of the Titan strongholds and she stared at them now and wondered what they must be like and if the men she had once cared for roamed these spaces.

'So we are gathered once again,' said Sveinn and his throaty tones rasped like a whetstone. 'The Pantheon's two Conflict Seasons await us for the twentieth year. From tomorrow, for a period of up to six weeks, the laws of the Raiding Season will come into force. Our inner Gates will be unlocked each night during the Conflict Hours of one until four to give access to our foe should they wish to sally forth and attack. During these hours, all troops will be weapons-ready within our halls and if you are required to leave Valhalla, the normal Rules of Conflict apply.

'As always, the Caelestia and the Curiate will place wagers on all encounters and all outcomes, so it is vital that you appreciate how forensically your actions – and those of your companies – will be analysed. Money will flow. A myriad of riches running in tributaries between rival hands. And this means that everything you do – every decision you make – *matters*.'

Sveinn's eyes settled on Kustaa. 'Welcome, Thane, to your first Conflict Council. I trust you are ready to brief us?'

Kustaa flustered retrieving a sheet of paper from a case and Calder took the opportunity to glance right. Bjarke loomed at the head of the table, arms folded, his beard freshly braided and golden hair strewn across his shoulders. He was wearing a simple tunic and leather jerkin, and a newly inked Valknut was emblazoned on his forearm. His face was screwed into a scowl of scepticism, but he kept his gaze rooted on the map.

With raw willpower, Calder forced herself to look beyond him, to the next man in the circle and she jolted physically at the sight of his eyes, hard sapphires, staring back at her. For an appalling second she was incapable of pulling away and her lips hung open as she gorged herself on his image. His stark white hair had been cut and his beard trimmed and his face had filled out from good living over the past six months, though it still bore a hyena's leanness as a lingering memory of Erebus and no amount of grooming could hide the violence coming off him in waves. The frost of his gaze slunk down her throat and clutched at her lungs.

'My lord, thank you,' said Kustaa, his paper clasped in front of him, and it was enough to bring her back. Skarde blinked once, then looked to the Thane and she was released.

'As you know,' Kustaa continued, oblivious, 'the Rules of the Raiding Season are drawn up fresh each year and the Caelestia has decreed that this time it will be very different from the last. While there was much excitement surrounding actions during the four Raid Nights of the Nineteenth, the resulting full-frontal clashes between both Palatinates' heavy lines was unforeseen and attracted much unwelcome attention. Such high-profile actions are not sustainable within the confines of the city and must not be repeated. It has been decided, therefore, that there will be only two Raid Nights this Season and they will be tightly regulated to ensure clear and limited confrontation.'

Bjarke guffawed and Sveinn had to signal that it was okay for his Thane to continue.

'I will now impart the Rules for the Twentieth Raiding Season.'

'Get on with it, man,' breathed Asmund.

'Both Palatinates will be given twenty-four hours' notice before each of the Raid Nights. For the first Night, the role of Valhalla will be entirely offensive and that of the Titans defensive. For the second, the Titans will attack and Valhalla will defend. On each Night, the designated attacker will field a single company of ten and will be permitted to select these from amongst its troops. The defender, by contrast, will field fifty.'

'Fifty!' exclaimed Bjarke. 'But that's just a quarter of our strength. What about the rest?'

'Jarl,' said Sveinn in tired tones. 'We have this every year. Our Thane reads the Rules and you get angry. Could we perhaps hear him out?'

Bjarke rubbed a fist across his mouth, but held his tongue.

'On the First Raid Night, Valhalla's Company of ten will be given a map and coordinates. Once at these coordinates, the ten must get within twenty metres of a radio frequency identification tag and it will reveal the location of a hidden cache. This cache contains another set of coordinates, which will take the company to a second cache and more coordinates. By this means, the company will find four caches and then discover coordinates to a fifth and final cache. Only when you have this *and* returned with it to Valhalla, can we claim the Asset.'

'What of the foe?' asked Asmund.

'On the First Raid Night, the fifty Titan defenders will not be told the coordinates for any of the caches. They will, however, know the broad location of the fifth and final cache and they will prepare themselves to defend this area and stop Valhalla's team.'

Kustaa paused and read down his sheet. 'On the Second Raid Night...'

'The positions are reversed,' Freyja cut in.

'Well... yes, in short.'

'And that's it?' Bjarke spat, glaring at the Thane as though it was all his fault. 'Just ten of us stumbling around looking for an RFID? No demand for my Hammer lines to be breaking heads?'

'It would seem not.'

Bjarke waved the response away angrily. 'One of these days Atilius and his monkeys are just going to tell us to sit down and play chess!'

Asmund picked his lip thoughtfully. 'Ten against fifty. I don't like those odds. Are we walking into a trap?'

'Yes and no,' said Freyja, who had obviously been briefed in advance. 'The Titans will arrange themselves around the location and if we are spotted then it will be a desperate fight. But I am informed the areas are large and the foe will not know the precise location of the final cache, nor will they know from what direction we will arrive. The previous coordinates and caches have been deliberately selected to weave the attacking company on a strange course and to bring them upon the final location from an unexpected quarter. Speed, stealth and cunning will be the order of the day.'

'What of the ten?' Bjarke challenged. 'How will they be selected.'

'We will need a strong mix of skills. Scouts, navigators, climbers, archers, runners, bulk for defence and guile for attack. So I suggest each of you nominates two or three from your regiments and we will chose from these.'

There was silence as each Council member mulled the information.

'Do we know the value of the Assets?' Skarde asked quietly.

'Only that this year their finding will affect our fortunes in the Blood Nights, not the Battle,' replied Kustaa and there were glances around the table at this.

'So,' said Sveinn. 'We will gather again in three nights with your team suggestions and we will determine the final ten. For now it is enough to know that we will need a Wolf to tear through our foe, so Skarde will lead.'

Calder's pulse roared in her throat. Bjarke turned to the man next to him with a surprised grunt and leaned into him, goading him with every cell of his bulk. 'Prisoner to Housecarl in a matter of weeks and now ordained as our leader for the Raids. Is there no stopping your rise, Wolf?'

Skarde need only have twitched the wrong muscle and fists would fly, but – for once – he refused the bait. Keeping his face rigid, he simply stared through the warrior breathing down his neck.

'Jarl,' Sveinn snapped and there was an interminable pause before Bjarke dragged his eyes to his king. 'Find me two good Hammers. The team will need them.'

Bjarke heaved his shoulders. 'You'll have them.'

'That's settled then. Thank you, Kustaa, for the briefing. Thegn Calder, we expect high things of you as temporary Raven Housecarl. The rest of you, brief your troops and make your selections. It begins.'

PART FOUR

CHAOS

XXVIII

The chosen ten gathered in Sveinn's Throne Room fifteen minutes before the one o'clock opening of the Gates, clad in iron and silver and furs, and armed to the teeth. Flames from the hearth played on shield bosses and chain mail, waxed bowstrings, feathered arrow shafts, vambraces, bone-handled seax knives, and longswords holstered in baldrics between each set of shoulder blades. Only spears were lacking, so these Vikings could be less encumbered for the hunt.

From the Ravens, three. Calder, Geir and new Thegn, Estrid. A surprise choice, but Calder had championed her, and Freyja – recalling the girl's speed with a blade in the vaults of the Armatura – had given her consent. They would be the company's eyes and ears.

Three too from the Wolves, Valhalla's hunter-killers. Silent, brooding Stigr, the man whose voice could break hearts. Ake, eyes black, skin white as bone, hair chopped away to nothing. And Skarde, dressed like Thor himself. Sapphire eyes, arctic beard, chain mail studded with silver and a rope coiled around his neck.

From Storm, two. Torsten and Gunnar, men with bows

over their shoulders, checking the fletching on their arrows in the light of the fire.

That left two places for Hammer. Bjarke had selected the champion of his Berserkers, Ingvar, broad as a bus and cloaked in bearskin. And another surprise package – Ulf. With none of the natural brawn needed for the centre of Hammer's shieldwall, the others had peered at him when he appeared in the Throne Room, but Ingvar had growled, 'Best damn navigator in the Schola.'

Sveinn sat quietly on his throne with a cup of warm spiced apple wine in his hand. At each Gate, the rest of Raven and Storm companies waited to shimmy onto the surrounding roofs and ensure no Titan scouts spied the ten leaving and attempted to fasten onto them.

Kustaa hovered beside his King, clutching a folded map and a discreet tracking device. The rest of the Council – Freyja, Bjarke and Asmund – watched from behind the throne and beyond the light of the flames lurked a Vigilis with a camera strapped to his helmet ready to film every act, every pause, every deliberation, every mistake made by this team.

Two minutes to Conflict Hours. Sveinn inclined his head towards Kustaa and the Thane stepped off the dais.

'The map,' he said, handing it to Skarde. 'Atilius has ensured it shows little detail. The roads are unnamed and there are no other features. The grid around the edges, however, is precise. If your navigator can interpret the unmarked roads, the coordinates will bring you to the correct location.'

Skarde took the map without unfolding it and held it behind him for Ulf to grab and open on the nearest table.

'And the tracking device,' Kustaa said and placed the second item in Skarde's hand. 'Use the map coordinates to bring you to general locations, then hope to god you can get this within twenty metres of an RFID tab on each cache. It will activate the tab and lead you straight to the cache where you will find the next coordinates. Have I made that clear?'

Skarde smiled sardonically. 'What *would* we do without you, Thane?'

Bustle from the Tunnels. Sveinn rose and glanced at his officers, then turned to the ten. 'It is time. The Gates are opening and Raven and Storm will be securing our perimeter from prying eyes. Provide the first coordinates, Kustaa.'

This time ignoring the Wolf, Kustaa handed a slip of paper to Ulf, who read the six digits and immediately began tracing lines along the edge of the map with a small ruler. The rest of the ten crowded round. The saliva in Calder's throat was sour and her stomach cramped. She fingered the bone of her seax handle nervously and eyed the back of Ulf's head.

'You have it?' demanded Skarde.

'Let the lad breathe,' snarled Ingvar.

Ulf strained over the map, sweat beading on his forehead. His ruler ran horizontally, then vertically and finally he nodded. 'I have it.'

'You better be certain,' warned Skarde.

'I *have* it. West, through the Gardens.'

Skarde rammed his helmet on and even his eyes were lost in the shadows behind the iron. The other nine did likewise, hoisted shields and checked their weapons one final time. The Vigilis released himself from the shadows, switched on his camera and fell in behind the group.

'The gods speed you,' called Sveinn. 'Retrieve that Asset and bring it back to me.'

Skarde bowed his head once and shouldered through the group. 'The North-West Gate. We go.'

When they saw the company heading their way, the Keepers checked their monitors for passers-by, then flung open the graffiti-riddled iron door onto Milne's Court and the cold hit Calder like a wall as they spilled onto the narrow close. Three hours earlier when she had arrived at Valhalla, the city had been hunkering down under an ominous indigo sky, but now there was snow in the air and the paving beneath their feet was already dusted white.

'Shit,' growled Ingvar and he was right, because they would show up black against this background and draw the eye of anyone foolish enough to be out on such a night.

Ulf led, clutching the map like a cherished keepsake, and Skarde ran beside him. They dropped down Milne's Court, turned west along Mound Place and then heaved and jumped over the garden walls below Ramsay Lane, treading through naked apple trees and frozen borders, then slipping and cursing their way down the slope below the Castle Esplanade to Princes Street Gardens.

Calder, Geir and Estrid moved instinctively to the front and spread out, while Torsten and Gunnar took the flanks and notched arrows without breaking step. Stigr and Ake loped behind, and Ingvar thudded and snorted at the rear, an axe strapped to his fur-clad shoulders.

They passed two Ravens among the trees, who gave them thumbs-up, and then they crossed the bridge above the railway and rounded the open-air theatre at the centre of the Gardens, which only two weeks earlier had jostled with

Hogmanay crowds. Ulf took them due west and climbed towards the junction between Lothian and Princes Street. The black mass of St Peter's reared up and he led over walls into the graveyards between this church and its cousin, St Cuthbert's, then slowed and flicked on a small hand torch to consult the map.

'Cover that light,' hissed Ake and Ulf hoicked his shield with one arm and Stigr stepped in close with his own shield.

'Well?' demanded Skarde.

'This is it. This is where the coordinates say.'

'So where is the damn cache?' said Ingvar between breaths.

'You.' Skarde pointed at Calder and flung her the tracker. 'Find it.'

Thrusting her shield high on her arm, she flicked on the tracker and watched concentric circles of green pulse outwards across the screen.

'Nothing.'

'So don't just stand there, get in range.'

She shifted right and scanned St Peter's, acutely aware of the Vigilis following her and filming every move. The tracker simply kept pulsing. She marched instead to St Cuthbert's, weaving between gravestones topped with a centimetre of flawless icing. As she slunk into the shadow of this church, a red dot began blinking on the left of her screen. She altered course and watched the dot inch towards the hub of the circles.

Geir was at her shoulder now. 'You have something?'

Calder strode to the eastern corner of the church, the dot hit dead centre, and there in the shadows beside the furthest buttress she spied a faint blue light.

'Is that it?' hissed Geir.

She knelt and fussed with a meagre box screwed into the stone. 'I can't see.'

'Ulf, get that torch over here.'

Ulf jogged over and Geir raised his shield for cover while the Hammer Thegn knelt beside Calder. For a heartbeat she smelt the sweat of him and remembered him high on the castle on the final Raid Night of the previous Season, intent on her murder. *Stop fucking about and just finish her*, had been his words and they had stayed with her ever since. She forced the memory aside and used the light of his torch to flick a catch on the box and pull it open. Inside was a wafer of plastic, taped watertight. With freezing fingers, she struggled to unseal it and extract a scrap of paper with six more coordinates.

Ulf forced the numbers into his brain, then leaned back and opened the map on his knees.

'Shit,' he said because it was getting wet with the snow and already flopping like a damp flannel.

'Here,' Calder said. 'Give me the torch.'

She held it for him as he tried to flatten the map and fussed with his ruler. Geir hovered over them and the others clustered in the snow – Gunnar, Torsten, Ake and Stigr scanning the night for movement.

'Do you have it?' pressed Skarde, shoving Geir out of his way.

'Not yet.' Ulf was flapping and, without thinking, Calder placed her hand on his and said quietly, 'It's okay. We have time.'

He glanced at her, his feminine lips and small eyes and reluctant beard clear even in the poor light. Then he focused again and flipped his ruler around the map's grid lines. Satisfied, he stabbed a finger on one spot.

'That's the place.'

'Where is it?' demanded Skarde.

Ulf tried to fathom the network of roads with no names or symbols. 'We're here – and these symmetric blocks are George and Queen Streets.'

'The circle is Moray Place,' said Calder.

'Yes, you're right and the next coordinates are just beyond that.' He tapped the map victoriously. 'It must be the river. The Water of Leith.'

'You certain?' hissed Skarde.

'As much as I can be in these bloody conditions.'

Skarde grabbed him by the scruff of his cloak and dragged him to his feet. 'Then lead us.'

It took them twenty minutes to slink past Charlotte Square and the western enclaves of New Town, waiting at each main junction to check for eyes. Thankfully the snow discouraged traffic, for the company could do little to hide their war apparel of shields and blades and mail. At last they came to the deep banks of the Leith and hoisted themselves over railings and down a steep tree-lined slope to the southern path. The snow was deepening and as Gunnar arrived from his position at the rear, arrow still notched, he looked back up the slope and said, 'Our prints are an open invitation for anyone who wishes to follow.'

'Then let's hope no one would be so stupid,' replied Stigr and there were mutterings of agreement, although he and Torsten lingered with Gunnar and kept their eyes peeled when the group moved off south. A few hundred yards along the path and Ulf slowed again.

'Are we here?' Skarde snapped.

'I don't know. I think so.' Ulf shrugged forlornly.

Skarde marched up to him and brought his helmet in so close that Ulf could smell a lingering sourness of ale from the Valhalla halls on his breath. 'Choose your words better, Thegn, or you'll be in that water and your mail will take you under forever.'

'It's too dark and there's nothing here to use as bearings. The coordinates on the map place the location halfway between India Place and Dean Bridge, but I can't see either in this light.'

Skarde spun on his feet and searched the figures around him. 'Thegn Calder, where are you?'

'Here,' she said without moving.

'Start tracking woman. Our navigator is a useless pile of shit.'

Once more she flicked on the device in her hand and watched the green circles. The river meant they could only go south or north along the path. She chose south and ran cautiously into the night. Ake came with her, Estrid too, and Ulf pulled himself together and struggled after them with the map. A building materialised and Calder could see a domed cupola of snow and Doric columns. It was St Bernard's Well, a Victorian architectural flourish housing a pump room. The red dot came alive again and she levered over railings and watched it glide to the centre of the circles. Looking up, she spotted another blue light at the base of a column.

She dropped to her knees and Ulf shuffled beside her. The same routine. Torch, ruler, map, coordinates. Skarde paced behind, the animal in him only just restrained.

'Where?' he hissed as Ulf rose.

'Ravelston, I think.'

'You think?'

'We stick to this path south. We can cross the river at Dean Village, then it's west into Ravelston.'

Ingvar swore. 'Where the hell is this damn wild goose chase taking us?'

Skarde grabbed Ulf again. 'Are you certain, boy?'

'Wolf,' warned Ingvar, a hand reaching behind his shoulder to finger the haft of his axe. 'Housecarl or not, you touch one of my Hammers again and I'll take your head from your shoulders.'

For a moment Skarde stared at the big berserker and the air was colder than the snow.

Then something whumped into Geir and he stumbled backwards. All helmets turned as he fell onto the track, his shield clattering and his free arm coming up to his shoulder. Black against the snow, an arrow shaft protruded below his collarbone.

'Titans,' Ake yelled and the company split.

Ake, Stigr, Torsten and Gunnar raced into the trees, while Ingvar charged back down the track. Skarde's blade rasped from the baldric between his shoulders as he stepped over Geir to secure the way forward. The Vigilis spun to take in what he could on his camera, then chose to follow the hunters and ran for the trees.

Ake took the widest circle, flying up the slope where the snow was thinner under the boughs. She returned to the iron railing separating the bank from the street and ran beside it. She had left her sword in its baldric and drawn the seax on her hip, because she knew instinctively this would be knife work. The first Titan was clambering back over the railings as she came upon him. He had time only to look up and then her blade took him in the soft gap between his cheek guards and his fish scales, stabbing into throat and shredding cartilage and tendons in a flood of hot blood. He collapsed towards the road, but she grabbed him and hauled him back into the trees to dump his corpse, her hand slippery with his life blood.

Fifteen metres along, the second peltast was vaulting the railings, but he stopped mid-leap and arched his back, a feathered shaft embedded in his fish scales. He struggled to keep clambering, but Torsten was there now to yank him backwards. The Titan kicked and yelled as he was dragged down the slope away from the road, then gurgled as Torsten's knife found the underbelly of his mouth.

The night went still. Torsten peered at Ake through the darkness. They had been lucky. This pair must have tracked them since the Gardens, but they were no longer in any condition to report Valhalla's route.

Below, Estrid and Calder had knelt beside Geir and eased his helmet from his head.

'I'm okay,' he grimaced.

'We have to get this out,' said Calder.

'No,' said Estrid firmly. 'Where's the torch?'

Ulf stumbled over. 'I have it.'

He shone the beam onto Geir's wound and they could see where the missile had driven the rings of his chain mail into his flesh. Delicately, Estrid plied a few of the broken ones away from the wound, but Geir snarled curses.

'Someone needs to pull this out,' said Calder again.

'We must not,' reiterated Estrid. 'The barbs on that thing

will do far more damage coming out and we might not be able to stem the blood flow. At the moment, the arrow head and his mail are blocking any heavy bleeding.'

Estrid yanked off her own helmet, tipped it upside down and tugged at the padded inner lining. With effort it came away from its stud fastenings and she wrapped it around the base of the arrow. Geir gasped and they heard Skarde swear from up the path.

'Leave the crying bastard. We don't need him.'

Ignoring him, Estrid unbuckled her belt and removed her scabbarded seax. Calder raised the prone Raven and Estrid looped the belt under him, then back over his other shoulder and secured it across the bloodied mail just below the shaft, so that it held the lining in place.

'It's rudimentary and won't last, but it's the safest option for now.'

Behind them the others were returning. Ake stooped to wipe her blade in the snow and no one had to ask if the hunt had been successful.

Skarde leaned over the injured warrior. 'This is a waste of time.'

'Can you stand?' asked Calder.

Geir grimaced and nodded, then heaved himself upright with the help of his fellow Ravens.

'Hold the shaft,' Estrid told him. 'Keep it firm.'

Geir complied and Calder threw a look to Ulf. 'Where now?'

'South,' he said pointing along the track. 'Dean Bridge is too much of a climb, but we can get him to Dean Village.'

'Can you make it?' Calder whispered to Geir, his good arm over her shoulder.

'Of course. And you leave me there.'

So they progressed. Down the track, under the vast arches of Dean Bridge and at last to the cluster of old houses that had once been a village separated from the city, but had long since submitted to the tide of expansion as Edinburgh flowed around it.

They left Geir seated beside the low bridge, the shaft sticking obstinately out of him. Footage from the Vigilis would alert the *libitinarii* to escort him to a Pantheon hospital before dawn. The snow kept falling and the clock kept ticking and the company of nine jogged across the bridge and followed Ulf into Ravelston.

XXIX

The third cache proved much simpler. Ravelston was suburbia and during a January snowstorm at two-thirty in the morning on a weeknight, the long length of Ravelston Dyke Road leading them spear-straight west was devoid of life, not even tyre tracks blemishing the snow. They ran fast, Stigr and Gunnar still glancing back every few strides and cursing the sight of nine sets of boot prints advertising their progress.

Ulf's coordinates took them along the lane to Murrayfield Golf Course and it was easy enough to see the well-lit patios around the clubhouse and to guess this was likely where the next cache would be found. Within minutes they had it and Ulf was brushing snow from one of the tables to lay his flimsy map and retrieve his ruler.

'Well?' pressed Skarde when Ulf looked up and stared into the night.

'That way. Due west. But…'

'But what?'

'There's no roads now and nothing on the map except a big blank space.'

'So?'

'So I've got the exact point of the next cache marked on

this blank space, but finding it in reality in these conditions with no visual markers is going to require the luck of the gods.'

Skarde peered west into the darkness. 'What's out there?'

'The golf course, but after that my knowledge of this part of the city is limited.'

'Corstorphine Hill,' said Stigr. 'That's what's out there. A long ridgeline running north to south.'

Ulf nodded. 'Then the fourth cache is somewhere on that.'

Ingvar cursed and shot a black scowl towards the Vigilis. 'That bastard, Atilius, will be laughing at us right now.'

'We aim for the summit ridge,' said Calder. 'Because if I was going to plant a cache on a hill, I'd do it on the top.'

There was logic in that and there were murmurs of assent.

'Set the course, Hammer,' Skarde snarled at Ulf.

The navigator checked behind at the lane they had run along and then turned his back on it. 'The lane runs due west and the cache is west from here, so we keep as straight a course as we can.'

To begin with the going was steady. The fairways were flat and studded with bunkers, but as the last vestiges of light from Ravelston faded, they closed ranks and jogged shoulder to shoulder lest they lose anyone.

'Use the damn torch,' grumbled Ingvar as he lumbered in the centre.

'Not here,' said Ake. 'If there's Titans on that hill, they could watch us the whole way until we ran onto their spears.'

They reached the perimeter of the golf course and came upon a dense barrier of hawthorn and alder. Their armour protected them from the worst of it, but they cursed and stumbled as unseen branches whipped at them and reached for their shins. Then they floundered down a short slope and found themselves in a ditch, their boots breaking through thin ice and sinking into mud. The night was blue with hissed profanities as their mail wedged them lower and their shields stuck. Blindly, they grabbed at grasses and gorse and hauled themselves up the far side, the stink of bog on their leggings tainting the air.

And then the climb began. They bent into the work, Calder, Estrid and Torsten in the vanguard, thumping into beech and sycamore branches and slipping in the snow that was gathering enthusiastically on this incline. The air that Calder sucked into her lungs was so raw it stung her throat, yet her spine was slick with sweat. Behind them, the Vigilis clung to the group like a limpet and she wondered what sort of images the Curiate would be able to see in these lightless conditions, but then she remembered they would also have access to satellite and thermal feeds. Perhaps, at this very moment, they were watching nine glowing Vikings and a Vigilis lumbering between the black fingers of the trees.

Perhaps too, the Curiate could see fifty glowing Titans waiting for Valhalla somewhere beyond the hill's crest, for this would be the fourth and penultimate cache and the Titans would be ranged in defence around the fifth.

At last, when their final reserves were unravelling, the slope relented and Calder brought them to a halt.

'Tell me this is the top,' panted Ingvar.

'It is,' confirmed Stigr, looking at the lights of Corstorphine and Barnton beyond.

Skarde shoved Calder in the back. 'Start looking.'

She flicked on the tracker, but there was no red dot. By feeling for the level ground, she began to inch north along the ridge and the visibility forced them to stick with her and shuffle together like some strange armoured beast. Nothing. After exasperating minutes, she turned them and they retraced their steps and searched south. Though they boiled with rage, no one spoke or cursed, for they knew this fourth cache must be close to the location of the fifth and the Titans could be just a whisper away.

At last, blessedly, her tracker blinked red and they only had to keep their course along the ridge and they would reach it. Sure enough, in the final yards a chestnut reared before them, spindly and naked in the winter cold, and there was the box with the blue light nailed to its trunk. The company breathed a ragged sigh of relief and four shields came round to cover Ulf while he plotted the coordinates by torchlight.

'South-west,' he whispered and his voice quavered with cold. 'Not far. The map is showing three tracks that curve over the lower slopes of this hill above those houses we can see at the bottom. The coordinates place the final cache where the tracks join at the highest point. That's all I can decipher.'

Gunnar made a sound in his throat. He was at the back of the group, peering out into the darkness. The company froze.

'You see something?' Stigr whispered and fingered his knife.

Gunnar was an age in answering, but then shook his head. 'No. Probably just the trees.'

'Right,' snarled Skarde. 'Lead us, navigator, and you better not fuck this up.'

'Eyes on,' said Ingvar. 'You see a soul up here on this sodding hill and you can wager it's a Titan.'

They dropped cautiously down the slope. Stigr and Ake watched the rear, Gunnar and Torsten the flanks, and Calder and Ulf led, groping between the trees and aiming for the homely lights of Corstorphine. A few yards behind, the Vigilis still strode wordlessly. He would not join the group, but neither did he make a sound to compromise them. The man must be fit and strong. A wraith trailing them whatever course they chose.

Suddenly Calder was aware of something in front. A mesh of lines, more uniform than the alder branches, too regular for nature, and rising high into the snow-filled sky.

'Shit,' Ulf whispered. He had seen them too.

'What is it?' Skarde demanded as they halted and the group knelt.

'A fence,' whispered Calder.

She stepped to it and reached out. The mesh was steel and strong, tensed to rigidity between regular concrete posts. She stared into the sky above and guessed it rose at least ten feet.

'What the hell is this doing here?' Invar growled, but no one had an answer.

Skarde thumped Ulf on the shoulder. 'You still saying the coordinates are on the other side?'

'Yes. Not far though. Six hundred yards max.'

Ake swore silently. 'Where the hell are the Titans?'

'They'll be somewhere close,' murmured Stigr. 'Mark my words.'

Ingvar crawled to the mesh and inspected it. 'My axe would take this down.'

'And it would bring all fifty Titans down on us too,' hissed Estrid, not shy to castigate the lord of Valhalla's Berserkers.

'Then we climb,' said Calder simply.

Ake examined her in the darkness. 'You and me last.'

Skarde thought to countermand her, but there was something in her tone that suggested finality, so he pushed Ulf forward. 'You first, navigator. If you break your neck in the fall, it'll be no loss.'

They shifted to the nearest concrete post and then knelt for long moments, listening to the night. The snow dampened everything and the hill was as silent as the grave.

'Lose your shield,' said Stigr and Ulf pulled it from his arm and dropped it.

'And give me your torch,' Ingvar commanded.

'I may need it.'

'Just give it to me.'

Ulf handed it over and then Stigr and Ingvar stooped against the mesh and he stepped into their clasped hands. With a single smooth lift, the big men scooped him high and he grabbed the top of the fence and used the post to manoeuvre himself over. Gripping the concrete, he stretched himself down the other side and then dropped. The snow cushioned his fall, but he still collapsed sideways with a yip.

'Shut up, you fool,' hissed Skarde. 'Or I'll cut your tongue out.'

Estrid went next and then Skarde.

'I'm staying,' said Ingvar through the mesh once the Housecarl was on the other side.

'You afraid of a fight, Hammer?' Skarde stepped to the fence in cold fury.

If the steel had not divided them, Ingvar would have

killed the Wolf where he stood, but instead he bottled his rage and rasped, 'If things kick off in there, you'll need a way out or they'll cut you to ribbons against this bloody fence. Look for the torch beam. I'll be here. Besides,' he whispered, nodding up at the mesh. 'No one's getting me over this.'

He spoke the truth and they all knew it, though Skarde swore and spun away. The others were lifted over and Ingvar was about to help Ake, when the Vigilis stepped forward and scrutinised them from behind his helmet. There was a pause and then Ingvar shrugged, 'We better get bonus points for this.'

The Hammer and the Wolf clutched the Vigilis' foot and raised him until he could scramble over the mesh, then Ingvar bent once more and let Ake stand on his palms. The Wolf maiden had assumed she would be last and had expected to climb the mesh without assistance, but Ingvar's change of plan made it easy. She balanced herself on the top of the concrete post and Ingvar passed up each shield for her to drop the other side.

'If all hell breaks loose,' she said to him through the mesh once down, 'light our way.'

'That I will, Wolf. But find the Asset first, so I haven't climbed this bloody hill for nothing.'

They left him and stepped off through the snow again. The trees were gone and they felt immensely vulnerable in this wide expanse of white. The world was silent, but a new scent caught their nostrils. An animal smell of damp hay and turds. A hundred yards and they came to a single mature sycamore and huddled against it.

'What now?' Skarde whispered to Ulf.

'Just maintain the line, I think.'

'Look,' said Estrid.

Ahead, perhaps two hundred yards, they could see dull orange lights behind hedging.

'It's one of the tracks,' said Ulf, perking up. 'They must be lit. We'll be able to see much better.'

'And so will the Titans,' murmured Stigr.

'Where *are* they?' mouthed Ake, staring around.

'And what the hell is that?' said Gunnar more loudly, turning them to where his eyes strained.

Something moved. A piece of the night shifted. Then there was a low rumble.

'A horse,' Torsten whispered.

Gunnar took a step forward and stared hard at the outline of the beast. There was something about its coat, a whiteness reflecting the snow, yet shadows like the mesh fence. 'That's no horse,' he muttered. 'It's a zebra.'

Ulf inhaled in realisation. 'We're in the zoo.'

The company stared at each other.

'That explains the fence,' said Estrid.

Stigr swore quietly. 'They're playing games with us.'

Calder was looking around. 'We need to get into cover. We're sitting targets here.'

No one could argue with that. Eyeing the zebra and wondering what else lurked unseen, the company jogged to the shrubs, climbed a smaller fence and pushed through to the edge of the track. It was tarmacked, low-lit every twenty yards and there was a sign pointing downhill reading *Chimpanzees* and *Penguins*.

The company knelt and Skarde reached through the greenery to knock Ulf's helmet. 'Where do we go, navigator?'

Ulf was breathing hard and it was obvious he was panicked. Skarde smacked him again and he forced himself to think. 'The map's useless, but approximate distances suggest we still have four hundred yards due west. We could follow the path up and it will curve round.'

'No paths,' said Stigr.

He was right. Far too bright.

'Then straight over,' pointed Ulf.

He began to move, but Skarde's hand arrested him. 'Take a care, fool. There are fifty Titans somewhere and there's only half the Raid Night remaining. It's now or never and they'll know it.'

'I've visited this place before,' whispered Ake, and Calder had visions of this wild Wolf maiden feeding meerkats. 'The main entrance is at the bottom of the hill. There's a secondary visitor entrance below us off a car park and a staff entrance on the opposite side. They'll be watching those like hawks. But our arrival from the hill seems to have surprised them.'

Calder recalled Freyja's words in the Council Chamber. *The caches have been deliberately selected to weave the attacking company on a strange course and to bring them upon the final location from an unexpected quarter.*

Skarde was about to signal the advance when there was a voice down the path. A single word of command and then silence. The eight Vikings froze, their ears on stalks. Long minutes passed, but nothing else was heard except a hooting of monkeys somewhere far away, which had no place on this bitter night in Scotland.

Finally Ake shifted to the edge of the path, stared downhill, then slipped across and into the shrubs on the other side. She listened then beckoned the others and one at a time they joined her. Only the Vigilis hunkered the other side and as he rose to cross, there was a cry from below. More voices took up the call, howling like the apes, and six Hoplites came running up the path.

Concealment abandoned, Stigr stood and his longsword sang from its scabbard behind his head. 'Go!' he pushed at Calder, as more Viking blades kissed the night. 'We'll hold them.'

Arrows thunked from Torsten and Gunnar, and two Hoplites crashed to the tarmac. Then the Storm pair shouldered their bows, drew swords and ran with Ake and Stigr to attack.

'Move it,' spat Skarde and dragged Ulf forward. 'You too, Raven, get that tracker out. Find the cache before they're all over us!'

Calder fired up the tracker and stumbled forward with Estrid and the other pair. Behind them the sounds of battle jarred the night and Ake's war cry came to them. No time for stealth now. Fifty Titan blades were on their way.

The four of them floundered out of the shrubbery and ran past tall pens housing hippo and rhino, then beside a dimly lit children's play area looking forlorn and unloved in the snow. They crashed through more borders and came to another path.

'This must be far enough,' gasped Ulf. 'We're at least six hundred yards from the fence now.'

Calder glared at the pulsing green circles on her tracker, then jogged fifteen yards up the path and suddenly the red dot began blinking like a heartbeat at the top of her screen. She wheeled left through bushes and it began to centralise, then she reached another barrier and stared through the steel bars.

Skarde came to her shoulder and yanked her round. 'What the hell are you doing, girl?'

'It's in there. The Asset's the other side of this.'

He looked up at the bars running twenty feet into the sky and tapering inwards. 'Not a chance of getting over that.'

They followed the barrier uphill and came upon a visitor seating area where the bars were interrupted by a wooden structure that housed a huge viewing window and a roof to shelter the public from Edinburgh's inclement climate. Calder assessed the roof and knew they could climb it and then lift at least two of them to the top of the steel bars beyond.

'Help me up.' She pointed to Skarde and dropped her shield beside the tables. He eyed her contemptuously, then disposed of his shield as well, stepped to the corner of the structure and stooped. She placed her hand on his helmet for balance and remembered this man punching her in the Valhalla showers and then – from nowhere – she thought of little Amelia. The memory made her gasp, for she stood on a frozen hillside amid monkeys and penguins with her hand on the father of her lost child.

There was no time to think further. Skarde was raising her and she grabbed at the roof of the structure and hauled herself onto it. 'Give me the rope.' She leaned down to him.

Again he paused and considered.

'Damn you, give it to me. I won't get out of there without it and you won't get your Asset.'

He tugged the coiled rope over his head.

'Secure it to something,' Calder hissed, the sounds of battle and pursuit coming ever closer.

'Here,' Ulf called. The tables were screwed into the concrete and he took the end of the rope from Skarde and tied it securely. Then the Wolf Housecarl threw the rest up to Calder. She wound the rope carefully again, stepped back and assessed the top of the steel bars ten feet above her, then threw the coils. They cleared the fence and unravelled the other side to land with a thump in the snow.

Behind her Skarde was already raising Ulf onto the structure, followed by Estrid. Then another figure emerged from the dark and for a moment Calder believed they were under attack. But it was the Vigilis, his camera taking in the scene. Dimly she realised he must have known the precise location of the final cache all along and come looking for them amid the carnage.

'Get in there and find it,' Skarde snarled from below, glancing contemptuously at the new arrival.

Estrid brought the other two close and said in low tones, 'I read the board. It's the lions.'

Ulf took a step back, eyes bulging, his jaw slack. 'No way,' he choked, shaking his head. 'I'm not going in there. Nothing will make me go in there.'

'Get moving, you arseholes,' hissed Skarde. 'Stop nattering like fucking housewives.'

Calder exhaled to calm her nerves, then took command. 'You stay here, Ulf. I'll need you to pull me back up.'

He nodded dumbly at that, sniffing snot from his lips.

'I'm coming too,' said Estrid and Calder regarded her.

'You don't have to.'

'Just get going.'

Ulf dropped to his knee and lifted Calder easily to the top of the fencing so she could perch where the bars curved inwards. Estrid came next. They sat and listened for many long seconds. Somewhere down the hill, blades clashed and harsh voices shouted, but in the enclosure all was peace.

'Maybe they lock them inside at night,' suggested Estrid. 'I hope so.'

Calder gripped the rope, levered herself over and rappelled down, then crouched until Estrid was with her. 'Straight ahead,' she said, consulting the tracker. 'It must be only ten yards.'

Silently, hearts in mouths, the two Ravens slipped forward, backs bent so low they were almost crawling. The ground sloped away and then in the faint light from the path, Calder saw another large tree and she no longer needed her tracker because there was the blue light. Gasping with relief, she edged towards it and that was when a new sound came to them, the sound of every nightmare.

A growl. Deep as Hades. A throaty rumble that was the distilled essence of the wild. The Ravens froze. Terror coursed down their spines. Every hair on their heads prickled and their hearts cannoned against their ribs.

Calder had no idea how long it was before she took her next breath. She could see the blue light so clearly, but her legs were immobile. Her body simply refused to advance.

'Calder,' Estrid whispered plaintively, her voice taut with dread, and Calder knew her companion could go no further.

The craziness of the situation overwhelmed her. What stupid, stubborn part of her had brought them to this point? How dare those bastards hide their Asset here.

Shakily she drew her seax and stared into the dark.

'Back,' she whispered to Estrid. 'Slowly. Don't turn away.'

Calder begged her terrified limbs to move and felt them

respond. Inch by inch, she crept backwards and felt Estrid shuffling behind her. The slope was only a few yards to the fence, but it felt forever. At any moment she was convinced death would come streaking from the night. In the Halls of Valhalla, she had conditioned herself to accept death, to face it bravely if it selected her. But not like this. Never like this.

They were at the fence.

'You have it?' Skarde's helmet pressed against the bars and his hand came through. 'Give it to me.'

Silently Calder shook her head and Skarde swore.

'You stupid bitches, get that Asset!'

'No,' said Calder without taking her eyes from the night.

Skarde stared at her for long seconds, realising the bars meant he was powerless to force her. 'Then rot in hell,' he spat and ran from sight.

Calder hunched frozen to the spot and it was Estrid who brought her back. The new Raven crawled to the end of the rope and Ulf was still on the roof, staring wide-eyed.

Forcing herself to move, Calder slunk to Estrid. 'You first.'

The other Raven shook her head. 'You're too important.'

Calder wanted to argue, but nothing came from her lips. She began to climb and, with Ulf hauling on the other side, it was only a few heartbeats before she was clambering onto the curved bars and dropping to the roof. A growl came again, louder.

'Drop the rope,' she pleaded and stared wildly at Estrid waiting below. 'Quick, for the love of god!'

Ulf threw it back as best he could and it wriggled down to her. She grabbed it and hoisted her legs. *Come on, come on,* prayed Calder and joined Ulf hauling once more. The Raven rose and then she was reaching for the top and Calder was half-laughing as she saw her safely onto the curved bars. Something heavy moved below, a flash of muscle whipped the night and was gone.

Estrid dropped to them and without thinking, Calder hugged them both.

Ulf was grinning beneath his helmet. 'I can't believe…'

He did not finish his sentence. An arrow thunked into his back and toppled him off the roof. He landed hard on the concrete and lay motionless.

Calder dragged her sword from its baldric and heard Estrid's blade come free. She crouched on the edge of the building and jumped, a pain flickering up one leg on landing, but she was able to stand. Bodies tore through the bushes and the Ravens prepared to sell their lives dearly. But it was Torsten and Gunnar.

'They are upon us,' Gunnar yelled and both turned with shields high and blades poised across the iron rims. 'Fly now!'

The Titans came stampeding and the Storm men locked shields and thrust the first of them backwards.

'Fly!' Gunnar yelled again, skewering the next Companion in the shoulder.

Calder bent over Ulf. He was lying on his stomach and an arrow protruded from his upper back, pinning his cloak to him, but he was conscious and moving. 'I'm not leaving you, Ulf. Can you walk?'

'I think so.' He tried to reach round and grab the arrow shaft.

'Leave it. No time.'

Calder and Estrid bundled him upright and shouldered an arm each, though he yelped like a pup. Their shields were still piled by the tables, but they could not delay. They ran, forcing Ulf to stumble between them, and Calder strained to remember their route. They pushed back through trees and shrubs and there were the rhino and hippo enclosures below them. She could see Titans running along the path beside the kids' playground, but the trio were above the foe and passed unnoticed. They reached the second path and paced down it as best they could until she saw the sign once more: *Chimpanzees* and *Penguins*.

Now they diverted left and found themselves on a viewing platform extending out above a snow-clad field. An information point said *Zebra* and she knew they were in the right place. They staggered to the end of the platform and looked down to the snow fifteen feet below.

'We're going to have to jump.'

Ulf groaned a protest, but voices shouted behind them as Titans rushed the walkway. Five of them. Companions from the look of their plumes, though she could not make out the colour in the light and prayed they were not the Band.

'Go!' she yelled and toppled Ulf over the side. Estrid thought to make a fight of it, but Calder grabbed her and they both leapt. The snow softened their fall, but the impact still tore up Calder's spine. She gasped and groped to her knees. Ulf was unhurt and already on his feet, swaying and staggering. The Ravens grabbed him again and lurched across the field. No arrows flew their way. No spears sought their spines. The Companions carried only their shortswords, but they were still coming. The first three were already dropping to the snow and Calder knew they could never outrun these steadfast pursuers. They would die in this place amongst zebra.

But then a mighty bellow and a new beast sprung from the night. Ingvar. Whirling his axe and cursing the gods, he laid into the three, slicing two in one mighty sweep and then taking the arm of the third. The remaining pair paused atop the platform and weighed the attractiveness of dropping onto an axe-wielding madman.

Calder ran. Ulf was gulping and spluttering on her shoulder, but his legs were pounding nonetheless. And before them was a tiny light. Ingvar had balanced the torch on a stone so that it would be a beacon in the dark. When they reached it they saw he had sliced the steel mesh asunder. He must have heard the night break with conflict and thought to hell with it.

They forced themselves through and stood gasping for breath and gazing back into the zoo. Ingvar was coming now. It had stopped snowing and they could see him lumbering across the white grassland. But there were Titans on the platform behind, silhouetted by the lights from the path. Many of them. Rallying and pulling themselves into order of attack. Ingvar arrived, heaving steam into the frigid air, and he swore joyously. His arms were lathered in blood and they held the mesh wide for him to barge through.

'What of the others?' Calder asked.

He wiped a bloody arm across his beard. 'That bastard Skarde's gone. Just came through and disappeared. I've seen none of the others.'

'We have to go,' warned Estrid. The Titans were massing and dropping from the platform.

The four Vikings fled up the slope to the crest of the hill.

As they reached it they saw two more figures bounding up from the southern flanks and they were sure this was the end. But it was Stigr and Ake, wild and shieldless. They demanded to know about the others. Calder said they had left Gunnar and Torsten deep in the zoo complex and Ake swore and made to run back, but Stigr grabbed her. They could see the ranks of Titans coming and sense prevailed.

'They'll see our tracks,' cursed Ingvar.

But it was not to be.

Somehow – miraculously – the Titans were confused by the plethora of footprints made by Valhalla's nine when they had been blundering around looking for the fourth cache. As the Vikings descended, they could hear their foe castigating each other, and they reached the golf course unchallenged. There, for the second time that night, Estrid inspected an arrow wound. Ulf's woollen cloak and mail had dampened the impact and his shoulder blade had stopped the iron tip burying deep. She could not tell if the bone had cracked, but decided the risk of blood loss was low, so – while the group closed around to hide the light of their little torch – she laid Ulf flat on his stomach, placed her hands on the shaft and pulled it from him. He gritted his teeth and made no sound and Estrid folded his cloak over the wound and used Calder's belt to secure it.

The Titans knew nothing of the route the Horde had weaved on their merry way to Corstorphine Hill and so the six survivors ran for the lights of the clubhouse and then slunk back along Ravelston Road.

Two lost. Two wounded. One bastard Housecarl.

And no Asset.

XXX

Despite the abundance of technological wizardry housed in Valhalla's Operations Support Unit, Aurora provided Oliver with the information he had requested from Odin handwritten on a slip of paper. Morgan Maitland – known as Olena, Captain of Companion Bodyguards in the Titan Palatinate – had last been seen on Pantheon-monitored CCTV running across the Royal Mile at 2.44 a.m. on 24 March two years previously, during the third week of the Blood Season in the Eighteenth Year, a pack of Wolves on her tail.

A natural inference would be that they had caught up and slaughtered her somewhere among the alleys behind Parliament Square, but the lack of a body for the *libitinarii* to collect suggested otherwise. Perhaps she had made it back to the Titan strongholds and they had secreted her away, but why would they do such a thing? Maybe she had been so badly injured that she had spent the last two years cosseted from the world in a Pantheon hospital? Possible, but Oliver's instincts thought unlikely. He was worldly enough to guess that a Caelestis like Odin would have fingers in many pies and if he wanted to find someone in an opposing Palatinate, he would not be empty-handed after two years.

Then there were the findings from Oliver's own search – or the lack of them. Everything he had checked for Tyler last year – insurance records, education databases, driving histories – all had been deleted, as though someone had been systematically eradicating Morgan's entire online presence. If this wasn't the work of Odin or the Titans, who else could have done it? Morgan herself? Covering her tracks? Disappearing?

Finally, there was the obscure chat room where someone called Olena Macedon using the online moniker *Torchlight96* had been posting about the Pantheon until 4 December in the Nineteenth Season, eight months after Morgan's last sighting on camera. If it was her, what had she been doing in between and why had she ceased messaging on that date?

He sat for an age, picking his upper lip and wondering why Morgan Maitland was such a prize for the Valhalla Caelestis. Kustaa had said it was because Odin wanted to help Tyler in his search for his sister, but having come face to face with the Caelestis and felt the force of his malevolence, Oliver knew this loathsome man did not have Tyler's – or Morgan's – best interests at heart. So why? Why did he want Morgan Maitland? Somehow Oliver understood that his own abduction and the murder of his parents – *the murder of his parents* – all came back to this need of Odin's to locate the Titan called Olena.

A seam of cold fury weighted his gut. He hated the man. Hated him. Hated him. And he would have his vengeance. All he could think was that if he discovered something about Morgan's whereabouts – something juicy, something that would make Odin beg and plead for it – maybe he could find a way to hurt him.

He pursed his lips and gazed at the back of Jed's scruffy head. 'Is it possible to see the personnel files on each warrior in Valhalla?'

Jed finished typing a sentence and turned to regard the lad. He was wearing a white T-shirt spattered artistically with gravy stains and when he leaned back with his hands on his head, there were sweat patches under his arms.

'No can do. That's confidential information held by Aurora alone. Why are you asking?'

'I've a friend in the Horde and I wanted to see which litter he's in now.'

Jed raised his eyebrows. 'A friend? I'd keep that quiet if I was you.'

'Is there a way I can send him a message? Some sort of internal email system?'

'Not one the likes of us can access. The Pantheon keeps its warriors' identities very close to its chest.'

Oliver brooded over this, then changed tack. 'What about local CCTV? Can we access that from here?'

Jed peered at him suspiciously, then relented. 'Not live feeds. Only the Pantheon teams can get into those. The thinking goes that if we could view live feeds from here on, say, Blood Nights, and see troop movements in real time, we might use it to our unfair tactical advantage. So we can only log into a library of clips, which Atilius' lot have deemed worthy of saving.'

'Could I look through those?'

Jed reached for a mini pork pie and bit into it. '*We* can. But not you. You don't have the clearance.'

Oliver clenched his jaw irritably. 'Okay then, can you help me search them?'

Jed took an age chewing his pie, then finally relented and signalled him over. 'Pull up a chair.'

He fired up the OSU's specialist server and clicked through a host of security screens before reaching the Pantheon's CCTV records for Edinburgh. 'What do you want?'

'Can you see if there are any clips from cameras on or around the top of the Royal Mile on 24 March, two years ago, after 2.40 a.m.?'

Jed peered sideways at him. 'This is this thing you're working on for Odin?'

Oliver nodded and the man shrugged. 'Okay, let's see what we've got.'

He input the date and the screen filled with files. 'Whoa, that's a lot more than usual. Let me see, third week of the Blood Season in the Eighteenth, but not a formal Blood Night.' Then he clicked on a few feeds and quietened for several seconds. 'This is the night of the Titan Raid into the cellars below Advocate's Close.' He peered at Oliver again. 'We were all pulled in here to work a night shift because Odin was convinced something was going to happen, even though it wasn't one of the six formal Blood Nights. The Horde was on full alert in the Tunnels and we sat at our screens seeing nothing and thinking the whole thing a fool's hunch, and then – there they were. A whole damn company of Companions creeping down to the cellar complexes below Advocate's. It's the location of one of the secret tunnels that give access to the lower reaches of Valhalla and Christ knows how the Titans knew about it. Odin sent Wolf and Hammer to stop them and it was a bloodbath down there. We had a camera mounted above the doorway and we witnessed the whole thing. Let me get this straight, you want to know if Atilius saved anything from CCTV in the surrounding area on *that* night?'

'I do.'

Jed inclined his head and turned back to the screen. 'Okay. What are we looking for?'

'A woman. A Titan officer.'

They spent an hour absorbed in the saved clips. Jed, increasingly intrigued, became as entranced as Oliver and they checked every recorded snippet, searching for this woman, even if just a shadow or a whisper of cloak. But the Pantheon had stopped saving footage after 4 a.m. when Conflict Hours finished. By that time there was new movement on the Mile as the first early shifts headed to work and still there had been no sign of the officer the pair sought.

Oliver returned disconsolately to his desk and sat with his chin in his hands staring moodily out at grey skies. In two hours his driver would be here to collect him for the return run to the Schola and maybe it was for the best because the day felt entirely wasted. He clicked on the folder of Tyler's old documents copied from his laptop and scanned cursorily through them, but most were just bills and paperwork from years ago, which Tyler had stored at the time.

And then Oliver's movements paused and his brow creased as he examined an energy bill from twenty-six months ago. It gave an address for a property on the Craigmillar estate, probably a flat, but it was the addressee that held his gaze. *M Maitland*. He flicked forward and found a phone and council-tax bill similarly addressed, but when he reached April of that Eighteenth Year, the name changed to *T Maitland*.

Oliver let out a low whistle. Tyler had never said he lived with his sister, but any fool could infer that Morgan had been the bill payer until she disappeared, when Tyler took over. Morgan Maitland had probably been living at that property with her brother.

'Jed.' He stalked to the shoulder of the other man. 'Do we have the capacity to check historic CCTV images that haven't been saved onto the Pantheon drives?'

Jed looked at him sharply. 'You mean hacking into private CCTV catalogues?'

'I guess.'

'Well, the answer's a robust no; we don't have the capacity, nor the protocols.'

'But...?'

Jed glanced at his other team members to check for eavesdroppers. 'But... some of us might know how to do it off the record.'

'So, maybe if I gave you an address, you might – off the record – be able to work your magical way into clip catalogues from nearby cameras on the night in question?'

Jed ran his tongue round his lips and took a long look over at her ma'amship in her office, then he leaned forward and began opening screens. 'First of all, let's make sure there's no trail for anyone to see what we're going to be searching. Okay – done. Now, give me the address.'

It took him four minutes to identify the two nearest cameras on the Craigmillar estate. 'All run by the same commercial surveillance company – and, bingo, looks like they use IP remote monitoring.'

Jed grinned because anything on the internet could be hacked. 'Every time a camera's sensors pick up movement, it sends the images over Wi-Fi to a remote monitor manned by some company watchman who can check if the activity warrants investigation. All these clips will be recorded and filed in case of future claims, but it depends if this particular company keeps footage from two years back.'

Oliver watched as Jed took them on a rollercoaster ride into the bowels of the company's secured archives and broke into their video library, then began searching the time stamps.

'Here we go. March twenty-fourth, a Thursday. Not much triggers the cameras between two and five in the morning, but then it starts to get busy.'

They opened each clip in turn, watching residents, drunks, foxes and cats take it in turns to set off the sensors as they wandered past. By the time they reached the footage after 6.30 a.m., daylight was unfolding over the estate and more people began coming and going.

'Wait,' Oliver said as Jed was about to move on from one particular clip time-stamped at 7.25 a.m. It showed a woman in a tracksuit walking fast towards the block.

'You see something?'

'I don't know. Just the speed she's moving and the way she's got her head dipped – like she's trying not to be recognised.'

'Might get a better view from the other camera.' Jed swapped and now as the woman strode past, she raised her head once to look ahead. Jed hit pause and Oliver stared at the grainy image. Memories of a framed photo in Tyler's flat came back. Of a happy shining moment at a graduation ceremony, when Morgan, Tyler and their mother had smiled for the camera.

'It's her,' he said.

Jed saved the clip to a USB stick.

'Can we keep looking?'

'You think there'll be more?'

'This shows her heading to her flat. It's where she goes next that holds the key.'

With another check around the office, Jed nodded and they continued searching. But Morgan did not emerge again and he grew impatient. 'We're going to have to call it soon. I need to do a couple of tasks before heading home.'

'Just a few more, please.'

He cursed quietly, but acquiesced.

It was the time-stamp for 10.13 a.m. that made Oliver grab the other man's elbow and his heart leap in his throat. 'There she is.'

Once more, Morgan walked past the first camera, this time dressed in a smarter coat and jeans, and weighed down with a kitbag. Next to her walked another woman. Oliver had never seen her before.

'Do you know who that is?'

Jed shook his head. 'Not a clue.'

They checked the other camera, but the women must have diverted because it captured nothing. They returned to the first footage and watched it several times before Jed saved it on the USB.

'Reckon that's our lot,' he said, handing Oliver the stick. 'Now get back to your desk. I've got some deleting to do.'

Oliver slunk to his corner and twirled the USB ruminatively in his palm. And with every turn a conviction took root in his gut that he had just witnessed the last known movements of Morgan Maitland.

The atmosphere in the Ephesus War Room was one of hollow triumph. Alexander had gathered his Titan commanders for a post-mortem on the First Raid Night and they were seated around a giant mosaic, which dominated the floor and depicted central Edinburgh in gorgeous, rainbow colours. There was muted satisfaction at the manner in which the Viking raiders had been sent scampering back to their Tunnels Asset-empty. Yet even an old and blunted blade could have cut the tension in the room because it was now three weeks into the Combat Seasons and no Raid Night success was going to suppress the issue that plagued their minds.

If the Titan Palatinate had a hundred and three Blood Funds to spend, their strongholds should be bursting with eager new recruits. Instead, their Brigades remained thin; only a smattering of fresh blood from the Schola now hefted sarissas with the Heavies and just ten new Companions worked at their sword-stroke in the Bladecraft Rooms. It was a travesty and the commanders wanted answers from their king.

Yet Alexander was at his most stubborn and confounding. They would come, he blustered darkly, just as he had done on each occasion he had been interrogated since the new year.

'When?' Cleitus demanded.

'When Zeus and I decide.'

'Oh come on,' Parmenion responded and Nicanor swore.

Only Agape and Simmius held their tongues.

'This is a pile of horseshit,' snapped Cleitus, his choice of analogy more befitting than he could ever conceive.

'Enough of your theatrics, Colonel,' warned the king. 'Your Companions have been strengthened.'

'By ten. I warrant thirty at least. Where are the rest?'

Alexander's eyes twitched furiously. 'As I have already said, the additional recruits are undertaking final preparations and will join your companies when Zeus decides. Until then, they are being held in reserve.'

Cleitus waved a fat finger. 'That's not what my sources tell me.'

Alexander eyeballed him. 'Your sources. *Your* sources! Just what do you mean by that?'

'That I am told there has been no further requisitioning of the Schola's fourth-year cadre.'

Parmenion and Nicanor exchanged glances and Alexander's fists balled and unballed, but it was Simmius who spoke. 'Since when, Colonel, do you have sources into my Schola?'

Cleitus grunted angrily, but did not press the point. Instead, Nicanor leaned his elbows on his knees, set his eyes on his King and said evenly, 'To confound it all, I have two troopers *missing* from my Heavies.'

'Missing? What do you mean, missing?' demanded the king.

'Just that. Simmius said he needed them a few weeks ago.'

'I too,' added Cleitus sourly. 'Menes tells me Maia from the Bodyguard is gone and that new one, Lenore. What are you up to, my lord king?'

Alexander's black eyes shifted to his Adjutant.

'My peltasts are a pair down too,' said Parmenion. 'And not just any pair. The Valhalla turncoats.'

All heads swivelled to him.

'The Wolfling traitors?' exclaimed Cleitus.

Parmenion nodded. 'Diogenes and Hephaestion.'

'They're gone too?'

'I laid eyes on Hephaestion at the *Agonium Martiale*, but that is all.'

Cleitus forced his fat carcass to its feet. 'Well – King – what games are you playing that you send your Adjutant to plunder the few forces we still command?'

Alexander rose to face his Colonel of Light Infantry and his hand reflexively sought a blade at his hip, though no weapons were permitted in the strongholds outside of Conflict Hours. Cleitus saw the motion and squared up across the mosaic map. 'You want to make something of this, my king?'

Alexander rained hate-filled eyes on him and took a step forward, but Simmius hurried from his station with raised hands. 'My lords, there is no need for this. I can account for each of your missing troops.'

Cleitus and Alexander glared at each other, but allowed Simmius to bustle onto the map between them. 'I understand your questions, but the explanation is simple. Zeus asked for a small detachment to accompany him on a series of engagements with members of the Curiate, so that he could illustrate the prowess of our Titan lines to these hugely important attendees. He felt a selection from each company would be most appropriate and so we chose two from the Heavies, two from the Companions and one from the Band.'

'And you took it upon yourself to make these selections

without conferring with their commanding officers?' Nicanor grunted.

'Or their king,' added Alexander and his voice was corpse-heavy.

'It was the Armatura, so there seemed no reason to trouble you.'

'And Parmenion's Wolflings?' snarled Cleitus.

Simmius took a breath. 'They are gone – thrown from the Pantheon.'

No one spoke for several heartbeats.

'Since when?' asked Parmenion.

'Since Zeus decided it was unbecoming to harbour Valhalla rejects.'

Cleitus twisted his lips and tried to get his head around this new information. 'Unbecoming? It was unbecoming that Agape didn't cut their throats on the beach when they attempted to surrender. Instead we escorted them all the way back here, fed them, gave them blankets to warm their lily-livers, then granted them the opportunity to fight for their right to join our ranks and kill two of my best Companions – and *now* Zeus decides it's unbecoming to harbour them?'

'He felt it was for the best going forward.'

Before Simmius could say more, Alexander turned on him, grabbed the front of his robe and dragged him across the floor to a table, pinning him on it. 'You knew about this?' he hissed, spittle flecking his lips. 'You knew about this and you didn't tell your king?'

'My lord...'

'How dare you!' The man's breath reeked of wine and his eyes burned. 'I should have you beaten for insubordination.'

Talon fingers curled into a fist and drew back to strike, but hands came around and pulled him away. Parmenion and Nicanor held him hard and waited while his anger mollified and Simmius was able to stumble upright and smooth down his robe.

'You are certain of this?' said Cleitus, as though nothing had happened. 'They're gone?'

Simmius adjusted the rope around his waist and nodded without looking up. 'I've already had their names struck and their accommodation cleared.'

Alexander breathed raggedly between his captors. Nicanor shrugged and released him. Parmenion returned to his seat and Cleitus scratched his balls gravely.

Only Agape remained unmoved and when Simmius finally lifted his head, their eyes met for the briefest of moments, like two swallows spinning high in a summer sky, there and then gone.

XXXI

Hephaestion stood with Boreas in his stall, rhythmically running a body brush down the stallion's neck until his grey coat shone with the oils drawn from his skin. The horse tugged on a hay net and regarded Heph with one coal-black eye, getting to know this man who rode him without saddle or stirrups and who took such care over his grooming.

From the other stalls could be heard the sighs and nickers of the rest of the horses as they enjoyed their feed and settled for the night. Outside the field had darkened and a cold, clear sky promised ground like granite by morning. The seven members of Zeus' new cavalry had spent the last hour sponging and brushing, picking hooves, combing manes, cleaning tack, laying straw and filling hay nets, but one by one they had returned to the farm for the evening, leaving Heph to enjoy the peace of the stables. There was something about the scent of the hay, the warmth of the big body and the gentle stirrings of the other stallions that brought such peace, so he was happy to take his time.

He pressed his face into Boreas' mane to smell his musk and the horse snorted, which might have been contentment, but more likely irritation. Either way, it made Heph smile because Boreas suffered no fools and Heph loved him all the more for it. He applied himself to the brushing again, focusing now on the withers, but Boreas raised his head and twitched his ears at a new presence in the stables.

Heph checked beyond the stall and spied Lenore bearing two beakers. 'Gin – I thought we both needed it, but I can see I'm intruding on something special.'

She balanced the beakers on a window ledge and came to join him in the stall, standing the other side of Boreas and peering at Heph across the stallion's great spine. She had showered and changed into jeans and a cashmere jumper and she scented the stables with rose. 'The others have begun their assault on the wine collection and Dio's cooking up a vat of chilli.'

'Dio's a star.'

'He feeds us like kings, god bless him.'

She placed a hand on Boreas' back and Heph glanced at her elegant fingers. Something heavy settled in the air between them and so he concentrated on his brushing and kept his head down.

'It's strange that we both ended up here,' she mused. 'Like we've been on similar journeys.'

'New Thegns,' he agreed. 'White Warriors and now fledgling cavalry. Were you also an Electi like me?'

'Yes. I was tracked by Simmius and a Venarii party and accosted outside my flat in New Town when I returned from the solicitors' I worked at. There were just four of us recruited last year, but in the end I was the only one who made it to the Oath-Taking and joined the Titans as a Dekarchos.'

'What's that?'

'A young officer. The same as a Thegn in Valhalla.'

Heph pondered this as he continued to brush Boreas. 'So were you a solicitor?'

'Just starting my training.'

'New Town? Solicitor? A nice respectable life. The sort it would be difficult to give up.'

'What are you implying?'

'Just that I suspect there's more to your story than that.'

'Meaning?'

'Meaning all of us here have less respectable stories. That's why the Pantheon wanted us.'

She lapsed into silence. Heph shifted his brushing to Boreas' flank and his hand came within a finger's length of hers, but she did not move it.

When he had first laid eyes on her a year ago on the field of the *Agonium Martiale*, he had felt a constriction in his chest, even though that initial meeting had revealed nothing more of her than ruby red hair shimmering in the flamelight beneath her helm. He remembered his visceral shock that the Titan White Warrior was a woman and during the subsequent weeks he worried for her on each Raid Night as his Valhalla comrades-in-arms conspired to bury their steel in her heart.

'I'm glad our journeys have brought us together,' she said, interrupting his reminiscences.

'You hated me once.'

She laughed, a peal that disturbed the horses and made Boreas once more raise his head from his hay. 'I did. You cheating White Warrior. I swore I'd make you pay.'

'So what changed?'

Lenore scrutinised him for so long that he looked up

from his work to see a smile flickering playfully on her lips. 'Maybe you did.'

He harrumphed at this and went to find a mane comb hanging on a nail beyond the stall and she removed her hand and stepped back to let him get at Boreas' long hair.

'You know...' She picked her words carefully. 'We all support what you're doing.'

He tugged at a snag in the mane and was silent for several moments. 'It doesn't feel like it.'

'If you mean Zephyr and Spyro, you have to understand, they're much-admired veteran soldiers with Seasons and kills under their belts and now you have them riding around a field saddleless and stirrupless in a seven-strong cavalry and their afraid we'll be the laughing stock of the Palatinate.'

'Is that what you think?'

Lenore ran her hand meditatively along Boreas' spine. 'No. But I do wonder sometimes what impact we can make.'

Heph ceased his combing and gave her his attention. 'I've seen what impact we can make. I travelled with Agape to the Kheshig summer-grazing grounds and from close quarters witnessed the charge of a ten-strong mounted arban. The speed and power of their attack was mind-blowing. The shock of their passing. Used at the right moment, pointed at the right spot and permitted the right momentum, I tell you, we could be devastating.'

He said the last words with such whispered conviction that Lenore was silent and a light danced somewhere far behind her eyes, but after a few heartbeats she broke her gaze and frowned. 'If you know where to look, sometimes clips sneak online that the Pantheon does not intend for public consumption, especially from the eastern Palatinates where security seems more patchy. I've seen a few mass attacks by Hun horse-soldiers and they don't have the impact on their Sultanate enemy that you're describing.'

'I've seen those too and I agree. But it's because Mehmed counters Attila's massed charges with closed squares of infantry many files deep. He arms his Janissaries with eight-foot spears and places them around the edges of each square. He fills the centres with Yaya bowmen who can loose arrows at a rate of fire comparable to the attacking horsemen. And he has his own müsellem cavalry – albeit much smaller – but enough to flank-attack the Huns if they become caught on the Janissary spears and lose cohesion. When *we* take to the field, we'll face Vikings arrayed in shield lines two or three deep at most, with only Hammer and Storm routinely using spears. We *can* break them.'

Heph stepped back to inspect Boreas, then returned the mane comb to its hook and claimed a beaker of gin. He plonked himself on a bale of hay set against the wall, knocked back a slug and wiped his lips with his arm. 'But we won't be breaking anyone if we can't become a cohesive unit.'

Lenore took the other beaker and then, after a moment's hesitation, perched next to him. 'You need to stop thinking like that. Zephyr's from the heart of the Phalanx frontline and Spyro's Band. These men don't take instruction lightly. So has it occurred to you that if they didn't have faith in what you are doing they might have cleared off long ago?'

Heph did not reply, but she had his attention and she twisted slightly on the bale.

'But here they are – here we all are – on this field at first light every day, listening to every word of advice, trotting in line, tightening into column, hefting spear and blade, weaving through fences, learning to steer with our thighs, taking things up to a canter without tack, and only stopping when the light fails and the horses need grooming.'

Heph pulled a face. 'Yeah, well that's all down to Dio.'

Lenore shook her head in exasperation. 'Heph, you idiot. It's *you* we follow. You're the one with the real vision – we all know that. We might be accomplished riders, but it's you who's thrown this new challenge at us – ride without saddle, without stirrups, like true Alexandrian Macedonians – and you've accepted nothing less. And, yes, we've hated you when the skill has seemed beyond us, but we've stayed true to your vision. We hurt for you, we bleed for you, we even dislocate bones for you and now we're tired to our very cores – but still we love it. Because this whole stupid plan has become a revelation, an addiction. I never realised what it could feel like to ride without the hindrance of leather tack and be at one with the horse beneath me, feeling his every twitch and shiver. I am a truer horsewoman than I ever believed possible – and it's been your bloody-minded determination that has got me here.'

Their faces were inches apart. 'Spyro and Zephyr aren't stupid,' she continued. 'They know Zeus wouldn't gamble on you if he had no faith. And, what's more, at the Blood Count in the Ephesus Gardens, every Titan watched you and Dio fight for your lives. And they saw Agape intercede on your behalf at the critical moment. Nestor acted dishonourably and deserved to die, but everyone knew Agape came into that circle to change your destiny – just as she stayed her sword when you surrendered on the beach.

Let's face it – anyone who's worth saving in her eyes must have something special.'

She lapsed into silence and they stared at each other. In that moment, with the pungent warmth of the hay and the rose scent of her and the gin in his belly, Heph wanted to lean towards her, but she dipped her lashes and inclined her face away. 'So what's your story?' she asked softly.

He tried to hide the shake in his voice. 'Mine?'

'You said we all have stories. At the culmination of last year's Battle, you were among the Wolves lining the crest of the beach and our Heavies and Companions were floundering in the water below. You could have held that position with ease until the klaxon. And yet you chose to step away and run around the flank of the whole Battle until you found the Sacred Band.' She laid her eyes on him again. 'That was *some* surrender. So I'm wondering, were you escaping your fears in Valhalla or seeking your dreams with us?'

She took a long, languorous drink of her gin, her eyes not leaving him.

He wrinkled his nose in deliberation, then inhaled and said, 'I was looking for someone special to me.'

'Oh,' Her body tightened and shifted almost imperceptibly from him.

'My sister. She used to be a Titan.'

Lenore's brows furrowed into a blade-sharp crease. 'But siblings aren't permitted in the Pantheon.'

'So everyone keeps telling me.'

'Have you asked Simmius about it? He holds all the information about Palatinate troops.'

'Not yet. I don't want to draw attention.'

Lenore was unconvinced, but she could see he would say no more, so she was quiet for several moments, then forced a breezy smile. 'Whereas leading the Titans' new Companion Cavalry will draw no attention at all.' He smiled at this and she nudged him and stood. 'Come on. Boreas and the boys want some peace and I can smell Dio's chilli from here.'

They crunched back over the frost-hardened field to the farmhouse, where a fire was blazing in the hearth and the kitchen was redolent with the rich odour of meat and spices. They joined the team around the table where they drank wine and cheered when Dio hefted a vast pan of steaming chilli onto the boards between them. As they ate, Heph shot glances at Zephyr and Spyro, and he saw their wine-warmed grins and – perhaps for the first time – he thought perhaps these men were happy to be here in this farmhouse, with this crew, sharing an enterprise to a destiny none of them yet knew.

Later, over pancakes and whiskies, Lenore found old pirate footage of the Hun and Kheshig cavalries in full war cry and the team pulled their chairs around the tablet screen and exclaimed and pointed and swore and laughed until finally the fire died and, one by one, they sought their beds.

'It's Waverley,' said Sveinn.

'So no bloody lions then,' Bjarke responded, eyeing Calder.

They had all watched the Vigilis' footage of her and Estrid clambering into the big cat pen and even though the failure to bring home an Asset was a strategic disappointment, the Valhalla Tunnels hummed with a sense of pride at the stone-cold bravery of the two Ravens. There were not many around the table in Sveinn's Council Chamber who would have traded places with them and they all knew it.

All except Skarde, who lurked wordlessly a pace back from the table with murder in his eyes. The video feeds did not lie and the Horde had seen its new Wolf Regiment Housecarl desert his troops and flee. It was ten months since his unprecedented arrival in the Palatinate and he had remained a man defined by the hell of Erebus, but since the Raid Night he was as much like a caged animal as the lions themselves, and just as dangerous. He smouldered with humiliation and every man and woman in Valhalla knew that one misplaced word, one ill-considered look, and he would break the invisible bonds restraining him and come at them with a killer's resolve. Even Bjarke kept his eyes to himself and refrained from his usual barbs, but he regarded Calder with a new admiration. *The past is the past*, his glances whispered to her. *You are a warrior now and you have earned your place at this table.*

'It hardly requires pointing out that this choice of location seems less than equitable,' said Asmund. 'As the Jarl says, Waverley has no wild beasts lurking on its platforms and it's a fraction of the distance from their strongholds compared to the long retreat our party undertook from Corstorphine.'

There was a murmur of agreement and Sveinn hoomed in the back of his throat. 'That's as may be, but Waverley has its disadvantages for an attacking party. For one, it's lit throughout the night and its wide-open concourses will do little to hide intruders. If we plan wisely, our fifty should be able to ring the station and make it impregnable. Kustaa – what do you have for us?'

The Thane retrieved his sheet of paper again. 'Much the same instructions as last time, lord. The ten-strong Titan invading party will be given coordinates to a hidden cache somewhere in the city. This will provide them with coordinates to a second cache and so on until they have the coordinates for the fifth and final cache. Although they do not know it, this will be hidden somewhere in Waverley station, a fact that we – as the defending Palatinate – have been told about in advance. Precisely where it is within such a large complex has not been revealed to us – and is for the Titans to discover.'

'What do we know about the station?'

'Just early research by my OSU, lord. Waverley consists of a primary island containing ticket office, waiting hall and retail units. Lines run east and west of this and there are twenty numbered platforms. The inner ones are mostly for local trains, with the outermost used for the intercity services to London and Inverness. There are five formal entrances. From Princes Street in the north, Market Street in the south, from Waverley Bridge in the west via North Ramp and South Ramp, and also the oft-forgotten footbridge in the far north-east corner giving access from Calton Road. We will need to patrol all these, although the station closes from midnight until five every night and gates are pulled across to seal it from rough sleepers.'

'They'll come from the roof,' Bjarke muttered.

'What makes you so sure?'

'Because they're pansy-arsed Sky-Gods and must always make an entrance. They'll jump off North Bridge and come across the roof. The whole damn thing's made of glass, so there will be air vents and skylights for them to sneak through.'

'They'll come from where the coordinates dictate,' said Freyja impatiently. 'That's the whole intent. Atilius will have planned a route that takes them on some winding, indirect journey and brings them to Waverley from a direction we least expect.'

The Jarl tugged his beard indignantly, but conceded the point.

'What else, Kustaa?' asked Sveinn, staring at the outline of the station on the Old Town map.

'The place is, of course, manned even when the gates are closed. Transport police, operations department, catering depot and cleaners, but Atilius has this all in hand. Station personnel will be detained in areas without lines of sight and cameras will be switched off until we leave. The tracks themselves will be filled with trains parked up until the timetable starts again after five and, as you said, lord, the concourses remain lit throughout the night so there will be few places to hide.'

'But remember,' Asmund spoke up, 'the Asset could be anywhere. It's easy to assume it will be somewhere conveniently central, but it could be hidden in the furthest darkest corner of the furthest darkest platform.'

There were nods at this.

'So,' mused Freyja, 'we may be fifty, but it's still a big area to cover. We'll need to split into threes, maybe even twos. That means when the Titans make their move, they could have the benefit of numbers at the critical moment of attack, so we must ensure each group is within hailing distance of another. We arrange ourselves so that a chain of alerts can bring all fifty of us to a single point within moments.'

'And I still say watch the roof,' added Bjarke. 'Bastards love heights, so keep your eyes up.'

'And also keep them peeled for a blue light,' said Calder and the Council looked at her. 'Each of the caches had a flashing blue light. Only small and hard to see, but anyone spots a blinking blue light, they need to make it known.'

'Understood,' said Sveinn, inclining his head towards her. 'Right – Kustaa – I want maps of this station. I want us neck-deep in blueprints. If a bird can get through a skylight or a rat up a drain, I want to know about it.'

'I will have them produced, lord.'

'Housecarl Freyja will review our order of battle and confirm the fifty when we next meet. And we will also decide who leads.' The King flashed a glance at Skarde, but his face was a frozen mask of resentment. 'We need to be on top of our game. We lost our opportunity to claim an Asset at the last Raid Night, so I'll be damned if this time we're going to allow Alexander's lot to slip through with one in their hands.'

'And be warned,' said Freyja. 'Because of the conditions, footage from the zoo night was poor, so the Vigiles will be all over those platforms like flies on shit, filming our every breath. Don't screw it up.'

XXXII

Freyja was right. When the Horde's fifty-strong defence arrived in Waverley for the start of Conflict Hours on the Second Raid Night, the place was crawling with Vigiles. During the preceding hour, they had rounded up those station staff not already given the night off by pre-warned bosses and herded them into the catering depot behind the main buildings. They had then requisitioned the primary operations rooms and commandeered camera control units and phone lines. Thankfully, the handful of transport police on duty had already absented themselves until four-thirty, by which time the warriors would have disappeared, the *libitinarii* would have cleared the detritus of battle and the station would once more be innocently empty.

Now – as the Horde arrived from Market Street and fanned out to agreed vantage points – the Vigiles loitered on the concourses, leaned over the walkways and rooted between carriages, until every field of vision, every line of sight, was covered by their helmet cams. This time the Curiate would not be denied their sporting drama.

Calder took up station on a footbridge above the main concourse and was joined by Sassa and Sten. After her heroics on the First Raid Night, Estrid, much to her chagrin, had been rested and new Thegn, Sten, was given this opportunity to prove himself. He looked anxious behind his helm, his eyes flitting and his throat swallowing, but he kept himself quiet enough and Calder was thankful. For her part, she had insisted she be included in the fifty and it seemed these days her opinions had weight, but now – looking down on the sleek lines of Waverley's twenty numbered platforms and the empty retail outlets and the ticket barriers standing open beneath the blank departure boards – this felt like an alien place for Valhalla and an ill-made selection by the Pantheon's planners.

Below them, Bjarke was dressed for war in mail and bearskin, a double-handed battle-axe over one shoulder. He gripped the haft and barked orders. This was a night for defence, for holding ground and repulsing invaders, and that required the big men of Hammer, so Bjarke was fizzing with fervour. Thirty-four of the fifty were from his shieldwalls, with ten archers from Storm and six hawk-eyed Ravens. In threes, he sent his Hammers to Waverley's platforms and entrances, with orders to plant their feet and let no one pass. Meantime, Storm split into pairs and found vantage points to rain iron onto great swathes of concrete.

Freyja was present too. Calder could see her by the ticket barriers in quiet conference with two of her more senior Ravens: Jorunn and Liv. She looked resplendent in her silver mail, black tresses tied into a rope and Raven shield strapped over one shoulder. Sveinn had not wanted to lose his principal adviser to the frontline, but both knew the defence of the station could not be left to Bjarke alone. It needed the finesse of her mind to scrutinise every eventuality and to think like a Titan. Where would they come from and what would they do when they first caught sight of the bright spaces of Waverley festooned with Vikings?

Calder was waiting to catch her eye, when suddenly the station's primary lights snapped off and the place was cast into the much softer gloom of its emergency illuminations. Somewhere in one of the operations rooms, Vigiles controllers must be determining the tableaux on which the night's actions would play out. Bjarke swore in surprise and voices could be heard up and down the platforms as patrols checked they could still see each other. Calder peered east and west along the tracks and debated whether this change was welcome. She had hated the shadowless glare of the main lights thumping off Viking helmets and exposing their every gesture, but now the twilight exaggerated the size of the station. Corners that had seemed innocuous, lurked in shadow. Distances that had seemed well judged, now stretched perilously between patrols.

Finally Freyja looked up and raised her arm at Calder.

'That's us – let's go.'

The three Ravens used lengths of leather strapping to stow their shields over their shoulders, then made their way to the centre of the footbridge. Sassa and Sten bent to let Calder place her boot in their hands and then helped her shimmy up iron girders above the handrail to a cramped maintenance crawl space that ran parallel to the bridge and was barely wider than her shield. Sassa followed, then they dropped arms for Sten and pulled him up kicking. After several metres on all fours, they came to a hatch in the roof. Calder yanked at a bolt and swore when it remained unmoved. Sten drew his sword and began hammering at it with the iron pommel. The noise reverberated around the station and anxious Viking faces turned up to them.

At last the bolt gave and Sten grunted in satisfaction. Calder heaved the hatch open and pushed her head through. Eight acres of steel and glazing extended in all directions, opaquely illuminated by the emergency lighting below and a cloud-harried moon above. At the far eastern end of the glass, the dark mass of North Bridge slanted up from the Balmoral Hotel to the high skyline of the Royal Mile, spanning Waverley's deep valley and connecting the hillsides on which sat Edinburgh's Old and New Towns. A night bus rolled down the bridge, but otherwise there was no sign of life. Calder eased herself out and perched on a steel support. She could see the platforms dizzyingly far beneath her feet and it took her a few moments to adjust. A breeze scurried over her and somewhere far away a siren wailed.

She waved the others up and sent them across the support beams in separate directions to crouch and wait. Calder herself remained beside the hatch because if anything kicked off, they needed sight and sound back down into the station. Checking her Ravens were settled, she scanned the expanse carefully. It was the third largest glass roof in Britain and no Titan should now be able to set foot on it without her seeing.

She glanced at the Balmoral clock. Three minutes fast as always, it read 1.38 a.m. and she wondered where the enemy might be, on what convoluted route they were being taken by the Pantheon's hidden caches. She remembered her own hunt for the caches with her Valhalla team. They had been ninety minutes into Conflict Hours before they discovered the fourth one and reached the perimeter of the zoo, but distances this time could be shorter and she figured they might have only another thirty minutes before the foe's eyes could be upon them. From where would they come? From the writhing alleys of Old Town and down the slopes? From the lightless embrace of the Gardens to the west? Or across North Bridge and rappelling onto this glazed roof?

The wind buffeted her hair and she pulled her cloak tighter. If the Titans came skulking across the glass, they would be ten against three. Unforgiving odds. She would have to pray her shouts would bring reinforcements rushing from the platforms.

And who would the foe send? Her mind reached for memories of Punnr and Brante, but cold logic dictated they would play no part tonight. The Titans would surely dispatch their crack hunters. The Companions and the Sacred Band. On the rooftops of Edinburgh, under winter-dark, wind-whipped skies, ten of those would be a match for anyone.

She signalled to Sassa and Sten and they waved back. There was nothing they could do except hunker down and watch.

Menes waited impatiently while his navigator bent over the fourth cache and plotted a new set of coordinates by the light of his torch.

'Well?'

'East north-east, sir. Four hundred paces.'

Menes bared his teeth. Of course, it had to be. He was old enough and savvy enough to guess exactly what had been on the Pantheon planners' minds when their bloody treasure trail brought his ten raiders to this spot. They had already been led on an expansive loop of central Edinburgh. From Thebes all the way down the Mile to the Palace, where the second coordinates sent them scurrying to the forgotten recesses of Calton Road and then the long hard climb to Regent Road above. Around the flanks of Calton Hill and into New Town, then the third cache directing them back to Princes Street, past the galleries on the Mound and finally this sudden drop to the railway tracks.

Now they clustered around the penultimate cache strapped to the base of a signal and every fibre of Menes' body told him the new coordinates would send them east, into the inky subterranean nothingness of the Tunnel looming at their shoulders.

'Four hundred paces along the tracks,' said Kyriacos, coming next to him. 'By my reckoning that takes us straight into Waverley.'

Menes nodded grimly and threw a black scowl towards a Vigilis hovering a few strides away. 'Practically into the bloody ticket office, the bastards.'

The ten comprised the cream of the Titans. Menes, as Captain of Companion Bodyguard, had overall authority and with him were three of his best lieutenants, hoplons strapped to backs, bronze finding means to glimmer despite the absence of illumination. Two places were taken up by peltasts bearing bows, while the remaining four were from the Band, led by their deputy commander, Kyriacos. Agape herself had been denied participation because Alexander would not risk his finest warrior against fifty Viking blades.

The navigator rose and flicked off the torch. 'I agree, sir.

Perhaps not as far as the ticket office, but four hundred paces east north-east will bring us well into the reaches of the platforms.'

Menes grunted and the ten Titans turned to face the gaping black hole of the Tunnel. 'How far in this?'

'Two hundred paces, sir.'

'And we're just supposed to pray that ScotRail isn't pissing about with any of its trains at this time in the morning?'

'Passenger ones shouldn't be running, but can't say about goods.'

Menes swore quietly. 'Two files, one each side. Hands on the walls to guide. If you've got the brains to count to two hundred, then do it, but quietly – and keep tight.'

With a long look in both directions, the Titan raiders and their limpet Vigilis stepped off and walked into the embrace of the Tunnel. The dark enveloped them. The air grew irredeemably colder and the bricks against their hands were slick with damp. Their war gear clinked and clanged and echoed around the confines, making them curse and hunch forward in a vain attempt to quieten their panoply. The edge of a hoplon caught against the brick wall, eliciting hissed threats from Menes, and after thirty paces the lead man walked into a steel pole and doubled over holding his helmet.

'Shut up, you fool,' whispered Menes from the other side.

Kyriacos placed a hand on his Band compatriot. 'You okay, Eusebius?'

The man grunted and took up position once more.

'Count us another thirty paces.'

Somewhere deeper into the hole, they heard a rumble and for a terrifying moment they were convinced a train was coming, but the rails beside them did not sing and they realised it must be a bus or lorry crossing the Mound above their heads.

They continued further and despite the cold, every trooper glistened with sweat. Rubble scrunched beneath their feet and someone stumbled into the person in front. Menes turned to peer behind and saw a small green light emanating from what he guessed was the Vigilis' helmet cam, no doubt filming with infrared. 'You let the Vikings see that when we get near, mate, and I'll stab you in the balls.'

The Vigilis said nothing, but when Menes next looked, the man had slowed and the light was much further behind.

At last they realised the darkness was relenting. A yellow aura reached for them and then, ahead, distant lights and an air that jostled with life once more. Menes held up his arm and the party halted and spread to peer at the cables and platforms beyond. Even from this distance they could see figures grouped into pairs and threes, limewood shields on their arms and the glint of iron.

'Showtime,' breathed Menes and spat. 'What's the tracker showing, Niketas?'

His navigator consulted the device. 'Nothing yet.'

'And the map?'

'I'm still saying another two hundred paces, sir, which will take us right past those guards and halfway up the platforms.'

Menes stepped to the shoulder of Kyriacos. 'What do you think?'

Kyriacos stared at the scene. He studied the roofs of the platforms. He calculated the heights of the verges on either side of the tracks. He peered at the overhead cables.

But, most of all, his eyes roved over an empty, lifeless train pulled into the platform numbered "20" on the outermost northern edge of the station. It was an intercity service, no doubt London-bound in the morning, and at least twelve coaches in length. Like a sleeping serpent, it stretched along the curving track and deep into the bowels of Waverley.

'I think,' he said, 'it's time to get creative.'

Freyja leapt lithely from a platform, followed by Jorunn and Liv. She crossed the tracks to one of the local trains parked up for the night, then dropped to her knees and peered underneath. Signalling to her companions, she crawled between the wheels and hauled herself out the other side. This brought her to the central platform, where two Hammers stood guard at the far end, staring into the night, hands on the pommels of their swords. With feline grace, she eased herself up and approached them from behind.

'If I was a Titan,' she said and they spun round swearing and reaching for their weapons, 'your throats would be cut.'

One of them – with a braided red beard and halitosis – spat dismissively and waved a brawny arm down the track. 'We're watching the western approaches. You're supposed to have the station covered.'

'How many Seasons have you been in Valhalla?'

'Four.'

'Four what?'

The man eyed her angrily, then said, 'Four, ma'am.'

'Then that's plenty long enough for you to know that the Sky-Gods only ever arrive from where they're least expected. One of you watch one direction and one the other. Cover every angle.'

The Hammers mumbled sourly and she strode around them and hopped down onto the next set of tracks, which she followed out from the station. The final tentacles of the platforms stretched beside her and then they were left behind and she was walking towards the black hole of a Tunnel beneath the Mound. She halted and stared hard into its darkness, held her breath and listened, then opened her mouth and inhaled slowly to taste the air. Jorunn and Liv came to her shoulder.

'What do you think?' Jorunn whispered.

Freyja was an age answering. 'Something about that tunnel. Something implacable.'

'Want me to check?'

But Freyja shook her head. 'No, too far away.' She swung round to examine the lights of Waverley. 'We'll make a circuit back along the southern perimeter and when we pass those two idiots again, tell them I'll have their heads on spikes if anything comes out that Tunnel and they miss it.'

Menes spat dismissively as the three Ravens turned away. The Titans had been crouching motionless in the blackness of the Tunnel, barely breathing lest it reveal them to the eyes of the Vikings.

'Timanthes died on the knife of that one in the centre,' Menes growled. 'Saw him fall with my own eyes.' There was a stir from his trio of Companions, a ripple of cold anger.

Towering above the station, the Balmoral clock nudged two-forty and Kyriacos slunk next to Menes. 'We should not delay. Every minute that passes, they will watch more diligently.'

Menes knew the sense in this. As the night slipped closer to the end of Conflict Hours, the foe would know the Titans had an ever-decreasing window to make their move. But still he waited, watching the receding figures of the Ravens as they steered onto the southernmost track. He had seen the bird on their shields and eight Seasons of campaigning had told him enough to know the eyes of these scouts were the sharpest in the Horde.

Keep moving, ladies. I'll take my chances with your knucklehead Hammer brethren.

The first platforms were a hundred paces from the Tunnel. A hundred paces of exposure, but Waverley's usual bright lights had been dimmed and the tracks were hemmed in by high walls and foliage, which blocked the glow of the city. Along the northern edge were two low-slung maintenance buildings blocking the line of sight of the Hammer pair loitering at the end of the central platform. Beyond them was a Vigilis and much further beyond him, perhaps another fifty paces, three more Hammers waited within hailing distance. If the Titans were spotted, the news would travel like wildfire through Waverley and every Viking blade would come hunting them.

The Ravens disappeared around the curve of the track and still Menes did not move, his eyes locked on the Hammers. One of them was angled away, peering up at the treeline to the north, but the other was staring straight down the track at them. Time flowed. The silence extended. *Come on, you bastards.*

At last, the man coughed, wiped a forearm across his

beard, swore in a low rumble and turned to his colleague. Menes felt for Kyriacos in the darkness and slapped his shoulder. Immediately the Band's lieutenant sprang forward, followed by his three troops and two of the Companions, and they spilled towards the first of the maintenance buildings. They had discarded their shields because now it was all about stealth and if they were spotted, they could never hope to make a fight of it.

The Vigilis made to follow the attackers, but Menes flung an arm in front of him. 'Don't you dare,' he hissed. 'There's cameras enough in that station and you won't be missed.'

The Hammers were still speaking and in the time it took them to laugh over some comment, Kyriacos and his team had their spines against the building. The Viking turned back, stamping his feet with cold, and resumed his inspection of the Tunnel, but he was a blind fool because the Titan assault party was already climbing to the roof of the maintenance shack.

Another long pause. Light leaked through the trees in the gap between the first and second building and now the damn Hammer was doing his job again. Menes bent and rummaged through the ballast at his feet, then kicked a leg back and flung a stone high into the trees above the southern flank of the railway. It thudded against wood and both sentries angled their chins towards the disturbance. On the other side of the tracks, the Titans dropped like cats, sped across the gap and ascended the second building.

Just thirty paces now to the tail of the London-bound train sleeping on the outermost platform, but thirty paces so close to the foe. Minutes ticked away. Menes thought to throw another missile, but chose to wait. A breeze caught in the trees and they creaked and sighed. A lorry trundled by on Market Street. And still the Hammers stood moodily, fists on pommels, shields held loosely at their sides. Finally, a voice from somewhere deeper inside the station and the pair glanced over their shoulders.

Kyriacos reacted like lightning. Down he pounced, landing with the agility of a puma, and then he ran, followed by the other five. Ten paces, twenty. The Hammers were shrugging and turning back, but the sleek contours of the train beckoned and, one after the other, the cloaked raiders dived into cover beside its wheels. Hearts hammered against ribs, so loud they were convinced they must be discovered, but the only sound that broke the silence was the hack of a Viking clearing his throat and spitting phlegm onto the concourse.

With practised ease, the Band's best climber sought the tiny bumps and notches on the smooth, featureless surface of the train and took herself onto the roof. In moments, another was beside her and arms dropped to ferry up the rest. Stomachs pressed against the roof, they waited while Niketas the navigator consulted his tracker and pointed east. Inch by inch, led by Eusebius, they began to crawl along the curve of the serpent train, edging ever deeper into Waverley.

Hunched and wind-whipped, Calder was frozen to her very bones on the glass canopy, when the first cry of alarm broke below her. More voices bayed as the pack picked up the scent. Calder forced her creaking knees to unfurl and stood to cast a gaze around the roof. Sten and Sassa were on their feet too, spinning on the spot to check every direction. Nothing. All clear. The attack must be focused on the platforms.

'On me.' Calder peered through the glazing to see Vikings running east, past the ticket hall and onto the platforms beyond. 'This is it – let's go.'

She flung herself back down the hatch and forced her way along the crawl space. Down again, onto the footbridge, Sten and Sassa behind her, and she was in time to see most of Hammer converging on Bjarke as he raced east along the platforms, bellowing and brandishing his war axe. Staring beyond him, she could see four Titans at the far end of platform 20. They were crouched around the base of a bench, fussing with something. *The cache. They have the cache.*

Vikings were streaming towards them. Bjarke leapt onto the tracks, swung between two trains and led his troops onto the outer platform, whooping with the joy of blood in his nostrils. The Titans waited and waited until they must surely be swallowed by their pursuers, then flung themselves to the tracks and sprinted east.

Calder ran to the head of escalators and began bounding down the stationary steel steps towards the concourse. Risking a glance up, she looked westwards down the platforms and there was Freyja and Jorunn and Liv. The final two Hammers came pounding past the trio towards the cacophony at the other end of the station, but the three Ravens were walking more slowly and something about Freyja's demeanour arrested Calder's momentum. The Housecarl was refusing to take the bait. Instead, even as she walked towards the ticket hall, she kept turning her head and looking behind.

And that was when Calder saw them.

Beyond Freyja, at the opposite end of platform 20, two figures jumped from the roof of the long train and their plumes huddled around a spot beneath an information board.

'Freyja!' Calder's sword sung from its sheath and pointed in the direction of the Titan pair. Her Housecarl followed the line of the weapon and saw the foe. With a cry, her blade also came free and she ran back down the concourse, Jorunn and Liv either side.

Calder's team bounded to the base of the escalator and stared east towards all the noise. The Hammers were chasing the decoy unit and only Vigiles hovered nearby, filming the Ravens, as though they already knew the hullabaloo in the east would lead to nothing.

'Come on,' she cried to the other two and they charged after their fellow Ravens.

Freyja, Jorunn and Liv were crossing the tracks and closing on their prey, but the Titans had what they needed. Their plumes swivelled to assess the threat and then they broke from their huddle and tore back down the lines towards the distant lurking mouth of the Tunnel beneath the Mound.

Calder avoided the temptation to angle towards the outer line and instead made up ground by tearing directly down the central concourse. Sassa was with her, Sten labouring a few strides behind. They reached the end of the concrete and flung themselves onto the ballast between the tracks. Freyja's party was fifty paces ahead and the Titan pair twenty beyond that. Already the Tunnel was beckoning them.

Calder never saw or heard the arrows. As the foe disappeared into the Tunnel's lightless embrace, Jorunn and Liv seemed to slam into an invisible wall and their bodies were thrown backwards. Time slowed for Calder. Her cry caught in her throat and though her legs still pumped like pistons, she made no headway towards them. The two Ravens floated backwards, carried on the night, their cloaks curving up around their shoulders and their blades dancing from their grasp. Freyja, oblivious and the Battle lust upon her, still tore towards the Tunnel and Calder screamed a warning to her, but the sound seemed only to reverberate around her own lungs.

Time came back.

Jorunn and Liv slammed onto the ballast with shafts embedded in their mail. Liv fell like a stone and did not move, but Jorunn rolled and curled and tried to right herself, though her legs would not obey. Calder's breath returned in gasps. Blood pumped behind her eyes. She charged past the fallen Ravens. Forty paces to the Tunnel. Almost there. Almost.

Freyja vanished into the crepuscular depths, her shield high, her blade across its limewood rim. Sightless, the Housecarl rammed into a wall of hoplons and was thrown sideways against the Tunnel's wall. She swung her sword blindly and stumbled forward. But the Titan six were accustomed to the dark and she was silhouetted by the station lights. They crowded her, shoved her, cut her.

And Menes had what he wanted.

'Payment for Timanthes, you heathen bitch,' he hissed and stepped to her with hard, fast violence.

Moments later, Calder raced into the stagnant depths.

Her foot caught on the rails, but she kept herself upright, only to stagger forward, trip on a fallen bulk and crash to the tracks. Hauling herself to her knees, she felt her way back and found Viking mail and long fine hair. Her nostrils filled with unmistakable scent. The same scent that she had known each night over dinner in the big house below Blackford Hill. The one that she had first smelt in training during the Armatura all those months ago, when it had floated gently above the sweat and fear and musk that had pervaded those vaults, sweetening the air incongruously as Halvar rumbled and swore at his useless Thralls.

Tears flooded her cheeks. The faintest light from the station smuggled itself into the gloom and Calder realised Freyja's eyes were glinting behind her helmet. Her chest moved and a bubbling gargle came from her throat. In a panic, Calder felt over her body and there was slick warmth pooling among the rings of mail below the curve of her breasts. Cursing, Calder bent close and tried to pull at the individual rings, but Freyja clenched in pain and her fingers found Calder's arm, telling her through their weak grasp to stop.

The Housecarl made to speak, but her lips could not find the words.

'Stay still,' Calder insisted. 'I'm here. We'll get help.'

Dimly she was aware of Sassa and Sten arriving and movement from further into the Tunnel.

Freyja was trying to speak again.

'Hush. Save your strength.'

But the Raven commander was raising her helmeted head, gurgling and spitting. 'Listen,' she gasped.

'Quiet,' said Calder, refusing to hear. 'The *libitinarii* are on their way.'

From somewhere, strength came to Freyja and her hand closed again on Calder's arm. 'Listen,' she croaked once more and some of her authority still clung to that word.

Calder put her helmet so close to Freyja's lips that she could feel the last warmth of her breath and the moist bloodiness of her mouth.

'Look to…' the Housecarl continued, but her voice trailed off in a groan. For several seconds she simply breathed.

Then she shaped her lips one more time and with her final oxygen – in the moments before Renuka Malhotra's mind filled with memories of her mother and her village amongst the orchards beneath the towering mountains of Himal Pradesh – she spoke the last three words of her life.

'Look to Erebus.'

XXXIII

It was cancer. Stage-three pancreatic, to be precise and he was damned if he was going to allow the specialists anywhere near him.

Sveinn sat in his favourite leather chair in front of a snapping fire in the Council Chamber, his elbows on his knees and a cup of warm apple wine steaming in one hand. These last few months the pain in his stomach was always present, but he found if he leaned forward it receded to little more than a weight somewhere beneath his ribs. In such a posture, he could almost convince himself it was illusory, a trick of the mind, an ache of age and nothing more.

They had said they must stop the cancer cells reproducing and he had told them where they could stick their chemotherapy, their radiotherapy, or any other kind of therapy. After leading the Horde for twenty years and witnessing fine people – much younger than him – cut down in their prime, he was not about to be the invalid king, rigged up to intravenous drugs to save his precious life, constipated and feeble, his silver locks coming away in handfuls. He would see out the Twentieth Season and during the months of the Interregnum he would assess his own stamina. If and when the time was right, he would inform

Atilius and prepare the way for the smooth transition to a successor.

And then he would do what he had spent more than a decade refusing to countenance. He would try to make peace with his son.

He drank the wine. It had become his favourite comfort. It warmed him, blurred the pain and lent him fleeting vigour. But not tonight. This time nothing could induce vigour because Freyja was gone. He stared at the flames. Somewhere above, another short February day was slipping away, the weak light escaping before it had ever really arrived.

When the first rumours had filtered into the Tunnels the previous night, he had refused to believe them. He had sunk onto his throne in the great Hall and let the noise wash over him, saying nothing, showing no emotion, until the *libitinarii* counts confirmed what he already knew. Then he had taken himself up to this room and if he had cried – if he had fallen to his knees and heaved great sobs of grief – it was an act no other living being would ever witness.

She had been in her ninth Season. One more and she could have departed the Pantheon with the honours accorded to a hero, but Sveinn doubted she would have left. Like all true warriors, the Pantheon was in her blood and she would have abandoned the shieldwalls only when her blade craft ebbed or her body lay broken. So perhaps this was the fate she would have chosen. Better to fall with a sword in your hand and a foe in your face, than to shrink with a cancer in your gut.

Maybe she had been a daughter to him, though she would never have known it and he would never dare have admitted it. From her early Seasons, when she had moved through the ranks, he had seen her promise and come to rely increasingly on her wisdom. No matter the predicament, Freyja always seemed to have the right words. Once – with the fire of Halvar leading his Wolves and the sagacity of Freyja commanding his Ravens – he had believed he boasted a Council of War that was the envy of his fellow kings. But look at it now. Such tattered remnants.

Hothead Bjarke, ruled by his passions. Reliable Asmund, a player in the cast, but never a star. Kustaa, ineffectual and so obviously Odin's puppy. Skarde, an oppressor by nature. A killer, but only of the weak. A man for whom the Pantheon's bloodletting was too honourable. And then there was Calder, now the Raven's new Housecarl. Sharp, resolute, audacious, but in only her second Season. Maybe she was one for the future. Perhaps greatness would come to her. Perhaps.

Try as he might, Sveinn could see no successor among that crowd.

It was Kustaa who had knocked timidly several hours earlier and handed Sveinn the formal results of the Raiding Season fresh from Atilius' command centre. Not only did these confirm the fatalities on both sides, they revealed at last the true values of each Asset. And this news could not have been worse.

It would seem that by successfully defending the Asset at the zoo on the first Raid Night, the Titan Palatinate would be free to engage all its forces in the coming Blood Nights. Conversely, by failing to claim that same Asset, Valhalla must confront the Blood Nights without its officer cadre. All ranks from Hersir and above must sheathe their blades and sit out the Conflict Hours, while their troops endured the challenges with a rudderless command structure.

If this news was not deleterious enough, by failing to defend the second Asset at Waverley, Sveinn's Horde would not be informed of the location for this Season's Grand Battle and would be permitted only twenty-four hours' notice to travel there. The Titans, by contrast, having raced through the blackness of the Tunnel beneath the Mound with an Asset in hand and the blood of a Housecarl on their blades, would be given the Battle's location forthwith and authorised to deploy troops at whatever speed and in whatever manner they so wished.

Sveinn heaved a deep sigh and watched the flames. It would be an arduous and bitter Blood Season to come and he would stand at the head of his Horde more alone than ever.

And somewhere, deep in his gut, death was coming.

Oliver had spotted the object five days earlier when Aurora called him into her office for a Friday update on his activities. Since then, a fresh idea had taken root in the folds of his brain and he had become fixated by the unexpected presence of this thing, lurking half-forgotten on one of the shelves beside her desk. Only now, as he watched her pull on a coat and head for the exit on some errand, did he sense this might be his opportunity.

He gave her a few minutes to get clear. When he pictured her striding past security to step into the afternoon sunshine, he rose from his seat holding an A4 folder of information he had been gathering during his months in the

OSU. It was mid-afternoon on a Wednesday and the place was like every other office in the city, a somnolent drone of air conditioning, the occasional ring of a phone, and energy-sapped heads drooped behind partitions, toying with their keyboards and counting the minutes until day's end. Jed was on the phone, his feet on his desk and his gaze angled out the window. Two more members of Tech were huddled together in soft confab and in the other units heads sprouted sporadically, but no one's eyes looked up.

Steeling himself, Oliver strode across the room and stepped inside her office. The place had a minimalist femininity and reeked of her perfume. Every surface was scrupulously clutter-free. A patterned silk scarf hung over the back of her chair and a vase of early daffodils took pride of place on the windowsill.

And there it was. Tyler's laptop, on a shelf beside him. Since the furore after he had last accessed it and discovered the fate of his parents, he was astounded it could be so casually laid aside.

In one steady movement he slipped it beneath the folder he was carrying, then swivelled on the spot and departed. He was convinced that everyone must now be staring at him, but when he reached his desk and looked up, the office was just as it had been. Jed still mumbled on the phone, his Tech colleagues still whispered, and no one gave a damn about the kid in the corner.

Oliver eased the screen open and powered up. The log-on history showed Aurora had been on it three times, snooping around to see what he had been up to. But after Oliver had made his dreadful discovery and before his grief swallowed him, there had been a few moments of appalled calm when he had somehow found the presence of mind to delete his history, remove the Wi-Fi connection and return admin rights to her. So she had been unable to find anything untoward.

He wished he had time to delve into the hard drive now, but she could be back any moment. Focusing his thoughts, he once more removed her admin rights, scanned for external Wi-Fi signals and logged on to the one that required no password. Clicking through some of Tyler's old saved documents, he found a bill dated three years ago, which was for a 60,000-mile service on his van and included his email address. If no one in this damn place would help him get in touch with Tyler through internal Palatinate communications, then he'd have to go rogue. Praying the email address was still current, Oliver logged into his own personal Gmail account and began to type.

Hi Tyler. How's Valhalla? Have you been involved in the Raid Nights? It's been so long since I saw you and I've such a lot to tell you. Get in touch as soon as you can. Oliver.

He pressed send and watched the note speed from the outbox. He waited long minutes to see if an undelivered warning would pop up, but his inbox remained undisturbed and eventually he allowed himself a sigh of relief. It seemed the message had flown successfully into the ether and somewhere out there it would be arriving on Tyler's phone. Oliver imagined his friend hearing the notification and he wondered where in the city he was at that moment.

His last conversation with Tyler had been sitting on the

stairs in the house on Learmonth Place, with a taxi waiting outside to whisk Tyler to the Grand Battle. That was almost a year ago and it felt like a lifetime. He wondered if Tyler had been back to the house. Did he know of the calamity that had befallen the Muir family? Did he wonder about Oliver?

Wherever you are, Tyler, pick up my message and write back.

Diligently, Oliver deleted the email, wiped his history, disconnected the Wi-Fi and returned admin rights to her ma'amship. Then he powered down, checked around the room and stalked back to her office with his precious cargo.

It was just before 8.00 a.m. and there were touches of spring in the air as a pale sun caught the first cream primrose buds beneath the hedgerows and sparkled on limitless dew-laden spider silk. A flock of grey geese had made camp in a neighbouring field and their coarse arguments could be heard in the stables where Heph held Xanthos steady while Dio crouched to wrap bandaging around his stallion's front legs between hock and fetlock. The horse had appeared discomfited in the last couple of days, so they had taken the precaution of putting stable bandaging below his knees for warmth at night, then changing to lighter wrapping each morning before exercise.

The rest of the team had already undertaken the daily 7.00 a.m. mucking out, refilled water, thrown up the horses' hessian night rugs and given them an early clean. Then they had dished out a first feed of oats and left them to ingest, while more oats – in the form of porridge – were prepared back in the farmhouse for the human contingent.

Heph watched his friend positioning the final wrapping and testing the ankle joint. Their times alone together were rare these days and he was happy enough leaning against Xanthos' muscle, while straw dust floated in the sunbeams around them.

'Are you pleased with our progress?' he asked.

'There's not much more I can do if I'm not,' grunted Dio, tucking in the spare ends of the bandage. 'It is what it is.'

'You've done an awesome job, Horsemaster.'

Dio stood and brushed straw from his knees. 'It's taken a lot to get us riding this proficiently without tack. I'll admit I've had fretful nights, especially in the early days when Zephyr and Maia seemed so lumpen.'

A cloud passed across his eyes and he stalked away to fill a hay net for Xanthos.

'Spit it out,' said Heph.

'I think we're ready to handle weapons,' replied Dio, his back turned.

'And?'

'And the truth is I've never done any of this before. I'm just going with my gut and what I've read about ancient cavalry craft. On horseback, the handling of lance and blade is fundamentally different from the way we fight on foot, even more so when we have no saddle to steady us.'

Dio came back with the hay and hung it for Xanthos. 'Alexander's cavalry will have grown up learning the skills of martial horsemanship from those around them, while we have only instinct and guesswork.'

'The blade craft of the team is already of the highest order, especially Spyro and Zephyr. Perhaps we will surprise you.'

Dio shrugged as he closed the stall on Xanthos. 'Perhaps.'

Heph punched him softly on the shoulder. 'Well, by my reckoning we still have a month before the Battle, time enough to make us Weapons-Worthy. If anyone can, it's you.'

Dio looked far from convinced, but before he could say more, the stable door flew open and a breathless Pallas burst in on them.

'Agape's here.'

It was true. When they emerged from the stable, there she was, standing by the gate, a silver Porsche 911 pulled up at a rakish angle in the courtyard. Her hair was loose, shining in the morning light and, in readiness for the Blood Season, she had once again dyed it blue, the colour of her Sacred Band. The rest of the team had spilled from the farmhouse, but she ignored them and waited motionless for the trio to trudge across the grass.

As Heph reached the gate, she stepped aside and he realised there was another figure standing beside the passenger door of the Porsche. Short, heavyset, his hands buried deep in the pockets of a black down jacket and his chin pulled into his thick neck to ward off the Scottish cold.

'Belgutei!'

Heph paced to the new arrival and held out a hand. Belgutei gripped it without smiling and then flung his paw back into the warmth of his pocket.

'What are you doing here?'

'I've come to check on the progress of you novices.'

'All the way from Mongolia?'

'When Agape asks, I will always try to find a way. Just

one weekend. I must be back before the jaguns assemble for the Blood.'

Heph found himself grinning like a fool. 'Can I introduce you?'

Belgutei cast a glance around the faces. 'I take it these are your endless lines of horse soldiers.'

'All seven of them.'

The Mongol shrugged and Heph turned to the others. 'Ladies and gents, this is Belgutei, the Jurtchis – Quartermaster – of the Kheshig Palatinate. And he's come from Ulaanbaatar specifically to watch us and give us the benefit of his wise words.'

The assembled Titans greeted this news in silence and Zephyr scowled. 'Why would the Kheshig think the Titan Palatinate needs wise words?'

Belgutei turned unhurriedly and squared up to him. 'And you are?'

'Zephyr,' came the bristling response. 'Brigade of Heavy Infantry, frontline in Alexander's Phalanx.'

'Well, infantryman. I am Horsemaster General of Genghis' cavalry jaguns, three hundred and fifty of the world's best mounted soldiers. And I've travelled for two days to see you ride because Agape asked me. Do you have a problem with that?'

There was a long, tense silence, then Spyro stepped forward and offered his hand to the Mongol.

'Spyro, Sacred Band.'

Belgutei accepted the handshake. 'Alexander's Sacred Band is much admired among our arbans.'

They were good words and the others began to introduce

themselves and there were cautious smiles of relief that here was someone with real cavalry experience come to witness their progress.

'You never cease to surprise me,' said Heph to Agape as the others led Belgutei into the farmhouse.

'I didn't think he would come, but there was no one else I could ask. Tengri and Zeus are happy, and Genghis won't notice him gone if it's just for a few days. Here – you can help me with these.' She strode to the car. 'And you, Dio,' she called.

Inside the minimal boot, extended by dropping the back seats down, several boxes had been stowed. She stacked them into the waiting arms of Heph and Dio, then slammed the boot and led them to a small outhouse.

'Is there news from the Raids?' Heph asked as he placed his boxes inside.

'We have performed well and claimed the necessary Assets. We hold the advantage in the Blood Nights and—' she stopped and forced them to look at her '—we know of the date of the Battle. You will be departing early for the Field. You have just two weeks to finish off here.'

'That gives us little time.'

'Then you'd better value Belgutei's every word this weekend and train for all the waking moments you have over the next fortnight. There will be no delays, no extra time, no second chances.'

Dio and Heph shared hesitant glances, then Dio pointed at the boxes. 'So what are these?'

Agape allowed herself a thin smile. 'You passed the test. You have Zeus' favour and so you are no longer a ragtag selection of individuals from separate Titan units. You are now our Companion Cavalry and these boxes contain your new armour and blades.'

She watched their eyes widen, but forbade them to speak further and swung away towards the farm's main door. When they reached the kitchen, Belgutei was seated at the table, surrounded by his new acolytes, consuming tea and porridge, though from his expression he was unimpressed by the lack of salt and butter in both.

Once their guest was fed, they took him to the stables and he inspected the horses and their accommodation. He grunted with satisfaction and shot Dio a look of respect. It was enough to make the tall man prickle with pride.

They spent much of the morning bringing the horses to trot and canter around the field under the watchful gaze of the Jurtchis, who smoked foul cigarettes and barked comments from the centre. Agape stayed for the first hour, but then nodded to Belgutei, retreated to her Porsche and left them to it. Over the course of the day, he stopped them repeatedly to demonstrate the importance of posture. How a saddleless rider must lock him or herself to the horse by the grip of thighs alone. How the upper body must be strong enough to operate separately from the lower limbs. He forced them to release reins and canter with arms at their sides. He made them imagine they were throwing lances, their legs gripped and steering, their waists fluid.

Zephyr was the first to fall. He hit the ground hard and lay winded and discharging a fusillade of expletives. On other days he might have stalked to the farmhouse in a blaze of fury, but he caught the steel in Belgutei's eyes and his anger cooled and he pulled himself back onto his mount, grimacing with pain and flexing his shoulders, but damned if he would be defeated.

Later in the afternoon, Maia and Pallas retrieved the lances from the stables and Belgutei took one and jumped nimbly onto the back of Xanthos. He wheeled around the field, getting the feel of the beast, then slowed him with his knees and talked them through the principles of light cavalry warfare.

'The Kheshig rides with saddles and stirrups, just as the Great Khan himself in the thirteenth century. But many of us have grown up on the steppes among horse stock and have known since a young age how to master and control a mount without tack. To fight in such a way is a very different proposition.

'A saddled rider can charge a stationary target and drive his weapon into the enemy by the velocity of his horse alone. Alexander's cavalry could not hope to do this and retain their place on the horse. Instead, they used their mounts to power through enemy lines at full charge, but kept their weapons high until they could wheel on the broken foe, slow their mounts and fight with lance and sword. Their horses gave them three advantages: speed around the battlefield; power through the foe; and height once the struggle turned to blade craft. You understand?'

The nods and muted assent were sufficient to make him lean over and spit derisively, then he kicked his heels into Xanthos' flanks and took off towards the fence line. As he neared, he steered Xanthos at a quick canter parallel to the perimeter, then slowed him hard and attacked a post with five short, fierce, lightning-fast jabs of his lance, three underarm and two over. The post stood resilient and undamaged, but everyone understood that each one of those jabs would have been a death wound to a Viking.

As the daylight weakened, Belgutei had them riding with lances. They cantered with blades high, then slowed the horses and lowered the iron points as though facing a horde of foot-soldier foe. By the time he finally relented, their backs were killing them and their arms throbbed. A Saab pulled into the courtyard and he gave instructions that he would return at 8 a.m. Then he released them to groom and feed the horses, while he marched to the car and disappeared back to somewhere more comfortable than the farmhouse.

That evening, they did not break open the alcohol. Instead, they baked flatbreads and wolfed a spicy chicken tagine that Maia had whipped up, then headed by torchlight to the stables. As the Jurtchis had detailed, they packed straw tightly into sacks until these were too hard to hit barehanded. Then they selected some of the spare horse blankets and wrapped them around each sack, binding them with lengths of cord. Zephyr and Spyro took the torches and went in search of loose fencing posts and carried six back to the stables where they checked them and used their sword blades to whittle each base into a rudimentary point. At first light the next day, they would secure these into the turf in a line across the field, then fix the blanketed sacks around the top of each. They wanted Belgutei to be pleased with their handiwork and anticipated his final day would have them devoted to hard lance and sword work.

Exhausted, they stumbled back to the warmth of the farmhouse, sank a few drams and collapsed into their beds.

XXXIV

Asmund's face was haggard when he opened the door of the Jaguar XF to allow Calder to join him on the back seat, but he attempted a wan smile of welcome as the driver pulled away from Mound Place and cut south towards the city's ring road. In the front, Bjarke's bulk hunched silent and still. Not so much as a turn of the head to acknowledge her presence. She peered at him in the glow of the dashboard and could see his downcast eyes, taking no interest in the journey they were sharing.

The Titans had made a fool of him. As Sveinn's senior Jarl, the Second Raid had warranted every ounce of guile and warcraft he could muster, but instead the blood had gone to his head, the Battle frenzy had consumed him, and he had led every last one of his Hammers on a stampede down Waverley's platforms in pursuit of a decoy unit, leaving Housecarl Freyja to track the real Asset and die on a Titan blade. The weight of her absence crushed each of them in that car and the driver wisely took them to the Blood Gathering of Scotland without word or hitch.

A few nights prior, Sveinn had required Calder's presence in Valhalla and had solemnly informed her that she was now Housecarl of Raven Company. It was a promotion she loathed, but she was the sole Raven Thegn and thus the only choice. After the bloodbath of the Nineteenth Season, the company she inherited was skewed towards callow new recruits. Of the five remaining from the Battle beach, Liv was dead, and Jorunn and Geir both recovering in the Pantheon wards, leaving only Sassa and herself with the experience of one Season or more.

Calder remembered Tyler describing the woman who had died beneath the denarii at last year's Gathering and as the car bore them to a magnificent mansion somewhere in rolling Borders countryside, she wondered what unpleasantries awaited. But this year, thankfully, there was to be no death. In the vast ballroom, she listened emptily to the words of Atilius and let the theatrics wash over her. The Titan cohort eyed her and she wondered if the man called Menes – Freyja's killer – was among them. She could see Alexander's jaw set in a rictus of triumph beneath his dress mask and guessed that the fleshy bruiser beside him must be Cleitus. Unlike at the *Agonium Martiale*, there were no niceties between the rivals. Sveinn kept his eyes averted, but she felt Alexander's sneer creeping over her flesh.

When the mournful music began and the dancers took their cue, she edged to the rear of the room and watched their slow hypnotic moves. Drink and drugs slunk into bodies and she noticed women waiting in the wings and guessed there must be other rooms in this place where the Curiate's every whim could be fulfilled. Once, perhaps, she would have disapproved, but as she watched the women speaking with some of the masked men and leading them in ones and twos to places more private, she realised she had no right to judge. After all, what was she, if not a woman putting her body on the line to entertain those who could afford it?

Feeling sick, she dumped her champagne flute on the tray of a passing waiter and stalked outside to gulp at the night air. She found a bench, ripped off her mask, wrapped her cloak around her and waited, the sounds of violins and exuberance filtering across the lawns.

At last Bjarke and Asmund found her.

'Let's get out of here,' the big Jarl growled and in that moment she would have followed him anywhere if it took her from that place.

In the coming nights, she dedicated every given minute to training her Ravens. The Palatinate had been informed of the results of the Raids and knew that the Blood Nights must be faced without Jarls, Housecarls or Hersirs. They had also been told that the Cull would be fifteen, a toll that was less than last Season, for which Valhalla was grateful for small mercies. Nonetheless, fifteen was still a hefty figure when measured in lives and eleven of the sixteen Ravens who began the Twentieth Season bore no Bloodmarks on their mail. Nine Drengr from the Schola and two Thegns fresh from the Armatura, they were all Vestales – Virgins – whose deaths were worth four Blood Credits, a sum that would draw the eye of every hunting Titan.

So, hour after hour, she and Sassa worked them in the Practice Rooms. The Blood Season was all about swordcraft. No spears, no arrows. The struggle would be close and personal, where eyes could recognise Bloodmarks and judge the worth of their opponent. Calder abhorred the inescapable fact that her promotion to Housecarl meant she must join Sassa sitting out the action and her Vestales would be released into the Conflict Hours like lambs to the slaughter. So the Ravens sparred until they could barely stand, first with heavy wooden training weapons and then with blunted steel.

In the rare intervals, Calder dragged her spent limbs up to Sveinn's Council Chamber and joined Bjarke, Asmund and Skarde, the flotsam and jetsam of Valhalla's once mighty Council of War. They came to the conclusion that the Horde's litters should be mixed and Sveinn saw the worth in this. While Raven and Storm boasted few warriors of experience in the lower ranks, Wolf still possessed the likes of Ake, Stigr and Unn, and Hammer's sheer size meant there were at least seventy Shields who could partake in the Bloods. So Valhalla would ignore the regimental structures and divide their ranks into bespoke litters, to ensure more experienced hands could stand alongside those without a Bloodmark.

One evening, in the gloaming before she was due in the Practice Rooms, Calder took herself to the house beneath Blackford Hill and let herself in via the back gate as she had done on so many previous occasions that summer. She still had a key and she ignored the garden apartment and went straight to the main house, where she unlocked the glass doors leading into Renuka's old kitchen. She flipped on the lights and her breath caught in her throat. She knew the *libitinarii* would have been there already, efficiently and heartlessly clearing the departed's personal items, destroying paperwork and removing all trace of the Pantheon, so Calder assumed the place would be scrubbed bare, reduced to a spartan shell ready for the next occupant. But instead, so much of Renuka's touch remained. The eclectic furniture, the vivid wall paint, even the watercolours of far-flung landscapes and the statues of Hindu deities.

'Is this all yours?' Calder had asked the first time she had set foot in the kitchen.

'The furnishings and the flair,' had come the reply.

She took herself to the front room where Renuka had taught her yogic asana postures and spoken of the seven chakras during their afternoons of Finding. Then she descended to the basement, where she discovered the gym equipment still in place, but the weapons and pells and Renuka's prized swords all requisitioned. She wandered upstairs, letting her fingers run along walls, taking in each room and remembering the voice of the other woman filtering through the house. Her Housecarl. Her mentor. Her friend.

When she reached Valhalla, she sought out Sveinn in his Chamber and asked him outright if – as a new Housecarl – she might be re-accommodated in Freyja's house. Sveinn squinted at her, but understood this was no request for more privilege or wealth or status. It was something far more personal. With a grunt, he said he would have a word with Kustaa and see what could be done.

The First Blood Night came at them headlong and before Housecarl Calder believed her charges were even remotely prepared, she found herself shepherding them through the Armouries in the minutes before Conflict Hours. The Horde would send out three units, comprising a total of nine litters. Estrid and Sten, along with five other Vestales Ravens were split among gruff Hammers and wordless Wolf hunters, all armed with broadswords and seaxes, and the leather on their limewood shields freshly painted with the Triple

Horn of Odin, rather than the symbols of their respective regiments, so the Titans would not know who faced them. Ulf was in the third unit, his shoulder heavily bandaged, and he inclined his head to Calder, acknowledging her promotion and recalling how she had helped him on the long flight to safety during the first Raid.

'Stick close to Hammer and Wolf,' Calder instructed her Ravens as she herded them into a corner of the Throne Room. 'Keep your shield high so the foe cannot see your lack of Bloodmarks and place your blade across its rim. Strike fast if fate allows, but do not be afraid to flee. There is valour in flight. Come back alive and you can stand another day.'

The units separated, one to North West Tunnel, one to South and one to East. Above ground a clear March sky winked with stars. And somewhere out there, on the rooflines running along the Mile, the Titans would be waiting to exit Ephesus and Thebes, Pella and Persepolis. Unlike the Horde, their officers would be present. Battle-scarred veterans like Nicanor and Agape and Menes.

Calder pulled on her helmet and checked her sword. She might not be permitted to go hunting during these Blood Nights, but nothing could stop her mounting the roofs above the Valhalla Gates and keeping watch for enemy scouts. Sassa had already headed to East Gate and Bjarke and Asmund were similarly attired for war with the same plan in mind. None of them could stand the thought of kicking their heels in the Valhalla halls while their troops risked life and limb on the streets of the Old Town.

Bjarke caught her eye as he swept back his hair and donned his helmet. She had watched him earlier while he fawned over his troops with a care and worry that she had never believed he possessed. A year ago, he might happily have killed her on the orders of Radspakr, but now, since the demise of the Thane and the arrival of Skarde, her trust in him had multiplied a hundred-fold.

She nodded curtly to him and marched up the North-West Tunnel, heading straight past the waiting litters and the obligatory camera-toting Vigiles, until she was the first by the Gates. The Keepers eyed her and watched the clock. Minutes now. Seconds. And then they were waving and the tiny graffiti-riddled doorway was opening onto Milne's Court and the Blood Night was on.

Calder burst out and began to climb, hoisting herself up well-used routes above the Gate until she could slink onto angled roof tiles and Edinburgh's night-time panorama opened up before her. There she crouched and strained her eyes for any movement that might betray Titan scouts. She was damned if she would allow them to settle into hiding places to report on the comings and goings of the Horde.

Her Raven charges dissipated into the night and in comfortable, opulent locations around the world, the Curiate and their hangers-on studied the live feeds, placed their bets and yearned for violence. And far, far above – up there where the stars burned bright – the gods toyed with destinies, casually deciding who would live and who would die.

Almost two weeks had elapsed since Oliver sent his email to Tyler and the lad was a seething mass of frustration. For all he knew, Tyler might have replied minutes after the laptop had been returned to Aurora's office, but since then Oliver had not had a single opportunity to retrieve it and check.

The damn woman never seemed to leave. Every morning when Oliver arrived from the Schola, she was already ensconced at her desk, drinking camomile and glowering. Each night, when the call came up that his driver was in reception, she was still rooted to her chair. Her meetings were held within the sanctity of its glass walls. Her comfort breaks were infuriatingly fleet. Her lunches comprised walnut salads, consumed behind her desk, alone and friendless.

What does she actually do? Oliver found himself venting. It wasn't as if leadership and direction flowed from her office. Her tangible productivity seemed woefully thin. He guessed she was being rewarded handsomely for running Valhalla's OSU, but perhaps even in the Pantheon – if you kissed the right arses and agreed with the right proposals and looked studious when the right eyes were upon you – you could coast through your work hours.

Finally, one blustery Tuesday morning, Oliver arrived to find the OSU devoid of her presence.

'Where's the boss?' he asked Jed who was sifting through his bag for a can of Coke and a breakfast pastry.

'Day off.' He pulled the tab on the can and the drink frothed, spotting his T-shirt. 'How *will* we manage.'

At eleven, Jed took a couple of his colleagues to one of the small meeting rooms and Oliver had his opportunity. Grabbing the A4 folder once more, he repeated his low-key amble to her office and returned with the laptop. No one noticed. No one cared.

Forcing himself to concentrate, he methodically went

through the admin rights and the Wi-Fi, then checked around. Jed could be seen in the meeting room, deep in animated conversation. Oliver brought up his Gmail and there was a single unread message at the top – but it was from someone called Callum Brodie. Cautiously, he opened it.

> Hi Oliver. Great to hear from you, lad. It's me – Tyler. Don't worry about the Brodie thing. They had to change my ID because – guess what? – I'm a Titan now! Long story which I'll tell you all about someday.
>
> How's your mum? How's Learmonth? I'm sorry I had to leave so suddenly. Changing Palatinates meant I couldn't stay there.
>
> My phone number had to get changed as well, so here's my new one. I can't promise I'll pick up, but text me when you want.
>
> Hope you're okay.
>
> Tyler
>
> PS. Hey, you'll never believe this – I'm learning to horse ride. Almost as good as the Huns now!!

Oliver stared at the screen and read the message over and over. Every sentence was a separate revelation. Tyler was a Titan? A change of identity. A new phone number. And – presumably – a new home, because he knew nothing of

Oliver's departure from the flats. Nothing of the murder of his mother. It seemed he may not have returned to Learmonth since his journey to the Battle last Season. And what was this – horses? Huns? Perversely, Tyler's message somehow distanced him more than ever.

Oliver made a note of the number, then closed down the screen and went through his exit procedure. When the laptop was safely back in its place on her ma'amship's shelves, he pondered the number, prodding at it with the tip of his pen.

Checking that Jed was still engaged, he turned to his terminal and pulled up a specific piece of Pantheon software. It could provide a live GPS location for most phone numbers and the OSU used it to keep occasional tabs on off-duty Valhalla troops. Jed had taken him through it several weeks earlier and he had even been tasked one morning with monitoring the movements of five Vikings, selected at random as part of Valhalla's routine surveillance.

Discreetly, he input Tyler's number and waited while the computer mulled over the information. Then the screen turned green and a blue dot blinked at its centre. Oliver frowned. If this was the location of Tyler's phone, the featureless surround suggested he was in the middle of nowhere. He panned out and a road appeared, then a small town with a name that meant nothing to him. He kept panning until, at last, he spied the M90 and Edinburgh appeared in the bottom corner and he was able to get his bearings. Tyler was somewhere several miles to the west of the motorway in what appeared to be rural Kinross.

He switched to satellite view and began to zoom slowly back in. Hills blossomed around the pulsing dot, then treelines and fields. Closer still and now he could make out a large house. He panned in further and he could see its roof and gables and a courtyard outside. The dot emanated from the heart of the building.

What are you doing there, Tyler? Is that where you live now?

Other buildings clustered in a neighbouring field, but they didn't look like houses and no vehicle tracks ran to them. He clicked to go closer, but the image began to lose integrity. There was something moving in the field. He leaned forward and squinted at the screen as though this would force the view to define itself. More than a single thing. Several. Moving across the field at speed, then wheeling around the edge and coming back again.

If he had not read Tyler's message, Oliver would have dismissed them as frolicking cows.

You'll never believe this – I'm learning to horse ride.

He watched the tiny black shapes traversing the grass. Perhaps Tyler had taken up a new hobby. Stranger things had happened. But the final line of his message kept replaying in Oliver's head. *Almost as good as the Huns now!!* You don't say that about a hobby.

Open-mouthed, he stared as the shapes wheeled again, hastening in great circles around the field. *Can those really be what I think they are?*

All that afternoon, Oliver mulled over his discovery. If the Titans really had invested in cavalry, it was a truly astounding development. The more he thought about it, the more he doubted the evidence of his own eyes, but it would explain the lack of numbers at the *Agonium Martiale*. He could barely control his excitement as he imagined the impact they might have on the battlefield and a new conviction settled in his gut. Odin must never know. Oliver must see to it that the bastard would never get a whiff of them. He must gain Odin's trust, help unveil Morgan's whereabouts, while steering him away from Titan plans.

Maybe – just maybe – Tyler might be the vengeance Oliver craved.

Alexander marched from the Ephesus Gardens and dropped down the stairs to his private chambers, his mind a bubbling cauldron of fury.

'Get me wine!' he yelled as he entered, knowing his pageboy would be lurking somewhere in the corridor.

He stalked around his desk and saw the lad had already set out two lines of coke on a fine blue ceramic tile. The King collapsed in his chair and contemplated the powder, then curled a finger through one of the meticulous lines and rubbed the drug into his gums. A hubbub from the Armouries seeped through the walls and he clenched his fists to stave off the urge to scream at them to hold their tongues.

It was the end of the Third Blood Night and Nicanor's returning Heavies had every reason to make a noise. It had all been going so well. On the previous two Nights, Sveinn's leaderless and rudderless Vikings had been overrun by Titan audacity and already seven of the necessary fifteen lives had been reaped: all at the expense of the Horde. Alexander's decision to save his Companions and Band for the forthcoming Battle, while sending out his Heavy Brigade to do the Blood Season's dirty work, had been looking increasingly like a tactical masterstroke, but now – tonight – disaster.

Two companies of Heavies had been on the roofs above the lower Mile, when they had spied a litter of the foe loitering under the archway of Bakehouse Close. The Titans had dropped to street level and swarmed into the Close, but were surprised to discover the Vikings already formed up in shieldwall. The Heavies took the fight to them and the two forces melded into close-quarter combat, shoving and hacking in the cramped darkness.

In those opening breathless moments, it was an even struggle, but if the Titans had held their heads and scouted the terrain before committing to the attack, they would have spied the other two Viking litters pouring towards the Close. The Heavies were trapped. Shieldwalls to the front of them, shieldwalls behind. Even two of the Vigiles were caught up in the press, their cameras providing the Curiate with raw, visceral footage of the carnage.

The *libitinarii* would confirm formal casualty numbers, but those Heavies who had made it back to Ephesus were claiming at least five were down for good. So now Alexander listened to their cursing in the Armouries, his face clamped into a snarl.

His pageboy entered with a goblet of wine and platter of cheese and apples, and Alexander grabbed the wine and drank deeply.

'Anything else, my lord?'

'No, get out.'

He forced himself to remain seated until the boy had gone, then exploded upright and paced the room, spilling wine in a fine arc. The bastards were blaming him. In

Pella and Thebes and Persepolis, they would be consulting the feeds and demanding to know why their King had not deployed his elite forces. All knew the Vikings were without their officers. So what better time for the Companions and Band to be sowing turmoil and reaping death?

Alexander dropped into his seat once more and skewered an apple with a small fruit knife. He cut a slice and munched on it savagely.

'Come,' he snarled in response to a thump on his door.

Cleitus strode into the chamber, followed by Menes, who stared at his King with unblinking snake eyes.

'My lord,' blustered Cleitus, dressed in a sagging tunic and crimson from the effort of climbing the levels to Ephesus. 'The worst possible news. At least five lost, while my Companions have been bound in our strongholds with their blades undrawn.'

'And you thought you'd come hot-tailing it up here from Persepolis just to tell me that.' Alexander stabbed at another slice of apple.

'I came to demand that your orders are changed for the forthcoming Nights. I will have my Companions where they should always be – in the thick of the action.'

'More wine!' Alexander hollered and regarded the new-comers bitterly, inviting neither of them to sit. 'By what authority do you have the right to demand anything of your king, Colonel? Do you have the ear of Zeus? Do you think you can dictate how I run this Palatinate? All I see before me is a fat man who can't even get up the stairs to address me in a proper state of decorum.'

'You will release my Companions,' said Cleitus hotly,

noticing the coke lines on the tile in front of the king. 'Or I will not be held responsible for my actions.'

'Are you threatening me?' The King watched him with hooded eyes. 'You think you have what it takes to make a formal Challenge?'

'Those are your words, my lord.'

'Listen to me, you prick. I may not have the strength of my younger years, but I would still run rings round you in the Challenge ring. I would fill your fat belly with so many holes, you'd leak fluids like one of the sprinklers in my gardens.'

Cleitus purpled at the insult. 'You cannot waste our advantage by holding back my Companions.'

'Not only will I hold them back, Colonel, I am packing most of them off to the Field before the next Blood Night.'

'That's madness,' shouted Cleitus, ignoring the pageboy who slipped around the aggressive stances of the visitors and approached Alexander with a second goblet of wine. 'To avoid another calamity like tonight, we must send out our best troops. We cannot afford to lose more lives before the new recruits finally arrive.'

Alexander surged from his seat. 'There *are* no more recruits, you fool!'

He aimed a furious slap at the person nearest to him, but he had forgotten the fruit knife still grasped between his fingers. The pageboy let out a high-pitched cry as the blade sliced across his cheek and halved his ear. Blood showered from the ragged wound and he fell backwards, grasping his carved face and blubbering in shock.

For a moment, no one moved. Alexander could feel hot

blood spattered on his arm. He stared at the little knife in his hand, then threw it aside with an oath.

'Get him out of here,' he snarled.

Menes grabbed the boy. 'Come on, lad. Let's get you cleaned up.' A centimetre higher and he would have lost an eye.

Alexander sat again and drank from the new goblet. Cleitus waited until the door had closed behind the pair, then said more evenly, 'What do you mean, there are no more recruits, lord?'

'Zeus has not spent the rest of the Blood Funds. He's holding them until next year when he believes he will be able to invest double the amount and take Valhalla by surprise.'

'And you've gone along with this madness?'

'He's Zeus! I don't pretend to understand Caelestia politics, but he owns this Palatinate and that means he can do what he bloody well likes.'

'So you're telling me we're going into the Battle with less than a hundred and forty troops, facing a rejuvenated and revitalised Horde with well over two hundred shields?'

'And that's precisely why I'm protecting the Companions and the Band. We need every one of them at the Battle. There can be no wastage of our elite troops during these Nights.'

The blood had drained from Cleitus' face now and he stared at Alexander. 'That muck is riddling your brain.'

'Get out,' the King snapped. 'Get back to Persepolis and prepare your troops for deployment to the Field.'

Cleitus swung on his heels without a reply.

'And, Colonel,' Alexander called after him, 'one word of this to anyone and I'll have you arrested and replaced.'

Menes was waiting outside and his eyes roved over the shocked expression of his commanding officer. The two men descended the levels to the exit and stomped back down the Mile in the thin light of a new dawn.

'We must rid ourselves of him,' Menes hissed. 'The man is a liability.'

'Rid ourselves of a king?'

'Rather one King than a host of our brightest blades. Leave me with the task. I have connections. I can ensure he disappears.'

Despite the lack of traffic, Cleitus halted at the junction with St Mary's Street and peered dourly down towards the Palace. 'No,' he said slowly. 'I have connections too and I know a better way.'

XXXV

In the days after Belgutei's departure, the company worked tirelessly at their lance- and sword-craft, and, in truth, it was an unerring mess. They possessed the skill to gallop their mounts past the pells, so close that their knees were in danger of snapping against the wood. They could also trot the stallions right up to the poles and strike fast with lance and blade, peppering the hay-filled sacks with deadly holes. But seamlessly combining these two components was beyond them. They would pull up too late from the gallop and be so far past the pells that a broken enemy line could weave together again before they had turned their beasts. Or they would pull up too abruptly and make their stallions rear back, exposing soft underbellies to a multitude of stabs in the heat of a real struggle. Sometimes they would strike while the horse was travelling at speed and hit the pells with such force that they cartwheeled over the rear of the horse and lay dazed on the muddied turf, cautiously feeling for broken bones.

Despite the shambles, Heph felt a burgeoning pride in this group of never-say-die individuals. It had been almost six months since they had first arrived at the farm. In that time they had seen no one apart from Pantheon drivers bringing supplies and ventured nowhere except for their brief appearance at the *Agonium Martiale*. Despite the arguments, the knocks, the freight of fatigue and the risk to life and limb, they had committed themselves to this project without exception. And in those final weeks, as they strove to master the weapon skills of Alexander's ancient cavalry in a fraction of the time given to their forbears, Heph felt a growing bond with each of them. A loyalty to a mutual goal. A pride in what this unit was and what it could become. An *esprit de corps*.

One morning, with clouds riding the winds above the Ochils and the scent of eggs poaching in the kitchen, Heph slipped to the outhouse and, one by one, retrieved the crates and placed them beside the kitchen table.

'It's official. We will not be returning to our old units. We are now a new company in the Titan order of battle. Alexander's inaugural Companion Cavalry.'

He could see the mixed emotions on their faces. They had hoped for this moment. They had worked for it painful day after painful day. Yet this announcement of the breach from their old units arrived suddenly and unequivocally and – for some like Spyro and Zephyr – it signalled the loss of honourable places in companies of distinction. Quietly they rose and opened the boxes and laid the contents across the table. Helmets with plumes the colour of blood, bronze cuirasses and greaves, leather shoulder guards, knee-length white tunics, strapped ankle boots, and double-edged, one-handed shortswords, scabbarded in horn and fixed to baldrics.

One of the cuirasses flaunted the contours of a muscled

torso and a necklace of vine leaves etched from shoulder to shoulder. Spyro picked it up and contemplated it, then stepped to Heph and held it out. 'A Captain's armour I believe, sir.'

Heph held the eyes of the man who had spent six Seasons in Agape's Sacred Band, searching for resentment or ridicule. But Spyro's expression was sincere and so he accepted the proffered armour with a dip of the head and a face impassive, though – in truth – his gut churned at the sheer madness of it all. Just his second Season in the Pantheon. Not even his first in the Titan Palatinate. And here he was – Captain of Companion Cavalry.

With a lurch, he wished his sister could witness this moment.

They separated to don their new attire and then stepped onto the bright, breezy courtyard, helms under arms, cloaks rippling, sun burnishing the bronze.

In the days that followed, something felt different. They still tussled with the pells and slipped from their mounts, yelling at each other and berating themselves, but the weight of the armour straightened their backs and lifted their chins. No more were they Hoplite or peltast, Phalanx or Band. Now they were in this together. One.

Gradually, hour by hour, the lances hit truer, the horses raced smoother. As each of them attacked a pell, two others pulled in tight to fend off imaginary foe. When they wheeled at the field margins, they turned in formation. As they galloped towards the pells, they moved sinuously from line to wedge, and they stormed through the line like an angry sea surging between rocks. At night, they huddled around the kitchen table, scrubbing clean their cloaks and tunics, combing the tangles from their plumes, and buffing their armour until it shone in the light of the fire.

It was a Thursday in the second week of March, mid-point between the Third and Fourth Blood Nights, when Zeus decided to relocate his cavalry.

The first the company knew of this was when their lunchbreak in the farmhouse was disturbed by the rumble of large vehicles and they stepped out to see two enormous horse carriers trundling up the puddled drive. The Titans were still cloaked and armoured, so Dio waved them back inside and he and Heph stripped off their cuirasses and re-emerged to greet the drivers dressed in their undertunics. But the new arrivals showed little curiosity. The most vocal of them – a little pot-bellied man with lank greying hair in its death throes – informed them through lips pursed around a cigarette that they had a couple of hours to prepare the horses, manoeuvre them into the transports and stow the necessary feed and equipment, then he and his team needed to be on the road by 4 p.m.

In the event, it was after 5 p.m. before the horses had all been encouraged into their stalls in the back of the carriers, with straw laid, water and feed in place and everything as Dio wished. Surplus supplies were stowed behind the stalls and armour and weapons were packed into the travel crates and loaded too. The forward sections of each truck contained kitchenettes and beds, so Heph assumed the company would be travelling with their steeds, but the man said his team would be using these spaces because they would be making the journey slowly and overnighting midway. Heph and his fellows should wait until after dusk when their own transportation would arrive.

Try as he might, Heph could glean no hint about their destination, except at one point the man used the phrase '*on the way up*', suggesting – as to be expected – that they were once more journeying to the wild, empty lands of the north. With a final careful inspection and a glower from Dio at the drivers that said: *Take care of my horses or I'll cut you from gullet to groin*, the carriers manoeuvred themselves out of the courtyard and set off.

The stables felt soulless as the company swept them and cleared everything away. Then in the dusk, they headed quietly back to the farmhouse and packed their things. Lenore and Dio cooked pasta and they all filled their stomachs for the long night ahead, then, on cue, they heard another engine and spied lights jolting up the drive. It was a fourteen-seater minibus with wide reclining seats.

As the others loaded their bags in the back and boarded, Heph caught Dio hanging back in the kitchen.

'You okay?'

The taller man shrugged wistfully. 'Another chapter closing. I've enjoyed it here. The fellowship around the table. The daily routines. The changing colours. The frost on the hills. The calls of the geese and robins and blackcaps and crows. The foxes round the bins. And our boys in the stables.'

'Like your own home up north.'

Dio considered this. 'Some of it,' he said with a thin smile.

'On to new chapters now.'

Dio laughed. 'Aye. And with you in charge I expect there'll be a few twists and turns in them yet.'

He reached for his bag and walked out to the hall. With a final look around and a gentle pat of the big table, Heph followed.

'Phones, watches, wallets,' said the driver when they boarded, jerking a thumb at a box on the first seat, which was already half full of deposited items from the others.

Heph removed his watch, powered down his phone and placed them on top of the pile. 'Here we go again.'

'Aye,' agreed Dio. 'Next stop 300 BC.'

Heph ferreted in his bag for his wallet and a pack of Marlboro, retrieved one cigarette, which he tucked behind his ear, and then discarded the rest.

'A final hit?'

'I figure I'm going to need one when we get there.'

'Wherever *there* is.'

The Pantheon chose on purpose to carry them north at night. Their unfolding journey and the route to their destination was not for their eyes. To begin with they hugged the M90 accompanied by other headlights, but eventually they turned on to quieter, snaking roads and the darkness swallowed them. Pallas lost himself in his headphones. Lenore and Spyro read. Zephyr, Maia and Dio reclined their seats and slept. While Heph stared past his reflection into the night. He remembered a similar crepuscular journey to an unknown destination, but that one aboard an executive plane crossing the fathomless Minch to the island chains beyond. He wondered if they would yet be taken to a plane or a boat, but hoped not, for the sake of the horses.

It seemed incredible that it was a year since he had travelled to the island and trained with Halvar and the Wolves on the beach beside the little church. He remembered nights swaddled in furs on flagstones, feasting around a fire and listening to Ake tell tales of Asgard and Ragnarök. Dio had told him of a saying in the British Army – *hurry up and wait* – and it was exactly how time felt during the last year. Everything that had occurred – his surrender, the duel with Alexander's champions, his new apartment, the breakfast with Hera, the splendour of Rome, the vast beauty of Mongolia, the arrival at the farmhouse – had happened as sudden, unexpected fits of change. Yet, in between, the days and weeks had passed in unremarkable, repetitive routine.

He must have slept. The bus was warm and the seats soft and the driver conveyed them unhurriedly along the invisible roads. When he woke it was still dark, but he pressed his nose to the window and thought he could make out the merest hint of light in the east. If that was the first blush of a new day, then they must have been travelling for over seven hours and he wondered that the driver had needed no break. There was something still so black about the land to the west, so featureless, that he suspected it could be water and for a few moments they passed through a semi-lit village and he caught the name Morar on a sign above a shop.

At last the bus slowed and they heard the indicator lights begin to click. Behind him, Dio woke with a harrumph and stared bleary-eyed around.

'Where are we?'

'Christ knows. Middle of nowhere.'

The bus turned off the road and trundled carefully through a gate and down a cinder track, then wheezed to a halt and the driver killed the engine. As the doors swung open, everyone rose and looked at each other questioningly. Beyond the windows waited nothing but empty darkness.

'Is this it?' demanded Zephyr of the driver.

'End of the line,' came the reply. 'Take your stuff and get out.'

They descended into a pre-dawn chill and a silence terrifyingly vast.

'I expected to see some of the others,' said Lenore. 'But we must be the first.'

Heph stepped away from the bus and breathed in the raw air. 'I suspect,' he ruminated, 'that we are to remain Zeus' little secret until the last possible moment.'

'You mean we're not at the Field?'

'We're probably close. It will be out there somewhere, but we won't be mixing with the rest of the Palatinate. If any of them are already here, they'll be far enough away never to know of our presence.'

'Just us again then,' growled Zephyr.

'Thank heavens we all love each other,' said Dio under his breath.

The doors of the bus closed behind them and the driver kicked the engine back into life. The vehicle swung around a tight turning circle and returned to the road. Gradually, as its rumble receded, light coalesced and they began to discern trees and the waters of a loch. Mountain masses revealed themselves. A sheep bleated and new shapes materialised between the trees. Heph peered at them and smiled thinly.

'I think I've found our accommodation.'

Lenore came next to him and sighed. 'Camping. My heart sings.'

'Of course, camping,' said Spyro, pushing past them and

heading down to the trees. 'How would you expect an army of Alexander to live?'

'It's not camping I object to,' she replied, trailing after him. 'It's camping in the north of Scotland while the Season still has one foot in winter.'

Heph watched the others meander to the tents, then took himself across the grass until he had an unbroken view of the dark waters of the loch. He wondered where Boreas and the rest of the horses had spent the night. They had become such a part of his everyday life that he felt incomplete without their presence.

He fumbled in his pocket for a lighter. Time for that final hit of nicotine.

Odin glared through the rain-spattered windows of his chauffeured Bentley as it waited at lights on its way to Quartermile. He still owned two properties in the city – an Edwardian detached on Morningside's Cluny Gardens and a five-bedroom penthouse overlooking Edinburgh's marina – but he had grown bored of both and now rented them out for extortionate sums. These days he preferred the variety of the city's best hotels. Zeus and his bloody wife were habitually ensconced in the Balmoral, so, more often than not, he plumped for a rather special suite at Prestonfield House beneath Arthur's Seat. It was a cluttered mix of four-poster beds, antique furniture, gaudy drapes, thick rugs and roaring fires, but he liked its old-world charm during the winter months.

He had spent almost a month on the other side of the pond, taking in the Super Bowl and then the Miami Boat

Show, where he had treated himself to a $185,000,000, 95-metre motor yacht complete with helipad, spa, infinity pool, six-person submarine and an underwater observation lounge. He'd never get around to using the goddamn thing, but what was the point of going to these shows if he didn't splash the cash? He drew on a cigar and wondered for the umpteenth time why he had located his Palatinate in miserable Scotland, when he could still be wintering under a Miami sun. At least by tomorrow he would be on his way to Moscow for the International Ballet Festival, although it struck him that if there was one place more miserable than Scotland at this time of year, it was probably Russia.

He had watched the Raid Nights from his Miami suite and sworn blue murder at Valhalla's inability to claim either of the Assets. Skarde, he decided, was a useful assassin, but worthless Housecarl, whose leadership of the Horde's unit during the First Raid was tantamount to gross dereliction of duty. He had brooded over the death of the one called Freyja. She had been an exemplary officer and her loss was far greater than simply the Blood Funds that Zeus would claim from her demise. Odin had also noted the rise of the woman known as Calder; Tyler Maitland's one-time confidante and someone he suspected knew more about his affairs than was healthy. Since he had last been present in Edinburgh, fate had conspired to place her on his Palatinate's Council of War. A Housecarl, admired by the troops and trusted by Sveinn. Odin exhaled a cloud of cigar smoke and wondered whether he should use this fleeting visit to disrupt that.

But what had really been playing on his mind, was the kid's discovery that Alexander's lines at the *Agonium Martiale* were down by at least seventy. Odin had put out feelers with his contacts in Atilius' teams and with a handful of the more pliable members of the Curiate, but no one seemed to know anything. Zeus was within his rights to hide his troops from prying eyes, but, nonetheless, it made Odin uneasy and he had spent frequent nights toying with a last whisky and wondering what the hell his Caelestis rival was up to.

The car finally broke free of the stop-start traffic and eased around the perimeter of the Meadows to Quartermile. Odin had not announced his return to Edinburgh and the first security knew of it was as he swept past the scanners. When he strode into the OSU, the boss was like a pheasant flushed from cover, bursting from her office in a flurry of squawks and hair-flicking. He told her to have coffee sent upstairs and cast his gaze around the room. The kid in the corner met his look and raised his eyebrows in a clear gesture that he wished to impart something.

'You,' said Odin, pointing a finger at him. 'With me.'

He held the doors of the lift while the kid grabbed an item from his desk and followed.

'You got anything more about Titan numbers?' Odin demanded once in his penthouse office.

'A little, lord. I have analysed CCTV images of coming and goings at the entrances to their strongholds and I see no obvious increase in footfall. It's not firm evidence, but it suggests Zeus has not filled his lines this year.'

'Pretty poor pickings for what I'm paying you.'

'You're not paying me, lord.'

'I'm not?'

'No one at the Schola is salaried. We're still under training.'

Odin pulled a face and sat heavily behind his desk. 'So what was that look about down there?'

'I *have* discovered something.' Oliver held up a USB stick. 'May I?'

Odin waved his permission and Oliver once more slipped around the desk to stand beside him, inserted the stick into the computer and clicked open a single image.

Odin stared wordlessly for long seconds. 'Where is this?' he asked at last.

'It's a still, captured from CCTV on the Craigmillar estate where Tyler Maitland used to live.'

Odin pointed a thick finger at the first figure. 'Is that who I think it is?'

'It's Morgan Maitland, lord. Taken two years ago on the morning of the 24th of March, hours after her disappearance from the Titan Palatinate and the last known sighting. But I don't know the other woman.'

Odin was silent again, his jaw flexing and tightening. 'That,' he said eventually, 'is Hera.'

'Zeus' wife?'

'The very same.'

'Then, Zeus must know where Morgan is.'

Odin nodded slowly. 'So it would seem.' He turned sharply to Oliver. 'Has anyone else seen this?'

'No,' Oliver lied, omitting to mention Jed.

Odin's fist came up and he grabbed Oliver by the scruff of his jumper. 'And it stays that way, you understand?'

'Yes, lord.'

Odin released him and waved him back towards the lift. 'I'll keep this stick. Oh – and, kid – good work. From now on you report directly to me. Whenever I'm on the premises,

I expect you up here. We'll get a laptop rigged up. You and me, we're going to find this woman and get to the bottom of this goddamn mystery.'

Once Oliver had gone, Odin remained examining the image, stroking his beard, a shard of cold anxiety weighting his gut. What the hell? If Zeus and Hera were behind Morgan Maitland's disappearance, then they must have learned of her treachery and knew that Odin himself had been running her as a spy. They would have realised why so many Titans had died during the Eighteenth and guessed that Odin had been making obscene amounts of money gambling on outcomes he had already fixed. If Lord High Jupiter were to learn of this, the consequences would be grave.

So why the hell had Zeus not played his hand already? It was two years since Morgan's disappearance, so what was he waiting for? Perhaps Morgan was long gone – executed most likely – but not before Zeus had pumped her for all the information he needed to ruin Odin. It made no sense and one thing Odin hated was uncertainty. What's more, the brother – Tyler Maitland – was now in the Titan Palatinate. Odin pondered the ease of his surrender at last year's Battle. Had Zeus had a hand in that duplicity?

Odin swung his chair round and stared out the French doors at his rooftop garden. All his life he had only ever known one way to stay on top. Strike first. If someone had something that threatened him, act fast, act without compunction, and take them down.

If Zeus really did know about Olena and Halvar's love and the treachery Odin had enforced upon them, then there was only one way forward. Odin must destroy his rival, before Zeus destroyed him.

He reached for his mobile and stabbed in a number. 'Kustaa,' he snapped. 'Cancel my trip to Moscow and get me Skarde.'

'I should throw you back into Erebus and have your balls fed to the rats.'

There was absolute silence on the other end of the line and Odin could imagine the cold hatred running through Skarde. The man must yearn to be there in front of the Caelestis, a seax in his fist, plunging the blade again and again through Odin's ribs. But such venom thrilled Odin. There was no more powerful feeling in the world than owning a man so dangerous.

'Your leadership on the First Raid Night was unworthy of a Vestalis, let alone one of my goddamn Housecarls. You ran from that mess at the zoo, you abandoned your troops, and your actions dishonoured me.'

'I will make it up to you, lord,' Skarde replied, the words barely escaping through clamped teeth.

'You will indeed or you'll be back in Erebus so fast your shit bucket will still be warm.' Odin opened the French doors and stepped from his office onto the rooftop garden. A pair of male blackbirds tussled noisily along the box hedging. 'I have a task for you. Get it right and we will put your performance at the Raid behind us.'

'What would you have me do?'

'Find that woman again. The new Housecarl.'

'The Raven, Calder.'

'Find out what she knows about Tyler Maitland. If that

bastard's still alive, I want to know where he is and I want to know now. Do whatever it takes.'

'Whatever it takes?'

'And Skarde – do this properly and Wolf Regiment is yours permanently. Understood?'

'Understood. And when it's over, do you want her alive?'

Odin thought about this, watching the blackbirds fight for the right to breed. 'No,' he said quietly. 'She's yours to enjoy. But make damn sure no one sees you. She disappears.'

'Yes, lord.'

Odin cut the line and stood gazing over the greenery of the Meadows, dappled with colour from early daffodils and crocuses.

His phone rang again and he swore, believing it was Skarde needing more clarification, but the number on his screen was different.

'Well, well. Cleitus.'

'My sources told me you're in the city.'

'Your sources are correct.'

'Can we meet?'

'My time is valuable.'

'You'll want to hear what I have to say.'

Odin mulled over this unexpected turn, then made up his mind. 'I'll let you know a time and place.'

He hung up and thrust the phone into his pocket. The blackbirds were still posturing and he watched them, lost in thought. A quote he admired oozed into his mind. *The Game's afoot*. Indeed, it damn well was.

Strike first. Strike fast.

XXXVI

The trees below them were alive with the sharp, staccato chatter of fieldfare gathering on the naked birch branches as evening settled. On the breeze-rippled loch a black-throated diver bobbed up, then just as quickly disappeared. Further out a squadron of Brent geese sailed imperiously east.

Heph and Dio had climbed a few hundred yards up the steep slope behind their camp and found some rounded rocks on which to perch and take in the view. The air was cool, but they had wrapped themselves in the heavy woollen cloaks that had been awaiting them in the tents on their arrival the previous morning. Beneath, they wore knee-length tunics, wool breeches and soft leather ankle boots of a type used by Alexander's troops, although these modern ones enclosed the toes, in a nod to the fact that this was north Scotland and not the shores of the Aegean.

'You got any sense where we are?' Heph asked, peering beyond the loch at snow-encrusted summits.

'You said you saw a sign for Morar when we were on the bus. So I'm thinking this could be the loch of the same name, which puts us about halfway up the western seaboard. The darkness is coming from our left, so we must be on the northern shore and facing south.' Dio swung an arm out to the right. 'Which means the sea isn't far off that way and probably the Isle of Skye.'

Heph pondered this information. Down in the woodland a light sparked and flickered bravely against the advancing gloom. Among the many items waiting for them when they had arrived were hand axes, and last evening Maia and Spyro had sent them searching for wood, then spent an age coaxing fire beside this wintry loch. They had also found sealed boxes containing an assortment of foodstuffs and they had pulled low benches around the flames and baked flatbreads to accompany a chicken and onion stew, followed by cheeses and honey cakes, washed down with flagons of wine. There were three tents, all rectangular and pavilion in style. The wooden frames were covered with thick, waxed canvas, which could be rolled back at one end to provide a broad opening. The two women took one, the five men another and the third was reserved for communal use. They had spent an uncomfortable night wrapped in coarse blankets on mattresses stuffed with wool. Heph had lain awake, cold canvas caressing his arm and the smells of the other men enveloping him, and he recalled the smaller tents of Valhalla on the blood island the year before. What he wouldn't give for that nice dry chapel floor and the reassuring presence of a leader like Halvar preparing them for the slaughter to come.

'Do you think there are more of us here?' he mused.

'Probably. Agape said the Titans had been told about the Field in advance, so Alexander has likely retained the troops he needs to contest the Blood Nights and sent the rest up here to prepare.'

Heph glanced around. 'I wonder where they're hiding.'

Dio nodded towards the darkening eastern skies. 'There's not much that way for miles except hills.'

Heph sensed his friend deliberating. 'But…?'

Dio shifted and jerked a thumb over his shoulder. 'But my money's on north. A half day's march beyond this hill should bring us to Knoydart.'

Heph shrugged. 'What's that?'

'A giant peninsula bounded on three sides by sea lochs and one of the last great wildernesses of Scotland. Not a bloody thing there. The empty quarter. The Pantheon could hide all its armies in there if it wanted. But we're not going to get over there without putting the horses on a boat.'

Heph swore. Trust the Pantheon to make everything so complex.

The horses had arrived the previous afternoon. The grind of heavy vehicles had broken the stillness and the little company had made their way along the shoreline and found the trucks pulled up outside a deserted, broken-windowed Victorian residence, overtaken by weeds. Beyond it, stood a renovated stable block and amid much kissing and patting and cooing, they led the horses to their new home.

Once the provisions and weapons crates had been unloaded, the trucks departed and the seven Titans fed their mounts and settled them in their stalls. Heph spent an age simply stroking Boreas' flanks, feeling his warmth and inhaling the musky hay-scent of his breath. Later, they walked them gently along the shore to give them a sense of their new surroundings, and it felt good, like the unit was whole again.

'A penny for your thoughts,' said Dio, eyeing him in the fading light.

Heph smiled thinly. 'I was just thinking about the horses and the twists that have led us to this place.'

'Aye. Another Battle to come and a different side.'

'And I'm still no closer to finding my sister. If she's alive, she could be anywhere and I don't know where to look any more.' He trailed off and stared at the dark waters of the loch. 'You realise Calder will be standing on the opposite side of the Field?'

'Of course I do.'

'I won't hurt her. I don't care what the bloody Pantheon demands, I'll never hurt her.'

'I know.' Dio heaved a sigh and rose from his rock. 'Enough of these wanderings. They do us no good.' He reached a hand down and pulled Heph upright. 'Come on. There's a cup of wine with my name on it.'

Bad news flowed swiftly during Conflict Hours.

Bjarke was in the Throne Room, mailed and bladed. All dressed for war and nowhere to go. The prohibition on Viking officers joining the fray maddened him and each night he went through the same ritual in the Preparation areas: cleansing, clothing himself in his war gear and blading up.

It was 3 a.m. on the Sixth Blood Night, the final hour of Conflict before the Grand Battle, and he had spent the time marching between each Gate to check on his guards and mustering the Hammer reserves in the Practice Rooms, making them work at the pells to keep their blood high, lest they be required on the streets.

The Council had agreed they should send the Valhalla ranks out in good numbers. No point in a litter here and a litter there, when no Jarl or Housecarl or Hersir could lead them and the Titans were making the most of the situation, coming at them with strong units and their officers at the head of the hunt. Thus far, the tactic had blunted the Titan attacks, but of the fifteen lives required during the Cull, thirteen had already been claimed and eight of these were from the Horde.

Now there was news of a fresh wave of assaults somewhere to the south of Grassmarket. The Viking contingent had been broken apart by a savage offensive and the first survivors were filtering back to the South-West Gate on Victoria Terrace, telling of Hammers down. Some even said Berserkers were falling.

Bjarke boiled with rage. 'Ingvar!' he yelled, striding through the Throne Room. 'Where are you?'

His Berserker Hersir appeared from the Practice Rooms on West Tunnel and clattered down the steps in his knee-length mail.

'Is it true?' Bjarke demanded.

'There's no stock in rumours, but the Ravens are saying Gorm and Troels are casualties.'

Bjarke swore ferociously. 'Get to South Gate and be ready for those who make it back along Cowgate.'

'What of you?' asked Ingvar, but Bjarke was already bounding up the steps to West Tunnel, shoving an expostulating Kustaa out of the way. He ran past the Practice Rooms and across the Western Hall, then took a left fork towards the South-West Gate. He knew the other officers were spending Conflict Hours on the rooftops above Valhalla, keeping watch for Titan spies in a vain attempt to feel of some value. Asmund was above North Gate on Warriston Close and the Raven Hersirs were somewhere to the east. He thought Housecarl Calder might be atop the western vantage points, but he had paid no heed to such movements during the hubbub before the litters were released.

At the Gate there were five of his returning Hammers, bloodied and beaten and wheezing from their flight.

'Where are the others?' Bjarke demanded.

'Still on Grassmarket,' came the reply.

'And you deserted them?' Bjarke was beside himself, spluttering with rage. It took every ounce of willpower not to punch the speaker and hurl all five of them back into the night.

'We were separated,' the man responded, as if that would cool his Jarl. 'It's chaos out there.'

'Get out of my sight!' Bjarke hissed and waded between them to the Gate. 'Open up,' he ordered the Keepers, then pushed his way out to Victoria Terrace without bothering to find a helmet. The place was deserted and there was rain in the air, just a light misting, but enough to leave the Old Town empty for the Pantheon.

He leaned on railings and stared down at the street below. Voices could be heard coming from Grassmarket. No words, just hoarse, heated syllables and the strident ringing of steel on bronze. Bjarke yearned to throw himself down the steps and charge towards the struggle, but he forced himself to grip the railings and stay put. Live by the Rules.

Die by the Rules. Valhalla had failed to gain the Asset in the lion enclosure and this was their punishment.

With another expletive, he spun on his heel and took a flight of steps up towards the Mile, then hoisted himself over a wall and began to ascend a steel ladder fire escape. Breathing heavily into his beard and sweat blossoming under his mail, he reached the top and carefully levered himself onto a short span of angled tiles. He hated these heights. The roofs were meant for lighter frames than Hammer Jarls and his heart thumped in his mouth. Give him solid ground to plant his boots and the smooth shaft of a war axe in his paws, but he had crossed these tiles before and knew the angle was safe enough if he kept his bulk forward.

He gained the apex and crouched with a leg either side, then lowered himself to a parapet. He could see more of Grassmarket now, but the rain smeared the view and he could still only hear the tumult coming from an unseen corner. He grunted and worked his way along the parapet until the roof opened onto a terrace and he was able to jump down and stand properly to peer into the night. Five figures raced under street lights on the eastern edge of Grassmarket and he could see enough to note their plumes and know they were Titans. He waited and watched, but the main action remained obstinately hidden. He wiped a fist across his face and tugged the damp from his beard.

The terrace was studded with aerials and A/C units and it curled away between the roofs, so he followed it in the hope of gaining an improved vantage point. He rounded a corner and stopped abruptly. Several paces ahead, in the darkest recesses beneath a chimney, he spied movement. For a second he thought it must be pigeons or even a fox, but then the limbs coalesced into writhing bodies sprawled on the wet concrete. There was a sob of anger and an answering snarl. *Titans*, he thought. *The bastards have one of our scouts.*

His hand dropped to his seax and he sprang forward, but his foot kicked a discarded helmet and it clattered against the stone balustrade. A face spun round at him and, even in the dark, he could see the startling white of the man's beard. Beneath him was another face, pale and horrified, blonde hair plastered by the rain. It took Bjarke only a heartbeat to recognise the posture of the man between the woman's legs and the pasty flesh of his arse above his half-lowered breeks. He saw the man's hand around her throat and the blood glistening from a scratch beside his eye. And Bjarke knew implicitly what act he had stumbled across.

Leaving his seax sheathed, he lunged forward, grabbed the man's shoulder and smashed a giant fist into his face. He felt the nose disintegrate with a soggy explosion and the man howled and tried to rise, but Bjarke's outrage was unsated. His fist came again. This time his knuckles burst an eye. Then he had the man by the hair and he was cracking his head against the chimney, while his foot sought to crush the naked groin into the concrete.

The girl grappled to her feet and clutched her throat where only moments before her attacker's fingers had been throttling the life from her. She watched the man's head being ground into the stone, then bent to retrieve a seax, which he had torn from her grasp when she first cut him.

'Bastard,' Bjarke was spitting. 'You bastard at it again. I *knew* nothing had changed.'

'Leave him,' gasped Calder, holding the seax shakily in front of her, but the Hammer was past hearing. His fist came again onto Skarde's chin, then he stepped back and aimed kicks at his groin. Skarde tried to draw his knees up for protection and curl into a foetal position.

'You want a piece of something,' Bjarke bellowed. 'You try a piece of me.'

He kicked once more, then shifted to plant a blow on Skarde's head.

'Jarl,' Calder said more firmly and stepped next to him.

Bjarke felt the cold prick of her seax against his neck and it was enough to cool him. For several long moments the night was still, broken only by the rasp of laboured breath and a soft keening moan.

Calder removed the blade and Bjarke gawked at her. Even in the poor light, he could see the marks of Skarde's grip on her throat and the livid scarlet of her bludgeoned cheekbones.

'Then you finish it,' he said simply, stepping away from the prostrate figure. 'Finish it here, Housecarl.'

Calder stared down at her attacker.

'Do it,' Bjarke insisted. 'Gut him. No Vigiles here. No cameras.'

'Who will lead the Wolves?'

'What?' Bjarke spluttered in surprise. 'What does that matter? Ake, Stigr. Any one of them is better than this piece of shit.'

Calder shook her head. 'No. We need him for the Battle.'

Bjarke turned to her and lowered his bearded face. 'Kill him, Calder. If you don't, you'll regret it.'

She took a long ragged breath, then shook her head again. 'No.'

Bjarke swore and strode away to glare out across

Grassmarket. Behind him Skarde was slithering and below he could hear troops returning. He spun back to Calder.

'Are you coming then, Raven?'

Calder sheathed her knife and bent to retrieve her helmet. She gave Skarde a final look and followed the Jarl back across the terrace. As they climbed the roofs, Bjarke was too angry to speak, but when they reached the ladder, he relented.

'You okay?'

'I'm fine.'

'Did he...?' He nodded towards her midriff.

'No,' she replied tersely and took his hand to clamber onto the rungs, but as they descended she asked, 'What did you mean *nothing has changed*?'

They reached the bottom and Bjarke paused. 'That's why he was sent to Erebus. Couldn't keep his cock in his breeks. Even attacked Freyja once. Sometimes the Pantheon discovers its moral backbone and acts with honour. When we heard Erebus had claimed him we celebrated hard in the ale halls and I thought I'd never lay eyes on the bastard again.'

Calder said nothing and they descended the steps to Victoria Terrace where a group of Hammers were stumbling back from Grassmarket.

'Gorm! Troels! They said my Berserkers were lost.'

'Whoever spread such lies needs their tongue removed, lord.'

Bjarke laughed and thumped them on the backs. 'That is good news indeed.'

'But we still lost two Hammers. So Atilius has his fifteen sacrifices.'

467

Bjarke placed a hand on Gorm's shoulder. 'Then I will have even more need of you at the Battle. We must avenge their deaths.'

He herded them through the Gate and turned to Calder. 'After you, Housecarl.'

Calder stepped past him, then paused and said quietly, 'Thank you for what you did up there.'

The Jarl rumbled incoherently and together they disappeared into Valhalla.

'Stupid sod's a nutjob,' taunted Gregor as he pulled a sweat-drenched T-shirt over his head to reveal his chubby adolescent chest.

The sparring was over for the night and the various year groups in the Valhalla Schola were filing back to the showers with aching joints. All bar one.

Oliver, as had become his wont, had selected two short wooden training blades and was striking a hanging pell again and again.

In the weeks and months since a van had taken him away from the Schola each day and returned him in time for the evening training sessions, it had become his routine to work on his blade skills until only he remained in the Arena.

Try as they might, the other Initiates could never get him to say where he was taken every day and why he was permitted to miss classes. Some were fascinated by his comings and goings, others resented his special treatment, but all agreed the routine was changing him. One night in the dorm, Gregor had attempted to beat the information out of him and found that his opponent hit back with a new violence. Gregor had pounded him hard and sneered when he returned to his own bunk, but secretly he had felt the pain of Oliver's blows and henceforward kept his attacks verbal.

Meghan watched Oliver over the weeks and saw an anger take root in him, which was masked only by the bottomless pain in his eyes. Sometimes they sat together in the late evenings after training and she thought he might open his heart to her, but he held his tongue and seemed content just to have her close. One time, keeping his eyes averted and without uttering a word, he had reached out for her hand and they had sat in silence while he gripped her palm.

'Shut your jabbering and get your sweaty arse into the showers,' Frog ordered Gregor, but his gaze was also on Oliver. He too could see the fury in the lad and it gratified him. Here was the sort of trainee the Pantheon needed. One with brains, but also now with violence. Frog watched as the wooden blades hit the pell time and again until the lad was gasping and scarlet.

He hates someone, the Hastiliarius thought. *Those blows are personal.*

Perhaps this whippet of boy – so timid and useless at the start of term – has the makings of a true Valhalla warrior.

Midnight at the top of the Mile.

The Blood Nights were over and all of Alexander's forces, bar a Companion rearguard, had already departed for the Field, but still Cleitus kept his head bent and his hat low on his brow as he marched the final yards. He was a big fellow and travelling unnoticed was a skill that eluded him. Odin, damn him, had a whole city to choose from, yet the bloody man had selected a venue in the heart of Pantheon territory, just a hundred yards from Pella.

With relief, he slipped into a tight wynd and negotiated its shadowed length until he reached a door that opened onto steps leading down into an elegant iron-framed conservatory. Beyond the glass, giant-leafed plants jostled for light and screened the interior from casual eyes, but he could just make out tables of ancient oak and the flicker of candlelight.

A solemn young lady of extraordinary beauty unlocked and stood aside to let him enter. The scent of sumptuous cuisine hung in the air as Cleitus descended the stone steps and he spied Odin reposing at a table, cigar in one hand, brandy in the other.

'You dine late,' the newcomer said gruffly.

'The night brings with it privacy.'

Cleitus noticed the two empty dessert plates and he shot a glance at the girl, but she ignored them both and took herself off to the interior of the restaurant. Odin waved a finger to the seat opposite and waited while the Titan officer removed his hat and coat and sat.

'A strange choice of setting,' Cleitus commented irritably.

'What are you bellyaching about?'

'It's not exactly a discreet location.'

'Bullshit. We all know Alexander's been thinning his troops, sending them off to the Field to prepare for battle. There can hardly be a Titan left in the city.'

'Just a company of my Companions and we'll be gone in forty-eight hours. The strongholds are locked and only Simmius will remain.'

'And my Vikings have no eyes for you, so quit your damn moaning and tell me what news can be so important that I must trade that exquisite piece of arse for your ugly face?'

Cleitus scowled, but checked a retort. 'Last time we met, you were earnestly interested in locating your pair of Valhalla deserters.'

'And no sooner had they killed your champions and earned themselves a place in your Palatinate, than you lost all knowledge of their whereabouts.'

'Well, I can confirm that they've been discharged.'

'Discharged?' Odin exclaimed.

'Gone. They're out the Pantheon and of no more concern.'

'You have this on whose authority?'

'Simmius divulged the news to Alexander. It was Zeus' decision. Seems he doesn't like second-hand Valhalla goods any more than the rest of us.'

Odin puffed on his cigar and glared at his guest. 'And you think this is *good* news?'

Cleitus puckered his lips, perplexed. 'I assumed the information would please you. Your renegades have had their comeuppance and are of no more consequence.'

Odin drummed his fingers on the tablecloth and took a slug of brandy to stop himself exploding. 'So you intrude on my evening once again to inform me of how little you know about my deserters. Is that all you have?'

Cleitus rained hard eyes on the Caelestis. The man was getting old. Behind all the braggadocio was a flaccid and rotting body. Permitted one opportunity on a battlefield and Cleitus would gladly carve him up. 'I bring other news, but it comes with a price.'

Odin rolled the cigar around his teeth and held his tongue.

The Colonel glanced behind to check they were alone, then leaned forward conspiratorially. 'Zeus has not recruited.'

Still Odin said nothing, so Cleitus waded deeper. 'Nicanor has thirteen new Heavies, bringing his Phalanx to eighty. And I have an intake of ten to resuscitate my broken Companion lines. But there remain seventy Blood Credits unspent. Zeus, it seems, is holding them until the end of this Season, when he hopes to combine them with new Credits won, to create a surge in forces that will take the Horde by surprise in the Twenty-First.'

'From whom have you heard this?'

'Direct from Alexander's mouth.'

'And you believe him?'

Cleitus was affronted. 'I am Colonel of Light Infantry. Second only to the King. He does not lie to me.'

Odin flicked ash onto his dessert plate, then brought the cigar close to his face so that the smoke wreathed his expression. 'Why are you telling me this?'

'Sometimes a man must decide which horse to back.'

Odin's eyes were talons in him. 'Explain yourself.'

'You have the numbers.'

'We've had the numbers other Seasons and you've not come kissing my arse before.'

'But never against a Palatinate so demoralised and a King so... unbalanced.'

'Unless I'm mistaken, the Raiding Season was a Titan victory. You stopped my warriors gaining the first Asset and you successfully claimed the second. In the Cull, ten of the fifteen sacrificial lambs were Viking. And, as we speak, most of your Palatinate is already camped at the Field, scouting the land, choosing stations and making plans. For what goddamn reason am I to believe you're demoralised?'

'Because at the start of this Season, every Titan believed we had the funds to equal the strength of Valhalla and now that belief has been snatched from us. Because our King is a paranoid junkie who cannot think without a hit. And because there are even rumours that Zeus is hoarding the funds because he's selling up.'

Odin froze. 'Come again?'

Cleitus shrugged. 'Only unsubstantiated rumours, but there's word that he wants out to the highest bidder.'

Odin stared at his guest, his gaze boring into him, sifting, searching for the truth. 'So what are you proposing?' he asked at last.

'Attack Alexander at the Battle. Send your Wolves for him and you will not find my Companion Bodyguard an insurmountable obstacle. Then kill him with a sword in the belly.'

Odin's brows came together. 'You expect me to believe that? You think I can't smell a trap when it's being laid?'

'I'm not asking you to do anything you're not already planning to do. I'm simply saying that if you try to get to Alexander during the Battle, you will find my Companions accommodating.'

Odin harrumphed suspiciously. 'And what do you want for this information, fair knight?'

'Honour and status in your new combined Valhalla Palatinate. The natural heir to Sveinn.'

Odin snorted, but said nothing. He stubbed out the

remnants of his cigar, sat back and regarded the man opposite. Silence reigned. From somewhere deep inside the restaurant came the sound of crockery being stacked. Then he leaned forward, reached for a bottle of brandy on a side table, poured a second glass and pushed it towards the Titan. 'Like you say, Colonel, I will be sending my Wolves and my Hammers and my Ravens into battle with the same orders I always give. If your lines should prove more malleable than usual, then maybe – just maybe – you'll have yourself a deal.'

In the candlelit privacy of the secret garden, the men clinked glasses.

'Do you still want me?' the woman asked when the fat man had left.

Odin glanced up at her. 'No, my dear. You may go.'

He poured himself another brandy and swirled the liquid around the glass until it spilled over the lip.

The Titan's news tallied with what the kid had discovered at the *Agonium Martiale*. The enemy were missing a whole heap of troops, which meant Zeus must be hoarding the Credits. And if he really was planning to quit the Pantheon, he must never be allowed to carry with him the secret of Odin's cheating in the Eighteenth.

He sat back and stared ruminatively at the night outside.

So this was it then. He must ruin his rival. Now or never. He must unleash his Horde and send them headlong for the throats of the foe. He must drench the field in blood. He must harvest lives. He must kill everything in his path until the blades of his Wolves kissed Alexander.

And then both the King of the Titans and his Caelestis must fall.

Strike first. Strike fast.

XXXVII

The Horde of Valhalla arrived on the eastern fringes of the Knoydart peninsula at first light on the day of the Grand Battle in five coaches.

It had been a night of jolting and twisting and turning on roads barely wider than the vehicles and Sveinn's warriors emerged groggy and sleepless and grumpy as hell to find themselves slap bang in the middle of nowhere. The air was sharp with cold. Mountains rose to greet the dawn and the ribbon of tarmac they had followed for hours tapered into nothing but a muddy track, as if it had finally given up trying to hold these five unwieldy burdens. From everywhere came the sound of hidden water, the tinkling and gurgling of streams beneath the grasses, a myriad of movement in a landscape that was otherwise utterly still.

The Horde loitered aimlessly, their cloaks wrapped tight and the bottoms of their breeks already getting damp, their faces creased into scowls and steam rising from their breath. Trestles were pulled from the backs of the coaches and a small Pantheon logistics team got porridge and flatbreads underway on giant gas burners.

'Ensure your Ravens fill their bellies,' Bjarke sidled next to Calder and muttered. 'There'll be no more until it's all over.'

They ate as heartily as they could, but the journey, the hour, the discomfort and the dread of things to come dictated that many stomachs refused to accept the offerings. Crates were unloaded, stamped with Regiment, Company and litter numbers, and the troops collected their war gear and found places on the hillside to help each other into mail, tug on vambraces, deck themselves in fur, strap sword belts or baldrics, and inspect their weapons for the hundredth time. Excess breads were stuffed into leather pouches and slung over shoulders. Some of the secret streams were discovered and flasks filled with brackish, peaty water. Finally, shields were hoisted and helmets pushed onto the backs of heads so that faces were not yet concealed.

Sveinn was there. Subdued, but regal in his gold-trimmed mail and black cloak, silver-streaked hair combed loose, a wolfskin across his shoulders and a Triple Horn hanging from his neck. Calder caught sight of Skarde lurking near his Wolves and gasped at the sight of his brutalised face. His nose was flattened, his eyes purple and swollen, and stitches trailed across his shredded brow. Unlike the others, he pulled his helmet fully down to hide his hideousness and the iron visage regarded her briefly, then turned away.

A Vigilis appeared further up the track and signalled. Sveinn cast an eye around his assembled two hundred, then grunted and waved them forward. And with that, the Horde advanced in loose column, dressed in its war finery, grasping spear and bow and shield, holding cloaks above the mud, and began the long trek into Knoydart.

The day unfurled. A bright spring sun gnawed at the shadows cast by the hills and stole the chill from the air. Sweat pooled beneath tunics and hands reached for flasks as throats dried. The column wound upslope, then dropped and followed low, boggy ground between high peaks. Water sprung from everywhere and the ground oozed and burped and gave way beneath the weight of their iron. The track dwindled to nothing, but still the Vigilis led them on.

Calder hauled herself through the mire, using the butt of her spear as a staff. Her mail pulled at her shoulders, dragged her down, so that her boots sank and her knees clamoured. Every step felt a labour. Plant her spear. Shift her weight. Heave her rearmost boot from the earth and plunge it forward. By mid-morning her stomach had long forgotten its porridge and she was desperate to halt, but she was a Housecarl now and while her Ravens straggled around her, she must not allow them to glimpse her fatigue.

Geir was back. His shoulder was still heavily bandaged and anaesthetised, but it didn't stop him grinning and cajoling the first-season Ravens and she was glad of his presence. Sassa and Jorunn were there too, though Calder wondered at Jorunn's recovery after the arrow at Waverley had laid her in the Pantheon wards for a month. She moved stiffly and looked ashen, but she refused to countenance missing the Battle, all the more so because Liv remained strapped to life support in those very same wards and would likely never return. Calder knew her experienced Ravens ached for Freyja and yearned for her Battle guile as they trudged to face their foe. Nonetheless, they accepted Calder's authority and looked to her for leadership and she swore to herself that she must not fail them.

The sun was nearing its zenith when they heard a whine above the squelching and heavy breathing and someone pointed. Heads craned up at the sky and they caught the glint of carbon fibre and realised the first of the day's drones had spotted them.

'Helmets down,' came the order from Sveinn, passed from litter to litter, and there were curses and V-signs flung at the thing. Its camera would be sending the images via satellites to every corner of the world, for those who paid handsomely enough to witness the action live.

Calder yanked her helmet on so that the eyepieces shielded her identity and she gave herself a moment to rest and close her lids. When she opened them, she realised the Vigilis had stopped by the base of a small slope and there was a single wooden-framed tent behind him, as well as benches and tables. A ragged cheer rippled through the ranks and the column forced itself the final yards. Litters requisitioned benches and those who could not find a seat pulled themselves to the drier ground up the slope and collapsed on the heather. Sveinn conferred with the Vigilis and then commandeered the tent, and for a while the Palatinate was nothing more than a rudderless crowd, content simply to sprawl now the journey was over.

Soon, however, the Hersirs began to marshal their litters. The sun was high in the sky and there could be only a couple of hours before the two o'clock klaxon, which would signal the start of the slaughter. Water was drunk, flatbreads unpacked and devoured, order resurrected.

Asmund found Calder and suggested she take a few of her Ravens up the hill and scout the lie of the land. She nodded, swallowed her bread and beckoned to Sassa and Estrid. They left their shields and bows with the rest of the company and used their spears to help them up the steep ground. As they reached the summit, she signalled for them to drop to their knees and they crawled the last yards. The land curved below them into a wide bowl of tussocky grass and heather, riven with tiny glistening streams and bounded by hills. A group of deer congregated near the centre, though they raised their heads at the sound of drones and began to trot for cover in the clefts of the slopes.

Calder's eyes were drawn by movement above the deer and she spotted a group of figures high on one hillside, pointing and conferring and assessing the land. For a moment, she thought they must be Titans, but then she caught the glisten of aluminium tripods and knew they were Vigiles. She ran her gaze around the crest of the land on the other side and saw more groups and then, on the hill at the far end of the glen, she realised a giant shaft had been driven into the ground and the banner of the Lion of Macedon hung from it, a playful upland breeze catching at its corners.

'It would seem this year our choice of ends has been made for us,' commented Sassa.

She was right, for this wide expanse of treeless land, rimmed by hilltop vantage points, was a perfect natural stadium and must be the Field. The Titans would have been there for days already, some, perhaps, for weeks. They would have walked the ground dozens of times, studying angles and obstacles, drainage and rock. They would know the direction of the prevailing wind and the arc of the sun. They would have examined conditions during rainstorms and watched where the water pooled and where the land remained firm. They would have wandered the streams and marked the best fording points. They had probably knelt just where Calder and her Ravens were now, picturing the

Field from that angle and deciding, irrevocably, that the other end was superior.

The sun was too high in the sky to be certain of direction, but it had been behind them for much of the trek and so Calder guessed they were now looking west, which meant by Battle's commencement at two it would be dipping into Valhalla's eyes. But beyond the valley, there was a cloud front building and she doubted the afternoon would be so bright.

A breeze whipped out the Lion of Macedon for a few moments so that all eyes could see the golden beast on its blood-red background. Coming to a decision, Calder stood and signalled for the others to rise as well. One group of Vigiles spotted them and began pointing. *Good*, she thought. *Enough of this hide-and-seek*.

'Tell Sveinn we have eyes on the Field,' she said to Estrid. 'And the foe are camped at the westward end.'

Estrid nodded and began to jog back down the slope.

'And fetch the banners,' Calder shouted after her. 'Let's wake those Titan bastards and let them know the Horde of Valhalla has come.'

It had been seven in the morning when a stranger arrived at the Companion Cavalry's little camp and disturbed their breakfast. He was dressed in civvies and was bareheaded, and he informed them that it was the day of the Battle, so they must prepare for departure.

'Where are we going?' Heph demanded.

The man pointed behind him. 'Over that hill. You'll be met on the other side.'

'Is there transport?'

'You carry everything you need. And you leave in an hour.'

The shock of the news brought a flurry of activity as they bustled back into the tents to retrieve clothing and arms.

'Don't discard your food,' warned Zephyr. 'Get it down you, no matter what.'

They choked on it as they struggled into their gear under the confines of the canvas. They had waited for this day. Prepared for it. Their armour was burnished and stacked. Their weapons honed to fighting edges and polished bright. Yet now the hour of departure had arrived, they were panicked and confused, breathlessly pulling on their panoply and worrying about the horses.

One by one, they emerged to find the man sitting quietly on a bench and he looked them up and down, taking in their tunics of white, their front-and-back bronze cuirasses, their long cloaks and the scarlet-plumed helmets they held beneath their arms. While they belted their swords, Spyro and Zephyr collected bread and flasks of watered wine and stowed them in shoulder bags.

The man rose. 'This is for your eyes,' he said, approaching Heph and handing him an envelope. 'Take a right at the lane and you'll find a track on the left. Be gone by eight. Good luck.'

He turned and walked back up to the road and Heph took himself a few steps away from the camp to open the envelope. Inside was a single sheet of folded paper and a note written in elegant script.

Hephaestion
  The Battle is upon us. After months of stealth, we must

reveal our secret. Yet, how we choose the moment and manner of this revelation determines the very success of our long project. Everything comes down to the instant you kick your heels into the flanks of your mount and show our hand.

In Battle, nothing sticks to plan. Everything turns on luck and raw emotion. But you must not lose your head. You are seven against two hundred, so you will have only one opportunity.

Before Belgutei departed, I met with him at Hera's request and he provided me with words of wisdom. Read them and take them to the Field locked in your head:

Wait. And wait again. Hold our secret until the single critical moment in the Battle.

Do not be distracted by the many different struggles on that field; focus only on the one that matters.

When you find it and you know the moment has come, hurl yourself at it with all the violence you possess.

Remember, you are nothing if scattered. Ride boot to boot and do not break.

Surprise, shock and speed. These are all that matter.

Fare you well, Captain. I have invested much in this enterprise, so I expect you to make it worthwhile.

We will be watching.

Zeus

Heph folded the note and tucked the envelope beneath his armour. The others were already traipsing along the shore, helmets in one hand, lances in the other. Alexander's ancient cavalry had ridden without shields, so they too would join the fray without such protection. Heph took a final scan around the campsite and followed.

It took them all of the hour to get the horses fed and watered and properly prepared. The beasts could sense the tension in the air and snorted and trembled and fussed over their oats. Dio realised they should be given a second feed before the Battle and cursed himself for not thinking of this before. He scurried around finding bags and filling them as best he could with oats while the horses watched him and guessed today would be unusual. The troops brushed them and whispered soothing words, then fixed harnesses and strapped the lion skins to their backs.

At last, they led them into the sunlight and each passed their lance to a companion while they mounted. Then they walked the horses to the lane and found the track over the hill.

Heph swore when they reached the summit and the scene opened up before them. Below were fields and a beach and a tiny wooden jetty protruding into a sea loch, which stretched endlessly east and west, but was little more than half a mile across. The land beyond swept away in folds of green and grey. The tide was high and a boat awaited them as they descended. It might once have carried cars, though now it was rusted and peeling, but at least the lowered stern meant the horses could be walked straight on.

The riders dismounted when they reached the beach and led their charges slowly down. The horses were nervous. They whinnied and stamped on the sand and a couple evacuated great clods of dung. But they trusted these humans who had devoted so many months to their care and, one by one, they allowed themselves to be walked onto the vessel.

The ferryman peered at his passengers through eyes pinched tight from years in the elements. His face was rutted with fissures and his hair steel grey beneath a knitted hat. A pipe was clamped between his teeth and he uttered not a syllable as they boarded. Heph thought he looked the epitome of an extra from *Whisky Galore*.

When they were finally all gathered on the deck, the stern rose and the engine coughed into life, making the horses twitch and stamp again. The little ferry and its strange cargo, puttered out into the loch and a breeze caught them. Heph assumed they were going straight over, but once they reached the centre of the water, the ferry turned to starboard and chugged along the length of the loch. The Titans peered at the far shoreline, but there were no signs of habitation and nothing moved. Beside Heph, Boreas pissed copiously onto the deck and Heph felt the urine puddling around his boots.

Eventually they rounded a small headland and another beach came into view. The ferryman eased his vessel towards it, slowed and then cut the engine altogether just as they reached the sand. The boat lurched and scraped to a stop, making the horses toss their heads and whinny again. Then the bow lowered and riders gripped the reins, whispered into the ears of their mounts, and led them slowly onto dry land.

Heph nodded to the ferryman and the man raised a finger towards a stone track weaving its way into the hills. Then he cranked the engine into reverse, raised the bow and slipped back onto the loch.

'It would seem it's that way,' said Heph.

Dio pulled a face. 'This is going to be some debacle if we can't find the Field or we get there when the damn thing's over.'

Heph looked round at his company. Pallas was fidgety with nerves, his mouth open and his eyes flitting everywhere. Spyro stood rigid, staring up the track. Zephyr had removed his helmet and was wiping his brow. Maia was talking to her steed, her face pressed to his. And Lenore watched Heph, her features pale, her hair tied back in a red ponytail that matched the sweep of her plume.

'Okay,' Heph said. 'The sun's already high. We probably have only a couple of hours, but we take it slow and let the horses dictate the pace. This is it then. Today's the day. Let's go surprise them all.'

He smiled and they grinned nervously back at him.

'Mount up.'

The Captain of the Sacred Band stood with Parmenion and Nicanor on the western hill and watched their sergeants bellow and chivvy the companies into formation. The Lion Standard had been moved downslope and now stood near a stream that wended its way around the left of the hill and continued its journey to the sea.

So much could depend on that stream. Further up the valley, the water was no more than a series of tributaries, which were crossable with a simple jump, but as the stream meandered its way down, it widened and deepened and became a key strategic feature as it finally bent and passed the Titan hill. Here they had spent two days finding stones and dropping them into the water to ensure they could shift their King back and forth across it, depending on which bank the main Valhalla attack materialised.

Below them, the sergeants were happy with the Phalanx

lines and permitted the Heavies to rest by unslinging their eighteen-foot sarissas and shoving the butts into the ground, then kneeling so that the shields strapped to their chests touched the earth and they could take the weight off their shoulders. They were drawn up ten wide and eight rows deep. Not enough. Hammer must possess a hundred and twenty spears this year and they could curl around the Heavies and tear into their exposed flanks.

Agape's Band and Parmenion's peltasts waited beside the Lion Banner. Thirty-four in total. Precious few, but they had the river. If events went badly, they would haul Alexander to whichever bank was the safest and defend it with their lives. The Companions were to the right of the Phalanx, grouped loosely into two units of ten. Their orders were to protect the flanks of the Heavies and stop any counter on that southern side of the Field, but it would be an unenviable task this year with the Wolves packing almost twice the number.

Cleitus and Menes were in close discussion and Agape watched them. For weeks the fat Colonel of Lights had been ballistic with anger about the lack of new recruits, but since his late arrival at the Field, he seemed more accepting and even animated about the struggle to come. Agape pursed her lips dubiously and supposed this must be a good thing.

She shifted her gaze up the empty valley. It had been a peaceful place over the last week. The Titans had erected a good camp behind their hill and eaten well and she had relished her time in the wilderness. But now the valley thundered. Three helicopters circled below the cloud base. At least a dozen drones zipped and whined in all directions. And on the northern and southern ridges, Vigiles teams clustered around cameras and jabbered into radios.

'Here they come,' declared Nicanor, breaking her thoughts, and, on cue, the Horde appeared over the eastern rim and spilled down to the Field. No ordered regiments here. No apparent discipline. They came in a mass of iron and shields and spear tips scratching the sky. Banners were raised at the foot of the hill. The Triple Horn, Raven, Wolf, Hammer and Storm, but from this distance Agape could not tell how these formations were arranged within the unruly throng. The jeers and insults came to them on the upland breeze and Parmenion whistled softly.

'There's a lot of the bastards.'

'Best part of two hundred,' growled Nicanor. 'We have a fight on our hands.'

'So when that klaxon sounds,' said Agape, 'you must move like lightning, Nicanor.'

'Aye. I know the plan. I just hope that lot over there go with it.'

Ten figures had separated themselves from the Viking mass and were striding across the Field, wielding axes and cursing and spitting. It was the usual Berserker antics and Agape paid them no attention.

'They must,' she replied. 'When your Phalanx moves, Hammer *has* to counter. Take the southern line and keep them on that side of the stream. But, whatever you do, don't allow them to move first or the game is up.'

They had debated the plan over many nights and Alexander – thank the gods – had discovered some of his old fire and announced that attack was indeed the only true form of defence. Against a foe so numerous, it would be catastrophic to allow Valhalla to come to them. The Titans must storm down the Field and take iron and fury to that end. Keep those Viking shieldwalls far from Alexander's banners and pray the Battle's hour passed swiftly.

Below them, Alexander was striding to his standard, accompanied by a sparse retinue of Bodyguards. Parmenion slammed down his helmet and turned to Agape with his hand extended. 'Well, this is it. Good luck, my friends.'

The three officers clasped hands and Nicanor and Parmenion headed down the slope to join their units. Agape delayed her descent and shot a long gaze around the perimeter of the valley, searching each cleft, each col, each lowland escape route for any sign of life. But nothing moved.

You better be out there somewhere, Heph. Or the gods are about to rip us apart.

XXXVIII

'Brace!' Nicanor bellowed and eighty sarissa butts slotted back into carrying slings and eighty bronze shields lifted from the earth.

'And rise!'

The Phalanx stood, their sarissas a forest of vertical shafts in this otherwise treeless valley. The Companions and peltasts howled their support, the helicopters roared overhead and the klaxon sounded.

'Phalanx, advance on me!'

One hour. One hour of blood and mayhem. And no one – not the kings, not the officers, not the entitled spectators and not even the Pantheon powers – had any idea how it would unfold.

Nicanor marched across the valley floor in the centre of the lead rank. His scalloped shield was strapped to his chest, leaving both hands free to keep his mighty eighteen-foot sarissa vertical. The ground was firm here. They knew this. They had checked it day after day. He strode hard and pressed the pace. They must claim the centre ground, then press the foe back into their own half. His shield jolted against his collarbones and his knees yelped. Already his shoulder muscles were burning with the effort of keeping his weapon upright as they forged over the uneven terrain.

He peered through the bronze sockets of his helmet and saw Hammer coming for them. The bastards were running. They were as eager to make ground as he was and he realised his Heavies would barely get halfway before the forces engaged.

Time to change.

'Spear!' he yelled in his loudest battlefield voice and he felt the lads either side of him drop a pace behind his shoulder. All along the line, each Heavy eased a step back from the trooper inside him and, though Nicanor could not see it, he knew the inner ranks would be opening, stepping towards the edges, so that they were now in a hollowed spearhead formation with their Colonel at point.

The Vikings were coming at them as a mob, but at thirty yards distant their Jarl and Hersirs bellowed commands and the pace slowed and limewood shields scraped together. They jostled into three ranks, the best part of forty across at the front. They could not hope to hold the Phalanx, but they would curve around it, as sinuous as silk, and try to get under the sarissas.

'Arms front!' Nicanor shouted.

The outer rank on both sides of the Phalanx's spearhead lowered their sarissas and couched them in their slings. The next rank inside lowered theirs between the shoulders of their comrades and the third rank did likewise. Now the Phalanx was a bristling deadly wall of thirty-six iron tips on each oblique edge.

'Choose your man and stick him. And do not stop!'

★

Ulf sucked air into his lungs and tried to quell a rising tide of panic. *Here they come again.* He remembered the hell of the Phalanx on the beach a year before as he crawled in the water while their shafts blocked the sky above and death reigned.

He was wedged in the second rank of Hammer, his shield pressed against the man in front and the iron boss of another shield thrust against his spine. His job should be to stabilise the first rank and jab his spear across the shoulders of the men in front, prodding for any weakness in assailants. But how could you do that when the enemy's weapons kept them fifteen feet away? So Hammer tactics had evolved and second rankers would throw their spears at the first opportunity, then use their free hands to grasp the probing sarissa shafts and tug the foe onto the spears of the front rank. That was the theory.

Men gasped and cursed around him. The air reeked of sweat and piss and even vomit, but it was nothing compared to the metallic tang of blood that would soon envelop them. They had raced across the ground when the klaxon sounded. Somebody up high – whether Sveinn or Odin – had demanded a full-out assault this year and Bjarke had led them running for the foe. Ulf could see him now at the centre of the front rank, shieldless, roaring his defiance and swinging a mighty war axe. Ingvar was similarly armed. They would attempt to cleave everything in their path and carve a way through the forest of iron.

Twenty yards. *Here they come.*

He felt the men around him dig in, heeling their boots

into the earth, shoulders against shields, and a rising intake of breath, though he was wedged so tight, he could barely expand his ribs. And then the sarissas arrived.

Months of Hammer training kicked in. The first rank dropped to their knees and burst forward beneath the forest of weapons. One man was too slow. He twisted his head to miss a first iron point, but the second took him on the helmet and bore him backwards. He had nowhere to go. The ranks behind held him too firmly, so his neck arched back grotesquely and snapped.

Even as Ulf watched aghast, another point passed his cheek by a whisper and he heard a soggy grunt as the man pushing into his spine caught it in his mouth. Teeth shattered and bloodied spittle soaked the nape of Ulf's neck. Desperately, he hauled his spear above the press and flung it towards the foe, then grabbed at the cherry dogwood shaft kissing his ear and wrenched it with every ounce of strength. He glimpsed the Titan on the other end stumble forward and a Viking rose to take him on his spear, but then the third rank of sarissas came driving at Ulf and he let out an involuntary cry of terror and his knees collapsed.

For the second time in his life the Phalanx's murderous canopy closed over him and their boots pounded towards him. He pulled himself out of the mud and dragged his sword from its scabbard, then raised his shield and pounded at the shafts that scraped along its rim. He forced himself into a half-crouch and launched forward at the marching legs. He stabbed into a thigh and his arm juddered as the blade hit bone. Yanking it free, he cut sideways and hamstringed another. Someone cried and a Titan collapsed on him, forcing him down into the path of the boots. A foot stamped on his helmet, another on his mail and then the full weight of the Phalanx was on him and although his mouth opened in a scream, the air had already been crushed from his lungs.

'Eyes on,' called Parmenion. 'We have company.'

A body of Vikings had crossed to the northern bank of the stream and were now approaching at a run. Forty of them, perhaps more. He squinted to make out their shields, but the designs were impossible to see at this distance.

Parmenion had used the newly placed stones to ford the river and had arranged his twenty peltasts on the northern side, facing east up the Field. Over his shoulder Alexander stood with Cleitus beneath his standard on the opposite bank, his jaw clenched. He was circled by six Heavies from the Bodyguard and beyond them was the reassuring presence of the Sacred Band, grouped silently, waiting to see how fortunes played and where they would be needed.

The Vikings were coming fast. The bastards were doing everything at the double. They obviously knew the Titan ranks were sparser than they should be and were determined to make their numbers count. 'Anyone see those shields yet?' Parmenion shouted.

'Looks like Raven to me,' someone said.

'Raven and Storm,' another confirmed.

'Good,' said Parmenion and he turned and nodded at Agape to signal the Band need not cross. 'Then it will be only a missile attack. Hold your ground and let them do their worst.'

★

With barely an hour to prepare and even less to take in the Titan battle formations, new orders had come from Sveinn. A change of tactics. Now everything was about speed and mass. Get to the foe and overwhelm them with Valhalla's additional numbers. Which meant, as Calder ran, she and her thirteen Ravens were armed with bows.

She tore ahead, determined to lead by example, though her limbs ached from the trek and her belly churned from hunger and fear. She locked her eyes on the foe and took in their scale armour, oval shields and helms without plumes, and momentarily wondered where on this Field Tyler might be. She had danced in his arms in Rome while he told her his name was Hephaestion, but he had omitted to say to which unit he belonged. Perhaps he waited for her now. Scale armour catching in the light. Javelin readied. Eyes boring into her from behind his bronze helmet.

Closer. The foe were going down on one knee with their shields high on their shoulders. So they knew what was coming. She yelled a command to her company and stalled her run, then notched an arrow, raised her bow and tried to calm her pounding heart. A single deep breath, released slowly.

'Loose.'

Fourteen arrows arced through the sky. With satisfaction, she heard their iron tips clang against bronze, but she was already notching a second. Another volley and a third and peltast heads were down.

That's when Asmund burst past her shoulder with his thirty-five troops. They used the seconds while the Titans were recovering to steal another fifteen yards, until they were close enough to see the jerk of the foe's eyes behind their bronze sockets, and then hurled their spears in a single devastating volley. Shafts embedded into peltast shields, thumped off helmets and tore into scale armour to find flesh and bone.

Three foe stayed down. The others rose and planted their feet with javelins couched. Beyond them, Asmund could see the Lion Standard across the river and Alexander staring back at him. Close. So damn close.

'That's them done,' shouted Parmenion. 'Regroup.'

Only it wasn't.

Storm had no intention of retiring. Their spears thrown, they drew swords and flung themselves at the thin line of peltasts with the promise of death. A bulky woman thumped her shield into Parmenion's, then dipped and punched her blade at his groin. Somehow he shimmied aside, but she followed with her shield and almost toppled him down the riverbank. She had thought him fallen and allowed a gap to open between them, but his back foot just found purchase and now he had the advantage with his six-foot javelin. He thrust it underarm and buried it blade-deep in her ample mailed stomach. Her cry was as high-pitched as a tern's and she fell to her knees and grappled with her wound.

As two more Vikings ran at him, he could not risk her finding the reserves to thrust a knife into his shins, so he jabbed her again, this time beneath an ear and she slumped lifeless. He just had time to wrench his bloodied javelin free before the next assailants were on him. A wild-faced man, lean as a fox, grabbed the rim of his shield with scrawny fingers and yanked it down. His accomplice swung his sword and it smashed into Parmenion's helmet, stunning him and making him collapse down the bank.

He hit the water and scrabbled for purchase, but then he was hit again by the full weight of his enemy and taken under. Fingers clutched at his throat. Water filled his helmet. His nasal guard struck stones and a knee rammed into his spine. He squirmed and fought, but the grip was iron. The stream was in his mouth, in his nostrils and hunting for his lungs.

Madly, he struggled for his shortsword and wrenched it free, then stabbed upwards. It caught on mail and he stabbed again and again until the water was crimson around him. The grip slackened and he wriggled from beneath the knee and launched himself for the sky to suck in great draughts of oxygen.

For a heartbeat he saw his broken peltast line in the water around him and then another Viking was launching himself off the bank, his blade coming for Parmenion.

'Agape,' he just had time to cry, though whether any sound broke from his lips, he could not tell.

'Back!' ordered Calder.

Sassa and Geir were already shouldering their bows and drawing blades to follow Storm into the fray. But her orders were clear. Storm had been loosed at the foe on the condition that Raven must become Valhalla's line of defence.

She yelled her command again and Geir cursed. They were so close. The Macedon banner hung just forty yards away. It would be easy to reinforce Asmund's troops and swarm across the river. He hollered in exasperation and glared at her, but beyond the banner and beyond Alexander, she could see the Band and understood how few Vikings would make it up that opposite bank.

She rallied her Ravens and herded them back east towards the Horde's own banners. Sveinn waited there with four Hammer Bodyguards and all of the Wolves. Ake nodded to her, but Skarde maintained his gaze upfield, his bruised and broken mouth a thin sliver of ice.

The Ravens shouldered their bows and retrieved spears from where they had stacked them, then Calder arranged her litters in a line in front of Sveinn's party and turned her attentions to both titanic struggles, one by the river and the other in the centre of the Field. Even at this distance, there was a stink on the air. The smell of fear and blood and excrement. Over the roar of the helicopters, came the din of iron on bronze and shrieks of fury and terror.

Calder glanced at Sveinn who was standing silently watching the action, a hand running absently along the mail on one side of his gut. She checked her Raven line, then gripped her spear shaft and swore beneath her breath that no one would pass.

Agape examined the battlefield.

The Vikings had folded around Nicanor's Phalanx and were cleaving into his flanks, but somehow he was still driving forward one step at a time. It was blood-drenched chaos, but it was chaos that remained resolutely upfield.

Parmenion's peltasts were in a death fight in the river.

Storm outnumbered them almost two to one and he needed reinforcing. But that would expose the Titans' centre.

Where are the Wolves?

She could see a Viking host beside Valhalla's banners and assumed it must be them, but why were they uncommitted? Did they delay for her? Were they watching the Band and waiting for her decision?

She glanced over her shoulder at the Companions. Menes still had them drawn up in two lines of twelve. It was enough. If the Wolves came down the middle, he would rush to engage and hold them halfway up the Field. The foe were more numerous, but he would keep them at bay long enough for her to send the Band in support.

Mind made up, she committed.

Her blade rasped from its scabbard. Kyriacos signalled the rest of the troop and they ran to Parmenion's aid.

Despite his pulverised eyelids, Skarde took it all in. He saw Agape's signal and watched the blue-cloaked Hoplites wheel towards the river.

On the final day in Edinburgh, Odin had given him personal orders in no uncertain terms. The bastard had been beside himself with anger at Skarde's failure to interrogate the Raven and disgusted at the sight of his broken face. But in those critical hours before the Battle, the Caelestis could turn to no other lapdog, so it would have to be Skarde. Accompanied by sly reminders of the horrors of Erebus, Odin informed him that his only chance of avoiding such a fate again was to follow his next orders to the letter. Kill Alexander. Nothing else would suffice. Kill him with a sword and only a sword. Odin had no goddamn need of fifty Blood Credits for the death of a King with a spear or an arrow. The fall of the Titan Palatinate was his only objective and that necessitated being close enough to bury a sword blade through Alexander's throat, or his gut, his ribs, his mouth. It did not matter, so long as he perished on that Field.

'Forget about the Companions,' Odin had growled. 'They will not trouble you.'

And now Skarde saw the bitch Agape and her Band finally leave the gate open.

With the merest flick of his arm, he signalled the advance and the Wolves slipped their chains.

Ake took two litters and swarmed around the outer, southernmost side of the Phalanx.

Unn was with her, though after the Wolf casualties of last year, many of the others were first-seasoners. They would have to do. They had trained hard enough these last months and had been selected for their combat skill. She led them across tributaries and splashing through great swathes of boggy ground, but she kept the pace unrelenting.

They rounded the battle between Hammer and the Heavies and could not avoid eyeing the slaughter as they passed. The Phalanx was still grinding forward, but it had lost cohesion. Everywhere Hammers were cutting into it, forcing themselves between the great sarissas and stabbing and scything. Many of the foe had dropped their shafts and drawn their own swords as the struggle became too close and personal.

A Hammer stumbled from the fray and fell as two Heavies pulled him back. He looked up at her with pleading eyes and she knew him from the ale halls of Valhalla, had even shared a song and drink with him recently, but her orders were to stop for nothing and get to Alexander's banners. She glimpsed his horrified expression and then he disappeared beneath the slashing and stabbing of his attackers.

There was a warning shout from her shoulder and she saw the Companions commit. Eleven of them, racing around the melee to block her advance. With a wild screech and a rictus grin, she flew at them. The first one she took with ease. Barely slowing her momentum, she kicked out at the base of his hoplon, tipping the upper rim forward, and then thrust her blade so far through his throat that it stuck in his spinal vertebrae. She wrenched it free just in time to parry a wild stab from another adversary and before the woman could recover, Ake punched her hard with the boss of her shield and they both fell. Her shield came loose, but she grabbed the Companion and rolled her in a flurry of hits with the pommel of her sword. Somehow Ake came up on top facing the wrong way. Her knees were pinning her enemy's arms, but all she could see were the Titan's legs. Without compunction, she stabbed between the thighs at her womanhood and dragged the longsword free in a welter of blood.

Then she was up and running again. There was no time to locate her shield, so she drew her seax with her left hand and stabbed at another foe and then she was through and there was just grass and rock and hillocks and beyond all these, Alexander's banner.

Without a glance behind, she howled and ran.

*

On the opposite side of the Phalanx battle, Skarde was also sprinting as fast as his mail and weapons would allow.

He was in the centre ground, following the middle line as straight as a die. The Hammers to the left of him, the stream to the right and Alexander three hundred yards ahead. Stigr was beside him and eighteen other Wolves, as hungry for blood as they ever would be.

He saw the final troop of Companions where they were positioned to cut straight across his path and he readied himself for the slaughter. But they weren't coming. Their officer – a lean hyena of a man – was holding them with a single finger raised by his side. The Wolves kept running. Closer and closer to the Macedon banner. And still the Companions waited.

Skarde's brutalised lips pulled back in an exultant leer as Odin's words came back to him.

On they ran. Nearer still to the King's group. Another twenty yards were eaten up. And then, finally, the Companions moved. But it would be too late. The Wolves were already past them and the way was open.

With a wild laugh, Skarde rejoiced at the whole bloody craziness of it all.

Ulf spluttered and spat globules of blood. Somehow he was alive and the boots of the Heavies were no longer grinding him into the earth. He raised his head and stared around. Bodies lay scattered beside him and the din and reek of battle continued unabated on all sides. Everywhere he looked, warriors fought in desperation and he realised he was in the hollow of the Titan spearhead.

The foe ringed him, but they had their backs turned and were struggling to hold their line and keep the Hammers at bay. Most of the sarissas had now been broken or discarded and the fight had descended into a heaving, cursing, spitting, brutal brawl with blades. A Viking broke through and Ulf realised it was Ingvar. He had lost his axe and was holding only a seax. He caught sight of Ulf and with a feral cackle launched himself at the backs of the Heavies.

Ulf struggled upright. There was no sign of his shield or sword, so he bent to grab a fallen spear and even as he righted himself, a Titan sprang at him and stabbed with his shortsword. The point tore into the mail on his left arm and severed the links just beneath the strapping from his previous injury. Hot, vivid pain shot through him and he yelled. The Titan withdrew his blade for a second attempt and Ulf swung the spear, cracking the shaft against the other man's helmet. The Heavy stumbled on one of the bodies and lost balance. Ulf lunged at him and thrust the spear so hard through his gut that the point embedded in the earth beneath. The man's mouth opened in a final snarl, then filled with blood.

Ulf wrested the weapon free. His left arm was on fire. The chain mail rings were entrenched in his wound and he wondered if his humerus was broken, but he could still hold the spear with both hands, so he thought it must be intact. In a welter of agony and despair, he waited as another Heavy came for his life.

But heads were turning now. Both sides were sensing the Wolves rushing past them and realising the path to

Alexander was unguarded. The huge Titan officer who had led the Phalanx began roaring and thrusting his blade towards the western end of the Field.

'Retreat!' he was shouting. 'Get back. Defend the King.'

Any last vestige of order disintegrated. The Titan lines broke. The Hammer attacks collapsed. The Battle dissolved into a melee of confused hacking and stumbling and shoving. Everyone began running towards the Macedon standard and Ulf was taken with the surge. He swung at a Titan next to him, smashing his spear butt into the woman's neck. Then he was punching and kicking at the figures in front, whether friend or foe.

Don't trip, a voice inside him was screaming. *Don't trip*.

To fall was to die.

Agape stood knee-deep in river water and cleaved the head of a Viking from his shoulders.

Yet even as she stepped for the next one, her warrior instincts called to her and she halted and cocked her head and listened. The song of battle still came clearly, but now its timbre was different, and though she could see nothing from her place in the river, she knew implicitly that the struggle had turned.

She leapt to a rock, pulled herself up and peered over the high bank in time to see the entire battlefield disintegrating and careening towards the standard of Macedon. At its head were the Wolves and she swore incredulously. *Where the hell is Menes? How has he allowed them to pass so easily?* A lone Wolf had pulled ahead of the tumult and was charging straight at Alexander.

'Band!' she cried. 'To the Colours.'

In a single lithe leap she was on the bank and racing to intercept the Wolf. Her Band surged from the river behind her, followed by a mixed crowd of peltasts and Vikings, still cutting and swiping at each other.

'Protect the King,' she yelled at the small group of Bodyguards as she tore by. Despite his helmet, Agape could tell Alexander was white with terror. Beside him, Cleitus was gesticulating wildly, though she could make no sense of him.

The Wolf saw her and his mouth split in a hideous broken leer beneath his helm. If he recognised his opponent as the Captain of the Sacred Band, he showed no hint of intimidation. Instead he flew at her with even more abandon and punched his shield boss into her hoplon with so much power and momentum that for the first time in her recent memory, she was taken backwards by the blow. Her boots scrabbled at the earth and through sheer willpower alone she arrested her collapse. Now he was in her face, a white-bearded, broken-toothed mass of muscle and hate. His blade came driving across the top of his shield and her parry only just deflected it past her helmet. She stabbed back, but he lowered his head and took the blow straight on the iron top of his own helmet.

His head came up again with a snake-grin on his bruised lips. 'I hope you got better than that, girl.'

The last Viking who called her *girl* had lost his balls and with a hoarse cry she shouldered her hoplon against his shield and shoved him backwards. A gap opened and she prepared to spring at him, but then the whole chaos was upon them and they were taken apart by a writhing river of bodies. He was still staring at her with raw hatred as the gap became too wide to bridge, so he shifted his focus and waded for Alexander.

Somehow enough Titans had got back to reinforce the Band and the Bodyguard, and a defensive circle pulsed and warped around the King. But the Horde was everywhere, skirting the circle, blades and spears thrusting between the Titans. Alexander was clinging to his standard as though it was the only thing keeping him upright. Cleitus was shouting and pointing his sword, but doing nothing of any value.

Agape felt the pressure of the enemy on every side. She would fight until her last drop of blood in this heaving, screaming, murderous tumult, but she knew irrevocably that Titan numbers were too few. They always had been too few. They had tried to take the fight to the Horde, but now the Vikings were on them and the enemy would not be beaten.

Zeus had placed his gamble and he had lost.

Heph, you bastard. Where the hell are you?

XXXIX

The seven members of the Companion Cavalry waited on a small col in the south-eastern corner of the Field and gaped at the carnage. They had arrived only minutes before and sat astride their mounts, trying to take in the situation.

The trek had been much longer than anticipated and the horses slow and belligerent. The stallions could sense their riders' nerves and the tension had made them flighty and obstinate, skittering forward along the track one moment, then refusing to go above a snail's pace the next. The sound of distant helicopters directed the party and told them the action must be getting under way, though they had no way of telling exact times. As their journey continued and the noise of rotors grew, the horses became even more nervous, shivering and snorting and dropping great balls of shit.

Soon the first ominous shrieks came to them on the breeze, but only when they pulled up the last rise and reached the col, did the scene unfurl. The Field stretched east, littered with dead and wounded, and on the slopes below them, those who could still carry a weapon were crushed in a heaving mass around the banner of Macedon. The struggle surged in and out like a winter's tide, at moments seeming so close to the King's banner that the Viking foe could surely reach out and touch it.

'We must go right now,' urged Spyro, ramming his helmet down over his face and couching his lance. 'There's not a moment to waste.'

'We hold,' countered Heph.

'Hold!' exclaimed Spyro. 'They're being murdered down there. We have to help.'

He clicked his heels and began to advance, but Heph wheeled out of line and blocked him. 'Don't you dare move without my command, soldier. I am Captain of this troop and you will await my order.'

Spyro glared at him. 'We wait any longer and it's the fall of this Palatinate.'

He made to take his horse forward again, but now it was Dio's turn to join Heph and block him. 'You heard the Captain, trooper. No one moves until he says so.'

Spyro swore, but relented and Heph turned Boreas to face the Battle again. Beside the banner, he could just make out the tall figure of Alexander standing amidst the mayhem. Heph had barely seen the man since he and Dio had been forced to fight for their lives in Ephesus and the sadistic, lunatic glare of the King that night was still locked in his memory.

A whine came to them from over the din and a drone appeared.

'Helmets down,' Heph ordered and they pulled their helms over their faces like Spyro.

The drone hovered before them, its cameras taking in every detail.

'Seems our secret is finally discovered,' said Dio.

And Heph thought of Zeus and Hera watching the live feeds right now, and all the other rich bastards around the world spluttering into their food and drinks as they realised the Titans owned a cavalry.

'Who are they? Who the goddamn hell are they?'

Odin sat in his penthouse suite above the OSU and stared at the screen, his arms extended above his head in a gesture of utter shock.

As agreed, a work station had been set up for Oliver and he had spent the last hour in the presence of the Caelestis. Now he stood beside Odin's chair, watching the Battle play out on a screen on the desk.

During the last weeks, Oliver had spent hours debating whether to show Odin the photo of Morgan leaving her Craigmillar flat with the unidentified woman. He loathed the possibility of giving the bastard one crumb of help, but had guessed the revelation might make Odin still more desperate, perhaps even force him to throw caution to the wind at the Battle.

So together they had watched the struggle unfold over the last fifty minutes and Odin had pounded the desk with exuberance as he witnessed his Hammers breaking the Phalanx and his Wolves tearing towards Alexander. By the time the chaos had surrounded the Titan banner, he was crowing with delight and even slapping Oliver on the shoulder.

And then the feed had switched and they were staring at

seven horsemen, plumed and cloaked and lanced, waiting motionless above the Field.

'Somebody tell me who the goddamn bloody hell those guys are!'

'It would seem,' said Oliver archly, 'that they are mounted Titans, my lord. Seven of them. And if I recall from my induction with your finance unit, horses cost ten Credits in the Pantheon. That's odd because I thought you said Zeus had *not* spent seventy funds this year.'

Odin lowered his arms and did not respond.

'This is madness,' exclaimed Spyro. 'We *must* go to their aid.'

'I said we hold,' snarled Heph and though the horses whinnied and stamped and shivered, the line obeyed.

The drone had been joined by two others and Lenore peered at them through her eye sockets. Her throat was dry and her stomach sour with dread, but when she shifted her gaze a few yards ahead to where Heph sat atop Boreas, she saw in his bearing, in the steel of his back, the square of his shoulders and the stillness of his helmet, the true authority of a Titan officer and, in that moment, she realised she would ride with him into hell itself.

As the Titan circle shrunk and every Viking blade reached for Alexander, Dio eased Xanthos next to Boreas and leaned across to whisper, 'I hope you know what you're doing.'

'So do I,' replied his Captain after a long pause.

Ulf was caught on the blood tide and all around him, madness reigned.

Companions and Heavies fought hand to hand with Hammer and Wolf in a myriad of individual struggles, while the ragged circle of Band and Bodyguard strove against Valhalla, like castles of sand facing the groping fingers of the sea. Bjarke was in the midst of it, sheeted in blood, still swinging his axe in giant arcs, so friend and foe alike feared for their heads. Skarde too, punching against the final line of defence like a maniac, driven crazy by the scent of his prey so close.

A Companion was shoved into Ulf and for a second they danced chest to chest, the man's eyes wide with terror. He was trying to join the defensive circle, but could find no way through. He grabbed Ulf's throat and used it to lever himself away an arm's length so that he could lunge with his shortsword. Desperately, Ulf flung up his spear and his opponent's blade cracked against the shaft. He shoved the man a step back, but could not adjust his spear in the press and in seconds the Companion was coming for him again. Ulf trod on a corpse, slipped in blood, and fell. The man was over him, teeth bared, blade back for the kill and then there was a holler and a brawny Viking arm buried a seax in his throat. His eyes blinked in shock and then the knife came free and blood fountained and he fell away.

Ulf grabbed his spear and used the corpse to grapple upright. He was shoved towards the line of defenders, but he scrabbled backwards because he knew implicitly that the circle had mastered a grim professional rhythm of short, punchy stabs to harvest lives and to venture too close meant certain death. He was jostled again. A blade whumped off his helmet and he tripped on another body. A shield beat at him and he righted himself enough to thrust his spear up and feel the jolt of iron breaking through leather and flesh, though he had no idea if he killed Titan or Viking. He ripped his weapon from the unseen victim, stumbled across two corpses, shouldered a female peltast from behind and then found himself, quite suddenly, staring over the shields of two Titan Bodyguards directly at Alexander.

The King of the Titans was no more than a dozen yards from him, clinging to his standard like an old man and his hoplon raised so that just his eye sockets and plume were visible above it. Wolves were attacking the guards, but in that heartbeat it seemed to Ulf that the bedlam softened and he had space. Space enough to bring his spear to bear and follow his instincts. With his last vestiges of strength, he flung the weapon between the heads of the defenders. It arced across the remaining yards, but then began to drop. The flight was too low and Ulf was already cursing his disappointment when the blade found Alexander's thigh beneath his shield and wedged itself in his scant flesh.

Ulf just had time to witness the King fold inwards, his hoplon drop and his beautiful plume arch down towards the wound, and then Ulf was thumped again from behind and his foot skidded on the blood-slick turf and he fell.

From his vantage on the col, Heph saw Alexander buckle. He hoisted his lance and looked behind him at his line of cavalry.

'Follow my pace. Follow my lead. Follow my orders. We go.'

He nudged Boreas forward. The stallion was shivering

with excitement, tossing his head and snorting. He was overjoyed to be permitted to move and began trotting vigorously down the faint track.

'Easy, boy,' Heph whispered. 'All in good time.'

He knew the others would follow in pairs. Lenore and Dio first. Then Pallas and Maia, with Zephyr and Spyro bringing up the rear. The drones tracked their progress and Heph knew his company must look spectacular. They had combed and primped their plumes and burnished every last inch of their bronze helmets, cuirasses, vambraces and greaves. The breeze would be spreading their cloaks from their shoulders. The horses trotted with high-kneed elation, their harnesses polished and their backs adorned with lion skins.

They reached the Field and the slope eased. Instinctively, Boreas stretched into a canter and Heph let him. He could sense Dio and Lenore on his shoulders and knew the others would be forming the backline of a wedge.

'Okay, boy,' Heph whispered down at the tossing mane before him and pressed his thighs into the stallion's flanks. 'Let's do this.'

Boreas accelerated into a full gallop. Heph clung to the reins. The ground reverberated. Great clods of earth spewed up behind them. And the first heads turned in the melee around Alexander's colours.

For the Companion Cavalry was coming and death flew with them.

Agape was deep in the slaughter of the defensive line when she heard Alexander yell and turned to see him collapse.

In the same instant a Viking blade came for her and she had to parry fast and strike back. When she could look again, Cleitus was over the King, heaving at the spear shaft in his thigh.

'No,' she cried above the tumult. What was the idiot doing? Surely he had enough experience to know never to drag a weapon from such a wound without proper assessment.

She hacked at an adversary, yelled at the Titans beside her to close up and ran to where Cleitus was already standing back with the spear in his paw. Blood pulsed from the ragged hole in Alexander's thigh and she guessed the injury. The tip of the spear must have pierced his femoral artery and every time his heart beat it pumped another salvo of his life's blood into the damp Highland air.

Agape flung herself to her knees and shouted at Cleitus to find binding, but he simply stood with his mouth open and gaped at her. Cursing she rose and cast her eyes around, but the only material she could conceive was the Lion banner fluttering above their heads.

Even as she thought to drag the standard from the earth, a new sound came to her – a thundering beneath her feet – and she turned to see horsemen flying towards the carnage.

Too late, Heph, damn you. You're too late.

But Heph was not too late.

In fact, he had timed the arrival of his cavalry to perfection and now all he had to do was carry out the scheme that had been with him since he first joined the Pantheon. The one that had sharpened when he breakfasted with Hera in the

Balmoral and then fully crystallised when he had first laid eyes on the seven beautiful stallions in the stables beneath the Ochils.

He had no intention of entering that bloody chaos before them. What good were seven horsemen in that bedlam? Indeed, what good were seven horsemen ever going to be against the massed ranks of the Valhalla Palatinate?

Gripping Boreas' reins in his left hand, he raised his right arm and pointed with his lance, then wheeled away from the struggle.

'What?' he heard Spyro exclaim and sensed the man pull out of formation.

'On me!' Heph turned and yelled at him and although Spyro blustered and shook his head in disbelief, he dug his heels into his mount and came after his Captain.

And now the full wonder of the charge was upon them. The stallions pounded the earth, their muscles worked in perfect rhythm and the months of training came together. Though there was nothing between horse and rider except a lion skin, the seven Titans sat firm and their lances did not waver.

They ate up that Field. Straight down the centre. With nothing before them except a last line of Vikings.

And the King of Valhalla.

Agape let out an exultant cry.

Her King lay mortally wounded at her feet and the foe were only a whisper away, yet the Battle was slowing and heads were turning to stare incredulously up the Field.

So she stood beneath the Lion banner and grinned from ear to ear. Because the idea was so beautiful.

Kill the King.

'Protect the King!' Calder shouted.

Her Ravens and the four Hammers were staring at the oncoming horsemen as though they were gods of war, so she took command.

'Notch arrows! Aim for the horses.'

She unshouldered her bow and grabbed at one of the arrows she had planted in the ground before her. Her hands were shaking and she could taste the fear smothering the others. They had been so far from the action. They had believed the Battle as good as over. And now these visions of war came at them and the ground reverberated beneath their feet.

She could barely fit the arrow to the string and she cursed herself. The last time she had been so clumsy was in the forest during her *Sine Missione* when she had shot her first bolt into Einar. Now she must call upon every ounce of calm and skill she had learned since then.

My god, come on, you fool. Don't fail me. This is death coming.

The arrow flew from nowhere and thunked off Heph's cheek guards.

He was so surprised, he dropped his grip on the reins and slipped sideways on Boreas, almost losing his balance altogether. Grabbing the stallion's mane and clenching his thighs for dear life, he wrenched himself upright again. The Viking archer was already notching another missile and furiously Heph guided his mount towards the figure and brought his lance to bear. The second arrow missed Boreas' neck by a whisper and whooshed past to tangle in Heph's outspread cloak, then his adversary dropped the bow and reached for a spear in the grass.

Heph kicked Boreas' flanks and bore down on the Viking, intent on impaling the bastard on his lance or letting Boreas trample him into the earth. He locked his thighs and kept his spine loose. Belgutei would have told him to slow and punch the foe with lightning jabs, but those lessons disappeared in the adrenalin rush of the moment. Horse and man were beyond slowing.

And then he glimpsed blonde hair curling beneath the Viking's helmet and a vision came to him, sharp and clear, of the friend he had deserted. Of the woman he might have loved.

He lunged at Boreas' rein and the horse tacked and passed so close that the beast's shoulder caught the Raven and sent her sprawling in the mud.

No sooner was Heph through, than a giant Hammer ran at him with a spear aimed for Boreas' heart, but the horse galloped straight through him, trampling him beneath his hooves with barely a loss of momentum.

And then there was Sveinn. The King stood twenty yards ahead beside his banners. His sword was undrawn and he held both hands clasped before him, his head high, eyes boring into the mounted apparition coming for him. Heph slung his lance aside and drew his shortsword and he could have sworn he saw a knowing smile on Sveinn's face.

I'm sorry. You were a good king.

And with that, he was upon him. He gripped his sword low and used Boreas' momentum to guide the blade through Sveinn's silver mail, through the leather beneath and onwards, piercing flesh, snapping ribs and severing organs. He released the hilt and left the sword embedded, then reined Boreas gently to a trot and turned him.

Heph's heart was pounding, his lungs heaving, his back sweat-soaked beneath his cuirass. And above him, the banners of the Horde of Valhalla flapped futilely on the breeze.

Odin turned in his seat and looked up at Oliver. His eyes were wide and bloodshot, his mouth opening and closing like a stranded fish.

Ever since Oliver had seen the satellite images of Titan horse riders practising on Perthshire fields, he had hoped and prayed that this secret cavalry might be let loose at the Battle and he had done everything in his power to encourage Odin to throw caution to the wind.

He looked at the Caelestis. The man was so shocked that he was having trouble understanding the ramifications of what had just occurred. He did not yet realise he had lost everything. Every vestige of power and influence gone with that one sword strike. He was yesterday's man. Friendless and pathetic. An ex-Caelestis who would be discarded by the Pantheon.

Imperceptibly Oliver's resolution consolidated. He had dreamed about this moment. Played it out in his head over countless nights in the Schola and now it was within his grasp. Act now or regret it forever. His heart thumped with fear, but his eyes hardened and his mind refused to consider all the myriad consequences.

'This,' he croaked, 'is for my mother.'

Maia was down and not moving, a spear shaft sticking from her chest like a flagpole. Pallas was grounded too and was crawling towards his horse as it lay screaming in its death throes. Zephyr was trying to control his rearing and whinnying mount. Lenore and Spyro were reining their winded stallions, and Dio had halted Xanthos and sat looking at Heph, his lance coated in blood.

The fight had flown from the whole field. The blood madness had opened its wings and escaped on the upland air.

Every single helmet, near and far, was fixed on Heph as he walked Boreas back to Sveinn. The King was prostrate on the ground choking on his lifeblood, Heph's sword still embedded in his chest. Heph dropped from Boreas and knelt beside him to take the cold, bony hand in his and squeeze it. He looked silently into the King's eyes.

And Sveinn stared back.

Oliver had pilfered the knife from the OSU's kitchen. It was small, but still strong enough for the task. Besides, he had spent hours perfecting the technique in the training rooms beneath the Schola.

He stabbed Odin in the throat, using an upwards motion to ensure the blade broke through the back of his mouth and pierced the medulla brainstem. Odin wheezed in shock and grappled for the knife, his eyes full moons of disbelief and his tongue lolling from his mouth.

Oliver stepped back and let him thrash for the weapon. The damage was already done, so the bastard could struggle all he wished.

Blood had spattered onto Oliver's shirt, but he had brought his coat up to the suite and he walked to the corner, pulled it on and zipped it up. Without a backward glance, he took the USB from the laptop and headed for the lift, while Odin collapsed to the floor and began bucking like a dolphin.

Downstairs the staff were so appalled by the outcome of the Battle they barely noticed Oliver's passing. Jed was gesticulating at his screen and Aurora stood behind him, her hands over her mouth and her face blanched of all colour.

'Hey,' said the man at security when Oliver exited the lift on the ground floor and strode by without a look. 'Hey!' he shouted again with more conviction.

But Oliver was already through the revolving doors and running up Middle Meadow as fast as his shaking legs would carry him.

The sound of the klaxon reverberated across the valley. Helicopters tossed the air into boiling cauldrons. Drones whined frantically. And from the other end of the Field the Titan Palatinate roared their triumph.

Heph stood and reached up to pat Boreas and the stallion shivered and snorted hay-scented breath into his face.

And in the vastness of Knoydart, two Kings died.

Author's Note

Dear Reader,

It is the end of the Twentieth Season and the dead of both Palatinates are strewn across the Field.

I must admit I've never set foot in Knoydart. It is known as Scotland's last great wilderness and the giant peninsula, stretching towards the Isle of Skye, is almost entirely inaccessible by road. Seasonal ferries can carry you to it, and each year adventurous hikers, seeking Munros and solitude, find their way into its lost glens. For my part, I sweated over maps, photos and descriptions until I could picture all the major folds of land and knew how my Battle would play out.

As for the Twentieth Raiding Season, it was a blast setting the action in Edinburgh Zoo and Waverley station. In a previous life, I worked at the zoo and had sometimes walked around the enclosures after dark. You can sense and smell the wild surrounding you. What better place to cast my protagonists into? I've never been in Waverley during the small hours and perhaps there is a bustle of comings and goings even then. So I may have used artistic licence to close it all down and give it the quiet needed to host a Pantheon Raid.

So where now? Two Kings dead. The fall of a Palatinate. The Pantheon thrown into turmoil. What will happen to Valhalla? Who will be the new Alexander? And how will our heroes survive when the Sultanate and the hated Huns come calling?

If you'd like to connect, please visit:
cfbarrington.com
Facebook – @BarringtonCFAuthor
Twitter – @barrington_cf
Instagram – @cfbarrington_notwriting

Thank you for coming on this adventure with me!

The final book in the Pantheon series – *The Bone Fields* – is released in 2023 and the whole damn game is about to go crazy.

C.F. Barrington

Acknowledgements

I wrote *The Hastening Storm* in two major stints during the lockdowns of 2020. The first focused on the Interregnum – the summer months when the Pantheon pauses – and the second threw me into the action of the Twentieth Season.

2020 was an awful year for so many and I was perhaps lucky that I could escape into the world of my characters.

For this – my third book – I have a new team at Head of Zeus. A huge thank you to my new editor, Peyton Stableford, who has been awesome keeping me on schedule and answering my questions, however daft. Thank you also to Laura Palmer, director of fiction at HoZ, for her faith in the Pantheon series, and to Polly Grice and all the marketing and digital teams at HoZ.

As always, huge gratitude to my inimitable agent, Laura Macdougall, and Olivia Davies at United Agents.

Once again, I love Dan Mogford's cover art. His furious skies have become a feature of the Pantheon series. I'm also indebted to Lydia Mason for her structural-edit skills on the first drafts of each book. Lydia has provided such insightful comments and coaxed me into making the story arcs and character details so much better.

As I have developed networks into literary circles, I want

to thank the bloggers, reviewers, festival organisers and readers who have loved the books, and especially fellow authors Matthew Harffy, Giles Kristian and Ruth Hogan for their advice and encouragement.

On a more personal level, I now have my very own Sacred Band of friends and family who have supported me throughout the series. The boundless enthusiasm (and beach barbecues) of Mike Dougan. Fellow creative spirit and mountain walker, Mark Clay. My first and most trusted reader, Dave Follett.

And, of course, my closest and dearest – mum, dad, Shireen, Steve, Sarah, Albie and Jackie. Love and thanks to you all. You are the inspirations and energies which keep the words pouring from me.

About the Author

C.F. BARRINGTON spent twenty years intending to write a novel, but found life kept getting in the way. Instead, his career has been in major-gift fundraising, leading teams in organisations as varied as the RSPB, Oxford University and the National Trust. In 2015, when his role as Head of Communications at Edinburgh Zoo meant a third year of fielding endless media enquiries about the possible birth of a baby panda, he finally retreated to a quiet desk and got down to writing.

Raised in Hertfordshire and educated at Oxford, he now divides his time between Fife and the Lake District.